**Praise for the romances of *New York Times*
bestselling author Virginia Henley**

Infamous

"Few authors combine historical personages and events with a passionate love story as brilliant as Henley."   —*Romantic Times* (4½ stars, Top Pick)

Unmasked

"Once again Henley has brought history to life—and another couple to true love."   —*Booklist*

"A merry chase . . . historical romance layered with a healthy dose of intrigue makes for a book that will keep readers unable to stop turning the pages."
—The Romance Reader's Connection

"*Unmasked* treats the events of history in a way that keeps the reader wrapped up in the story."
—Roundtable Reviews

"Henley's gift for bringing remarkable women to life in colorful, turbulent times is what turns her romances into keepers. Henley heats up the pages with her love scenes, and her skill at portraying actual historical personages with humanity while maintaining historical accuracy wins our minds. Henley knows what historical romance is all about and always gives the readers what they want."   —*Romantic Times*

continued . . .

Insatiable

"Dangerous games, Machiavellian manipulations, and political maneuverings. . . . Lusty and lavish."
—*Booklist*

"As twists of fate contrive to keep the two apart—intrigue, backstabbing, the bubonic plague—readers will hanker for them to live happily ever after."
—*Publishers Weekly*

"If you like history-rich characters that come to life in your own imagination . . . then Ms. Henley is one author you cannot dismiss!" —Romance Designs

Undone

"Heartstopping excitement, breathless tension, and tender romance." —*Rendezvous*

"All the sensuality and glitter of a more traditional romance, but enriched by the plot's complexity and the heroine's genuine growth." —*Publishers Weekly*

"A gently suspenseful tale . . . filled with satisfying historical detail and actual characters from this intriguing period." —*Booklist*

"Extraordinary characters, rich historical details, and a romance . . . [set] the pages on fire."
—*Romantic Times* (Top Pick)

NOTORIOUS

Virginia Henley

A SIGNET BOOK

SIGNET
Published by New American Library, a division of
Penguin Group (USA) Inc., 375 Hudson Street,
New York, New York 10014, USA
Penguin Group (Canada), 90 Eglinton Avenue East, Suite 700, Toronto,
Ontario M4P 2Y3, Canada (a division of Pearson Penguin Canada Inc.)
Penguin Books Ltd., 80 Strand, London WC2R 0RL, England
Penguin Ireland, 25 St. Stephen's Green, Dublin 2,
Ireland (a division of Penguin Books Ltd.)
Penguin Group (Australia), 250 Camberwell Road, Camberwell, Victoria 3124,
Australia (a division of Pearson Australia Group Pty. Ltd.)
Penguin Books India Pvt. Ltd., 11 Community Centre, Panchsheel Park,
New Delhi - 110 017, India
Penguin Group (NZ), 67 Apollo Drive, Rosedale, North Shore,
Auckland 1311, New Zealand (a division of Pearson New Zealand Ltd.)
Penguin Books (South Africa) (Pty.) Ltd., 24 Sturdee Avenue,
Rosebank, Johannesburg 2196, South Africa

Penguin Books Ltd., Registered Offices:
80 Strand, London WC2R 0RL, England

First published by Signet, an imprint of New American Library,
a division of Penguin Group (USA) Inc.

First Printing, May 2007
10 9 8 7 6 5 4 3 2 1

PUBLISHER'S NOTE
This is a work of fiction. Names, characters, places, and incidents either are
the product of the author's imagination or are used fictitiously, and any resemblance to actual persons, living or dead, business establishments, events, or
locales is entirely coincidental.
    The publisher does not have any control over and does not assume any
responsibility for author or third-party Web sites or their content.

If you purchased this book without a cover, you should be aware that this
book is stolen property. It was reported as "unsold and destroyed" to the
publisher, and neither the author nor the publisher has received any payment
for this "stripped book."

The scanning, uploading, and distribution of this book via the Internet or via
any other means without the permission of the publisher is illegal and punish-
able by law. Please purchase only authorized electronic editions, and do not
participate in or encourage electronic piracy of copyrighted materials. Your
support of the author's rights is appreciated.

*Dedicated to the memory of my mother, Lilian.
She was wise, shrewd, blunt, witty, and brave.
I miss her every day.*

After a thirty-five-year reign, King Edward Planta-genet dies, leaving his only living son, Edward II, to inherit the throne. Under the father's rule, England grew and prospered. Wales and Scotland were conquered and subdued. Peace was achieved with France through several strategic marriages, including the new king's own marriage some ten years earlier to his child bride, Isabelle, princess of France. But King Edward II is not his father. He cannot control the country with the fierce authority his father wielded. Early in his reign he loses Scotland to Robert Bruce at the Battle of Bannockburn. Edward's distractions are infamous and numerous, and he allows his favorites to gain wealth and power at the expense of his nobles and barons. In the year 1322, far from London, at the vast de Beauchamp holdings in Warwick, it is becoming increasingly clear that the monarchy is in peril.

Chapter 1

"I cannot believe you are a woman grown, Brianna de Beauchamp. When I was last at Warwick four years ago you were a child." Roger Mortimer clasped the young girl's hands and kissed her brow, then held her away from him so he could have a good look. "I was present when you were born. I never would have believed such a scrawny little scrap would turn into a rare beauty."

Brianna raised her lashes and smiled at the darkly handsome Mortimer. He was easily the most charming male she had ever known, and her heart began to beat wildly. Her older brother, Rickard, was married to Roger's sister, Catherine, and was a captain in Mortimer's army.

"Your eyes would melt a heart of stone and render a strong man weak as water." Mortimer spoke with complete sincerity.

Brianna had the soulful, soft brown eyes of a doe, fringed by thick dark lashes tipped with gold.

"Mother doesn't think me a woman, nor does Father. They think at sixteen I am still a child."

"Nonsense! I was wed at fourteen and a father at fifteen. Your mother attended my wedding."

"You had your boy Edmund when you were fifteen?" Brianna asked in amazement.

Roger threw back his head and laughed. "He wouldn't be pleased to be called a boy. Edmund is a man of twenty-one and his brother, Wolf, is twenty. They patrol the Welsh Marches when I'm in Ireland."

Brianna's eyes lit with curiosity. "Wolf?"

"He found a motherless wolf cub a few years back and kept it. He's had the name ever since." Mortimer grinned and shook his head. "I can't believe it's been more than sixteen years since that night at Windrush. Where have the years gone?"

I was born at Windrush? Why the devil wasn't I born at Warwick Castle? Brianna wondered. Her thoughts were interrupted by her mother's arrival.

The elegant Countess of Warwick swept briskly into the hall. She encountered a servant bringing ale to their guest and lifted two tankards from his serving tray. "Well come, Roger! It's lovely to see you again." She handed him a tankard and lifted the other one to her own lips. "Is Lady Mortimer not with you?"

"Nay, she remained in Ireland. She has vast landholdings there and lives on a grand scale. I believe she prefers it to Wales."

"We've all heard of your victories in Ireland. Rickard corresponds regularly. You look every inch the conquering hero."

A year after Robert Bruce had defeated young King Edward and his English army at Bannockburn, Scotland's king had sent his brother, Edward, to Ireland to free the Irish from English rule. The King of England had chosen his fiercest Welsh Border Lord, Roger Mortimer, to put down the Irish insurgency. Mortimer was an outstanding military leader and within four months he had taken back Dundelk, then taken Ulster. He had remained there for the past four years as Ireland's justiciar.

Roger grinned, while his light gray eyes took in every detail of her beauty with frank male appreciation. "You have a knack for making a man feel like a conqueror, Jory." He took her fingers to his lips. "Your husband is a lucky devil."

Jory de Beauchamp rolled her eyes. "Here comes the devil now."

Warwick, now in his fifties, was still an imposing figure. The white at his temples contrasting with his black hair, and the deeper lines of his dark face were his only signs of age.

"I've put your men in the barracks beside the armory. Your capable sons have taken charge of stabling the horses and don't need my interference. Let's sit by the fire, where we can be comfortable. There is much to discuss."

Brianna, displaying good manners, withdrew from the circle, but she had no intention of leaving the hall. She sat down in a window embrasure where she could hear everything her elders said. *I shouldn't . . . but I shall!*

Mortimer stretched his long legs toward the fire. "I was surprised to learn you had withdrawn from court."

"The Despencers are the only ones with access to the king. Father and son are determined to gain political supremacy over all the earls and barons in England." Warwick's features hardened. "Our presence there became untenable."

"It broke my heart to leave Isabelle. I have been a lady of the queen's court since she arrived from France when she was thirteen. As you well know, we became dearest friends. She adored Brianna, and they became like sisters. Then Hugh Despencer dismissed me, along with the queen's other loyal ladies."

Mortimer clenched his fists. "It is beyond belief that Edward has another degenerate favorite after what happened over Gaveston. That the queen is forced to accept him would gag a maggot."

"When we rid Edward of Gaveston, the king turned

to Isabelle and fathered her children like a normal husband. At that time the elder Despencer, head of the King's Council, stood firmly with the barons. Then, last year, the avaricious swine spied his chance and made his son chamberlain of the king's household, and parliament appointed him to the council. After that it didn't take Hugh Despencer long to become the king's new favorite," Warwick said with disgust.

"Once a pederast, always a pederast!" Mortimer bit back a foul oath.

Pederast? I know not the meaning of that word, but I warrant it means something bad. Brianna decided she would ask her mother, but not in the presence of her father. *He would keep me innocent forever.*

"The avaricious Despencer is the reason I returned from Ireland. He stole two manors from young Hugh Audley by registering them in his own name, and is doing his best to appropriate certain estates that were granted to me. Hugh Despencer covets the lordship of Gower, which lies along his lands in Glamorgan. Gower belongs to John Mowbray, but Despencer claims he never got a license from the king. He's urged Edward to declare it forfeit and grant it to him." Mortimer flung out his arm in a flamboyant gesture. "Since when did a Welsh Marcher baron ever need a license from the King of England for his land? Marcher barons have had the privilege of Welsh land for centuries!"

Roger Mortimer has such a commanding, royal presence. He is exactly what a king should look and sound like, because he is a descendant of King Brutus from the Arthurian legends. She sighed.

"Obviously Despencer is trying to build a large lordship for himself in what has always been the Marcher barons' power base." Warwick made no effort to hide his contempt for the Despencers.

"Exactly!" Mortimer said grimly. "His aggrandizement is a direct threat to all the Marcher lords. Our independence and even the lands and castles we own are at stake."

"Mowbray didn't surrender his land, surely?" Warwick asked.

"He adamantly refused, so the king sent men to take it by force. I immediately went to Westminster to persuade the king from the folly of a direct attack on Marcher privileges. When he would not listen, I sought audience with the queen to ask if she would use her influence. It was then that Isabelle told me all the power is in the hands of Edward's catamite!"

"The barons hate and detest the Despencers," Warwick declared.

"They are brutal and greedy and Hugh has an insatiable desire for land and wealth," Jory added.

"The earls of Hereford, Mowbray, Audley, and d'Amory have joined with us Mortimers to form a confederacy against the Despencers. I have come to rally the barons to join us. Together we can and we *must* utterly destroy them."

Warwick nodded. "We'll go to Lancaster and enlist his support." He looked up as a tall youth fashioned in his own image entered the hall. "Here's Guy Thomas. He must have been only ten or eleven the last time you saw him. He has grown apace."

Brianna took advantage of the distraction of her brother to slip from the hall unnoticed. Her feet carried her in the direction of the stables. If a score of mounts belonging to Mortimer's men were being accommodated, she wanted to make sure that her palfrey, Venus, was kept safe from the other horses.

She got only as far as the courtyard when the sight of two snarling, growling canines who looked as if they were about to kill each other filled her with dread. "Brutus! No!" she screamed, and without hesitation threw herself between the combatants and flung her arms about her father's black wolfhound. Her eyes widened in horror as she looked at his opponent. "Hell's teeth, it isn't a dog at all, it's a wolf!"

A male descended upon her and roughly dragged her away from the two animals. "You stupid girl! Have you no common sense?"

Furious, she drew back her hand and slapped his dark, arrogant face. "How dare you bring your wild beast to Warwick?"

He grabbed her hand, forced it behind her back, and stared down at her with fierce gray eyes. "My wolf is tame, which is more than I can say for you. They are only challenging each other to test the boundaries. Let nature take its course," he ordered.

To Brianna's amazement the two long-legged animals circled each other with their lips drawn back to show their fangs; then they stopped and stood eye to eye, growling in their throats. When both stood their ground and neither backed away, it was a standoff. She raised her eyes to stare at the intense, dark face of the male who held her in his iron grip. "Take your hands from me, Wolf Mortimer."

"You know my name." He let go of her wrist. "You have me at a disadvantage, mistress."

She raked him with a haughty glance. "And always shall." *How in the name of God could this uncivilized lout be the son of Roger Mortimer, who is the epitome of chivalry?*

"Brianna, is that you?"

She swung about to look at the tall young man who spoke her name and realized he must be Edmund Mortimer. He had been a gangling youth the last time she had seen him. "Indeed it is, Edmund. Welcome to Warwick." She gave him a dazzling smile, hoping it would affront his loutish brother. "They are serving ale in the hall. You must be parched. Come, Brutus!"

The wolfhound trotted to her side and Brianna

turned and said coldly, "Keep your wild beast in the stables. He is not welcome in the castle."

"She is a bitch," Edmund corrected gently.

"She is indeed," Wolf Mortimer declared. "A bitch who needs taming." He touched his cheek where she had slapped him, then threw back his head and laughed insolently.

Brianna took Edmund's arm and walked briskly toward the castle. "Your brother is uncouth."

He looked down at her apologetically. "I'm afraid it is a Mortimer trait."

"I don't believe that. Your father is one of the most charming men I have ever met, and I'm not the only female to think so. He is renowned for his fatal attraction."

Wolf Mortimer stared after the pair until they entered the castle. The impact of the beautiful female had been like a blow to his solar plexus. The moment she slapped him, a raging lust ignited and ran through his veins like wildfire. His nature was both impulsive and decisive, and he knew instantly that he wanted her. Not only was she exquisite to look at, but she was all fire and ice. She was a spirited female who would give as good as she got, rather than being meek and submissive, and the thought excited him. *I recognize your towering pride, since I have the sinful trait myself, Brianna de Beauchamp. Your challenge is irresistible!*

At the evening meal Brianna's brother, Guy Thomas, almost two years younger than she, sat with Mortimer's sons. Their talk was all about horses and hunting and weapons. Brianna had chosen to sit with her mother's ladies, rather than up on the dais, and it gave her an unimpeded view of her parents and their guests.

Her mother, Jory de Beauchamp, was an exquisite

beauty who easily held the attention of every male in the hall, including their guest of honor, Roger Mortimer.

Brianna gazed at the handsome Marcher lord with her heart in her eyes. Her glance was suddenly drawn against her will to Wolf Mortimer. *The pet wolf is not the only reason for his name. He has the look of a dark, lean predator. I warrant he is both dominant and dangerous when the mood takes him. His pale gray eyes are startling in his swarthy face. When the bold devil looks at me his gaze is so penetrating, he seems to discern my thoughts.* Brianna gave a delicate shudder of distaste and forced her eyes away from him.

Her mother's ladies were speaking of how much they missed being at the Queen's Court. Brianna missed Queen Isabelle and longed to see her again. She began to daydream about how lovely the gardens would be at Windsor Castle. Before the month of March was over, spring would arrive. The queen always had exciting masques portraying Queen Guinevere and King Arthur, and she and Isabelle had fun choosing the costumes and playacting in the roles. There was lively music and dancing and Brianna was at an age to attract a great deal of male attention and had never lacked for partners.

Brianna also missed the company of Prince Edward, whose household was at Windsor. She often rode out with him and shared in his hawking lessons and watched as he was taught swordsmanship and how to shoot with a longbow. She sighed and wished they could soon return to Windsor. She longed to see Queen Isabelle's new baby. Joan had been born in the Tower of London and would soon be a year old.

Her thoughts were brought back to the present when she realized that the meal was over. Her mother rose from the head table to withdraw and leave the men to their wine and their plans. This was the signal for her ladies to retire and Brianna left also.

She went upstairs to her mother's chamber, eager to get answers to some of the things she'd heard today that puzzled her. She watched as her mother removed her emeralds and locked them safely in her jewel casket.

"I always assumed I was born in this castle, as was Guy Thomas. Why was I born at Windrush?"

Jory, caught off guard by her daughter's question, gave her a half-truth. "Your father and I had a quarrel." Her green eyes sparkled with amusement. "I withdrew to my own castle of Windrush to bring him to heel."

Brianna laughed merrily at the absurd suggestion that her father could ever be brought to heel, but she knew her mother was an enchantress, and wanted to be exactly like her.

Jory picked up her brush. "Any more questions?"

"Yes." Brianna's admiring glance lingered on her mother's beautiful silver-gilt hair. "What is a pederast?"

Jory's eyes widened. "Come and sit down and I'll brush your hair. You were listening today when your father and I were talking to Roger."

Brianna sat down at the dressing table before the mirror. "Of course I was listening."

"It refers to a man who loves males rather than females."

"King Edward loves males? What about Queen Isabelle?"

Jory sighed. "It's a long story, infinitely sad and disturbing, but I suppose you are old enough to hear it."

Brianna watched in the mirror as her mother applied long soothing brushstrokes to her red-gold hair.

"When Edward married Isabelle and brought her from France, she was only thirteen years old. They had separate households at Windsor until she was old enough for the marriage to be consummated, and I was chosen as one of her ladies. Young Isabelle was madly in love with Edward and thought him a golden god. He hardly noticed her. He had eyes for only his favorite, Piers Gaveston, who had been placed in the prince's household when he was a boy. When King Edward learned of the immoral relationship between his son and Gaveston he banished him. But the moment the old king died, Edward brought Gaveston back to court."

"When I was a little girl, I remember that Edward and Gaveston were always together. No wonder Queen Isabelle detested him."

"We all hated Gaveston. He manipulated Edward like a puppet on a string. He was greedy and grasping and had a sycophantic entourage of Gascon relatives and friends who bled the king dry. He paraded about in the Crown Jewels, and Edward even gave him the jewels that Isabelle received as wedding presents."

"Edward actually fell in *love* with Gaveston?" Brianna asked.

"For Edward it was more than love at first sight, it was complete surrender. He showered him with gifts and lands and titles, and Gaveston turned the king against the barons."

"When did Isabelle learn that Edward loved Gaveston?"

"When she walked in on them and found them in bed together. Her naive innocence was stripped away in an instant. She was devastated and wrote to her father. The King of France contacted Thomas, Earl of Lancaster. Since Thomas was England's high steward and the second greatest power in the land, King Philip charged him to become the queen's champion and rid Edward of his lover."

"What happened?" Brianna hung on to every word.

"Parliament banished Gaveston, more than once, but each time Edward brought him back again. The last straw for me came after my dearest friend, Princess Joanna, died. The king immediately married his sister's daughter, young Margaret, to his lover so that he would get all the lands and castles that her father, Gilbert de Clare, had left her."

"I can remember how upset you were. I thought it was because Joanna had died, but now I see that it was more."

"Margaret was like my own daughter. Edward married her to a monster and there was nothing I could do about it. The king ruled by divine right, but in truth it was *Gaveston* who ruled!"

Brianna, who had heard disturbing gossip about Gaveston's death over the years, whispered, "Did Father murder him?"

Mother's and daughter's eyes met in the mirror. "Good God, no! Rumors have laid so many deaths at your father's feet and none of them are true. Parliament tried Gaveston and found him guilty on forty different charges such as counseling the king to do evil, stealing the Great Seal of England and using it for his own purposes, and urging the king to civil war. Gaveston fled to his castle of Scarborough, which the king had given him. He finally surrendered to Pembroke, on condition that his life be spared. Pembroke and his soldiers brought the prisoner to Warwick. I remember that night so well. Thomas of Lancaster arrived and demanded custody of Gaveston. I knew how much Lancaster hated him and knew what he would do. I used all my feminine wiles on your father to keep him at Warwick that night."

"Were your suspicions correct?" Brianna whispered.

Her mother nodded. "As soon as they were on Lancaster land, Gaveston was executed and Thomas took full responsibility." She put down the brush and sat on the bed. "I was vastly relieved that young Margaret was widowed from Gaveston. The following year she married Hugh Audley, the young Marcher baron who was worthy of inheriting the earldom of Gloucester through his wife."

Brianna stretched out beside her. "Tell me the rest."

"In his grief over the loss of Gaveston, Edward reached out to his wife because he had no one else to turn to. Isabelle knew he had always been a weakling, but she felt compassion for his anguish and she comforted him. In her innocence she thought that at long last, Edward had begun to love her. They became man and wife in more than name and she had Prince Edward, followed by her other children. Though they were not in love, their relationship was at least amicable and polite and lasted almost ten years. All seemed well and fine until the greedy, grasping Despencers made their move. The elder Despencer, who was on the King's Council, appointed his son Hugh to the post of Chamberlain of the King's Household. Hugh Despencer soon slipped into Edward's bed and the trouble started all over again."

"They are sodomites," Brianna said in a shocked voice.

Her mother rolled her eyes. "Wherever do you learn these words? Your father would run mad if he heard you."

"That word is in the Bible," Brianna said innocently. "I sensed there was something peculiar about Hugh Despencer." A lump came into her throat. "Poor Queen Isabelle must feel so alone. She must miss us as much as we miss her."

"It is infinitely sad. She has never known a man's love. In the early years of her marriage she worshipped Edward with her whole heart. I cannot count the number of times I held a sobbing Isabelle in my arms to try to comfort and soothe her. She was sick with jealousy that the handsome young king gave all his love and attention to Gaveston and could spare none for her. After his favorite was permanently removed, Edward turned to Isabelle as if he were seeing her for the first time. She was generous enough to forgive him, naively believing he was cured of his aberration. She did her duty by the king and gave him children, and the outside world began to believe that their king and queen had a normal marriage. But now that he has shamed and humiliated her once more with Hugh Despencer, her marriage is finished."

"I would never allow myself to fall in love with a man unless he had proven that he loved me," Brianna declared fervently.

Jory smiled at her daughter's innocence. "You cannot control love, darling. It controls you. The heart wants what it wants."

As Brianna made her way from the Master Tower, she was deep in thought. The things she had learned tonight answered so many of the questions that had puzzled her about the royal couple. Their relationship was cool, polite, and distant; nothing like the passionate affair between her father and mother.

She went down the hallway that led to the Lady Tower and her own room. When she got to the junction leading to the east wing that housed the guest chambers, she came face-to-face with Wolf Mortimer. She stiffened as she saw his companion.

"I forbade you to bring your wolf into the castle!"

He looked at her with tolerant amusement. "I usually ignore orders from females."

Brianna gasped. "How dare you refuse to obey me?"

He tried valiantly not to laugh at her. "I was brought up with a gaggle of spirited sisters who continually tried to rule the roost. I've been handling women and their whims since I was five. I'm not about to start obeying female orders at my age."

"I am *not* one of your sisters."

"No, you are far more vain and spoiled."

The bold devil looks as if he enjoys goading me.
"Your manners are atrocious, Mortimer!"

"While you have the manners of a fine lady, Brianna de Beauchamp. Go back to the nursery where you belong."

"Nursery!" Brianna cried in outrage.

"Only a baby would be afraid of Shadow."

"Afraid? I'm not afraid of your wretched wolf."

"Prove it," he challenged.

Her towering pride outweighed her fear. After a slight hesitation she held out her hand. The silver she-wolf sniffed it cautiously while its golden eyes assessed her.

"Your scent doesn't alarm her," he declared.

"Hers doesn't alarm me. The stink of her *master*, however, offends me to high heaven." She thrust up her chin and swept off. The sound of his mocking laughter followed her down the hallway.

Chapter 2

Just as dawn was breaking, Brianna entered the stables and saddled Venus. She was an avid horsewoman, much to her father's delight, and he had promised to endow her with his castle of Flamstead in Hertfordshire where he crossbred his distinctive and much-sought-after Warwick horses, renowned for their speed and strength.

She saw the outline of a tall male as he entered the stables. The light was dim and she suspected it was Wolf Mortimer. The sharp retort died on her lips as he drew close and she saw that it was her cousin, Lincoln Robert de Warenne.

Her frown turned into a smile of surprise and delight. "I had no idea you were here!" She welcomed his warm kiss of greeting and the ardent look of admiration he bestowed upon her.

"It was near midnight when we rode in. The River Nene was swollen with the thaw and the bridge was out."

"I warrant Uncle Lynx was cursing a blue streak."

"Actually, he showed a deal of patience. Said he'd encountered worse in Scotland and it gave him a chance to teach his sons how to deal with adversity."

"So Jamie is here too?"

He nodded. "The young devil's still snoring under the covers."

"Would you like to ride out with me?"

"You know that's why I came to the stables at this ungodly hour." He made no secret of the fact that he was highly attracted to her. "My horse cut his leg last night. I was hoping you'd take a look at it—no one knows how to treat their ailments better than you, Brianna."

"You flatter me beyond reason. All my herbal cures I learned from your mother. My concoctions do well enough, but Aunt Jane has a mystic ability to commune with animals that I haven't perfected yet."

Brianna inspected his horse's leg. "The cut looks clean."

"I washed it the minute we arrived," he assured her.

"An ointment made from briony will do the trick. I keep a large pot of it here in the stables." She retrieved the ointment from the shelf and applied it to the cut while Lincoln Robert held the animal's leg still. "It will stop the wound from fretting. Choose one of the Warwick horses. Your mount should heal in a couple of days."

The pair rode side by side, falling into an easy lope so they could talk. Lincoln Robert spoke of accompanying his mother to Scotland so she could visit her family. "Plans aren't firm yet, but I was born there, so I'm a native Scot."

Brianna glanced sideways at his mane of tawny hair and green eyes. "You look more like a lynx to me," she teased.

He laughed. "The de Warenne curse!"

"I too would love to visit Scotland. My mother spent almost as many years there as your father. It would be a great adventure."

"It's only talk at the moment, but if she does decide to go, I'll suggest you come with us—Mother would love to have you."

"Thank you, Lincoln. I adore Aunt Jane. She's so sweet, gentle, and even-tempered, compared to my mother and me."

"I admire a fiery temperament."

Brianna laughed ruefully. "I have inherited my mother's temperament, but not her lovely silver-gilt hair, alas."

"Your hair is beautiful. The morning sun burnishes it to molten red gold."

"No more—you will turn my head. Only yesterday I was accused of being vain and spoiled. I'll race you back!"

The pair galloped neck and neck. Because of Brianna's lighter weight and expert skill she arrived in the castle courtyard just ahead of Lincoln. It was filled with men readying their horses, and when she saw that Wolf Mortimer was there, she deliberately lifted her face toward Lincoln Robert and gave him a radiant smile. "You are so gallant. You let me win!"

He dismounted in a flash and came to her side. He held up his arms and she came down into them, managing to display her petticoats and her long, black riding boots.

Warwick arrived, accompanied by his brother-in-law, de Warenne. Lynx reached out his large hand and ruffled Brianna's hair. "How's my imp of Satan?" he teased.

"This week I am contemplating the convent."

"Don't be a nun, Brianna," he said with a straight face. "You'd have to cover your glorious tresses." He spoke to his son. "We are on our way to Kenilworth, then Pontefract. Go and tell your brother to hasten or we'll leave without him."

Brianna intended to go with Lincoln Robert, but just then Roger Mortimer emerged from the stables mounted on his black stallion. He cut such a handsome, gallant figure that the sight of him rooted her feet to the ground and she gazed at him with undis-

guised admiration. His teeth flashed white in his dark
face as his two sons, Edmund and Wolf, fell in beside
him. She sighed and unconsciously ran the tip of her
tongue over her lips. She caught herself and blushed.
Suddenly, she felt someone's eyes on her and glanced
up to find that they belonged to Wolf Mortimer. His
penetrating stare read her thoughts. She was mortified
to see him grin knowingly.

Brianna went up to her chamber to change from
her riding dress and found the tiring woman who had
once been her nurse, making her bed. "I'll do that,
Mary. Sit down, there's something I want to ask you."

"And what would that be, Mistress Inquisitive?"

"I only just learned that I was born at Windrush.
Why did you never tell me?"

"I don't remember, lovey," she said evasively.

"Mary, that is a deliberate lie. I know that Father
and Mother had a quarrel and she went running off
to her own castle. I want to know what their quarrel
was about."

"It was all a silly misunderstanding," Mary said
lightly.

"A misunderstanding about what?" Brianna persisted.

Mary sighed and gave in. "A wicked Welsh serving
woman, who had come to Warwick with your father's
first wife, gave your mother ale that had been dosed
with pennyroyal. Luckily, your mother didn't drink it,
or you wouldn't be here, lovey."

Brianna gasped and went pale. "She tried to *abort*
me?"

"I suspect the woman was daft in the head."

"But why did my parents quarrel?"

"Your mother thought Earl Warwick had dosed the
ale, and she ran off to Windrush to protect you."

"But why on earth would she think Father wanted
to abort me?"

Mary hesitated as she searched for an answer that would satisfy Brianna's curiosity. "Women with child are often plagued by strange notions. Earl Warwick immediately sent the servant back to Wales. And then he came riding to Windrush to set things right. It was all a terrible misunderstanding."

Brianna smiled. "Thank you for telling me, Mary."

When the woman left, so did Brianna's smile. *Mother thought my father wanted to be rid of me . . . She left Warwick Castle to protect me. Why would she suspect such a thing? Could it be possible that Father didn't want me?*

Brianna was horrified at the thought, and rejected the idea immediately. She wished that she hadn't relentlessly pursued the subject. *Of course he wanted me! Father loves me with all his heart.*

When the nobles arrived at Henry Plantagenet's castle, only five miles north of Warwick, they felt themselves fortunate to find his brother, Thomas, Earl of Lancaster, at Kenilworth. This saved them the long ride to Pontefract.

They gathered in the Great Hall and enjoyed the hospitality of a meal while Lancaster and his brother listened to Mortimer's grievances about Hugh Despencer taking land and castles that belonged to the Marcher lords.

"It isn't only the Marcher barons who are affected by the insatiable Despencer greed. If any man owns aught they desire, they imprison him and confiscate it. Their political power is dangerous and must not be allowed to continue," Thomas declared.

"My sentiments exactly," Mortimer said. "I have formed a confederacy with Marcher barons Hereford, Mowbray, Audley, d'Amory, and my uncle Mortimer of Chirk, who has been the Justiciar of North Wales for years. I have come to ask the support of Warwick and Lancaster. We must pledge to form a powerful alliance before we are ruined."

"We must be resolved to force the king to dismiss Hugh Despencer. There is no time to lose. This paramour is far more devious and clever than Gaveston ever was," Warwick warned.

"We are faced with an impossible choice," Roger Mortimer pointed out. "The Marcher barons have always been staunch Royalists. To rise up against a lawful king is treason. But Hugh Despencer is proving ruinous. He is determined to rob us of our time-hallowed privileges and we cannot allow it to continue."

Lancaster glanced at his brother, Henry, and then he nodded. "We will stand with you against the Despencers." Thomas was not known for his decisiveness. He had the clout of five earldoms and could have been the power behind the throne, if he had asserted control over the young king from the beginning. "What do you propose is the best plan of action?"

Warwick said, "I warrant the best plan is to mount an offensive against the Despencers on the Marcher lands in South Wales. I will return with you, Mortimer, and bring a force of men."

"Thank you. I have an army, but will need to recruit more."

Lynx de Warenne pledged to send troops the moment he returned home to his castle of Hedingham. He had recently inherited the earldom of Surrey from his late uncle, John de Warenne, and commanded a large number of men-at-arms.

"I pledge to bring men if you need them," Lancaster promised.

"Done. I believe I have everything I came for," Roger Mortimer said decisively. "I thank you, gentlemen."

On the ride back to Warwick from Kenilworth, Wolf Mortimer maneuvered his mount so that he was riding beside Lincoln Robert de Warenne. "I have been admiring your horse."

"It isn't mine. It's a Warwick horse I borrowed to ride out with my cousin Brianna early this morning."

"I saw you racing. You were gallant to let her win."

"I didn't. She won fair and square. Brianna rides like the wind. She has a wealth of knowledge about horses. Her father crossbreeds them at Flamstead, an easy riding distance from Windsor when she and her mother were at the Queen's Court. I miss her company."

"Your castle of Hedingham is in Essex, some distance from Windsor, is it not?" Wolf asked.

"Yes, but Hedingham is only a few miles from Flamstead. We have spent a good deal of time there together."

It was obvious to Wolf that Lincoln de Warenne was infatuated with Brianna. He spoke of her in a proprietary way. *I sense that there is an understanding between them.* His dark brows drew together momentarily in deep concentration, and then they cleared. *Poor de Warenne—you will be doomed to disappointment when I steal the prize away!*

"I thought I'd have at least a week's peace and quiet when you departed," Jory teased her husband. "Why are you back so soon?"

"Lancaster was at Kenilworth. Mortimer got his pledge."

"Thomas was no doubt making the rounds of the wealthy castles he recently inherited from his wife's late father."

"I envy him Derby. Some men have all the luck," he taunted.

"Ah, but do you envy him Alice de Lacy?"

Warwick grimaced. "Not often. I suppose I'll have to content myself with beauty." He dipped his head and kissed her.

"I sincerely hope you were served a hot meal at Kenilworth. All you will get here tonight is cold fare."

"I'll make you hot for me," he murmured.

She slapped his hand as it reached for her bottom.

After the meal, Guy Thomas challenged his de Warenne cousins to a game of dice and the Mortimer brothers elbowed their way in. When Wolf began to win, young de Beauchamp was most impressed with his skill and watched his every move. The dice matched whatever call he made, no matter how carelessly he spun them across the table. "How do you do that? What's your secret?"

"His secret is luck," Edmund Mortimer said. "My brother has the devil's own luck."

Wolf Mortimer had inherited the gift of second sight and other intuitive powers from his Celtic ancestors. He was grateful that Edmund had not revealed his real secret.

Wolf looked at the earnest young face of Guy Thomas. "I feel compelled to tell you the truth." He smiled gently. "It's not luck, it's practice."

Guy Thomas glanced up and saw his sister. "Brianna, come and watch—Wolf Mortimer has an amazing skill at dice."

She had wanted to draw closer to the group of young males who were having great fun and hadn't seemed to even notice her. She moved toward the table and stood beside Lincoln.

"Would you care to hazard a throw, Mistress de Beauchamp?" Wolf Mortimer held out the dice, his gray eyes challenging her.

Lincoln voiced his disapproval. "Brianna has no interest in playing dice—she knows nothing of games of chance."

"Course she does," her brother declared. "Who do you think taught me?"

Wolf knew she would not be able to resist, especially when told she should not indulge.

Brianna looked at her cousin and said lightly, "I shouldn't . . . but I shall! Thank you for making my decision for me, Lincoln." She took the dice that were held out so temptingly on Wolf Mortimer's palm. "What was your last throw?"

"I rolled a ten."

She looked directly into his eyes and saw the bold challenge. "I can beat that." She cast the dice with the aplomb of a goddess bestowing a favor on mere mortals, and then walked away as if she were completely confident of the outcome.

"Double six!" Her brother laughed. "Now, that was luck."

Wolf's eyes gleamed with admiration. "No, that was pride." He scooped up the dice before anyone else could touch them. He knew that traces of Brianna's essence would be left upon them and, if he chose, he could use it for his own purpose.

Jory de Beauchamp was enjoying a rare conversation with her brother before they retired. "Poor Lynx, you chose an unfortunate time to visit. The moment you arrived, you were whisked away and embroiled in the trouble of others."

"The shameful way the country is being run affects all of us. The barons must stand together. Edward is so weak and feckless. The Despencers have usurped the king's royal power. We must take it back from them—we have no choice."

"Now that you have inherited the earldom of Surrey, you must find the burden of your responsibilities much heavier."

"Not really. I've been earl in all but name for some time because of our uncle John's ill health."

Jory placed her small hand upon his large one. "Yes, he relied upon you for so much, and you never let him down."

"That's debatable, Minx. The Earl of Surrey as well

as his cousin Pembroke were always staunch king's men. Now that the earldom is mine, I'm taking the side of the barons."

"The Earl of Pembroke is the king's godfather. He made vows that he will not break, no matter how dishonorable Edward becomes. You are doing what is right and just," she assured him.

"I actually came to ask your advice. Jane hasn't seen her family in over sixteen years and I know she would dearly love to return to Scotland for a visit. Since there is a signed truce in effect, do you think such a journey would be safe?"

"I see no physical danger, but would it be politically advisable? You surely don't imagine King Edward has forgiven the barons who refused to take their troops and fight at Bannockburn?"

He grinned. "Lancaster, Warwick, Arundel, and de Warenne. We were within our legal rights to refuse. The king did not get Parliament's permission to go to war with Scotland."

"That was the excuse you used. You and Arundel were boyhood friends with Robert Bruce. Your lands in Essex ran together."

"Before we left Scotland, I swore an oath to Robert that I would never again take up arms against him. I suspect Warwick refused to fight at Bannockburn for love of you, Jory."

"Well, he may have wanted to kill Robert for having once been my lover, but Guy truly believed that the Bruce was the rightful King of Scotland." She quickly changed the subject. "Rickard answered the call to arms, as did Roger Mortimer. They have always been loyal to the king."

"At least spending the years in Ireland kept them out of the barons' continual quarrels with the king."

"Until now. Where is the thanks for all they have done? The king turns a blind eye while his lover, Despencer, steals their land in the Welsh Marches."

"Well, we can make no plans for Jane to visit Scotland until this trouble has been resolved. Perhaps next year. Do you have no desire to see Scotland again, Jory?"

"No, none. My heart belongs to Warwick."

Lynx knew that his sister meant Warwick the man and not the castle. "Here he comes. I will bid you good night."

As Guy and Jory ascended the stairs of the Master Tower, her husband took her hand. "I'm sorry your visit with your brother was cut short, love."

"I considered asking him to stay longer, then decided against it. I know Lynx is eager to go home to Jane."

"It's the very devil when you're in love with your wife."

Jory began to unfasten her gown. "Is it indeed? Most men don't have that problem."

"Let me do that." Guy removed her gown and caressed her bare shoulders.

"Mortimer for instance. His wife, Joan, remained in Ireland. He told me she prefers it to Wales because she lives on a grand scale, but I happen to know that Roger transformed both Wigmore and Ludlow into veritable palaces. In Wales, Mortimer lives like an independent prince. They *choose* to live apart. They have been estranged since their youngest daughter was born."

Guy disrobed quickly. "Their families wed them so young, they had no say in the matter." His eyes followed her possessively as she hung her gown in the wardrobe.

"The marriage was to gain land and castles for the ambitious Mortimers. It wasn't a love match, though they have certainly produced enough children."

"Yes, Mortimer is a good father. He made excellent matches for four of his daughters with the sons of England's wealthiest nobles."

"He will be ambitious for his sons. I hear he has

approached Lord Badlesmere, who owns Leeds Castle in Kent. He's arranged a betrothal between his heir, Edmund, and Badlesmere's daughter. The girl's mother is a de Clare and Mortimer knows that family owns almost half of Wales."

Warwick swooped up his wife and carried her to their bed. "Enough of Mortimer. Are you trying to make me jealous of the virile devil?"

Jory reveled in the prolonged foreplay. His kisses and caresses always thrilled her to her very core. When Warwick made love to her, he made her feel beautiful and special and her body responded to his every touch. After an hour of lovemaking, they spent together and Jory stretched languidly with satisfaction.

Guy's arms came about her again and pulled her against his body. She was surprised to feel his hard erection against her belly. "You are extremely amorous and possessive tonight, my darling. What stirs such deep passion?"

Suddenly, Jory went very still.

"You are leaving me! You are returning to Wales with Mortimer to fight the Despencers."

"I am." His deep voice was implacable. "My dearest love, I have no choice. The barons have pledged to stand together."

Jory's heart contracted. *What if it's civil war? It could be a fight to the death!* She took a deep breath and masked her fear. "Of course you must go. Mortimer could not have a stronger ally."

Wolf Mortimer sat on the edge of the bed, the pair of dice held loosely in his hand. He conjured a picture of Brianna de Beauchamp in his mind and concentrated upon it until it came into sharp focus. Then he freed his thoughts to seek out her chamber so that he could enter and observe her with his inner eye.

He smiled in the darkness as he watched her ready

herself for bed. When she removed her shift and revealed a pair of firm, high breasts, a wave of pleasure
washed over him. When she donned a night rail that
concealed her nakedness and covered her long slim
legs, he experienced a moment of disappointment.

The young beauty stepped before a mirror and
began to brush her lovely red-gold hair and his enjoyment returned. He watched her lay the brush down
and approach the bed. To his surprise she did not pull
back the covers, but sank down onto her knees. He
heard her voice, earnest and contrite.

"It was wrong of me to call the wolf wretched. I did
not mean it. I truly love all animals. She is a beautiful
creature." Brianna whispered the wolf's name with
reverence. *"Shadow."*

Wolf glanced down at the silver wolf that lay at his
feet. "She is thinking of you and speaks your name.
Go to her."

The animal arose and padded to the door. Wolf
Mortimer, silent as the night, followed her.

The next morning, Brianna was awakened by Mary.
"Are you all right, lovey? You're usually up and about
at this hour."

"I feel fine, Mary." Brianna threw back the covers
and got out of bed. "I had the strangest dream. Some
great wild beast—I think it was a lion—threatened the
safety of everyone here at Warwick, so Father and
Guy Thomas went off to hunt it. A dark angel came
to me and enfolded me in his wings to protect me. I
felt safe and warm and had no fear, even when the
beast approached. The dark angel turned into a wolf
and savaged the lion. Then it lay down beside me to
guard me until I awoke."

"That's simple enough to interpret. The threat of
the lion is the king, and your father is preparing to
leave for the Marches."

"Preparing to leave? I had no idea!" Brianna dressed immediately, dragged the brush through her tangled curls, and tossed her hair back over her shoulders.

"What's this?" Mary picked up a small silver disk that lay amongst the covers and handed it to her.

Brianna examined the small object that looked like a medallion from a dog's collar. She turned it over and saw it was inscribed with a name. "Shadow," she whispered, as fragments of her ethereal dream scattered and moved just beyond her recollection.

Brianna hurried to the Great Hall where she found her mother conversing with their castle steward, Mr. Burke. "Is it true? Is Father returning with Roger Mortimer to the Welsh Border country?"

"Yes, my dear. He's readying the men-at-arms now. We need not worry; he will leave a strong guard to protect Warwick. When they are ready to depart, we will see them off together."

Brianna noticed that her mother was unusually pale this morning, yet she gave no hint that she was the least bit troubled. "You have so much courage. I promise to put on a brave face when Father leaves."

Guy Thomas came rushing into the hall, unable to hide his excitement. "Father says I may go too!"

Brianna saw her mother's face blanch at her son's words.

Jory opened her mouth and closed it again while she gathered her thoughts that had been thrown into sudden disarray. She composed herself quickly. "I'll come and help you pack the things you will need."

He squirmed. "Please . . . I'm going on a man's mission, I don't need my mother to hold my hand."

Mr. Burke cut in smoothly, "I will advise you on what to take. We must make haste, you don't want to hold up the other men."

Jory looked at her daughter. "He's fourteen."

Brianna sought for strengthening words. "Roger Mortimer was wed at fourteen, and a father at fifteen."

"I suppose Warwick was that age too when he wed the first time. Why do they rush headlong into manhood? Why can they not wait?"

"The same reason we cannot wait to become women."

Jory's smile was tremulous. "Real women wear their best gowns and jewels and hold their heads up proudly when their men depart. It gives a lasting impression that we believe they are invincible, that they will win every battle and return home victorious."

Brianna spied Lincoln Robert and his brother, Jamie, who were carrying out their packed saddlebags. She hurried to their side, her heart in her mouth. "Are you riding to the Welsh Borders?"

"Unfortunately, no—I'd give anything to go with them. Father has promised to send troops, so we are returning to Hedingham," Lincoln said ruefully. He smiled down at her. "However, it pleases me beyond measure that you are concerned for my safety."

Brianna felt relief, though she understood Lincoln's regret. Like all young males he was eager to prove his manhood in armed conflict. "I'm sorry you are leaving. I shall miss you." Impulsively she hugged him. "Take good care of yourself. You too, Jamie. Say hello to Aunt Jane for me."

Two hours later, mother and daughter, gowned in velvet and fur capes, with emeralds glittering at their throats, stood proudly in the courtyard as the mounted men cantered by. The Warwick banners, each displaying a golden bear against a field of black, fluttered bravely in the stiff breeze. The de Beauchamp ladies raised their hands and waved as the Infamous Warwick, with his son at his side, departed.

How could I have doubted your love for me? May God keep you both safe and return you to us with all speed. The feeling of deep pride for the great courage they displayed helped to ease some of Brianna's apprehension. She had had a private good-bye with her father earlier, as had her mother. This public good-bye was for all the men.

Following the Warwick men-at-arms, Roger Mortimer, flanked by his sons, rode by and gallantly saluted the ladies.

Wolf Mortimer, his helmet tucked beneath his arm, his black hair streaming in the breeze, caught and held Brianna's gaze. His challenging gray eyes held a promise that this would not be the last time they would meet.

Brianna was clutching the small silver medallion so tightly, it felt as if it were burning a hole in her palm. She sent up a silent prayer: *Please keep his wolf safe.*

Chapter 3

"King Edward has given Lundy Island to Hugh Despencer!" Wolf Mortimer had just returned to Wigmore with a large troop of men he had recruited. The castle now bulged at the seams with Mortimer men-at-arms from Ludlow and Chirk. Henry de Bohun, Earl of Hereford, was there with his own army and also men recruited by Adam Orleton, the powerful Bishop of Hereford. The other Marcher barons had assembled an additional army, and the commanders were gathered in Wigmore's Great Hall.

"Christus! Lundy Island will give Despencer control of the Bristol Channel." Roger Mortimer was outraged.

"There's more." Wolf handed his father a missive.

Mortimer scanned the parchment. "The king is mobilizing troops and has ordered all royal castles in Wales to prepare for war."

Warwick warned, "The king has done this on the advice of the Despencers. It puts the Marchers in open rebellion against the Crown instead of against the Despencers alone. It could prevent some barons from supporting your cause even though they resent the Despencers' influence."

"Did Lynx de Warenne send men as he promised?" Wolf asked.

"He did," Mortimer replied. "I have put your brother, Edmund, in charge of his men-at-arms and you will command his Welsh archers along with your own."

The Earl of Hereford banged his fist on the table. "The avaricious Despencers have been planning this for some time. Now I see why the elder Despencer took over Queen Isabelle's castle at Marlborough." De Bohun had come into his earldom of Hereford as well as the post of Constable of England on the death of his father. Though he was widowed from the king's sister, Elizabeth, he was first and foremost a Marcher baron. "I've fought my whole life to preserve de Bohun lands and castles from the Welsh, I'll be damned if I'll let the Despencers have one fucking yard of it."

"This army they are gathering will march to Bristol. I suggest we move our forces from Wigmore to Hereford's castle of Goodrich and then stay put and let them make the first move. If they take *one* castle, we will descend upon them with fire and sword," Roger Mortimer declared.

A deafening shout, ripe with bloodlust, erupted from the throats of the entire assemblage.

The king's strong force marched westward and took control of the queen's castle of Devizes, which was within a dozen miles of Marlborough Castle. At Easter the king's army arrived at Bristol and Edward and Hugh Despencer took up residence at Gloucester. From there the king issued a warning that the Marchers were not to attack the Despencers' holdings. On the last day of March, the king summoned them to Gloucester.

When the Marcher barons ignored the summons, Edward then ordered them to convene at Gloucester the second week of April.

Roger Mortimer consulted with the other Marcher barons in Hereford's castle war room. They were amused that the king had summoned them twice. "Give me suggestions for our reply."

"Answer the summons with a legitimate reason why the Marcher barons will not attend the king," Warwick advised.

"Tell Edward that we refuse to come into his presence while Hugh Despencer remains in his company," Hereford suggested.

Mortimer put pen to paper immediately. "Excellent idea. It's time we made some demands of our own."

Wolf spoke up. "Insult their pride, if they have any. Demand that Hugh Despencer be placed in Thomas of Lancaster's custody until Parliament can hear our grievances."

Laughter reverberated around the room, as Mortimer and Hereford, the two leading Marcher barons, signed their demands with a flourish. They were all spoiling for a fight and hoped to get one by baiting Edward and his lover.

It did the trick. When the king read the insulting letter, he issued a writ confiscating all of the estates that belonged to Hugh Audley and his wife, Margaret of Gloucester, and gave them to Hugh Despencer.

The Marcher barons retaliated swiftly. On the first day of May they launched a devastating attack on Despencer lands in south Wales. By the middle of May, Mortimer and the vast Marcher army had taken back the castles of Caerphilly, Cardiff, and Newport. Then they swept across Glamorgan and Gloucestershire with fire and sword, burning newly planted crops and ravaging all the property that the greedy Despencers had accumulated. They took possession of sixty-three manors and seized thousands of sheep, hogs, oxen, cattle and five hundred horses.

Wolf Mortimer began to notice that young Guy

Thomas de Beauchamp sought his company at night around the campfires. The boy was eager for advice to improve his fighting skills and it was apparent to Wolf that the young lad wanted to emulate him. Wolf was patient and explained the best tactics to employ in a castle raid, but knew the safest place for Guy Thomas was riding alongside Warwick where his father's vigilance would protect him.

Young de Beauchamp showed little fear and one afternoon as they rode toward Whitney Castle, Wolf Mortimer saw that Guy Thomas was at the head of the pack and Warwick was nowhere in sight. The men on the walls began to shoot at their attackers, using flaming arrows that had been dipped in pitch and set alight.

Wolf's mouth went dry. He crouched low in the saddle, set his spurs to his mount, and thundered across the turf in a direct path to de Beauchamp. Just as he arrived a flaming arrow thunked into Guy Thomas's saddle. It missed the lad by an inch, but set ablaze his hair that was hanging below his helmet.

Wolf, gripping his mount with his knees, plucked out the arrow with one hand, snatched up the horse's reins with the other, and rode as if the devil himself were after them. When they were a safe distance from the castle, Wolf knocked the lad from the saddle, jumped down, and rolled him on the ground to smother the sparks that still smoldered in his hair.

"You have more guts than brains!" Wolf growled.

A white-faced Guy Thomas stared up into the gray eyes of the man straddling him. "Don't tell my father."

Wolf pulled off Guy's scorched helmet. "I won't tell him that you were reckless enough to reach the castle before the others."

Guy Thomas grinned, gingerly touching his burned neck. "I'll tell him that—don't tell him I was too slow to dodge the arrow."

Wolf cuffed him across the ear, then stood up and whistled for their horses. When both animals obeyed the summons, young de Beauchamp gave him a worshipful glance. "That's another trick you must teach me."

"First, I'll have to teach you to stay alive, you young fool!"

By the end of May the Marcher barons had taken back all that belonged to them and more besides. King Edward and Hugh Despencer fled back to London. As they traveled east they were met with jeering crowds and surly, disapproving Londoners. It was a marked contrast with the cheers that Queen Isabelle evoked when she rode out. The people loved their beautiful young queen as much as they hated the Despencers.

On Hugh's advice they moved into the impregnable Tower of London for safekeeping and the king ordered Isabelle to her own apartments in the Tower. In mid-June the king put the tower of London into the queen's custody. It was a wily move, since Edward and Hugh knew that the people would never attack the fortress if it were in Isabelle's keeping.

The Marcher barons, flush with victory, rode north to meet again with Lancaster at his magnificent castle of Pontefract. They held a private parliament and the earl reconfirmed his alliance with the Marchers. At the end of June they issued a condemnation of the Despencers and vowed to have them disinherited.

"I propose we give the king a month to rid himself of his favorites. If he does not banish the Despencers, I intend to take my army to London and expel them by force," Mortimer declared.

"We must make it clear that our threat is directed at the Despencers and not the king's person, or we could be charged with treason," Warwick warned.

Wolf Mortimer made a suggestion. "If our forces

wear livery bearing the royal arms it will show our loyalty to the Crown."

His father agreed. "Spread the word. We march in one month."

"Though Lancaster's castle of Pontefract is renowned for its lavish hospitality, I don't believe Thomas will be overjoyed to host *all* the Marcher barons for a month," Guy de Beauchamp pointed out. "I shall spend the time at my own castle and offer Warwick's hospitality to any who wish it until we march south."

Roger Mortimer grinned. "I accept your generous offer."

"Could I billet my men at Warwick?" Hereford asked. "We have our own campaign tents."

Warwick nodded. "I shall send a message to my wife, telling her to expect us."

Wolf stepped forward. "I volunteer to deliver the message, my lord earl." He smiled inwardly. He had spoken to Brianna in a dream last night and forewarned her that he would visit Warwick.

The early July day was warm and Brianna had spent the morning visiting Warwick's ailing inhabitants and dispensing her herbal curatives. In the afternoon she had taken Venus on a five-mile ride along the lush banks of the River Avon. On her way back she decided that her horse deserved a swim before she returned her to the stables.

She slipped down from Venus at a place where the rushes grew tall and the water was fairly shallow. A small skiff that she and her brother used for fishing was moored to a willow and it rocked gently as a pair of waterfowl glided by.

Brianna unsaddled Venus and watched her palfrey wander downriver a short distance, then watched her walk to the water's edge and dip her head for a drink. Brianna sat down in the skiff and removed her boots and hose. Her eyes followed an iridescent dragonfly as it hovered above a bright yellow kingcup, then swooped down to the water.

Brianna loved the River Avon and the cool water lured her. She gave in to temptation almost immediately. She removed her dress and, wearing only her shift, waded in until the water was breast high. She laughed when the ducks quacked a protest at being disturbed and paddled off.

As Wolf Mortimer approached the castle he purposely focused his thoughts on Brianna. His mind searched about for where she would be on this warm afternoon. His keen intuition told him that she was outside the castle walls, and when Shadow loped off toward the river, Wolf knew where he would find her.

He slid from the saddle, tethered his horse, and walked down toward the water. As he moved silently through the rushes, seeking his quarry, his senses became drenched with her.

Brianna heard a rustle and glanced toward the riverbank. She saw nothing and thought it may have been a bird or a small animal. When she heard the rustle again she raised her eyes and scanned the rushes to see what was disturbing them. She shivered slightly as she experienced the sensation that someone was watching her.

Her first emotion was not fear; it was anger. "You sniveling coward, sneaking about to spy on me. Show yourself instantly!"

She watched the rushes move apart and saw two bright golden eyes staring at her; then the creature raised its head and gazed at her over the rushes.

She laughed with relief. "Shadow! How on earth did you get here?" Brianna suddenly stiffened. *If Shadow is here, Wolf Mortimer cannot be far behind. How prophetic that last night I dreamed the arrogant devil would return to Warwick.*

"You skulking swine! I know exactly who it is, so

you might as well stop hiding." She waited for a drawn-out minute, her gaze riveted on the rushes, but they remained absolutely still. "Where the devil are you, Wolf Mortimer?"

"I'm behind you."

Brianna gasped. The low murmur was directly in her ear. She spun about, startled and furious. Her foot slipped out from under her and she made a desperate grab for him so that she would not fall beneath the water.

Wolf's strong hands clasped her beneath her armpits and kept her head from going beneath the surface, and then he set her firmly back on her feet.

Her breasts rose and fell with indignation at being handled in such an undignified manner. She stared, mesmerized, at the rippling muscles of his chest and arms. "You are naked!"

"You noticed," he said dryly and waded toward the riverbank. He climbed out, careless of his nudity, yet fully aware that she was staring at his bare buttocks. He was a man who enjoyed being naked. He was totally at ease without his clothes, never feeling threatened or vulnerable as others did when they were bare. It was the animal side of him. It felt natural, and like most animals he was well furred. He flung his long, black, wet hair over his shoulder and picked up his linen shirt.

"No need to thank me, Mistress de Beauchamp."

"It was *your* bloody fault! You sneaked up on purpose, just to startle me and amuse yourself."

"Alas, I was doomed to disappointment. It wasn't the least amusing to see you flail about because you were afraid of getting your face wet."

"Afraid? Afraid of getting wet? You must be jesting! I am an accomplished swimmer, Welshman."

"That sounds suspiciously like bravado. Can you swim across the river?"

Her chin went up. "Of course I can."

"I'll race you," he challenged. He dropped the shirt and began to run, splashing through the shallow water until he reached her.

"I shouldn't . . . but I shall!" Brianna's eyes widened. *The bold devil has a dragon tattooed on his thigh!* She blushed. *I've never seen anything so shameful.* Brianna turned quickly and dove beneath the water, heading toward the middle of the river where the tide ran more swiftly. She battled the current with long, strong strokes, thoroughly enjoying herself by showing off her prowess. They touched the other bank at almost the same time. Wolf Mortimer's dark face threw her an insolent grin, and then he dove beneath the surface. When his head emerged, he was halfway across the river and her heart sank. Determined not to give up, she put her head down, stroked powerfully with her arms, and kicked strongly with her long legs.

He was sitting on the riverbank when she arrived.

"I'm wearing a shift—you had me at a disadvantage."

He gave her back her own words. "And always shall." His gray eyes filled with admiration. "I will never let you win out of gallantry, Brianna. That would be an insult. Take pride in how well you acquitted yourself, and know that in the future, if you prevail in any challenge with me, it will be a worthy victory."

"Are all Welsh Borderers this arrogant?"

"Only Mortimers, I warrant." He cocked an eyebrow. "Are all shifts this transparent?"

Brianna crossed her arms over her breasts. "You Welsh devil!" She ran to the skiff to retrieve her clothes. When she emerged through the rushes respectably dressed, she found herself alone. The image of his lithe, hirsute body, however, was indelibly imprinted in her mind. She could see the sun-bronzed muscles of his chest and his wide shoulders as if he were still standing before her. And the dragon! She could definitely see the dragon. She told herself it was because Wolf Mortimer was the first naked male she had ever seen and determinedly ignored her wildly beating heart.

"Wolf Mortimer, welcome to Warwick. I hope you bring us good tidings." The countess kissed him on both cheeks and unfolded the letter from her husband.

"We met with success, my lady, but I'm sure you would prefer to hear the details from Lord Warwick. He has generously offered his hospitality to some of the Marcher barons and all should be here by tomorrow or next day at the latest."

Jory's eyes scanned the paper. "So he informs me. I see he has invited the Earl of Hereford."

Wolf saw something flicker in her green eyes and tried to identify it. It wasn't anger, nor was it fear. It was more like a memory from the past that disconcerted her. The Countess of Warwick had such a serene confidence, he was surprised to see it waver. She summoned Mr. Burke and handed the steward Warwick's communication. "They'll start arriving tomorrow night."

"Hereford is bringing his own campaign tents," Wolf told Burke.

"Very good. I'll plenish your chamber, my lord."

Brianna arrived on the scene. "Is Father coming home?"

"Very soon, darling. Wolf was good enough to bring a message." Jory looked at her daughter's dripping tresses and then her glance was drawn to Mortimer's wet hair.

Wolf bowed. "Ladies." He had seen the countess's curious glance. *Now she has something else to disconcert her.*

*   *   *

Warwick Castle, its stables, and its surrounding pastures were filled to capacity. It was almost time for the evening meal and Jory de Beauchamp, with Brianna at her side, stood in the Great Hall to welcome their noble guests.

Roger Mortimer arrived, accompanied by a much older man with a craggy face and iron-gray hair. "Do you remember my uncle, Lady Warwick? You met at my wedding many long years ago."

Jory's smile was warm and welcoming. "How could I forget the other Roger Mortimer?"

The older man took her fingers to his lips. "I'm called Mortimer of Chirk so none will confuse us. You look as young and radiant as you did two decades ago, my lady."

"Thank you, sir. This is my daughter, Brianna de Beauchamp."

Brianna tore her gaze from the handsome Mortimer and smiled at the older male.

"A rare beauty. Is she spoken for?"

Brianna laughed prettily. "Are you interested, Lord Chirk?"

"A beauty and a charmer. Your daughter knows just how to flatter an old man. Takes after her mother, I warrant."

Mr. Burke led them away and Brianna saw her mother put her hand to her throat as if she were suddenly unsure of herself. Curious about who could have such an effect on her mother, Brianna stared at the trio of males who had just entered the hall.

The countess stepped forward and held out her hands in an effusive welcome. "Lord Hereford, it is an honor to welcome you to Warwick. These tall young men must be your sons."

Brianna saw the earl gaze at her mother with longing. *Good heavens, he looks as if he's in love with her.*

The Earl of Hereford took the Countess of Warwick's hand to his lips. "Jory, you look exactly the same. I should never have let you get away." He cleared his throat. "Yes, these are my sons. John and Humphrey de Bohun."

The handsome brothers were tall, fair-haired replicas of their father. When Brianna smiled, both looked at her hungrily. A sudden thought struck her. *Mother's first marriage was to a de Bohun.* She took a closer look at Hereford.

The steward, who had seated the Mortimers, now returned for the Earl of Hereford and his sons.

Brianna could not contain her curiosity. "What did the earl mean when he said he should never have let you get away?"

"I was wed to his brother, Humphrey de Bohun. When he died in battle, the old earl wanted me for his second son," Jory explained.

"The old earl wasn't the only one who wanted you. De Bohun is still in love with you."

"Nonsense." Jory blushed. "When I refused the offer, he wasted no time marrying a royal princess."

"Was Elizabeth Plantagenet your friend?"

"No. Joanna was my friend . . . Her sister, Elizabeth, had her own household and her own ladies. The de Bohuns gave such loyal service to the late king, he rewarded them with his daughter."

"Hereford's sons are rather handsome, and become even more attractive when you consider their mother was a royal princess."

"Ah yes, until you remember there is a streak of something akin to madness in the Plantagenet bloodline."

Brianna thought of King Edward and shuddered. "Here's Father."

"At last! He was only gone four months, but to me it felt like four years."

Warwick caressed his daughter's cheek, and then enfolded his wife in his arms. "Have you seen Hereford?" he asked anxiously. "Those were such unhappy years for you. I hope that seeing him didn't dredge up sad memories."

"Of course not. It is so good to have you home, my darling."

They have eyes only for each other. 'Tis plain to any who see them together that they are still in love. Brianna spotted her brother and welcomed him home. "You look different, Guy Thomas."

"I'm older. I'm almost fifteen and I've fought in the raids that took back Welsh castles," he said loftily.

"I mean your hair. What did you do to it?"

"I cut it."

"So I see! Come, you can sit with me at dinner and tell me all about your adventures."

"Sit with my sister, when I have a chance to sup with Wolf Mortimer? You must be jesting." His eyes searched out his hero. Then he noticed the scowl on her face and tried to make amends. "Don't look so fierce, I'll ask him if you can join us."

"I wouldn't dream of imposing myself," she said sweetly. Brianna walked a direct path to where the de Bohun brothers were seated. They jumped to their feet immediately.

"John . . . Humphrey . . . could you possibly make room for me? Did you really take back all the castles in the Welsh Marches?"

Chapter 4

Though Wolf Mortimer hardly glanced in Brianna de Beauchamp's direction throughout the meal, he was acutely aware of her. She focused all her attention on the Earl of Hereford's sons, whom he knew well. She listened attentively to John de Bohun, then conversed at length with Humphrey. She laughed with one brother and accepted wine from the other, completely captivating them and wrapping them around her elegant fingers.

Wolf's composure was not ruffled by the performance being played out before him. He knew it was prompted for his benefit and he was both flattered and amused. As the meal drew to a close, however, an errant thought insinuated itself in his mind and he could not rid himself of it. In a few short months, Brianna would be seventeen and Warwick would be receiving offers for her. *Four of my sisters were wed before they reached Brianna's age, and Katherine and Joan will likely be betrothed once they turn twelve.*

Wolf knew of at least three men around his own age who would be eager for a match with the infamous Earl of Warwick's daughter. Two of them were before him now, vying for the beauty's attention. The third was the Earl of Surrey's son, Lincoln Robert, who most likely had the advantage. As well, there could be others that he hadn't even thought of. He made up his mind in an instant and followed his father as he left the hall and sought his chamber.

"Come in, Wolf." Roger Mortimer turned his attention from the map he intended to study. "Have a seat if there is something you wish to discuss."

Wolf took a chair and stretched his long legs before him. Roger poured both of them tankards of ale, then sat down to listen.

"Father, you made a good match for your sister, Catherine, when you wed her to Rickard de Beauchamp. Have you ever considered another match between Mortimer and Warwick?"

"I have. It's crossed my mind more than once. A second blood bond between our houses would be advantageous to both families. But your sister Katherine is not yet twelve and Guy Thomas is only fourteen. There's plenty of time, I warrant. Warwick's lad isn't his heir, so that puts him at a grave disadvantage, but young Kat is not the reigning beauty of the Mortimer litter so she may have to settle for a younger son."

The unintentional barb pierced Wolf's protective carapace. He was well aware that he was at a grave disadvantage by not being Mortimer's heir. He swallowed his pride and gathered his courage. "I wasn't thinking of Warwick's son, I was thinking of his daughter, Brianna de Beauchamp."

"Aye, a prize indeed. I could kick myself for betrothing Edmund to Lord Badlesmere's girl when my heir could have had Warwick's daughter." Mortimer shrugged. "The betrothal's been formalized; there's naught I can do unless *you'd* like to seduce Badlesmere's wench and carry her off?"

He knew his father was only half jesting, and his pride was badly stung. "I'm a wolf, not a bloody sacrificial lamb," he said coldly. "Good night, Father."

Roger Mortimer stared after his namesake. He wasn't the least obtuse. What virile male, especially a hot-blooded Mortimer, would not be tempted by Brianna de Beauchamp? He saw the way Wolf looked at Warwick's daughter, the studied indifference that masked the hunger. Roger didn't want his favorite son to be disappointed by a refusal. There were many heirs to earldoms from which her parents could choose a husband, and not the least of these was Lynx de Warenne's son, who was now heir to the earldom of Surrey. *If you want something badly enough, Wolf Mortimer, you will find a way to get it.*

Mortimer was working with Warwick at the castle forge. Each took pride in being able to shoe his own horse.

"Your lovely daughter Brianna will soon be seventeen. Is she spoken for?" Roger asked.

"You mean spoken for in marriage?" Warwick's brows drew together. "No, she is not yet formally betrothed."

"Perhaps there is an understanding between the de Warenne family and your own?"

"There is nothing definite, but I warrant there is an unspoken understanding between Jory and Lynx to wait and see if the young couple develop a natural affinity for each other. I prefer to leave the matter to my wife. She has very strong feelings about betrothals. Jory is adamant that Brianna not be betrothed before she is seventeen and not marry until she is at least eighteen. Jory and I wanted to marry, but her family didn't tell her that I made an offer for her. Instead, they forced her to wed Humphrey de Bohun. Jory has vowed that such a fate will not befall Brianna."

"Most of us have arranged marriages."

"You needn't tell me. I had two before I found love and happiness. I am certain of one thing—Jory will never push our daughter into an arranged marriage,

especially if Brianna has any qualms about the man."
He cleaned his horse's hoof with a rasp. "You've had
more experience in these matters than I—you've married off at least four daughters, I believe."

"I made good matches for them—I didn't consider
their qualms," Roger admitted. "Rather, I considered
the castles their husbands would inherit. Not long ago
I wed Margaret to Lord Berkley's heir and I have an
understanding with Lord Audley to betroth his son to
my daughter Joan when they are old enough. The next
in line is Kat. I saw her eyeing your son Guy Thomas
when we were at Wigmore Castle."

"You have given me food for thought. It seems like
only yesterday they were children. I am beginning to
feel ancient."

That night in bed, Warwick brought up the subject
of their children's betrothals. "I'm not saying we
should be in any hurry to get them married. But perhaps it is time we looked about us and made a list of
prospective families for possible matches."

"Brianna and Lincoln Robert seem perfectly suited
to each other. I can foresee a betrothal there, perhaps
when she turns seventeen, if we let nature take its
course, darling."

Warwick nodded. "He's a good man. Now that he
is heir to the earldom of Surrey, perhaps we should
formalize their betrothal, once Brianna turns seventeen. I cannot envision a better match for her than
Lincoln Robert."

"No. It would be an ideal match for both our
families."

"Mortimer hinted at Guy Thomas for his daughter
Katherine."

"Good heavens, our son is only interested in swords
and armor and learning to become a warrior at the
moment."

"Aye, he's more interested in fighting than fucking,

unlike his father." He drew his hand up the length of her silken leg, and it wiped betrothals from his mind.

Jory, however, pondered the subject for the next few days. Just before the month was up, when the men would be taking their armies south, she brought up the subject with her daughter. They were in the castle's vast stillroom where Brianna was hanging up bunches of herbs to dry.

"In the not too far distant future, we shall have to start looking about us for a suitable husband."

Brianna stared at her mother in disbelief. "You surely don't mean a husband for me? You have always drummed into me that I must be at least eighteen before I wed."

"You'll soon be seventeen, darling, and we will no doubt be receiving offers for you."

"You know as well as I do that I am going to marry Lincoln Robert someday. I wouldn't consider any other for my husband."

"Well, that pleases me beyond measure. Your father thinks that since Lincoln is now heir to the earldom of Surrey, we should formalize your betrothal when you turn seventeen."

Brianna suddenly realized how soon that would be, and something inside her rebelled. *I will go straight from the protection of my father to the protection of my husband.* "I will soon be seventeen years old, and every one of them has been sheltered!" Brianna declared passionately. "I've never been anywhere or seen anything. I don't want to go from being a child to being a wife with nothing in between. I want some independence like you had!"

"Like me?"

"Yes, you lived in Wales and then you lived in Scotland—places I've never even seen. When you were my age you left your family and went away to court to be a lady in waiting to a royal princess."

"You were in Windsor with me at Queen Isabelle's Court."

"Mother, I was there as your child, not as a lady in waiting."

"So you think I have you tethered to me on a leading string!" Jory took a deep breath. "I went to Wales as a bride, an unwilling bride, married to a stranger. I went to Scotland as a widow. I want to protect you from making the foolish mistakes I made."

Brianna was suddenly riven with guilt. Jory was the most loving mother in the entire world. "All I want is a small taste of freedom, a chance to make my own choices for a year. Then I shall be perfectly content to wed Lincoln Robert and become a devoted wife."

Jory let out a relieved breath. *She takes it for granted that Lincoln Robert will be her husband. We have naught to worry about.*

Wolf Mortimer paced the battlements of Warwick Castle deep in thought. Tomorrow they would ride south and tonight was his last chance to communicate with Brianna de Beauchamp. Though he had seen her every day, they had never been alone together since that afternoon in the river. It seemed as if the de Bohun brothers stalked her and she did nothing to discourage their company. If she went to the mews, the falconer was with her; if she rode out from the castle, a groom attended her; if she visited the garden, her mother's ladies were ever present.

Wolf placed his hands on the crenellated wall and gazed up at the stars in the night-black sky. He had never explored the full depth of his powers and did not know all the capabilities they encompassed, or their limitations. He had always refrained from using them on a whim. Until tonight.

He focused all his concentration on Brianna. His mind's eye saw her clearly. She was asleep in her bed and she was dreaming. Gradually, he took control of her dream and spun a new story for her to explore. Once more she was indulging in a game of chance. As she won each throw of the dice, her confidence grew and she risked higher stakes.

The moment she became reckless, she lost. She refused to pay her debt and instead, she woke up. She sat up in bed and threw back the covers, slightly disoriented. *Was I gambling in the hall before I came to bed, or was it just a dream?* Brianna was unsure because the details were so vivid.

She reached for her bed robe and put it on over her night rail. The room seemed to trap her. She had an urge to get some fresh air and then the need to escape became compelling. She felt a strong desire to go up on the castle battlements. She longed to see the stars and feel the warm night air on her face. Brianna had never before experienced such a yearning. Until tonight.

She moved silently, determined to disturb no one as she ascended the tower stairs that led to the ramparts. She stepped out and moved slowly along the crenellated wall. She stopped to gaze up at the stars and sensed that another was there in the darkness. Strangely, she was not surprised. Somehow, she had known all along that she would not be alone. She sensed the presence was overtly male and though she tried to deny it, she knew his identity.

Brianna wanted to turn and run. If she did not withdraw now, perhaps escape would be impossible. Yet because retreat was not in her nature, she hesitated.

"You have come to pay your debt in private."

"What debt could I possibly owe you, Wolf Mortimer?"

"A gambling debt."

"I didn't gamble tonight."

"Are you suggesting that I dreamt it, mistress?"

Her pulses quickened. *We could not have had the same dream.* "I won every roll of the dice!"

"Until the last throw. Then you lost and refused to pay your wager."

She tossed back her hair. "I misremember the wager."

"That is a lie." Wolf emerged from the darkness and stepped close. "You remember it as clearly as I do."

She looked up into his compelling gray eyes and could not deny it. "Then take your damn kiss and be done!"

Wolf held her gaze. "I could have *taken* a kiss, or whatever else I desired, any time I wanted. Our wager was that you *give* me a kiss. It must be a gift of your own free will."

She raised a defiant chin. "I . . . cannot."

"Ah, I see your problem. You don't know how. You have never kissed a man. Until tonight."

"Of course I have." *Lincoln Robert has kissed me . . . but not on the lips.* She saw him smile knowingly as if he read her thought.

"I clearly see your dilemma. You are not averse to giving the kiss, providing it is the most memorable kiss I have ever received, and how can you be sure if you've never done it before?"

Brianna wondered briefly if she was still dreaming. She deliberately touched the crenellated stone and found it rough beneath her fingertips. *This is no dream.*

"The answer is simple. Let your instinct guide you. Your animal instinct," he suggested boldly.

Brianna gazed at his mouth. It was sensual and wickedly tempting. She raised her eyes to his. They were smoldering gray, lit with invitation, and suddenly he was right. To her great consternation she did want to kiss him, but it must be the most memorable kiss he'd ever experienced. Her pride demanded it.

Slowly, she lifted her arms and entwined them about his neck. She went up onto her toes and leaned her body into his, resting her soft breasts against the hard muscles of his chest. She opened her lips and raised her mouth until it was almost touching his. She paused, as their warm breath mingled. She looked directly into his eyes, and then slowly lowered her lashes until they rested on her cheeks. She waited until his lips touched hers and then she yielded sweetly to the hot demanding kisses that almost devoured her.

When his possessive mouth finally set her free, Brianna lifted her lashes and smiled triumphantly. "I still haven't kissed you."

"No. That pleasure awaits you. I'll collect the debt next time we meet," he promised. "Sweet dreams, Mistress de Beauchamp."

By the last day of July, Mortimer, Hereford, and the rest of the Marcher barons arrived at London with their forces clad in green livery and bearing the royal arms. They surrounded the city and the Tower of London, where the king had taken up residence. On August 1, Lancaster, Warwick, and some of the other barons joined Mortimer. The powerful Kentish baron, Bartholomew Badlesmere, of Leeds Castle, whose daughter was betrothed to Mortimer's heir, allied his forces with Lancaster's. All demanded that the king hear their complaints against the Despencers.

In a panic, Edward summoned the Earl of Pembroke, who was the head general of his army. He had just returned from France with his new bride, Marie de Chatillon, who was Queen Isabelle's cousin. Pembroke immediately answered the king's summons and then arranged a meeting with Mortimer and Lancaster. As he listened to their complaints, he could not deny that they were valid. The Earl of Pembroke was a man of honor, who had sworn his allegiance to the king, but he saw clearly how destructive the Despencers had become. For the good of the realm, he knew the favorites must go.

"Sire, the Marcher lords and the barons cite eleven articles against the Despencers. They have usurped your royal authority, they have incited civil war, they have perverted justice, they bar the magnates from your presence, they commit violence and fraud, and they alienate the king from his people."

Pembroke gathered his courage and straightened his shoulders. "Sire, I advise you to accept the barons' demands and make peace with them."

King Edward stubbornly refused and dismissed Pembroke.

The Earl of Pembroke met again with Lancaster and the Marcher barons. Roger Mortimer stepped forward and, with his considerable charming persuasiveness, set forth a plan. "The people of London love Queen Isabelle and that gives her power. Her Grace wields far more influence in this realm than she realizes. If she will approach the king, supported by you and by all the bishops, and beg for the people's sake that her husband show mercy to his subjects by banishing the Despencers and making peace with his lords, it would be difficult for Edward to refuse. The king would not lose face if he gallantly gave in to his queen's pleas."

Everyone, including Pembroke, agreed the plan had great merit. Roger Mortimer signaled his son Wolf, who bided his time until he got Pembroke in a quiet corner. Then he delivered the second part of Mortimer's suggestions, which was far more persuasive, especially coming from the dark, compelling son of Mortimer who had the intimidating looks of a predator.

"My lord earl, I devoutly hope you can persuade His Grace to the wise course my father suggests. If the king does not banish his favorites, the barons will renounce their homage to Edward and set up another in his place."

"Another?" Pembroke knew he referred to the king's son Prince Edward Plantagenet.

Wolf leaned in closer and lowered his voice. "If their demands are not met, the Marcher barons plan to burn to the ground all the royal buildings between Charing Cross and Westminster Abbey."

During the next week, Pembroke went back and forth between the king, the queen and the bishops.

"Sire, the barons are threatening to set London ablaze. They are ready to renounce their homage to you and put Prince Edward on the throne."

"That power-hungry swine, Lancaster, is at the root of this. He has never supported me as king of this realm!"

The threats so alarmed the king that he agreed to give Isabelle and the clergy an audience.

Pembroke then went to the queen.

"My lord earl, many times I have begged my husband on bended knee to rid himself of his favorites, to no avail. I am willing to do anything to get the hated Despencers banished, but I doubt that Edward will even listen."

"Your Grace, Roger Mortimer has united the Marchers and the barons. He and Lancaster have surrounded London with their formidable forces. The king has no choice but to capitulate to Mortimer's demands. He will be able to save face if he accedes to your pleas rather than cave in to the Marchers' threats."

Isabelle caught her breath. "Roger Mortimer has done this?" A glimmer of hope ignited in her breast. *How powerful he must be to bend the King of England to his will. He must have the courage of a fiery Welsh dragon to pit himself against the authority of the Despencers. How gallant that he is willing to risk all to make my life more bearable.* "Roger Mortimer . . . Roger Mortimer." She invoked his name as if he were her savior.

The audience with Queen Isabelle and the bishops proved successful. Her intervention allowed the king to capitulate. He summoned the Marchers to Westminster and icily agreed to send away his favorites.

The following week Parliament sentenced the Despencers to exile and forfeiture of any property they had accumulated. They also were forbidden to return to England without Parliament's consent.

Without the wily and powerful authority of the Despencers behind him, the weak king was utterly deflated. On August 20, Parliament issued a writ pardoning Lancaster, the Mortimers, and the other Marcher barons who had risen against the king.

Isabelle could not believe her good fortune. She decided to go to Windsor and spend the late summer in her favorite castle. She would be with her beloved son Prince Edward, who resided at Windsor with his tutors. It was an excuse to get away from a husband she loathed. When she arrived she would go to the chapel, get on her knees, and pay homage to Roger Mortimer, a man more worthy than any saint.

Chapter 5

"Believe it or not, Roger Mortimer pulled it off without shedding a drop of blood," Guy de Beauchamp told his wife and daughter. "The Despencers have been banished, and the Marcher barons have been issued pardons for rising up against the king. Lancaster and I left immediately, but the Marchers are awaiting official writs that their lands have been restored to them."

"That's marvelous news, darling. Isabelle will be the happiest lady in England." Jory lifted her face for her husband's kiss. "Roger Mortimer could charm the ducks off the pond, but beneath his velvet glove is a fist of steel."

"Aye, beneath the polished surface, Mortimer is tough and hard-bitten, but it's a damn good thing he is."

"I'm going to miss Wolf Mortimer," Guy Thomas said wistfully.

"Wolf Mortimer is an uncouth lout. I'm surprised Father allows you to associate with the arrogant devil," Brianna declared.

"The Mortimers will be celebrating a wedding tomorrow."

"A wedding?" Brianna asked sharply.

"Roger Mortimer's son is marrying Lord Badlesmere's daughter," Guy Thomas informed his sister.

Brianna's face went pale. "Wolf Mortimer is to marry?"

Jory noticed the alarm in her daughter's voice and exchanged a look with Warwick. "No, no, darling. It is Mortimer's eldest son, Edmund, who is to wed Elizabeth Badlesmere."

"You look relieved," her father teased.

"I am relieved for Elizabeth Badlesmere. Edmund Mortimer is civilized, which is more than I can say for his brother."

That night before she retired, Brianna spoke with her mother. "Now that the Despencers are banished, I'm sure the queen will return to Windsor. Can we not go and visit with her? The gardens will be beautiful. In late summer, everything will be in bloom."

"Your father has only just arrived home. I think I'll give it a couple of days before I broach the subject. I too would dearly love to spend some time with Isabelle."

"Why don't you suggest we go to Flamstead? You know how the horses draw him. I don't think he'd be averse to spending time at Flamstead, while we visit Windsor."

"I must caution you, Brianna, that this will only be a *visit*. Much as I love Isabelle, being caught up in the intrigue, strife, and machinations of the royal court has lost its appeal for me. I prefer to spend my time with your father at our own castles. I have no intention of returning to court as the queen's lady."

Brianna gathered her courage and plunged in. "Do you think I could take your place in the queen's service?"

Jory smiled. She understood perfectly her daughter's desire to leave the nest, to spread her wings and become her own woman before she took on the role of devoted wife and mother. "You would make a perfect lady in waiting for Isabelle."

Brianna's eyes shone with excitement at the prospect. "You are the best mother in the world!"

"I'll talk to your father. I'm sure he will be eager to visit Flamstead and we can also visit Lynx and Jane at Hedingham."

"That's a lovely plan. I can't wait!"

At Leeds Castle in Kent, the wedding ceremony had been celebrated and the newlyweds had sought their nuptial chamber at midnight. The celebrations, however, went on long after the couple had withdrawn. It seemed that half of Kent had been invited to join in the revelry. By four in the morning, though, the castle had quietened. The villagers had staggered home, the inebriated guests had finally sought their beds, and even the servants had fallen asleep in the vast kitchens or the Great Hall.

A lone figure prowled the courtyard. Earlier, Wolf Mortimer had joined in the merriment, carousing with the best of them. He had been pursued by a bevy of females, taken a different partner for every dance, and slipped away for dalliance with more than one buxom wench. But as the night advanced, he grew more sober with each passing hour. Though Leeds was like a lovely mythic castle in a fairy tale, perched on the edge of its own delightful Kent lake, Wolf experienced an ominous feeling, as if a dark shadow had fallen over Leeds Castle, and he could not cast off the sense of foreboding that clung to the very stones.

He became aware of another presence and was not surprised that his father had come to join him on his lone walk. They fell into step in the darkness and without words Roger Mortimer became attuned to his son's mood.

Finally he asked, "What is amiss?"

"I have a sinister feeling about this castle. Was it not a royal castle once upon a time? How did Badlesmere come into possession of Leeds?"

"It belonged to Queen Isabelle, but when the king made Badlesmere steward of the royal household, he gave him Leeds in exchange for Adderley Manor in Shropshire."

"Since Shropshire is in the Marches, I warrant it was Hugh Despencer who wanted it." In deep thought, Wolf rubbed the black bristles sprouting on his jaw. "The king won't forgive Badlesmere, a steward of the royal household, for allying himself with Thomas of Lancaster. He could seek revenge and retaliate."

"Badlesmere prepared all his castles for war before he joined Lancaster. He was ready for an attack on Leeds." Roger placed a reassuring hand on his son's shoulder. "The danger you sense has passed. We have drawn Edward's sting. Without the Despencers the king is impotent."

"What makes you think they will stay parted?" Wolf asked.

"I have confirmation that the elder Despencer has reached Bordeaux, and Hugh Despencer's ship was seen heading into the Channel. Edward knows it will mean civil war if they return."

"Hugh Despencer has his own vessels, and is a master of the seas. He and King Edward could meet secretly at any port."

"I'll drop a word of caution in Bartholomew's ear to leave Leeds Castle well guarded."

The next day, Wolf took his brother aside. "Edmund, I don't wish to alarm you unnecessarily, but I have a feeling your father-in-law may be a marked man. I sense trouble at Leeds Castle."

"Then I had better stay here with Elizabeth."

Wolf nodded. "Father is cautious. The Marcher barons will take their time withdrawing. When we get as far as Oxford our forces will likely stay put for a while just in case trouble raises its ugly head."

Queen Isabelle had no sooner departed for Windsor than a secret missive was brought to the king from Hugh Despencer. The next day Edward left London and traveled to the Isle of Thanet, just off the coast at Ramsgate.

Edward embraced his lover as if they had been parted for years. "Hugh, my dearest love, I cannot eat, and I cannot sleep without you. Tell me that you forgive me, I beg you. It wasn't my fault! The bloody barons forced me to sign the banishment papers."

Hugh pouted sulkily and did not allow the kisses that Edward craved. "Swear to me that you will be avenged against the Marcher lords who took my lands and the barons who forced you to exile me? Only then will I find it in my heart to forgive you, Ned."

"You know I will do anything that is within my power. I lust for revenge against Thomas of Lancaster. He has always thought he should have been king in my stead. He would like to see me deposed. He would like nothing better than to set Prince Edward on the throne and rule himself as regent!"

Hugh fed the fire of Edward's hatred. "It was Lancaster who murdered your beloved Gaveston and he will not rest until he has done the same to me."

"I will never allow it. I will protect you with my life!"

This time, Hugh allowed himself to be caressed and fondled. "We must think up a plot that will bring them all low, Edward."

"I cannot think of anything save making love to you at the moment. You alone know how to soothe me. Let me love you, and then we will concoct a plan worthy of our enemies."

Hugh plied him with two goblets of full-bodied red wine, then drew him into the bedchamber. He removed his garments with a deliberate slowness that was calculated to inflame the king. Finally, he stretched himself naked on the bed and watched with veiled contempt as Edward threw off his own clothes in a frenzy of need.

Only after much persuasion did Hugh roll to an accommodating prone position. "Ned, you know what I like, first," he said coyly, taking the stopper from a flagon of scented oil.

Edward dutifully massaged and caressed his lover's buttocks, though he needed no foreplay himself and was nigh to bursting.

Finally, with a satisfied smile of manipulation, Hugh drew up his knees, raised his bum, and presented himself for penetration.

Hugh was so tight. Edward moaned with pleasure. He had no idea why most men were attracted to females when there was absolutely nothing more seductive than the stimulating body of a young male.

Edward came hard and fast because he'd been forced to abstain for a time, and one ejaculation did not nearly satisfy him. Hugh was a master of manipulation, however, and knew exactly how many times the king needed to spend before he was drained of his lust and became malleable clay in his hands.

Hugh arose from the bed and poured Edward another goblet of wine. The king sat on the edge of the bed and opened his legs in avid anticipation. Hugh dipped his fingers into the potent red liquid, anointed the large, bulbous head of Edward's cock, then handed the goblet to him. Hugh went down on his knees between the king's thighs and licked the droplets of wine with his tongue. Then he took him whole into his mouth and sucked rhythmically, watching Edward writhe in ecstasy. As the king felt his orgasm

start he began to swallow his wine, and it was the
signal for Hugh to swallow the royal elixir that always
made him feel omnipotent.

A short time later, they lay curled together in the
bed. Edward had spilled all his seed and now it was
time for Hugh to plant his own seeds in the fertile
ground of the king's mind.

"What you need, Edward my love, is a *just cause*
to move against the Marcher lords and those other
barons who have supported your enemies."

"I was outraged that Badlesmere, a steward of my
royal household, turned his coat, joined Lancaster, and
supported my enemies!"

"You must take your revenge against the Kent
baron and his family. If your cause is *just*, the people
will support you."

"The people hate me. They give their love and support only to Isabelle." Edward's voice was filled with
petulant self-pity.

"The people are like sheep, Ned. With a little manipulation they can be led in any direction. We must
use this blind devotion they have for Isabelle to our
advantage."

"You have been blessed with a quick, brilliant intellect that I do not possess, Hugh. Explain how I can
take advantage of the people's love for the queen."

"Badlesmere will have prepared his castles for war
and will be expecting an attack on his main seat at
Leeds. If you send an armed force to take back Leeds
because you have restored it to Queen Isabelle, its
rightful owner, Badlesmere's castle guard will attack
them. The confrontation will rally the people to champion the queen against Badlesmere. The outrageous
slight to your beloved consort will give you just cause
to take up arms against Badlesmere."

"But I want bigger fish than Badlesmere—I want
the Marcher barons and most of all I want that swine,
Lancaster!"

"And you shall have them, Edward my love. When the bigger fish come to the aid of Badlesmere, you will net them all and punish them for the disobedience and contempt they committed against the beloved Queen of England."

"It's a trap!" At last Edward understood the plot.

"A trap that gives you just cause to be revenged against the enemies of the queen, enemies who just happen to be your own."

"All I have to do is tell Isabelle that Leeds Castle is hers once more. She loves the place so much, I am certain she will want to visit before winter sets in. I will provide her with an armed guard as escort for her own protection."

"Edward, your brilliant intellect far outshines mine."

"My dearest Jory and Brianna . . . welcome to Hedingham. I was overjoyed when I got your message yesterday that you were at Flamstead and were coming to visit us." Jane de Warenne's face, wreathed in smiles, told them how happy she was to see them again. "Jory, you look exactly the same, not an hour older than when I saw you last, but, Brianna . . . oh my, you have blossomed into a beautiful noble lady, exactly like your elegant mother. It is no wonder that Lincoln Robert has not stopped talking about you since he returned from Warwick."

Brianna, thrilled that she lingered in Lincoln's thoughts, blushed prettily. "That was more than four months ago, Aunt Jane, I'm sure you exaggerate."

"Not even a tiny exaggeration. He's been up on the battlements since first light watching for your arrival. Any moment he will come dashing down the stairs to greet you."

Jane's words proved prophetic as her eldest son arrived before she finished her sentence, prompting everyone to laugh aloud. "You are just in time to carry our guests' luggage upstairs. Brianna, I want you to have the chamber your mother occupied when she lived here at Hedingham."

"Jane, you are always so thoughtful, not to mention sentimental. Your hospitality is ever warm and welcoming." Jory kissed her sister-in-law's cheek. After all these years she still marveled that her brother Lynx had had the good sense to make the gentle Scottish lass his wife. Though he had been heir to an earldom, he'd chosen a commoner to be the mother of his children.

Lincoln Robert hoisted Brianna's trunk to his shoulder. "We do have a staff of servants to do this, but Mother believes menial chores strengthen the character."

Brianna threw him an admiring glance. "It certainly strengthens the muscles." She picked up her jewel case. "I shall come upstairs with you . . . Lead the way."

Lincoln let the trunk slide from his shoulder to the wide bed. "Mother has little concept of how a countess should delegate responsibility to her staff. She has no ladies in waiting and instead she makes friends of the kitchen maids and sewing women."

"She wasn't brought up noble, and that is what your father loves about her. She is sweet and kind with no false airs whatsoever. She is without ambition and has never even visited the royal court, let alone sought a position there. Her husband and her sons are her life, her entire world. You are fortunate indeed."

"I agree, Brianna, that I am blessed to have such a mother, but I am heir to a great earldom and seek higher qualities in a wife. Qualities that befit a countess, such as noble blood, a fine education, and a certain refined elegance that sets her high above other females."

"A paragon indeed," she teased.

"Qualities that you have in abundance, Brianna."

"Flattery begod!" she said lightly, trying to dispel the air of seriousness that had settled about them.

"Don't swear, Brianna. It detracts from your loveliness."

Brianna raised her brows in amusement. "Bugger, bugger, damn, and bugger! Don't try to make an angel out of me, Lincoln Robert. It makes me want to scrawl rude words on the walls."

He laughed ruefully. "You take delight in teasing me."

"Perverse delight. It stops you from being stuffy. And speaking of stuffy, let's let some fresh air in." Brianna could not bear the sensation of being stifled. She turned to the window, drew back the drapes, and saw the shutters were closed.

Lincoln's arms moved around her to unfasten the iron bolt. The shutters swung open and the scent of lemon verbena wafted into the chamber. Brianna deliberately turned in his arms and smiled invitingly into his green eyes.

When Lincoln took her by the shoulders and set his lips to hers for their first kiss on the mouth, Brianna felt triumphant. *It works every time.* "Why did you never do that before?" she whispered.

"You are a gently born lady. I did not want to give you a disgust of me, Brianna."

"Perhaps I would be more disgusted if you didn't want to kiss me," she teased.

"We shouldn't be here alone in your bedchamber, my sweet. I don't want to blemish your reputation or your innocence."

She wound a strand of his tawny hair around her finger. "Not even a little?" she tempted wickedly.

"You are a minx, like your mother. I shall have to keep a tight rein on you."

"Tight rein? You make me sound like a filly you intend to ride."

He groaned and turned away from her, trying valiantly to control his physical response. "Come, I will take you back downstairs. I should go and greet your father and your brother. They are more than likely at the forge looking at the new shields our armorer has designed."

At the evening meal, Brianna was amused to see that Lincoln Robert was once again eager to be close to her. He took the seat beside her and served her with all the most succulent pieces of game. As they sat flanked by their two younger brothers, their conversation and laughter flowed easily, and Guy Thomas proudly answered all the questions the de Warenne brothers asked about his exploits in the Welsh Marches, when he had helped to take back the castles and properties that the evil Despencers had stolen from the barons.

Brianna saw her parents as well as Lynx and Jane cast glances at their table and knew that she and Lincoln Robert were being discussed. She smiled inwardly, happy that the parents of her future husband already loved her. They were like one family, and Brianna felt blessed that she would not be wed to a stranger when she turned eighteen as her mother had been.

After dinner Brianna and Lincoln played backgammon. She won the first game and laughed with glee. But when she won a second time, she suspected that her partner was deliberately losing. "I believe you could have won that game if you had tried, Lincoln."

He covered her hand and squeezed it gently. "You enjoy winning so much. I enjoy seeing your eyes gleam with victory."

The two younger boys were playing an uproarious game of fox and geese. Jamie's hunting dog kept stealing the pieces from the board and when they chased after him, the clever hound dropped them in Jane's lap for safekeeping.

Lynx laughed. "Stalker is supposed to be Jamie's,

but all the animals at Hedingham believe they are the sole property of Jane."

The next day Lincoln looked everywhere for Brianna and finally found her in the castle stillroom with his mother and her young maid, Rose. "I should have guessed that Mother would be monopolizing you," he teased.

"You are quite wrong. I am the one who begged your mother to help me make some verbena-scented candles. I love the fragrance of lemon."

Jane smiled inwardly at her son's interruption. She knew he was enamored of Brianna and had wondered how long it would take for him to run her to earth. "Rose dear, fetch me one of the small flagons of verbena oil I have distilled."

Rose brought the small bottle to Lady de Warenne.

"Try a few drops of it in the water when you wash your hair. I'll have Rose take it up to your chamber."

"What a lovely idea. Thank you, Jane . . . thank you, Rose."

"It's such a warm sunny day, I warrant it is an unconscionable waste to spend it indoors," Lincoln declared. "I was hoping you would ride out with me around Hedingham. I'd like to show you the river and the woods we acquired last year."

"I would like that above all things. It will take hours for the wax candles to set. I don't need to stand vigil over them."

"Why don't I get cook to pack you a lunch, then you won't have to come rushing back here to eat?" Jane suggested. "My son has the appetite of an ox and, like most male animals, is at his best when regularly fed and watered."

"I'll go up and change. Don't leave without me."

"No need to hurry, Brianna. I'll saddle Venus for you."

Brianna changed into her green riding dress, pulled on her boots, and made her way to the stables. She realized it may have been wiser to use the feminine trick of keeping him waiting, but she knew there was no need to pique Lincoln's interest in her. He made no secret of the fact that he was enamored of her.

She felt his hands linger at her waist after he lifted her into the saddle. "Did you remember the food?"

"I did. My saddlebags are filled with tempting delights."

She threw him a saucy glance. "Perhaps it's a good thing your mother warned me about your appetite."

The pair rode slowly, their stirrups almost touching, so they could talk, as their horses cantered over the vast Hedingham holdings. The orchard trees were laden with fruit and Lincoln picked them each an apple. He watched in fascination as Brianna bit into it with relish, then licked the juice from her lips.

It was harvest time and they rode past fields of wheat and barley that had been scythed and bundled into sheaves. The hay too had been cut and stacked so it could dry for a few days in the September sun before being gathered and stored for the winter. Their horses flushed a covey of wild game. The birds had been gorging themselves on the scattered seeds.

"We should have brought the dogs," Lincoln said.

"Oh no, it thrills me to see the birds take flight and know they are in no danger. The iridescent feathers of the pheasants are brilliant in the sunshine." She spied a blue-green tail feather on the ground and impulsively dismounted and picked it up.

Lincoln dropped from his saddle, plucked the feather from her fingers, and stuck it into his tawny hair. "It's a cock feather, far too vivid for a well-bred lady." When she tried to snatch it back, he danced away from her. "Catch me if you can."

She was after him in a flash, joining the game with

zest. She grabbed his shirt with one hand and jumped high enough that her fingers were able to filch the feather from his locks.

His hands encircled her waist and she dropped to the ground and tried to scamper away from him. He clung tight and the pair of them rolled against a haystack, knocking it over and scattering the hay stalks all about them.

He pinned her beneath him and as he gazed down at her, his laughter fled and his face became serious. "Brianna, I think you know how I feel about you."

She laughed up at him. "Not really. Why don't you tell me?"

"I'd much rather show you." Lincoln bent his head and kissed her full on the mouth.

The kiss put her in a decidedly playful mood. "I concede," she said breathlessly, adorning his hair with the vivid feather. "You have presented me with irrefutable evidence that you are the *cock* and I am the hen."

"Brianna de Beauchamp, you say the most outrageous things."

"Therein lies the attraction, mayhap." At his quick frown, she said, "Surely I don't shock you?"

"Sometimes," he admitted.

"Yet you don't consider that rolling me in the hay is shocking, Lincoln Robert de Warenne?"

He looked down into her eyes. "Are you shocked?"

"Not yet, but the day is young." She grinned up at him with mischief brimming in her eyes. She quickly wriggled out from beneath him and ran to her horse. By the time he got to his feet, she had mounted. "Perhaps when we get to the woods you can try again." She touched her heels to Venus and they took off, leaving her silvery laughter dancing on the breeze.

For their midday repast Lincoln chose a shady spot where the river skirted the edge of the woods. Brianna

sat down on the grass dotted with lacy white saxifrage
and purple Michaelmas daisies. She immediately removed her boots and hose, so she could wade in the
water. "You will have to add impulsive to my faults."

"I'll add it to the things that make you irresistible,"
he said gallantly.

She moved to the wide river's edge. "Oh, how
lovely . . . the fish are darting about like silver
daggers."

"We bought the river for the fish and the woods for
the game. They help supply Hedingham with food."

"How prosaic and practical. Don't spoil my illusions. I imagined they were acquired to add a romantic atmosphere."

"Let's eat, I'm starving. We can wade later." Lincoln emptied his saddlebags of the food that had been
wrapped in linen cloths.

Brianna joined him on the grass. "What are the
tempting delights, Scotsman? D'ye have a haggis hidden under your kilt?"

Lincoln gave her a quelling glance as he unwrapped
freshly baked bread and soft cheese. "I have venison
pies and quince tarts—I also brought a flagon of
wine."

"Ah, now you're talking. Mother prefers ale, but I
have recently discovered wine and I like it exces-
sively." Brianna nibbled on some cheese and enjoyed
a pie, while Lincoln devoured everything else. He had
a man's healthy appetite and she took pleasure in
watching him eat. Each time she drained her cup of
wine, she held it out to be refilled.

After her third cup, she lay back among the wild-
flowers, replete and happy. The wine filled her imagination with daring thoughts as Lincoln Robert stretched
his great length beside her. He leaned on an elbow and
gazed down at her.

The corners of Brianna's mouth lifted in a secret

smile. *You want something. Dare I hope you will challenge me to a naked race across the river?*

Lincoln threaded his fingers into her dishevelled curls, and touched his lips to her wine-red mouth. "I love you, Brianna. Will you marry me?"

Chapter 6

"Lincoln Robert, you know I will." She looked up into his green eyes that held a trace of uncertainty. "Surely you had no doubt of my answer? I've always known you would be my future husband."

His uncertainty vanished in an instant and was replaced with a look of happy relief. "I needed to hear you say it. After all, you are the daughter of the Earl of Warwick and I've recently come to realize the danger in simply taking it for granted."

"Danger?" she puzzled.

"Now that you are of marriageable age your father will be receiving other offers for you. The Barony of Warwick is both powerful and wealthy with its many castles and vast landholdings. You are a prize that will tempt every noble in the land."

"Because of my father's name and wealth?"

"Absolutely."

"How very flattering," she teased. "You, of course, are the exception. You love me for myself."

He searched her face. "You know I do. But I'm a man, Brianna, and I must be practical. I am responsible for providing for our future. Father has promised me a castle of my choosing when I wed. I am torn between Wigton, near the Scottish Border, which has obvious appeal for me, or Farnham Castle in Surrey that Father inherited from Uncle John de Warenne."

"You've never been to Wigton Castle. I think you should see it before you decide."

"It could be a year before I get to travel to Wigton," he protested. "I must decide now, my dearest."

"But it will be at least a year before we marry."

His brows drew together. "What do you mean, a year?"

"Mother has always been adamant that I be at least eighteen before I marry."

"But that's ridiculous! I just asked you to marry me and you accepted."

"Lincoln, I thought you were talking about the future. We are so young . . . We have our whole lives ahead of us."

"I'm nineteen. I want a wife now—I want sons."

"That's one of the reasons Mother wants me to wait until I'm eighteen. She thinks seventeen too young to have a child."

He ran an impatient hand through his hair. "We'll go and talk to her—we'll persuade her to change her mind."

"But I happen to agree with her." She reached out and touched his cheek. "Lincoln, am I not worth waiting for?"

He groaned. "Of course, sweetest. But so much can happen in a year." He gathered her close. "What if someone tries to steal you away from me?"

"Impossible," she whispered. "I put my heart in your keeping, Lincoln. I pledge you my love."

Her words lightened his mood. "I won't give up," he vowed. "I give you fair warning I intend to overcome your resistance."

When they arrived back at Hedingham, Brianna went inside to freshen up and change her clothes before the evening meal, while Lincoln Robert took their mounts to the stable. Inside he found his father discussing the purchase of horses from Warwick.

"I'm glad I've found you together. I have a dilemma and hope you will conspire to help me. I asked Brianna to marry me today and happily, she said *yes*."

Lynx grinned, pleased at the news. "I see your dilemma. You should have first made a formal offer to her father here."

"Yes, I am aware of the correct procedure and I apologize for not seeking permission before I proposed, but I wanted to make sure that Brianna felt the same way I did." He looked at Warwick. "I'm making a formal offer for your daughter now, sir."

"Warwick is a tough negotiator. When he married Jory, he actually managed to talk John de Warenne into giving her Chertsey Castle in Surrey. I have no doubt your lovely bride will cost me an arm and a leg," Lynx jested.

"Brianna said her mother would not let her wed until she is eighteen. I need you both to help me change her mind."

Lynx threw up his hands in mock horror. "My sister Jory has a will of iron. Once she makes up her mind about something, she is tenacious as a terrier. I'll broach the subject, but I think it will take a man of Warwick's courage to challenge her."

Both father and son looked at Guy de Beauchamp, who had remained doggedly silent on the subject.

"Jory and I have discussed our daughter's future marriage, and we agree that a match between you and Brianna would be ideal for both families. We could not ask for a finer husband for our daughter. Since she is almost seventeen, I see no reason why you could not be betrothed for a year, but I know her mother is opposed to Brianna marrying before she is eighteen."

"Can't you help me change her mind, sir? To me a year seems like an eternity."

"Splendor of God, do you know how fortunate you are in being able to marry a lady of your own choosing? Neither Warwick nor I had that luxury. Our marriages were arranged. We did not get to know our brides until after our vows were exchanged. I warrant that a year is a short space of time to curb your impatience."

Brianna found her mother and Jane in Hedingham's lovely solar. When she found them alone together, she had an overwhelming desire to confide her exciting news.

"Lincoln Robert asked me to marry him and I said yes!"

Jane jumped to her feet and enfolded her niece in loving arms. "That's wonderful, though I must admit it is no surprise. My son speaks of you constantly. I am so happy, Brianna. I love you dearly . . . You are the daughter I always wanted."

"When I told him we would have to wait until I was eighteen, he was grievously disappointed."

"Well, I think that is a wise decision. I was eighteen when Lynx and I were handfasted and I conceived immediately. I think seventeen is too young for motherhood, though many noble ladies are wed at fourteen or fifteen."

"I'm sure Lincoln Robert can be persuaded to wait a year for you. Your father actually waited more than five years for me, and Warwick is certainly not known for his patience," Jory declared. She looked at Jane. "Brianna would like to spend a year at court with the queen before she gets married. Hedingham is close enough that she and Lincoln will be able to visit with each other throughout the year."

"That's true. Promise me you will come often?" Jane invited.

That night in the hall, when the subject of Brianna

and Lincoln Robert's future marriage was discussed, Lynx de Warenne championed his son's cause. "Why don't we draw up the contract and betroth them formally? That way, perhaps my son will stop worrying that you will entertain other offers for your beautiful daughter."

"I have no objection if Jory agrees," Warwick declared.

"And I have no objection if Brianna wishes it. They make a perfect couple," Jory declared.

Lincoln Robert took possession of Brianna's hand and murmured, "I'd like us to be formally betrothed, sweetest, but I give you fair warning I shall still try to persuade you to marry me, long before you are eighteen."

"I shall like being wooed," she whispered seductively.

The Earl of Warwick and the Earl of Surrey negotiated late into the night. In the end a contract was drawn up giving Farnham Castle, in nearby Surrey, to Lincoln Robert. In addition, Lynx de Warenne agreed to give Wigton Castle, with its wealth of sheep, to Brianna on the day the young couple wed. It was also put in writing that Lynx's eldest son would inherit Hedingham along with the earldom, and Guy de Beauchamp legally bequeathed his beloved Flamstead Castle along with its herds of horses to Brianna.

The following evening, the two families gathered in the castle's small library where Hedingham's business affairs were conducted. Tall candles lit the chamber and illuminated the legal document that lay on the polished oak table awaiting the signatures of the young couple. The betrothal contract, as well as being a mutual promise for their future marriage, laid out in detail the properties that Brianna and Lincoln Robert would receive on the day they were joined in holy matrimony. The document must then be witnessed and signed by both sets of parents.

Lynx de Warenne dipped the quill in the inkwell. "Though you know what we have agreed upon, I urge you to read the contract before you sign it, Brianna."

She smiled up at Lincoln. The warm glow of the candlelight emphasized the rich tawny color of his hair. She took the quill from Lynx, and knew that her future husband would look exactly like his father when he was fifty. The realization pleased her.

Her eyes scanned the words on each page of the crackling parchment, and then she signed it with a bold flourish.

Lincoln Robert stepped up beside her and he too carefully read the legal document. After he signed the betrothal contract, he captured her hand possessively and lifted her fingers to his lips while his eyes paid homage to her beauty.

They watched their parents come forward and affix their signatures as witnesses. A betrothal ceremony required no exchange of vows or verbal promises of undying love, devotion, or fidelity. It was simply a straightforward binding, legal contract.

To make the memorable occasion more personal, Lincoln Robert reached into his doublet and pulled out a small box. "It's a betrothal ring to wear as a token of my love."

Brianna caught her breath and opened the box. "Oh, it is an emerald . . . my favorite jewel." She held out her hand so that Lincoln could do the honors. She knew that emeralds were the traditional stones of the de Warenne family, handed down through the generations. "Mother has a large collection from which she generously allows me to borrow from time to time. I am thrilled to finally have an emerald of my own. Thank you, Lincoln."

"I believe a betrothal calls for a toast. I know some of you prefer ale and some wine, so I asked the steward to provide us with both tonight," Jane declared, moving to a side table.

Jory spoke up. "I believe I will forgo ale on this very special occasion. Let's toast the betrothed couple with wine."

Guy de Beauchamp enfolded his daughter in his arms and dropped a tender kiss on her bright curls. "Remember that you are still mine. I don't have to give you away for another year," he murmured softly.

He loves me with all his heart. How could I have ever doubted?

Her father looked into her eyes. "If anything or anyone mars your happiness, come and tell me."

She went up on tiptoe to kiss his cheek. *As if anyone would dare do anything that would earn the wrath of the infamous Earl of Warwick.* "I love you, Father."

"Where shall we have the wedding?" Jory asked. "Flamstead is closer to Hedingham than Warwick and would be more convenient."

Father loves Flamstead. "Yes, let's hold the wedding at Flamstead," Brianna agreed.

An hour later, when Brianna was readying herself for bed, Jane slipped into her chamber. "I too have a gift for you, but I wanted to give it to you in private. Though I know your mother will approve, since I painted one for her years ago, I'm not sure about your father. He frowns upon superstition and would likely scoff at the idea that a Celtic artifact has powerful mystic properties that can guide and protect you."

Brianna took the small silk bag from Jane, and could feel the oval shape of the object inside. "Oh, how lovely. You have painted me one of your Celtic touchstones."

"When you saw them on my worktable in the solar the other day, I could see your fascination. The moment you left, I decided to design one especially for you."

"The touchstones you paint with flowers, goddesses, and Celtic crosses are all extremely beautiful, but I hope you chose a symbolic animal for me."

"When you love animals so much, it was an obvious choice."

Brianna slid the flat, oval stone threaded with a delicate leather thong from the silk bag. She held it on her palm and gazed down, enthralled at its beauty. The symbolic animal Jane had painted for her was a silver-gray wolf with golden eyes.

"The she-wolf is a Celtic emblem of power, intelligence, and secret knowledge. She is the chosen companion of the earth goddess Sironi. The she-wolf is a superlative mother, fierce, protective, and loving. She will guide and protect you on your journey through life."

"She is lovely. I can already feel her power. I thank you from the bottom of my heart!"

"I'm so glad you like her. Good night, my dear. Sleep well."

When Brianna was alone she gazed down at the touchstone, amazed that Jane had chosen the she-wolf for her emblem. She traced the exquisite creature with her fingertip. "Shadow . . . Shadow."

She set the touchstone down on the table beside her bed, but once she slid beneath the covers, she picked it up and slipped the thong over her head. The wolf lay in the valley between her breasts, close to her heart. It wasn't long after Brianna fell asleep that she drifted into a dream.

She heard a sound in the distance that made the hair on the nape of her neck stand up. She raised her head from her paws and listened intently. The howl came again, stirring her senses and calling to the wild spirit that lay hidden, deep within her. She got to her feet slowly, silently, as her innate wariness cautioned her to use her eyes, her ears, and her keen sense of smell to alert her to the dangers that might lie in wait for her outside her den. The howl came again and the call to the wild was so tempting, so compelling, that it was almost irresistible.

With an age-old wisdom bred into her through generations of clever, wily ancestors she carefully weighed the risks involved. Her natural reluctance gradually eroded, replaced by the knowledge that the adventure that awaited her promised to be glorious. Her restless spirit hungered for excitement. Her every instinct thirsted for a soul mate.

Silently, she moved from her safe haven into the shadowy, moonlit night. She slipped between the trees to where the ground began to slope upward, following an invisible trail that lured her to her destiny.

Suddenly she saw him and stopped dead in her tracks. His black silhouette was outlined by the moonlight as he stood on the summit of the hill with his head thrown back. He was the most magnificent male she had ever seen. Instinctively, she knew the dark wolf would be dominant and dangerous, but she was ready to follow wherever he led.

He scented her presence, turned to look at her, and howled a welcome that was elemental and primal. She drew closer, answering his call, and saw that his sleek pelt was black, his eyes a fierce light gray. He took a step toward her and she growled a warning in her throat. He ignored her warning and his tongue came out to lick and taste her. She nuzzled his neck, accepting him.

Side by side, they loped down the hill, running faster and faster in a wild frenzy of joy, relishing their freedom, ecstatic that they had found each other. They covered miles of territory, over fields, through streams and woods until dawn began to lighten the sky. They

*flushed a covey of birds and playfully chased them,
though they had little interest in hunting at the moment.
The game of mating was far more pleasurable and held
them in its thrall. Exhilarated by their nightlong dash,
they found a clearing in the heart of the forest.*

*He stretched his sleek body in the grass and she lay
down beside him, admiring his dark male beauty. She
felt the primal heat of arousal in her belly and rolled
playfully onto her back, yielding to his dominance in
alluring age-old feminine submission.*

Brianna awoke with a start. She sat up and saw that
the first flush of dawn light was inching in through the
open shutters, illuminating the lovely chamber that
had once belonged to her mother. She felt the touchstone against her breast and it evoked a memory of
her dream. "I was dreaming about Shadow." A frisson
of delight rippled through her as she remembered
more about the dream. "No, I dreamed that I actually
was Mortimer's she-wolf." Suddenly, she blushed and
her delight turned to dismay, for she knew with a
certainty the identity of the dark, dominant male who
had lured her to indulge in the reckless, uninhibited
mating game.

Brianna deliberately dismissed the dream from her
thoughts. This would be her last morning at Hedingham. After the noon meal, her father and brother
were returning to Flamstead Castle while she and her
mother were off to Windsor.

Brianna had promised Lincoln Robert that she
would ride out with him before she left, so that they
could enjoy a private farewell. When she arrived at
the stable, she heard laughter and identified the voices
of her betrothed and his brother Jamie.

"There's one sure way to make Brianna beg to
marry you long before she turns eighteen," young de
Warenne declared.

"And what might that be, genius?"

"Get her with child, of course."

Brianna was stunned at the blunt advice she had inadvertently overheard. She wanted to slap the young devil's face.

"My own thought exactly!" Lincoln replied, laughing.

Very bloody funny, I don't think! She turned on her heel and left the stable, but halfway across the courtyard she saw the humor in the situation. *They'd die of chagrin if they knew I'd overheard them.* She wasn't naive enough to think males didn't discuss sexual matters; it was likely their favorite topic. Upon reflection she decided to return to the stables. This time, however, she made enough noise to alert them.

Lincoln Robert came to greet her immediately. "Good morning, sweetheart. I've saddled Venus for you."

"How thoughtful you are. Good morning, Jamie. It does my heart good to see brothers get along so well. Why don't you join us on our ride? Lincoln and I would both enjoy your company."

Jamie glanced at his brother. "I don't think—"

"I insist . . . I won't take no for an answer." She watched the smile leave Lincoln's face, and hid her amusement.

"I'm afraid I must decline, Brianna. Father will have my scalp if I run off and—"

"Oh, go on . . . I'm jesting, for God's sake. As if we want a chaperone along to observe our tender good-byes."

He laughed with relief and left them to their own devices.

"You should have seen your face. It turned dark as a thundercloud. I was only teasing." She licked her lips. "I enjoy teasing you, Lincoln."

When he lifted her into the saddle, she gave him a provocative, come-hither look. "Catch me if you can."

By the time he finished saddling his own mount, she

was out of sight. He didn't catch up with her until he reached the orchard.

Brianna dismounted and reached up to pick an apple. The one she wanted was beyond her reach, so she climbed into the tree. "I forwent breakfast this morning, so we could ride out together." She picked two apples and bit into one with gusto.

Lincoln was out of the saddle in a flash. He came to the tree and lifted his arms in invitation.

Brianna took another bite and slowly licked the juice from her lips as she contemplated his invitation. Without warning, she sprang down into his arms and her momentum carried them sprawling to the ground. Lincoln rolled until he was in the dominant position. She held out the other apple and murmured seductively, "The woman tempted me."

He covered her mouth with his and kissed her hungrily. He was fully aroused and pressed his hard erection into her soft belly. He lifted his mouth from hers and gazed down at her with speculative eyes, as she lay supine between his thighs.

"There's one sure way to make me beg to become your wife," she whispered temptingly. "Make love to me and get me with child."

Lincoln groaned and sat up. "Christ, Brianna, you heard us talking in the stables this morning."

"Indeed I did, Lincoln Robert de Warenne. And I hereby give you fair warning that I have more good sense than to allow you to seduce me." Her eyes sparkled wickedly. "For at least another year," she added saucily.

When she made no move to get up, he leaned back over her. "Because you'll be gone within the hour, I have an overwhelming urge to kiss you as you've never been kissed before."

Brianna was filled with the wisdom of Eve. They had already fought over her wanting to become a lady in waiting to Queen Isabelle, and she knew how much he disapproved. "It's because I'm going to court. You have an overwhelming male need to put your brand on me."

"Yes, I do," he admitted. "It's because you would tempt any man to madness." His lips crushed hers possessively.

Lincoln Robert stood in Hedingham's courtyard long after Brianna had departed. He cursed under his breath. He had never felt as frustrated in his life. Brianna acted as if she had done him a great favor in agreeing to the betrothal, when in fact it was the other way about. *I'm the heir to the earldom of Surrey! A betrothal entitles me to certain rights that she took great delight in denying me. The cock-teasing little bitch has had me in a state of arousal for days.*

Lincoln eased his swollen cock into a more comfortable position and spied Rose, his mother's serving girl, walk across the courtyard with a basket over her arm. His eyes followed her with speculation and he closed the distance between them.

"Where are you going, my pretty maid?" he teased.

Rose blushed at the handsome young heir. "I'm going to the orchard, my lord. Cook needs some pears."

You have a lovely pair! "Rose, I think I'll come with you and make sure they are ripe."

Chapter 7

"Jory! Brianna! I sent a message to Warwick, imploring you to return to Windsor. I thank you from the bottom of my heart for coming so quickly." Isabelle was overjoyed to see the Countess of Warwick and her daughter.

The de Beauchamp ladies went down before the queen in deep curtsies. "Your Grace."

The queen raised them immediately. "You must call me Isabelle, as you always did, when we are among ourselves."

"We didn't get your message," Jory explained. "As soon as we heard the Despencers were sent into exile, we made plans to come."

"We persuaded Father to visit his castle of Flamstead, so we could come to Windsor. I thought about you every day and I long to see baby Joan."

"She is a beautiful baby. The children will be so excited to see you when they waken from their nap." Isabelle stared at Jory's daughter with unconcealed admiration. "Brianna, it has been more than a year since last I saw you. You are no longer a girl, you are a lady . . . a beautiful lady."

"I decided she was old enough to learn the truth about Hugh Despencer, so there is no need to pick and choose your words, dearest Isabelle. After we were dismissed and sent home to Warwick, was it unbearable for you?"

Isabelle's blue eyes revealed her vulnerability as she remembered the indignities she had been forced to suffer. "Sometimes I fear the walls have ears. Come, let us go into my private sitting room where we can be comfortable, and I will tell you all."

The queen's steward served them wine and discreetly withdrew.

"On Hugh Despencer's orders, all my ladies were dismissed and the loyal French servants, who came to England with me when I was married, were sent home. I was allowed to keep only my steward, Montebus, and his wife, Beth, who was my only lady of the bedchamber. I was deprived of my musicians and my dressmakers. One by one, all the castles that were in the queen's dower were taken from me. First it was Brotherton in Yorkshire. Then it was Leeds nearby in Kent, which I dearly loved and visited often. After that Marlborough and Devizes were taken from me. Despencer took all my rents and revenues and kept them for himself. I had no money to run my household or pay my servants, not even Matilda my washerwoman."

Brianna was appalled. "Your Grace, you are the Queen of England. Did you not complain to King Edward about the shocking way that Hugh Despencer was treating you?"

"I tried . . . on the few occasions I was permitted to see my husband. Edward insisted that because of his father's wars, England's coffers were empty. He told me that as chamberlain, his dearest friend Hugh was forced to institute economies in the royal household. He grudgingly agreed to pay for the children's nursemaids, for which I was thankful."

"The avaricious bastards grew rich at your expense," Jory declared passionately. "When Warwick told me they took back sixty-three manor houses and thousands of sheep and cattle that the Despencers had accumulated, I was outraged at their greed."

"I was well aware of the Despencers' power since they were the principal members of the King's Council, but I had no idea of the vast lands and properties they had unlawfully amassed or the wealth they had stolen from the Marcher lords and the barons of England."

"Now that the hated Despencers are exiled and forbidden to return without consent of Parliament, you must forget about them."

"Jory, I will *never* forget!" she whispered fiercely. "I loathe and detest Hugh Despencer with every ounce of my being. Exile is too good for him. I wish him dead!" The ice-hard expression on Isabelle's beautiful face softened. "I owe an enormous debt of gratitude to Warwick and Thomas of Lancaster and to Roger Mortimer, who came all the way from Ireland to deliver me from my enemies."

"Ridding England of the Despencers was brave and heroic," Jory agreed, "but it was in their own best interests, Isabelle."

"To me they are saints," the queen insisted.

"Roger Mortimer is the most gallant man I've ever known." Brianna's face was radiant as she remembered the last time she had seen him mounted upon his black stallion.

"His handsome looks and his charm are enough to turn any woman's head and have captured my daughter's imagination. But the qualities I admire most are his strength and determination."

Brianna and Isabelle exchanged a look that told Jory both females were in danger of losing their hearts to the virile devil. She deliberately changed the subject. "The Earl of Pembroke wed your cousin. I would love to meet her."

"And so you shall. Marie is here at Windsor. You

will both love her. Her Parisian gowns put mine to shame. I haven't had the pleasure of any new clothes for a very long time. Alas, what beauty I had has faded. I have become pale and wan. When I could no longer bear to look at myself, I had my mirrors covered."

"Dearest Isabelle, your beauty has not faded," Brianna insisted. "You have an ethereal, delicate look that makes your face exquisite."

"Do you really think so, Brianna?" Isabelle asked uncertainly.

"It is not any lack of beauty that is the problem here. It is your complete lack of confidence," Jory insisted. "What the devil have those cruel swines done to you, Isabelle?"

The queen smiled tentatively. "Life will be good again, soon, I hope. Some of my musicians are back and I have just had my royal barge returned to me. We will be able to go out on the river again and perhaps my son Edward will join us. Please tell me you will stay here at Windsor with me for a little while so we can enjoy what is left of summer?" Isabelle pleaded.

"Thank you, Isabelle. I will be delighted to stay until the end of September, but Brianna's dearest wish is to stay a whole year and serve you as a lady in waiting."

The petite queen's eyes lit with pleasure. "Brianna, would you really do that for me? I've been so alone . . . You have no idea what your company and your friendship would mean to me."

"Your Grace, it is my great honor to serve you. You are the Queen of England, beloved by everyone."

"Not everyone, I'm afraid." Her small hand fluttered to her throat, and it tugged at Brianna's heartstrings to see how unsure of herself the young queen had become.

"I can't wait to see Prince Edward. I warrant he

will easily outride me by now." Brianna had ridden out regularly with the young prince when her mother had been part of the Queen's Court.

"Edward has grown so tall, you won't recognize him. I am told that he is the image of his grandfather, not just in looks, but in his personality also. Everyone remarks upon it."

"Then you have good reason to be proud of him," Jory said.

Isabelle summoned her steward. "I'd like you to plenish the same rooms that the Countess of Warwick previously occupied. When she leaves they will belong to Lady Brianna, who has graciously consented to serve as my new lady in waiting."

Two hours later the de Beauchamp ladies had unpacked and their rooms, adjacent to the queen's chambers in the Upper Ward, looked as if they had never left. Brianna opened the windows that overlooked Isabelle's private garden. "I'm so glad these familiar rooms will be mine. Windsor is such a lovely castle."

"You will have your work cut out for you," Jory told her daughter. "The greatest service you can do for Isabelle is to restore her confidence. She is far too vulnerable and unsure of herself at the moment. It will do her a world of good to have a trusted friend in whom she can confide. You will serve as a perfect role model . . . You have an abundance of vitality and self-assurance, Lady Brianna de Beauchamp."

"That is because you have always set such a glorious example for me, Mother."

Jory smiled, pleased at the compliment. "Try to instill some of it in Isabelle. A queen should possess a regal confidence."

"I will do my best," Brianna promised.

"That's all any of us can do. Let's go and see the children. It's been so long, perhaps they won't remember us."

When Brianna and her mother returned to Isabelle's apartment, they found her holding her last-born, Princess Joan.

The tiny one-year-old had a heart-shaped face like her mother. "Oh, she is so beautiful . . . She looks exactly like you."

"Thank you, Brianna. She is such a happy baby. Ah, here come John and Eleanor. My son is now six."

"And Eleanor is four." Brianna swooped up the child, who immediately chortled and tangled her fingers in the tempting red-gold curls. "She remembers my hair!" Brianna was delighted.

Prince John of Eltham carried a wooden sword and thrust it into all the chair cushions. Isabelle smiled indulgently. "He wants to be just like his big brother, Edward."

Jory pretended to be afraid of the fierce warrior, and the child laughed with glee. "You have beautiful children, Isabelle."

"I love them so much. They have helped me keep my sanity during the dark times when I was in despair."

The following day, Isabelle introduced her French cousin. "It gives me great pleasure to present Marie de Chatillon, the new Countess of Pembroke. Marie, this is my dear friend Jory de Beauchamp, Countess of Warwick. She is the wonderful lady who befriended me and took me under her wing when I first came to England . . . and this is her beautiful daughter, Lady Brianna."

Though Marie was not a great beauty, her clothes lent her an enviable elegance. Jory greeted her warmly. "Lady Pembroke, we are distantly related through marriage. Your husband is a cousin of my late uncle, John de Warenne. I am delighted that you have joined the Queen's Court."

"Lady Pembroke, it is apparent by the lovely gown you are wearing that you will be a font of information about the latest French fashions," Brianna declared. "You put us all in the shade."

"Please call me Marie. In Paris the latest style for gowns is fitted sleeves, tight bodices that are nipped in at the waist, and full billowing skirts."

"It looks elegant on you, Marie, but I'm afraid the new fashion would do little for me," Isabelle said wistfully.

"Your Grace, you are wrong!" Brianna insisted. "The fashion was designed for a lady with a petite figure like yours. On you it would look extremely graceful and feminine. I urge you to be fitted for such a gown. I wager you will set the fashion and other ladies will be so envious they will copy you."

Encouraged by Brianna and Jory, Isabelle was fitted for some new gowns, and Marie instructed the queen's sewing women in the latest Parisian styles.

The September weather was glorious. Brianna enjoyed every day at Windsor as Queen Isabelle began to exercise her newfound freedom. One by one, the noble ladies who had been dismissed from the Queen's Court returned. Lady Marguerite, the twenty-year-old daughter of Lord John Wake, recently restored to the queen's household, arrived and Arbella Beaumont, daughter of Isabella de Vesci, one of the queen's original ladies, eagerly took her mother's place. Maude FitzAlan, the sister of Richard, Earl of Arundel, also returned to Queen Isabelle's service. Once again, the lovely chambers of Windsor Castle began to ring with laughter and merriment.

At the urging of Brianna and her other ladies, Isabelle agreed to an outing on the river. The royal barge was outfitted with bright new cushions and a gold-fringed purple canopy to shade them from the sun. Hampers of food and wine were taken aboard and the queen's musicians were brought along to provide music. Isabelle spoke with Prince Edward's tutors and arranged for her son to join her on the river excursion.

As the royal barge moved out into the river, Brianna sat down beside Isabelle. She had brought the queen's cloak in case Isabelle became chilled. "Was Prince Edward able to join us?"

"Yes, but the moment he came aboard he went belowdecks to watch the men who man the oars. He loves ships and he is at an age where strength and physical skills impress him."

"If he is anything like my brother, he would much prefer a lesson in rowing to one in Latin."

The young prince came up on deck and joined his mother. "You look happy today. The fresh air has put roses in your cheeks." His eyes lit up as he recognized the young beauty who curtsied to him. "Brianna, I heard a rumor that you were visiting Windsor. I demand that you come and ride with me before you leave."

"I'm not leaving. The queen has invited me to be a lady in waiting." Brianna smiled at Prince Edward, amazed at how much he had grown since she had last seen him. Though he was younger than her brother, his tall athletic build belied his age. He had the striking Plantagenet features of his magnificent grandfather, and resembled a young golden god. *He was born to be King of England, and what a splendid king he will be!*

"That's wonderful news. You are the only lady of my acquaintance who is knowledgeable about horse breeding. One of these days I intend to visit your castle of Flamstead and see for myself the famous Warwick horses."

"We would be honored by your visit, Edward."

"Oh, look." Isabelle pointed to the fields where the men were cutting the grain with long, curved scythes and the women followed gathering, binding, and stacking the golden crop. "It's harvest time. Autumn is such a lovely season. Listen, they are singing!" The queen moved to the rail for a better view and the people in the meadows stopped what they were doing to gaze at the royal barge. Suddenly, they realized that it was the Queen of England who was sailing down the Thames from Windsor to London and they began to wave and cheer.

Edward joined Isabelle at the rail. "The people love you, Mother." He raised his arm and waved back at the harvesters. Then the queen too lifted her hand and waved to the people.

Brianna watched as Isabelle's face became transformed with pure delight. *This is the very best thing that could have happened to restore her self-confidence.*

As the stately royal barge glided down the River Thames past Chertsey and Richmond the people in the villages rejoiced at the sight of their queen. Their reception was mild, however, compared to the reaction from the throngs gathered on the wharves and streets as the royal vessel approached the Tower of London. Wild shouts, whistles, and cheers of adulation spread along the river embankment as Londoners paid homage to Queen Isabelle the Fair.

On the return trip to Windsor, the queen and her ladies enjoyed the food that had been prepared in the vast kitchens and brought aboard in the early morning for the alfresco luncheon. Brianna poured wine for Isabelle and noticed that her face was flushed with pleasure because her subjects had clearly demonstrated that they held her in high esteem.

During the last week of September, Queen Isabelle and her ladies took advantage of the superb weather. They spent their days outside, riding in Windsor's great park, hawking in the nearby forest or gliding on the River Thames to fascinating places like Runnymede and Maidenhead.

The company and the outings had an extraordinary effect on the queen. Her forlorn manner began to disappear. Hopelessness was replaced by anticipation. Her spirit became lighter, she began to smile and laugh, and her shining beauty returned in full measure.

"Warwick has sent an escort of six to safeguard my return to Flamstead." Jory did not want either Isabelle or Brianna to feel sad that she was leaving Windsor. "I warrant my husband has given them orders to abduct me, if I delay my return."

"I am so reluctant to part with you that I have decided we shall accompany you as far as Saint Albans. It is less than a half-day's ride and the views of the Chiltern Hills will be breathtaking at this time of year."

"That is a lovely idea," Brianna agreed. "If you send word to Father, he could meet us there and I will be able to say good-bye."

"I should like a chance to thank the Earl of Warwick in person for helping to vanquish my enemies," Isabelle said.

"I shall dispatch a letter to Guy immediately, advising him of our plans. He will be most honored to receive your thanks and happy to see with his own eyes that you are flourishing."

Two days later, Queen Isabelle, Brianna, and Jory, escorted by a small cavalcade of Warwick men-at-arms and royal grooms, rode into the courtyard of the ancient Abbey of Saint Albans.

Brianna lifted her hand to shade her eyes from the midday sun. "Father is here before us," she said happily.

"Warwick is eager to get his wife back," Isabelle declared, as a trio of males strode across the courtyard. "You are a most fortunate woman, Jory."

Guy de Beauchamp bowed to the queen, then moved to her side and held up powerful arms. "May I have the honor, Your Highness?"

Isabelle bestowed a radiant smile upon the infamous earl and allowed him to lift her from the saddle.

Guy Thomas, who had accompanied his father, went directly to his mother's stirrup and helped her to dismount.

Brianna's smile of welcome was wiped away as she recognized the third man. *Wolf Mortimer, what the hellfire are you doing here?* When the dark Borderer made no move to aid her from the saddle, she was acutely annoyed . . . She had wanted the satisfaction of rejecting his offer. Her irritation deepened when she realized he wasn't even looking at her. His attention was riveted upon the queen, as she graciously thanked the Earl of Warwick for his service to her.

Brianna stared as her father beckoned Mortimer and presented him to the queen. Her eyes narrowed as the dark devil took Isabelle's hand and kissed her fingers with a gallantry he had obviously learned from his father. He kept his voice low and she could not hear what he said to the queen, but she heard Isabelle's words clearly. "Please tell your father that the Queen of England will be forever in Roger Mortimer's debt."

Brianna felt chagrin when she realized she was the only one still in the saddle. One of the Warwick men, Simon Deveril, stepped forward to attend her and she gifted him with a grateful smile. "Thank you, Simon. Would you be kind enough to see that Venus is watered before our return journey?"

"I will take good care of her, and you also, Lady Brianna. The Earl of Warwick has assigned me to your service."

She started to protest, then thought better of it. *Father loves me . . . It's only natural that he wants to protect me.* She smiled with commiseration. "Poor Simon, you have my sympathy."

Brianna hurried to catch up with the others.

"The Benedictine Monks of the abbey have a large

brew house. Saint Albans's ale is famous in these parts," Warwick told the queen. "It will quench your thirst after your long ride. I'm told they use it in place of holy water," he said with a straight face.

Brianna watched the queen take her father's arm and laugh up at him. *Isabelle is a natural coquette . . . She is starved for masculine attention.*

When they entered the abbey, the abbot who was head of the Benedictine order, along with a number of brown-robed monks, came forward to welcome the queen to Saint Albans.

Brianna smiled as her brother sought to distance himself from the holy men by joining her. She pounced on him immediately. "What the devil is Wolf Mortimer doing in Father's company?"

"He came to Flamstead to buy a horse. He's on his way to join his father and the other Marcher lords at Oxford. Since this is the route he would take, Father invited him to ride with us. He jumped at the chance to meet the queen."

Brianna experienced a pang of disappointment. She had imagined that Wolf Mortimer's sole purpose in coming to Saint Albans was the chance to see her. She blushed at her own vanity.

"Is it official? Are you now a lady in waiting to the queen?"

"Yes, my wish came true. Oh Lord, did you see which way they went? I'm supposed to attend her at all times." Brianna picked up her skirts and hurried down the long nave. She went beneath an archway and found herself in a vaulted chamber with many exits and a stone staircase that led up into a high tower. She gazed about, perplexed.

"Mistress de Beauchamp, I see you are admiring the abbey. Did you know that it was built with stone from the ruins of the ancient Roman city of Verulam?"

She was disconcerted; he seemed to appear from nowhere. "I don't need a history lesson from you, Wolf Mortimer." *Splendor of God, why does his very presence provoke a sharp response from me?*

"You are right. A lesson in manners would benefit you far more." He made no effort to hide his amusement.

She felt an overwhelming desire to wipe the mocking laughter from his face. Her eyes were drawn to his mouth and it angered her that she remembered his kisses. He looked so much like his father, yet at the same time there was a marked difference. Roger Mortimer's manner was polished and charming. The man before her had an aura of animal virility, tightly leashed. Deep down, she feared that she must keep up her defenses lest she succumb to the dark devil's compelling attraction.

"Did my father tell you that I am newly betrothed to Lincoln Robert de Warenne?" She uttered the words, hoping they would invoke a protective shield about her.

"An ideal choice." He allowed the amusement to reach his eyes. "Such an upright youth will enjoy teaching you manners." Inside, his gut knotted with disappointment to learn the proud beauty was betrothed. That de Warenne was heir to an earldom added to his misery. "I warrant he thoroughly disapproves of you joining the Queen's Court."

The truth of his words stung her. "I didn't seek his approval. I am my own woman."

"Poor lad. You will ride roughshod over him."

She raised her chin. "Damn you, Wolf Mortimer. How dare you call Lincoln Robert a lad? He is only a year younger than you are!" She saw the folly of her words the moment she uttered them. They underscored the vast disparity between the two males. De Warenne would come up the loser in any comparison with the fierce young warrior who had patrolled the Welsh Borders for years and looked as if he'd cut his teeth on a sword.

Brianna's breasts rose and fell with her agitation. She stiffened with indignation as she saw his intense gray eyes gaze at her bodice. "What the devil are you staring at?"

"You are wearing a Celtic touchstone, painted with the image of Shadow." He reached out to touch it. "The likeness is amazing."

She felt suddenly breathless and licked her lips. "The she-wolf is a symbol of power, intelligence, and secret knowledge. My aunt Jane, who is Scottish, painted it for me to guide and protect me on my journey through life."

He looked into her eyes. "Do you believe in mystic power, Brianna de Beauchamp?"

"Yes, I do," she whispered.

His fierce expression softened. "So do I." He held out his hand. "Come, I will take you to the queen."

She hesitated, remembering their encounter on Warwick's battlements when he had vowed to collect a kiss from her the next time they met.

He read her thoughts and smiled wickedly. "I'll wait for the kiss, and all the other things I intend to have from you."

She drew in a swift breath, not knowing if she was relieved or disappointed. "You are a Welsh devil, Wolf Mortimer."

He rolled his eyes. "You have no idea, English!"

Chapter 8

"The king is here!"

Brianna heard the dismay in Isabelle's voice. The moment they entered Windsor's Upper Ward on their return from Saint Albans they saw King Edward's attendants everywhere. Brianna dismounted quickly, turned Venus over to Simon Deveril, and went to the queen's side. She kept silent until Laurence Bagshot, the queen's groom, helped Isabelle to dismount. When he moved off toward the stables, Brianna gave her a reassuring smile. "Don't be alarmed, Your Grace . . . The hated Hugh Despencer will not be with him."

Isabelle reached for her hand and Brianna was surprised to find it ice cold to the touch. When she felt the queen tremble, she realized that she must do something to bolster her confidence. She led the way to Isabelle's royal apartment, sat her down in a comfortable chair, and poured her a glass of wine.

"Why does he not leave me in peace? I had such a lovely day—why did he have to come to Windsor and ruin it?" Isabelle hissed. "I won't go down to the hall for dinner tonight. I shall keep to my rooms—we can dine up here."

Brianna was appalled. She knelt to remove Isabelle's boots to give her time to think. *I know what my mother would say, but do I dare speak my mind to the Queen of England?* Brianna bit her lip. *Isabelle is relying on me to be her friend and her confidante. If I don't speak up, she will forever cower in her warren like a frightened little rabbit.*

Brianna took a breath and plunged in. "Your Grace, you are making a grave mistake. You are the Queen of England. If you wish to be treated with dignity and respect, you must *act* like a queen, *dress* like a queen, and *speak* like a queen. You must wear your regality like a cloak. When you go into Windsor's Great Hall to dine, your entrance should make everyone gasp. It is a high honor to sup with a queen. Remember that you are honoring them with your presence. Never allow any to forget it for one moment. Not even the king . . . nay, *especially* not the king."

Isabelle listened intently as she drank her wine.

"You are the mother of the future King of England. King Edward should treat you with deference and show you his gratitude for giving him such a splendid heir to the throne. Prince Edward will no doubt dine in the hall tonight. Take your rightful place beside him on the dais. Your son will be delighted to see you."

"Perhaps Edward came to Windsor to see his son."

"Of course he did," Brianna assured her. "Though you believe the king's presence has ruined your day, you must not let him know it. You must never, ever cower before any man—it will give him power over you. If my mother were here now she would say, *If you lie down and make a doormat of yourself, the world will wipe its muddy boots on you.*"

Isabelle laughed tremulously. "That is exactly what Jory would say. Your mother is a wise woman."

"Let me call the servants and order you a bath. Then I will help you choose a spectacular gown fit for a queen. Summon Marie and your other ladies and we will all attend you in the hall tonight. You won't be alone for one moment. If your confidence starts to slip, remember how the people cheer when they see you aboard the royal barge. Londoners speak of you as Queen Isabelle the Fair. Let tonight be a new beginning for you."

In less than two hours, Isabelle stood before a full-length mirror. Her reflection told her that she did indeed look regal. "My gown, jewels, and especially the way you have done my hair, have given me a measure of confidence . . . at least on the outside." The deep blue taffeta had tight sleeves with jeweled cuffs. Its fitted bodice showed off her tiny waist and petite figure to perfection. A coronet studded with sapphires held her golden tresses away from her heart-shaped face, but allowed a few delicate tendrils at her temples.

Brianna opened the door, spotted a page boy in the corridor, and immediately assigned him a task. "If you do your part well, I will reward you with a silver sixpence." She picked up a royal-blue velvet cushion with gold tassels and thrust it into his small hands. "We are on our way to the Great Hall to dine. You will follow behind the queen and place this cushion on her seat. Then you will bow very low to Queen Isabelle before you withdraw. Do you understand?"

The boy nodded solemnly, liking the attention and keen to earn the promised reward.

"Let me see you bow," Brianna directed. "Very good." She turned her attention back to Isabelle and gave her a warm smile of encouragement. "Think of it as a performance where we all have our parts to play. Marie, Countess of Pembroke, who holds the highest noble rank, should walk beside the queen and the rest of us will follow. Keep your heads high, ladies, and don't forget to smile."

Marguerite, Maude, and Arbella were wearing their newest gowns, copied from the latest French styles worn by the Countess of Pembroke. Brianna, however, had chosen to wear her plain gray silk. The dress was usually a flattering counterpoint to her glorious red-gold hair, but tonight she covered her bright curls with a demure silk head veil. She did not want to draw attention to herself, or be recognized by the king. He had been complicit in dismissing her mother from the queen's service, and Brianna was exercising caution so it wouldn't happen to her.

When Isabelle entered the Great Hall she stopped to gather her courage. To those already present, however, it looked as if the queen had paused deliberately until all eyes were upon her. It caused a stir among the king's attendants and it caught the attention of Prince Edward, who was seated on the dais next to his father.

Young Edward smiled with pleasure. "Mother!" The prince immediately got to his feet as he had been taught to do by his tutors. The king's attendants followed suit and stood respectfully for the beauteous Queen of England.

The king, sprawling in his chair, imbibing wine, his second favorite indulgence, turned his head toward the entrance and saw the queen. Prompted by the example of the courtiers present, and mindful of his agenda, Edward arose and waited for Isabelle to come forward.

Brianna nudged Marie, impelling her to advance into the hall. She let out a relieved breath when Isabelle matched her cousin's steps. Brianna gave the page a gentle push and smiled as the boy fell in behind the queen with more dignity than a bishop.

Up on the dais, Prince Edward greeted his mother with a welcoming kiss. The page boy proudly placed the cushion upon the queen's seat, stepped back, and solemnly bowed.

The king lifted Isabelle's fingers to his lips in a show of gallantry and waited until she sat down before he resumed his own seat. The Countess of Pembroke curtsied to King Edward and sat down beside the queen.

Brianna led the other ladies in waiting to the first table below the dais, where she could quietly observe the royal couple. She noted with satisfaction that tonight, Isabelle looked every inch a queen. Her glance was drawn to King Edward, and she studied him with dispassionate eyes.

Indulgent living has aged him beyond his thirty-eight years. His body is flabby and soft beneath his fashionable garments. His eyes are pouched from drink and his mouth is weak and petulant, like that of a spoiled woman. Brianna suppressed a shudder.

Edward lifted a careless hand, and a servitor stepped forward to refill the king's goblet.

"When I arrived, I was surprised to learn you were not at Windsor," he drawled. "Where were you, Isabelle?"

"Some of my ladies and I decided to ride out to Saint Albans Abbey. I gave alms to the abbot to thank him for prayers on my behalf." Isabelle was quite used to speaking half-truths to protect herself. She regularly went on pilgrimages to Canterbury and other towns with great cathedrals and religious shrines. It was often her single means of escaping the odious presence of her husband and Hugh Despencer.

Edward was the only male in the hall who was indifferent to the queen's delicate beauty. To him she looked like a pretty doll. She stirred no personal interest in him, and her value was solely the goodwill she engendered with the people. He could not control his feelings of resentment over her popularity, yet at the same time he knew the esteem in which his subjects held her was a political asset he could not afford to lose.

Edward was mindful of the reason for his visit. "When you ride out with your ladies, Isabelle, you give little thought to your safety. I warrant I have been most negligent in providing you with adequate protection."

I prefer your negligence to your attention.

"I have ordered a small troop of royal guards to accompany you on your travels. I'm sure our son would be happier if his mother had a military escort to protect her."

Since the king solicited the prince's approval, Isabelle could hardly refuse. "Thank you, Edward," she said graciously.

Dining with her husband had effectively killed Isabelle's appetite. She was unable to banish her apprehension, yet she played her role as queen like an accomplished actress, tasting every dish set before her. She said little, but smiled often, and listened to the conversation Edward was having with their son.

"I'm on my way to Portchester Castle, Hampshire."

"Doesn't that overlook the Isle of Wight, where the fleet is anchored?" Prince Edward had a good grasp of geography and a keen interest in ships.

Thank God he's leaving. The farther the better! Isabelle's apprehension eased enough for her to enjoy her dessert. She finished her slice of pear tart covered with thick clotted cream, then watched with pleasure as her son devoured two helpings.

"I have some news I'm sure will please you, Isabelle." Edward held out his goblet for another refill.

She held her breath. Edward's news seldom pleased her.

"Leeds Castle is once again yours. I signed the official papers restoring it to you last week at Westminster. Traditionally, Leeds has always been part of the queen's dower, and I know the castle is a particular favorite of yours."

Isabelle could not hide her delight. "Thank you, Edward. That is most generous of you." *He is trying to make amends for the humiliation I have suffered. Or perhaps now that the hated Despencers have been removed from the Council, the other members are righting the wrongs done to England's queen, by restoring my property and revenues.*

Isabelle hoped it was the latter. She lowered her lashes so he could not read her thoughts. *You have no special friend now that your disgusting favorite has been banished. Don't try crawling back to me because you are lonely. I foolishly forgave you once, but never again. I wouldn't lower myself to spit on you!*

Edward was suddenly lost in his own thoughts. Soon he would be with Hugh. He closed his eyes, savoring the anticipation. *Portchester Castle will make an ideal residence where Hugh can come and go at will. The Solent and the Isle of Wight will give his vessel fast, easy access to the English Channel and there are scores of inlets where he can come ashore unobserved. How clever he was to think of it!*

Edward opened his eyes and glanced at Isabelle. He congratulated himself on how well he had played his part tonight. With any luck, he had set the wheels in motion that would turn the tide of ill fortune that had almost drowned him of late. Hugh's plot to capture the people's support and goodwill, which they lavished upon the queen, was both clever and cunning.

I have baited the trap with Leeds Castle. Isabelle's eyes are sparkling with anticipation. She has no idea that Hugh and I have chosen her as our instrument to avenge ourselves against our enemies. Edward raised his goblet to salute his gullible queen.

"I want to thank all of you for your help tonight." Isabelle smiled happily. "I could not have done it without your encouragement and support. You were quite right, Brianna. I masked my intimidation and, lo and behold, my apprehension gradually melted away."

"You looked very beautiful tonight, Your Grace," Marguerite Wake declared. "Each time you lifted your hand, your jeweled cuffs sparkled in the candlelight."

"The jewels Marie lent me, and my elegant new gown, imbued me with a confidence I did not possess at the start of the evening."

"You looked completely poised and self-assured sitting up on the dais with the prince and the king." Brianna removed the sapphire coronet Isabelle wore and handed it to Marie. "Do you have no jewels at all, Your Grace?"

"I have a few pieces of jewelry left, but I was forced to lock them away and hide them in my apartment in the Tower of London for safekeeping."

"It is unthinkable that anyone would dare steal the Queen of England's jewels," Marie declared with disbelief.

"Most of the indignities I suffered at the hands of Hugh Despencer were unthinkable, Marie. I'm glad you were not here to witness them." Isabelle kicked off her slippers. "*Eh bien*, I am determined to put it all behind me, like a bad dream. Good night, ladies, I thank you from the bottom of my heart."

Isabelle took Brianna's hand, signaling her to stay.

"Let me help you with your gown." Brianna unfastened the row of small buttons that ran down the back of the bodice.

"The king is on his way to Portchester Castle in Hampshire. We should be rid of him by tomorrow. I cannot believe my good fortune." She stepped from her gown and did a little pirouette.

Brianna smiled. Isabelle looked like a young girl tonight. Up on the dais, the king had looked twice her age.

"Edward has restored Leeds Castle to me!" Isabelle could not contain her excitement any longer. "I doubt it was from the goodness of his heart—Edward has no heart. Most likely it was the Council prompted him to do it. Tomorrow we will make plans for a visit. It's like a fairy-tale castle; you will love it."

"I hear tell it has a beautiful lake."

"Yes, the lake has two islands connected by a bridge. The castle on the inside is like a luxurious palace. It even has a marble bathing room. The other island has a pavilion enclosing a courtyard garden with a carp pond and a lovely tiered fountain. The first King Edward built it for his queen."

"It sounds delightful . . . I've never been to Kent."

"The hops will be ripe and the hedgerows ablaze with flowers. It's October tomorrow . . . We must go before the weather changes."

Brianna's thoughts darted about like quicksilver as she lay in bed, savoring the fact that at last she was a lady in waiting to Isabelle, Queen of England. *Wishes really can come true! At long last I am following in Mother's footsteps. She left home when she was exactly my age to become a lady in waiting to Princess Joanna, right here at Windsor.*

Saying good-bye to her parents at Saint Albans today had brought a lump to her throat. She loved them dearly. They had taught her to embrace life, and were now willing to let go of her, so that she could make her own decisions and move confidently forward into the future. It was exhilarating to be part of Isabelle's court and tomorrow they would make plans for a visit to Leeds Castle.

That's where Edmund Mortimer was married not long ago. Leeds Castle sounds like a most romantic setting for a wedding. Lincoln Robert and I will be married at Flamstead—not nearly as romantic.

Brianna's imagination took flight, as she pictured herself wearing a beautiful wedding gown and a jeweled coronet with a sheer, billowing veil. She drifted into a dream and found herself standing before an altar that stood beneath a pillared pavilion in a lush garden. She could smell the fragrant jasmine that twined about the pillars and hear the splash of the pretty, tiered fountain as she smiled up at Lincoln Robert, who stood proudly by her side.

"Dearly beloved, we are gathered together here in the sight of God to join together this man and this woman in holy matrimony."

Brianna and Lincoln solemnly pledged their vows and plighted their troth, one to the other. She lowered her lashes modestly as the bridegroom took her left hand in his and slipped a wide gold band onto her third finger.

"With this ring I thee wed, with my body I thee honor, and with all my worldly goods I thee endow."

Brianna's lashes flew up. The voice did not belong to Lincoln Robert; it belonged to Wolf Mortimer. *"You!"* she cried.

"Who else?" he demanded.

She stared up into his dark, dangerous face with disbelief and desperately tried to pull her hand from his. His grip was so powerful she could not free herself.

He turned and pulled her after him and Brianna had no choice but to follow where he led. He took her across the bridge that led to the other island where the fairy-tale castle stood. He swept her up into his arms and carried her inside. He strode across the Great Hall toward a magnificent staircase and set her feet to the floor.

Breathless, she fled up the stone steps, desperate to escape. But as she ran, her bridal garments began to fall away and she felt panic because she feared that by the time she reached the top, she would be naked. She saw a golden door and knew that beyond it lay the bathing room. She flung open the door, then slammed it closed and leaned her forehead against it, weak with relief that she was safe.

When she caught her breath, she turned and gazed in wonder at the beautiful black marble bathing pool. The warm, perfumed water lured her to its edge and she bent down to touch one of the delicate pink water lilies that floated on the surface. She saw her reflection in the pool and realized she was naked. She watched in fascination as the water began to ripple from something gliding beneath the surface.

Brianna smiled her secret smile, no longer afraid. She knew exactly who was causing the water to undulate. She saw the dark head surface and watched as he flung his long, wet hair back over his shoulder. "You!"

"Who else?" he demanded with a wicked leer and held out his hand. "Come to me, Brianna Mortimer."

In the morning when she awoke, the ephemeral dream immediately began to scatter and fade, though she tried to cling to the remnants as they floated beyond her reach. She remembered only that her dream had been deeply pleasurable and she was left with a luxuriant feeling of well-being. Brianna stretched languidly and realized that she was bare. "That's strange. I'm certain I put on my nightgown last night. I've never slept nude in my life."

She threw back the covers and remembered that Isabelle wanted to make plans to visit Leeds Castle. "Leeds Castle." The moment she murmured the words, her dream came back to her in vivid, shocking detail. She rubbed the back of her hand across her lips to wipe away his kisses. "Damn you to hellfire, Wolf Mortimer!"

Chapter 9

"I can smell the spicy fragrance of hops on the breeze." Brianna rode abreast of the queen and the Countess of Pembroke. Isabelle's other ladies, Maude, Marguerite, and Arbella, rode behind, and a number of royal servants and grooms followed in the rear. The military escort that King Edward had insisted upon rode at the head of the queen's party as it departed from Wickham in Surrey where the travelers had spent the night.

"All of Kent smells like that at harvest time," Isabelle declared. "Lady Otford was most hospitable, especially on such short notice and with the added burden of a dozen king's guard."

"She told me it was a great honor to have you at Wickham Hall."

"Brianna, I think we should give Leeds Castle advance notice that we are on our way. Would you kindly ask the captain of the guard to send a messenger ahead to let the castellan know we will be arriving in a few hours?"

As Brianna spurred her horse forward, Marie remarked, "Your subjects should not need advance notice, Isabelle. Every castle in England should be eager to accommodate you, day or night."

"I was taught manners at the French Court. It never hurts to be gracious, Marie."

An hour later, the captain of the king's guard approached the queen. "Your Grace, the messenger I sent to Leeds Castle has returned. He said the constable did not believe the queen had sent him. The insolent fellow said Lord Badlesmere is away and that he has strict orders to permit no one to enter the castle."

"But Leeds does not belong to Lord Badlesmere. The king has returned ownership of the castle to me. Obviously, no one has informed the castellan. Send word that I shall be there in about an hour and the fellow will be able to see for himself that it is indeed Queen Isabelle and her ladies who wish to enter."

The captain saluted the queen and ordered his guards to follow him at full speed.

"It is unthinkable that the Queen of England should be refused entry to her own castle," Marie declared.

"I'm sure that whoever is in charge will not deny me courtesy and hospitality when they see that it really is their queen."

"Perhaps you should have sent a groom wearing the queen's livery. A military soldier bearing arms may have alarmed the castle guard. They could suspect an attack," Brianna suggested.

Isabelle laughed. "They will clearly see their mistake when I arrive." She urged her horse to speed up into a gallop and Brianna quickened Venus's pace to keep abreast of the queen.

Two of Isabelle's grooms and Simon Deveril rode forward. "Is aught amiss, Lady Brianna?"

"The Leeds Castle guard doesn't believe it is the queen and her ladies. They've been ordered to let no one enter."

"A harbinger should have been sent days ago to ensure that all was in readiness," Deveril reproved.

"It was a last-minute decision. Queen Isabelle

wanted to come before the cold October winds
arrived."

The lovely castle and the lake came into view just
as the afternoon light was starting to fade. Isabelle
and her retinue drew rein at the end of the causeway
and the captain of the guard rode back to meet them.
"Lady Badlesmere has been left in charge. She insists
you seek lodging for the night elsewhere, Your
Grace."

"Kindly inform Lady Badlesmere that I will speak
with her," Isabelle directed. The guard saluted and
returned to the castle. "Her husband is steward of
the royal household," she told Brianna. "As soon as
she recognizes me, she will realize she has inadvertently offered grave insult to the Queen of England."

Isabelle spurred down the causeway and the others
followed. "My God, the king's guards are forcing
entry!"

Arrows from the castle walls flew past Isabelle, and
found their marks in the two grooms at her side.
Simon Deveril grabbed Brianna's reins and forced
Venus to retreat.

"Simon! Attend the queen! I'm away." Brianna
grabbed Marguerite Wake's reins and dragged her
horse around and the two rode hell-for-leather back
down the causeway. Deveril clutched the reins of the
queen's palfrey and slapped the rump of Lady Pembroke's mount in a grimly determined effort to protect
both the queen and the Countess of Pembroke.

The captain, and the king's guards who were still
alive, made a quick retreat. Four of his men lay dead
at the castle gate.

Up on the crenellated parapet of Leeds, Lady Badlesmere went pale. The moment she had given the
order for the castle archers to loose their arrows, she
saw Isabelle. "The queen!"

"Christus, madam, what have you done?" Edmund Mortimer demanded.

Maggie Badlesmere turned to her new son-in-law. "I didn't believe it was the queen! You know we've been expecting a raid on the castle. Armed men were forcing entry!"

A grim-faced Edmund Mortimer declared, "To attack the Queen of England is unpardonable, madam. You have just committed an act of treason!"

"I was obeying my husband's orders. Badlesmere joined forces with Thomas of Lancaster—you Mortimers also belong to this alliance against the king," she accused.

"Nay, madam, the Marcher lords and the barons too were careful to make plain we were opposed to the Despencers, not the king. Surely you know the penalty for treason?"

"You must go and find Badlesmere. He must return to Leeds Castle immediately and protect us from retaliation."

"As soon as it is full dark, I will slip away and get word to Badlesmere what has happened here." Edmund Mortimer feared that retribution could be both swift and harsh. His brother Wolf had warned him that he sensed trouble at Leeds Castle. Edmund desperately hoped that his father and the other Marcher barons had not yet left Oxford.

He went below and sought out his bride. "Elizabeth, as soon as dark falls, I must leave the castle and get word to your father about what has happened here. I'm taking you with me."

"No, Edmund, don't go! Danger waits outside these walls."

"I *must* go. Royal guards were killed at your gate. Your father must bring his men to defend Leeds or it will be taken. Get ready—wear a dark cloak. I will take you to safety."

Elizabeth burst into tears. "No, no! I must stay with my mother and my sisters. Leeds Castle is impregnable. Edmund, how can you ask me to imperil my life by leaving this stronghold?"

Edmund, frustrated beyond words, wanted to slap sense into her. Instead he drew her into his arms. "Don't cry, Elizabeth. Once I alert your father, he will bring his Kent forces to protect you." He added reluctantly, "If you feel safer here, I will go alone."

Queen Isabelle and her ladies took refuge at the priory in the nearby town of Maidstone. The abbess and her nuns occasionally accommodated noble travelers on their way to Canterbury, but the two small bedchambers were woefully inadequate for the Queen of England and her ladies.

Brianna urged Maude, Marguerite, and Arbella to take one of the rooms. "Marie and I will attend the queen. Try to get some rest."

Brianna poured Isabelle a goblet of sacramental wine brought up from the priory's cellars. "Your Grace has suffered a nasty shock . . . We all have. The wine will soothe your nerves."

"We were lucky to escape with our lives." A tear ran down Isabelle's cheek. "My groom, Laurence Bagshot, fell dead before my very eyes. I cannot understand why on earth we were attacked."

"Your Grace, 'tis obvious they did not believe it was you."

"Brianna, please call me Isabelle. Marie, do stop pacing."

Marie was absolutely livid over what had happened. "The Badlesmere woman *knew*! She was in charge of the castle and insolently suggested the queen find accommodation elsewhere."

Brianna searched for an answer. "I warrant she believed that Leeds Castle still belonged to the

Badlesmeres—apparently no one informed her its ownership had been returned to the queen."

"That is of little consequence," Marie declared in outrage. "The laws of hospitality demand that the queen be made welcome in any castle in England. All unlucky enough to be in residence at Leeds Castle today will pay for this!"

Brianna thought of Edmund Mortimer and his bride, Elizabeth, who had been wed at Leeds such a short time ago. In light of the circumstances she decided to keep the knowledge to herself.

"The captain of the guard is undoubtedly riding to King Edward with the news that the queen has been attacked, but I intend to inform Pembroke," Marie declared. "My husband is commander of the king's forces. He will be the one to force Leeds Castle to surrender and he will arrest those within. I shall go down immediately and ask the abbess for pen and paper."

When they were alone, Isabelle drained her goblet and poured herself more wine. She looked at Brianna and whispered, "What if Edward lied to me about the reversion of Leeds Castle?"

Brianna drew in a swift breath. *Lady Badlesmere certainly defended the castle as if she owned it. When the king's guard tried to force entry, she ordered the attack.* "Isabelle, why would he lie about such a thing?"

"He knew I would come," she whispered. "He dangled the bait before me, knowing I would not be able to resist the temptation."

"But that would be deliberately putting your life in danger."

"It wouldn't be the first time," Isabelle murmured sadly.

When Marie returned, Isabelle said, "I don't think you should send an alarming message to Pembroke tonight. Let us wait until morning. We cannot remain here another night, there are not enough beds and my poor servants have been left in the stables. We need to decide where to go, and what course of action is best in this matter."

"It is too late. I've already dispatched the letter with one of your servants. Rest assured Pembroke will know what is best."

"I'm so sorry I decided to visit Leeds Castle—it has stirred up a hornets' nest. I wish we were all safely back at Windsor."

"Isabelle, you mustn't blame yourself in any way. You need a good night's rest. Let me help you with your gown." Brianna folded the queen's garments and tucked her into bed. She and Marie shared the second bed in the small room.

In the middle of the night, Brianna heard Isabelle quietly sobbing and it tugged on her heartstrings. *How infinitely sad it must be to know that your husband does not love you . . . I warrant it is even more devastating to know that she cannot trust him.*

Before dawn lightened the sky, Brianna went down to the stables to speak with Simon Deveril. "How long will it take us to get back to Windsor?"

"That is out of the question, Lady Brianna. The safety of Queen Isabelle, as well as your own and the other ladies', falls squarely on my shoulders. What was left of the military guard slunk away in the night."

Brianna looked at the queen's servants lying in the straw. "We need better accommodation."

"I suggest Tonbridge Castle, just a few miles west of here. It is a strong fortalice and, since it belongs to the Archbishop of Canterbury, will be well provisioned and luxuriously furnished."

"In keeping with his vow of poverty," Brianna said solemnly.

"Churchmen these days don't even pay lip service

to celibacy, let alone poverty." He jerked his thumb at the servants. "I'll get this lot on their feet and start saddling the horses."

*   *   *

As Isabelle and her retinue rode toward Tonbridge, it was obvious the word had already spread that the queen and her party had been attacked and some of her servants murdered. The people of Kent gathered along the roadways, showing their steadfast loyalty and offering their staunch protection to their beloved Queen Isabelle the Fair.

They arrived at Tonbridge Castle just before the midday meal. Brianna breathed a sigh of relief when she saw how well Queen Isabelle was received. Though Walter Reynolds, the Archbishop of Canterbury, was not in residence, his legion of well-trained servants had been taught how to treat royalty. She knew that if it were necessary that they remain for a long period of time, they would be made welcome.

"I cannot get over Tonbridge," Brianna said in wonder. "The castle is guarded like a fortress. The bedchambers are so numerous and furbished so luxuriously, it smacks of decadence."

"I quite agree, but I'm not about to complain." Isabelle helped herself to a sweetmeat from a solid silver dish. "Every meal served has been like a banquet. By comparison, I realize just how meager and paltry my royal table was over the past year. 'Tis clear that Hugh Despencer did not impose his economies on the archbishop. It takes a deal of wealth to live in such splendor."

At Portchester Castle, King Edward and his lover were also indulging their appetites, when the captain of the military guard assigned to Isabelle brought the king the dire news that the queen had been attacked at Leeds Castle.

"Attacked? What do you mean? Speak plainly, man."

"Sire, Badlesmere was away and Lady Badlesmere insolently told the queen to seek shelter elsewhere for the night. I ordered my men to force the gate and the harridan ordered her archers to shoot us. They killed two of the queen's royal grooms and four of my guards." The captain fought a suspicion that Edward had known he and his men would be shot if they tried to enter Leeds Castle. "Queen Isabelle and her ladies were forced to flee for their lives and take sanctuary in a nearby priory."

"This is outrageous! The Badlesmeres will rue the day they attacked my beloved wife. To use arms against the Queen of England is an act of treason and they will pay the price!" Edward crashed his fist on the table and knocked over his goblet. The dark red wine spread like blood. "When did this happen?"

"Forty-eight hours ago, Sire. I have ridden two nights and two days to bring you the news."

"You did well, Captain." Edward's voice was filled with satisfaction. "Tell my steward that I order him to plenish you a room and a meal."

The captain saluted and withdrew, convinced the king had sent him to provoke the owners of Leeds Castle into an act of treason.

When they were alone, Edward turned to Hugh with a smile of delight on his face. "The trap I set worked like a dream!"

"Now you have your just cause to take up arms against Badlesmere, Ned. But if you intend to net the *bigger fish*, you will need to gather an army greater than theirs."

"I'll hire mercenaries to supplement Pembroke's forces."

"That's good, but it's only a start. As word spreads about the insult to your *beloved consort*, the people will become incensed. Tomorrow, you must order a general muster of all men between the ages of sixteen and sixty. Then you must return to London, so you can take command."

"You know how I detest kingly duties. I much prefer to remain here with you, my love."

"We part now so that we can be together permanently, once you regain your royal authority over all your enemies and extract a just revenge for what they did to me."

"I swear I will avenge you, Hugh, and vow to restore all the properties they took from you, and more besides. Just name it, and it shall be yours."

Two days later, on Hugh Despencer's shrewd advice, King Edward made his way slowly from Portchester to London. He stopped at every village and hamlet along the way, firing up the people's anger at the way Queen Isabelle had been assaulted in Kent. With every mile he traveled, the king recruited more men-at-arms.

When Edward arrived in London, he summoned Pembroke. By this time the earl had already received the message from his wife cataloguing the treasonous assault the queen and her ladies had suffered at Leeds Castle, and he was readying his forces to march.

"I have mustered enough angry men to double the ranks of our standing army. I command you to lead them into Kent and lay siege to Leeds Castle to punish the disobedience and contempt against Queen Isabelle by certain members of the household of Bartholomew Badlesmere. I will make an example of the traitor!"

"Father! Thank God I found you!" Edmund Mortimer had ridden the hundred miles from Leeds Castle to the City of Oxford on a horse he had stolen from a Kent farmer.

Roger Mortimer stood beside his campaign tent, pitched outside the city on a bank of the River Thames. He saw the exhaustion on his son's face. "What's amiss?"

"Trouble at Leeds Castle, as I foretold." Wolf Mortimer caught his brother as he slid from the saddle.

"I have to find Badlesmere. He must ride to Leeds to protect his family. Do you know where he is?"

"Take him inside," Roger instructed Wolf. He summoned one of his men. "Find Badlesmere and fetch him here." Mortimer entered the campaign tent and poured his son a tankard of ale.

As Edmund thirstily quaffed the ale, he knew he must leave out reference to the queen if he had any hope of rescuing his wife. "The king sent a military force to take Leeds. Lady Badlesmere defended the castle and gave the archers on the wall orders to shoot. They killed six of the royal guards and forced a retreat, but they are bound to return with a larger force."

Roger cursed the king. "Lady Badlesmere has every right to defend her castle. She is a de Clare, a family that takes its property rights seriously. Since our families are now united by marriage, we have an obligation to support them." Mortimer paced the tent, hating to be confined. "I'll go and speak with Hereford. The Marcher lords must stick together. Come and get me when Badlesmere arrives."

When his father left, Edmund's voice betrayed his apprehension. "I tried to get Elizabeth to leave with me, but she was afraid and wanted to stay with her mother and sisters."

Wolf stared at his brother silently, while his mind's eye showed him the alarming scene that had taken place at Leeds Castle. He saw Brianna de Beauchamp and his gut knotted that she had been so close to mortal danger. "Elizabeth has reason to be afraid. You forgot to mention the royal guards were escorting the queen and her ladies."

"My reckless mother-in-law gave the order to shoot before she saw the queen. I informed her she had committed an act of treason, but the deed was done. I thank God no harm came to Queen Isabelle or her ladies."

"Edmund, you were present. You too have committed an act of treason. Your expedience in leaving has likely saved your neck."

"Do you intend to tell Father that Lady Badlesmere ordered an attack on the queen?" he asked with trepidation.

Wolf shook his head. "No, Edmund. *You* will tell him."

Chapter 10

"How on earth did you know where we were?" Brianna was surprised to find her parents in Tonbridge Castle's courtyard when she emerged from the stables.

"The moment Simon Deveril gave you safe escort here, he rode to Flamstead. We were about to return to Warwick when he brought us the disturbing news." Guy de Beauchamp enfolded his daughter in his arms.

Brianna looked up into his face and saw the concern written there. *He really does love me deeply.*

"Deveril assured us you and Isabelle and her other ladies were unharmed and safe here at Tonbridge, but we had to see for ourselves." Jory kissed her daughter with relief.

"Come, Isabelle will be so happy to see you." Brianna took her parents to the large solar where the queen was writing letters.

"Jory . . . my lord earl . . . the news of our ordeal has reached you."

The countess curtsied. "Your Grace, how are you faring?"

"Don't be formal with me, Jory. You are my dear friend. I was in deep shock when two of my grooms were killed before my eyes. We took sanctuary at

Maidstone Priory, but your man Deveril suggested Tonbridge Castle would be more suited to our needs. I am most grateful to him."

Over the midday meal, Isabelle, Marie, and the other ladies recounted the events of the fateful afternoon at Leeds.

"As we crossed the Kent border, we encountered Pembroke and an exceedingly large army on their way to Leeds Castle." Warwick noted that though the Countess of Pembroke was elated at the news, Queen Isabelle appeared troubled.

After the meal, Jory took her daughter aside. "I don't suppose we can dissuade you from Isabelle's service, though that was your father's first protective instinct. At least we are satisfied you are in no danger. The entire country is ready to protect the queen."

"Thank you for understanding. Simon Deveril is a most competent guard."

"That's why your father chose him." Jory embraced her daughter. "We won't be with you on your birthday, but at least we know you will be warm." She took a parcel from her baggage.

Brianna opened it to reveal a sable cloak lined with blue velvet. "Oh, it's the loveliest thing I've ever seen." She put it on and pulled up the hood. "I adore beautiful clothes."

Jory winked. "Like mother, like daughter. Enjoy it, darling."

When her parents were ready to depart, Brianna accompanied them down to the courtyard. "Father, Isabelle voiced a secret fear to me that I realize she won't speak of in front of Marie or the others. She suspects Edward lied when he told her Leeds was hers again. She fears the king gave the guards orders to provoke the attack. I don't understand. Why would he do such a thing?"

Warwick's brows drew together. "Such a ploy would

split the barons. Badlesmere threw in his lot with Lancaster and the Marcher lords. Most of the earls will take the queen's side. You have given me food for thought, Brianna. Don't fret, the queen is in no danger, though I can't say the same for the Badlesmeres or those who support them."

As Brianna waved farewell, she thought of the Mortimers. *When Wolf Mortimer met Isabelle at Saint Albans she said,* Please tell your father that the Queen of England will be forever in Roger Mortimer's debt. *Yet Edmund is married to Elizabeth Badlesmere. I pray this trouble does not pit brother against brother.* Brianna pictured Wolf Mortimer, and she shuddered. *He would make a formidable enemy.*

"Badlesmere is nowhere to be found. His men struck camp early this morning. Rumor has it there was trouble in Kent."

Roger Mortimer nodded at his lieutenant. "He's no doubt ridden to protect his castle of Leeds." He turned to Hereford. "I'll move farther south in case he needs backup. You need not come."

"We're in this together. There's power in numbers."

Mortimer returned to his tent. "Badlesmere has already left. Wolf, give orders to strike camp. We'll follow the River Thames south to Reading, skirt the Chilterns, and then ride east into Kent. It will take us a few days to get to Leeds Castle."

Wolf Mortimer gave Edmund a piercing glance, then left the tent.

"Father, the military captain who came to Leeds said the *queen* was seeking shelter. Lady Badlesmere didn't believe it and told him she had orders to permit no one to enter the castle."

"Maggie de Clare doesn't suffer fools gladly. Get some rest, Edmund. We'll be ready to ride in two or three hours."

*   *   *

"You are rather pensive today, my love." Guy de Beauchamp searched his wife's face as they rode side by side on their journey to Warwick. They had spent two days at Jory's Castle of Chertsey before they left for home, inspecting the size of the harvest to make sure the animals had adequate fodder for the coming winter. "Is it because you disagree with my decision to remain neutral and not join Pembroke?"

"If I disagreed with your decision, I would have opened my mouth and said so," Jory declared.

"Your brother Lynx rushed off to Kent to show his support for Queen Isabelle. Are you sure you're not angry with me?"

"Over the years I have learned to trust in your wisdom. You must have just cause for your decision."

"I pledged my word to the Marcher barons. I cannot go back on my word. Mortimer, Hereford, Lancaster, and I swore a bond to stick together. I would never break a pledge. It is a principle I live by and one I have taught my children."

Jory nodded. "We also have a bond of marriage with Mortimer and he has one with Badlesmere. Yet I know you support Queen Isabelle . . . Remaining neutral is the wisest course to take."

"When we get to Oxford, I'll meet with Mortimer."

An hour later, the Earl and Countess of Warwick saw a large force of fighting men moving toward them. "Hellfire, it looks like Mortimer is on the march. Unfurl our standard," he ordered.

Reading Abbey was nearby and Jory and her serving women went inside to refresh themselves while Warwick, Mortimer, and Hereford conversed in the walled courtyard.

"I'm eager for news. What has happened?" Roger asked.

"On Edward's orders, Pembroke took his large

army into Kent and drew up his forces before Leeds Castle. The king has stirred up a vast amount of public support. Hundreds of Londoners, as well as men from the surrounding counties, have all surged into Kent. The earls of Arundel and Richmond, as well as Edward's half brothers, Edmund of Kent and Thomas of Norfolk, have joined Pembroke to avenge the insult and abuse of their queen."

Roger Mortimer's eyes narrowed. "Are you telling me Queen Isabelle truly was at Leeds and Maggie Badlesmere attacked her?"

"You didn't know?" Warwick asked.

"I thought it was merely rumor."

Warwick shook his head. "If you ride into Kent to support Badlesmere you will be defeated and likely charged with treason. The besieging forces must number close to thirty thousand. The entire country is eager to avenge their queen."

Hereford looked at Mortimer. "I warrant Lancaster won't defend Badlesmere against the queen."

Roger Mortimer said decisively, "Nor will I. Out of respect for Queen Isabelle, I won't go to relieve Leeds Castle."

"A wise decision. My brother-in-law Lynx de Warenne is among the thousands who have gathered in Kent, but I have chosen to return to Warwick."

Hereford went to give word to his lieutenants that they would go no farther.

Warwick drew Mortimer aside to impart a confidence. "My daughter was with the queen at Leeds. I rode to Tonbridge Castle, where they are now safely ensconced. Isabelle believes the military escort Edward provided had orders to deliberately provoke the attack on her party."

Mortimer's dark brows drew together. "A clever plan to split the barons. He cares little about Badlesmere. He's after us."

"The plan is too shrewd for Edward alone."

"Christ Almighty, Despencer must be secretly advising him!"

"Exactly. Leeds Castle cannot hold out much longer."

"My son's wife is there," Mortimer said with regret.

"Pembroke is in charge. He is too honorable to harm women."

Mortimer nodded. "I thank you for the news, my friend. We will make camp here and await events." Roger mounted his horse and went in search of his sons.

When he saw Edmund, he was out of the saddle in a flash. He raised his arm in fury and clubbed his son across the side of the head, felling him to the ground. "Whoreson! You knew the queen was at Leeds Castle."

He glanced up and saw Wolf striding across the grass. "Did you know about the queen?" he demanded.

"I did," Wolf said curtly, and braced himself for a blow.

Mortimer took a deep breath, though it did little to assuage his anger. "I won't strike you. Loyalty to your brother is obviously an honorable thing in your eyes." He looked at Edmund, still on the ground. "Where is *your* bloody loyalty?"

"His duty is to his wife. You cannot fault him for that."

"Can I not? His duty was to bring Elizabeth out of Leeds."

"She was terrified—she refused to leave," Edmund muttered.

"*Refused?* She's a woman, for Christ's sake! Wolf or I would have dragged her out by the bloody hair if necessary."

Edmund lowered his eyes as shame washed over him.

*　　*　　*

When King Edward realized the besieging forces surging headlong into Kent numbered close to thirty thousand, he rushed to Leeds Castle to take charge of the siege.

Maggie Badlesmere, badly shaken that her husband had not come to her defense, grew more frantic by the hour. As well as her children, including newly wed Elizabeth, Badlesmere's sister, and her son, Lord Burghersh, were inside the besieged castle. Since his brother had been appointed to the powerful bishopric of Lincoln by the king himself, Burghersh offered to negotiate terms with the Earl of Pembroke.

King Edward, suddenly power mad, refused to negotiate, and in early November, Leeds Castle surrendered. Edward exacted a savage vengeance. He ordered the constable and his twelve archers hanged before the castle gates. Then, over Pembroke's objection, he took Lady Badlesmere, her children, and the other family members into custody. He ordered that they be imprisoned at Dover Castle, whose impregnable walls were twenty feet thick.

The king issued a proclamation: *I have made an example of Leeds Castle so that no one in future will dare to hold fortresses against me.*

During the following week, all Badlesmere's castles surrendered to the king and the search was on for Lord Badlesmere, who had gone into hiding.

"A great cavalcade is approaching," Brianna announced. "Perhaps it is the Archbishop of Canterbury. The trumpets are sounding a fanfare."

Isabelle rushed to the tall windows of the solar. She and her ladies had been at Tonbridge Castle for more than a month and knew nothing of what had been happening outside its walls.

"It's the king." Isabelle made no effort to hide her disappointment.

Brianna also heard the note of trepidation in her voice. "Don't be intimidated, Isabelle. You should go down to greet him in the Great Hall. If he has to seek you out in the solar, it will look as if you are hiding. We will all remain with you when you receive him, Your Grace."

A half hour later, Queen Isabelle, looking both regal and serene, stood in the Great Hall. The light from the crackling fires in the hall's huge fireplaces reflected on the jewels hastily borrowed from her ladies.

Edward strutted in with a dozen attendants in tow. He beckoned the castle's steward. "Wine for everyone! I have vanquished my enemies and we will drink a toast to my great victory." It was the king's first military success since he had been crowned and he was intoxicated by it and swollen with pride.

Showing great poise, Isabelle bowed her head and her ladies went down in graceful curtsies. "I bid you welcome, Sire."

He spread his arms wide. "I have avenged the brutal assault on you, Isabelle. I have stripped Leeds Castle of anything of value, including its provisions, and I have brought them to lay at your feet in compensation for the vile ordeal you suffered there."

"Thank you, Sire." Isabelle's voice was calm, concealing her inner turmoil.

"When Leeds Castle surrendered, its ownership reverted to the Crown. It is my gift to you."

His attendants applauded his magnanimous gesture.

Not by word or look did Isabelle show the contempt she felt. He had given her Leeds Castle when it was not his to give. Now that it *was* his, she didn't want it.

"Where's that wine I ordered?" Edward demanded.

A dozen servants hurried into the hall bearing silver trays that held wine-filled crystal goblets, and cheers erupted from Edward's attendants.

"I'm going to faint," Isabelle whispered.

Brianna swept up a goblet of wine and pressed it into the queen's hand. "No, you must *not*!"

Isabelle took two quick gulps of wine and felt its restorative warmth seep along her veins. She drained the goblet and a red rose bloomed in her breast. It bolstered her confidence and she saw clearly that by the time dinner was served, Edward would be well into his cups, as indeed he was most nights.

That's when I'll ask him if I can return to Windsor because I want to be with the children. I haven't seen them for more than a month and I miss them sorely. If I ask when he is drunk, in front of his sycophantic attendants, he will not be able to deny himself the grandiose gesture of granting me my wish.

The following day, Walter Reynolds, the Archbishop of Canterbury, arrived at his castle of Tonbridge. He had more attendants in his entourage than King Edward.

The queen, with her ladies at her side, kissed the archbishop's ring. "Your Excellency, please accept my deep gratitude for the hospitality you have so generously provided to me, my ladies in waiting, and the people who serve me."

"I am honored that you chose Tonbridge Castle for sanctuary in your hour of need. It is a privilege indeed to offer my humble hospitality to the beloved Queen of England." Reynolds was well aware there was nothing *humble* about it. "Please stay as long as you desire . . . My castle is your castle."

The king replied for the queen. "Unfortunately, my wife must return to Windsor tomorrow. She has been away from the children for over a month. The Earl of Pembroke and the other nobles who gallantly rode into Kent on her behalf will assure her safe escort. I, however, intend to enjoy a visit with you here at

Tonbridge. I never tire of looking at the treasures you have collected over the years."

Walter Reynolds knew immediately that Edward wanted something. He had been part of Prince Edward's household at Kings Langley when they were little more than boys, and he owed his appointment as Archbishop of Canterbury to the king. He knew he would have to accommodate Edward, if he was to continue living in splendor.

Queen Isabelle's party left the next morning, and that night Edward closeted himself with Reynolds in his magnificent library.

"I want you to summon a convocation of the clergy to Saint Paul's Cathedral to formally annul the sentence of banishment on the Despencers."

"On what grounds could it be formally declared null and void, Your Grace?" Walter Reynolds asked carefully.

"*You* are the fucking Archbishop of Canterbury. I have every confidence that you will find just cause, Walter." Edward helped himself to his friend's imported French wine.

Reynolds steepled his fingers as his mind searched for a religious excuse that would hold water. Finally, he said, "The sentence of banishment could be annulled on the grounds that it did not have the unanimous support of the bishops."

"Brilliant!" Edward refilled the jewel-encrusted chalice and saluted his friend. "Waste no time. Summon them to Saint Paul's by the first of December. I'm sure I don't need to emphasize that until it is a fait accompli, I rely upon your discretion in this sensitive matter, Walter."

"I insist that you ride with your wife, Lord Pembroke. Marie has seen very little of you lately." Isabelle did not want to hear the gory details of the surrender of Leeds Castle. She was secretly appalled that Lady Badlesmere and her young family had been imprisoned and was tired of listening to Marie's righteous insistence that the harridan deserved to be hanged.

Before the queen's party left Kent, however, two more prominent earls, along with their forces, joined the entourage. Richmond and Arundel flanked Queen Isabelle and she graciously thanked them for their loyal support.

By the time they crossed into Surrey, the king's young half brothers, Kent and Norfolk, caught up with them and decided they too would travel to Windsor. Edmund, Earl of Kent, was attracted to the fair-haired, blue-eyed Marguerite Wake, and he maneuvered his mount so that he could ride between Marguerite and Brianna.

"Lady Marguerite, your ordeal at Leeds Castle must have been terrifying."

"Indeed it was, my lord earl. I would have been killed, if Lady Brianna had not snatched my palfrey's reins and forced her back down the causeway."

He turned to look more closely at Brianna and when he recognized her, his eyes widened. "Mistress de Beauchamp, I am delighted to see you back at the Queen's Court." He called to his brother, the Earl of Norfolk. "Tom, come and see who is here."

Norfolk joined them. "Brianna! I had no idea you were back at court. You have blossomed into a rare beauty."

"It's Lady Brianna, if you don't mind, and I can still beat you in a horse race," she teased.

The royal brothers grinned as their hot glances swept over the two ladies in waiting. "Christmas season at Windsor promises to be rather festive," the Earl of Norfolk remarked.

Brianna smiled her secret smile. *I have given my*

heart to Lincoln Robert. Thomas of Norfolk will have to find another lady to amuse him when he learns I am betrothed.

Though the hour was late when Isabelle arrived back at Windsor, she could not resist visiting the nursery wing where her children had already been put to bed. It warmed Brianna's heart when young Prince John threw his arms about his mother and told her he had missed her. Little Eleanor was so excited she jumped up and down on her bed and giggled delightfully when Brianna told her she could jump better than a frog.

Isabelle kissed baby Joan gently. She was sound asleep and her mother did not want to disturb her.

As they left the nursery, Brianna saw the tears glistening in Isabelle's eyes. "Don't cry . . . They love you with all their hearts."

The nobles who had escorted Isabelle and her retinue back to Windsor Castle took up residence in the chambers that were always reserved for them. The Earl and Countess of Pembroke had a suite of rooms in the Round Tower and Marie had permission from Isabelle to withdraw with her husband for a few days.

When the king summoned Pembroke to Westminster, Marie rejoined Isabelle and the other ladies. She was eager to relate the things she had learned from her husband that the queen was unaware of.

"The Marcher barons left Oxford intending to support Badlesmere, but when Roger Mortimer learned about the attack on the queen, he sent a message to Pembroke pledging that out of respect for Queen Isabelle they would not go to the relief of Leeds Castle."

"Thank God Roger Mortimer is a man of honor. There could have been a terrible battle in Kent if he had brought his forces to aid Leeds Castle," Isabelle said with relief.

"Roger Mortimer's heir, Edmund, is wed to Elizabeth Badlesmere. Their loyalties must be torn." Brianna felt great empathy with the Mortimers. "It must have been a difficult decision to make."

"After the castle surrendered, Roger Mortimer sent another message from Reading offering to mediate for the prisoners, but Pembroke told me the king flatly refused his offer," Marie said.

Brianna was surprised to hear that Roger Mortimer and his forces were at Reading. *That's only a dozen miles from here!* Brianna pictured him as she had last seen him mounted on his black stallion, and it made her pulse race. Her thoughts gravitated to Wolf Mortimer and she wondered why she and the dark Borderer were always at odds when they encountered each other. *The Welsh devil tries to goad me on purpose . . . and always manages to spark my anger.* Brianna's innate honesty made her admit she did the same to him. *I made a point of telling him I was betrothed to Lincoln Robert simply to annoy him.* She sighed. It hadn't seemed to bother him in the least.

The nobles who were eager to show their loyalty to Queen Isabelle now congregated at Windsor Castle. Richmond, Arundel, and the other married earls were joined by their wives and daughters. In the evenings the Great Hall was filled with music and laughter, and after dinner there was dancing.

The queen and her ladies began to plan for the Christmas festivities, and Brianna was relieved that Isabelle looked happier. "Do you suppose the king will come to spend Christmas at Windsor?"

"Thank heavens, no!" Isabelle murmured. "He always celebrates the festive season at Kings Langley. It has become a tradition."

Brianna knew that Langley had been Prince Edward's residence when he was a youth and could only imagine the debauched atmosphere of the all-male household.

After dinner, the Earl of Richmond bowed to the queen and led her out in the dance. Edmund of Kent immediately asked Marguerite Wake to partner him, and his brother Norfolk managed to persuade Brianna to dance.

"Will you be spending Christmas at Windsor, my lord, or will you go with the king to Langley?"

Tom leaned down to speak in confidence. "Edward isn't going to Langley this year. Now that he has gathered such a large army, he intends to make full use of it. He is determined to reclaim his royal prerogative and deal with the barons who rebelled against him and defied him."

Brianna's heart leaped into her throat. She lowered her lashes so that Norfolk could not see her alarm. *Does he mean Lancaster? Nay, Thomas is the king's cousin and has royal blood. Edward is going to seek revenge against Roger Mortimer, who led the rebellion! His punishment will be terrible—he will have no mercy.*

Chapter 11

"I must rid myself of this ominous foreboding."
Wolf Mortimer spoke his thoughts aloud to Shadow, who stood beside him on the bank of the Thames, not far from where the Marchers were camped. His clothes felt constricting, so he removed them, knowing his spirit could commune more freely without the impediment of his garments. He shook his head to banish the gloom, hoping the dark clouds that had gathered in the evening sky were coloring his mood.

Grateful that Welsh mountain streams had inured him to the cold, Wolf dove into the river and cut through the water with powerful, clean strokes. The Thames, however, did not cleanse away the feeling of menace; it clung like a cobweb he could neither wash away nor ignore.

Wolf climbed from the water and shook himself. He was reluctant to voice his premonition to his father, lest it become a self-fulfilling prophecy. It was full dark now and he stared with unseeing eyes into the blackness. He willed himself to relax, giving up control so that his unconscious mind could leave the present and penetrate the future.

He saw Edmund's wife, Elizabeth, and knew that

though she was confined, she would survive. Her father, however, wore a noose—a portent of certain death. He conjured a picture of the king, but it was the degenerate male at Edward's side who wore the crown. For the Mortimers he sensed sinister threats from both east and west, and betrayal from the north. He saw his father in the jaws of a closing trap, and knew snares lay in every direction. Death awaited three Marcher barons, but before he learned which, he felt something brush against his leg. His hand reached down and touched Shadow and he was jolted back into the present. He dug his fingers into his animal's thick silver fur and knew that her life too was threatened unless she found a safe haven.

Wolf heard the distant but ominous rumble of thunder in the west, coming from the direction of the Welsh Borders. Jagged lightning flashed in the east, a sure warning that the danger from London was closer and more deadly. He dressed quickly, knowing he could remain silent no longer.

Don't rush off, it may arouse suspicion. Brianna schooled herself to patience and did not leave Windsor's Great Hall until Isabelle and her other ladies departed.

As Brianna hurried to her chamber, her mind darted about like quicksilver. She knew she must warn Roger Mortimer of the king's intent and had formed a plan while she had been dancing.

Brianna lit the candles and, as she dipped a quill into the inkwell, she warned herself against using Roger Mortimer's name.

My Dearest Lord:
  I beg you take heed of my warning!
  The army will not be disbanded but will be used to bring the Marcher barons to heel. He

> *seeks revenge and retaliation and I fear he will*
> *show no mercy.*

Brianna folded the unsigned letter and melted wax to seal it. She put on her dark green velvet cloak, pulled the hood up to conceal her bright hair, and slipped from her chamber. She took the outside steps that led down into the Upper Ward and, moving slowly, avoiding the pools of light from the outside torches, made her way to the castle's Lower Ward. By the Norman gate were the lodgings of the guards and grooms and she hesitated for a moment, wanting to be sure she chose the right room before she knocked. A sudden flash of lightning revealed the Warwick bear and staff device on a door and her knees felt weak with relief.

Simon Deveril opened to her knock and Brianna quickly slipped inside. "It's me . . . Don't light the candles."

"Lady Brianna, what's amiss?" He knew she would never venture outside at midnight without great provocation.

"Simon, I just learned of a vile plot against the Mortimers. The king intends to use the forces he has gathered to take revenge on the Marcher barons. They are close by at Reading. Will you deliver this letter of warning into Roger Mortimer's hands?"

"Are you sure of this, my lady?"

"The king's own brother, Thomas of Norfolk, confided it to me. There is no time to lose—they must flee!"

"I'll go now." He took the letter.

"I didn't sign it, so be sure to tell him it comes from Warwick's daughter, Brianna."

"He will recognize me as Warwick's man."

"Simon, I thank you with all my heart. Perhaps you can keep ahead of the storm."

"The storm's over London. It will likely move out
to sea. There's no need to thank me. Mortimer is a
kinsman of Warwick."

Brianna returned to her chamber and readied herself for bed. Before climbing beneath the covers, she
sank to her knees and said her prayers. She asked that
Simon Deveril be guided to the right place and that
Roger Mortimer would heed her warning. She prayed
that the divine spirit would protect all. She gave
thanks that Deveril was willing to risk danger to do
her bidding, and then she thanked God that her father
cared enough to provide her with a Warwick man
whose devoted service she could rely upon.

Brianna lay in bed with her eyes wide open, too
tense to sleep. In spirit she was with Simon on every
mile of his journey. She tried to calculate how long it
would take him to get to Reading, then wondered
how much time would elapse before he located Roger
Mortimer. She began to worry that Simon might not
find Roger at all, but quickly banished her pessimis-
tic thoughts.

*When will Simon get back to Windsor? If all goes
well, he should certainly be back by morning*, she assured herself. Brianna tossed and turned for hours in
a vain attempt to sleep. Finally, she imagined she saw
the first faint light of dawn creep into her chamber,
and all thoughts of sleep fled.

She threw back the covers impatiently and got out
of bed. She poured cold water from the jug, washed,
cleaned her teeth, and began to dress. To save time
she put on the same clothes she had worn yesterday.
She gave her tangled hair a cursory brushing, slipped
on her cloak, and pulled its hood over her disheveled
curls. *I'll go down to the stables and wait for him.*

When she got outside she realized the sky only
hinted at dawn, and Brianna guessed that it was some-

where between the hours of four and five. The stables at Windsor were vast, designed to hold over a hundred horses, and since the castle was at present occupied by many nobles and their families, she knew every stall would be filled. She was thankful that none of Windsor's servants or grooms would be up and about yet.

When Brianna went inside, she breathed in the miasma of horses, hay, and manure. It was a smell she had known all her life and it was somehow comforting. She was surprised and also vastly relieved to see that Simon had returned. She picked up her skirts and hurried toward him, anxiety written all over her face. "Did you find him?" she asked breathlessly.

"I did, m'lady." Deveril jerked his thumb in the direction of the box stalls at the back of the stables. "You have a visitor."

Her brows drew together in perplexity. *Who could it be?* Her heart began to hammer. She was reminded of her early morning meetings at the stable with Lincoln Robert and fancied he had come to visit her.

She lifted the latch on the wooden door of the first box stall and stepped in. The lamp was unlit and it was dim inside, but Brianna needed no light to identify her black-clad visitor.

Wolf Mortimer and Shadow stood motionless at the back of the stall. Brianna was so shocked that she was speechless.

"Hello, English." His greeting was irreverent, as always.

"You should be gone—the danger is real!" Brianna said angrily.

"I know," he said gently. "My future is uncertain, my road fraught with danger. I seek a haven for Shadow."

She stared at him in disbelief. "You are asking *me* to find a safe haven for your wolf?"

He looked directly into her eyes. "I have no other."

Brianna's vision had adjusted to the dimness and she saw his stark features clearly. *This man with his towering pride would only compromise it for love of this animal. It is costing him dearly to ask a favor of me.* "You honor me."

"I do, Brianna de Beauchamp." He knelt and fixed a lead to his wolf's collar.

Her mind quickly searched for an answer to the dilemma. "I will take her to my mother's castle of Chertsey, close by in Surrey."

"I thank you." He put the lead in her hand.

Brianna suddenly realized how much courage it took for him to part from his beloved wolf. He moved toward the stall door.

"Wait!" She removed the Celtic touchstone from around her neck and handed it to him. "Keep Shadow's likeness close to your heart."

He took it from her and slipped the thong over his head. "I thank you." Again he turned to leave.

"Wait! There's something else I must give you." She knew it was impulsive, even reckless, but something compelled her. She feared they might never meet again and did not want them to part while she owed him a debt. She closed the distance between them, stood on tiptoe, and lifted her mouth to his. She gave him the kiss willingly, generously, allowing her animal instinct to guide her. Her hood fell back and she felt the power of his strong fingers as he threaded them into her disheveled hair. Heat leapt between them. Brianna could hear her heart beating wildly in her ears and the taste of him sent her senses reeling.

Brianna stood mesmerized long after the kiss had ended. She didn't remember him leaving. One moment he was there, the next he had disappeared into the dim shadows. The stall door opened and Simon Deveril stepped inside.

"I promised to take his wolf to Chertsey for safekeeping."

He did not question her sanity; instead he said simply, "The fastest way is by river. Come, I will hail us a wherry boat."

When they arrived at her mother's castle, the elderly steward greeted her warmly. He had always had a good deal of patience with the animals she had brought him when she was a small girl. He had helped her nurse many a rabbit back to health, then made sure she set them free once they were strong enough to eat and hop about.

"Mr. Croft, this is Shadow. She belongs to a Warwick kinsman who cannot keep her with him for the next few months. I've brought her to Chertsey because I know you will give her a safe home. The wolf is highly intelligent and when she visited Warwick Castle, she was extremely well behaved."

The steward let Shadow sniff his hand. "Mrs. Croft will be in her glory. Our old dog died a month ago and we miss him something fierce. We'll take good care of this one."

"I know you will, Mr. Croft. I'm now lady in waiting to Queen Isabelle at Windsor, so I promise to come and visit Shadow."

"Come to the kitchen and have some breakfast before you leave."

"Thank you. Lovely as that sounds, I must get back to Windsor."

Wolf Mortimer did not waste time returning to Reading, but rode directly north from Windsor. He knew that by day's end he would catch up with the Marcher barons who were moving with all speed to meet with Thomas of Lancaster.

Last night lingered in Wolf's thoughts. When he had returned to camp from his midnight swim, his father

summoned him and handed him the message from
Brianna de Beauchamp. The news confirmed the visions he had experienced. "We must heed this warning. Grave danger threatens. Edward *will* bring his
force against us."

"I don't fear the feckless cocksucker!"

"Hugh Despencer set the trap at Leeds Castle.
When it was successfully sprung, the king became
power mad and he lusts for revenge. Hugh Despencer
once again holds Edward by the balls, and is now
plotting our downfall."

"Experience has taught me to believe the things you
foretell. You prophesied trouble at Leeds the night
Edmund wed Elizabeth Badlesmere. This time I will
heed your warning. Give the order to break camp. We
will leave now. I'll pass the word to Hereford, Audley,
and d'Amory."

Wolf Mortimer's thoughts came back to the present
and his fingers closed over the Celtic touchstone. *I
was right to trust my instincts about Brianna de Beauchamp. Beneath her fiery temperament, she has a heart
of gold.*

Wolf caught up with the Mortimers sooner than he
expected. Hereford and the other Marcher lords had
fled with amazing speed, but Roger's progress had
been impeded because his uncle of Chirk was ailing.
In the Chilterns he had doubled over with pain and
vomited blood.

Wolf conferred with his father and Edmund. "Take
the men north with all speed. Leave us a packhorse
with a tent and fodder. I'll remain with him, and we'll
catch up when he's well enough to travel."

Roger Mortimer, decisive as always, agreed. He
would not jeopardize his or Chirk's forces because of
one man's illness.

Wolf pitched the small tent in a sheltering stand of
fir trees and made his uncle a bed with saddle blan-

kets. Then he went off in search of wood betony. He found some and though the leaves were withered with the cold, it was the white thready roots of the plant that were beneficial for all manner of stomach ailments. He made a fire and boiled the roots in water from the stream. To make certain his patient slept, Wolf added a few drops of distilled poppy, which he always carried in his saddlebags.

When the brew cooled, he propped up Chirk, held the cup to his lips, and made certain he drank every drop. Softly, he crooned a Welsh ballad until the older man dozed; then Wolf withdrew and fed the horses. His heart was heavy—deep down he knew that Mortimer of Chirk was one of the three Marcher lords who would not survive. Yet he sensed that his death was not imminent. *That cruel bitch, Life, is not done with him yet. The poor old bugger will have to endure a few more months of suffering before his mortal spirit finds release.*

Wolf sat down before the fire and stared into the flames. He put up a barrier to guard his mind against more visions of the future. Instead, he thought of Brianna. His mouth curved in a half smile. *Her kiss was not only warm and generous, it was indeed the most memorable kiss I have ever shared.*

On the boat ride back from Chertsey, Brianna made a conscious decision not to tell Isabelle about King Edward's plans to go after the Marcher barons. Now that she had warned Roger Mortimer, she felt completely confident they would all be long gone by the time Edward's forces began to search for them. And now that she had alerted the Marchers, even if it did come to a fight they would easily defeat the king's forces, as they had done before.

Brianna and Simon walked briskly from the river and entered Windsor's Lower Ward through a gateway in the west wall. She knew that she must change her clothes and join the others without delay. Today, Isabelle and her ladies would be decorating Windsor's Great Hall for the Yuletide festivities.

"Simon, I thank you with all my heart for your help." Impulsively she hugged him, then picked up her skirts intending to run to her chamber. Before she took one step, she saw the tall figure of her betrothed striding toward her.

"Lincoln Robert! What a lovely surprise." She gave him a dazzling smile, hoping he would not question what she was about.

He did not return the smile. "I can believe you are surprised. Who the devil is your companion?"

"He is not my *companion*," Brianna denied. "Deveril is a Warwick man my father sent to Windsor to guard me from danger. And that is exactly what he did when I accompanied the queen to Leeds Castle."

"Thank God you came to no harm. My father and I were so outraged, we took de Warenne men-at-arms into Kent and joined Pembroke in the siege," he said proudly.

You and thirty thousand others. Brianna was immediately ashamed of her thoughts. She reached out and took his hand. "That was most courageous of you, Lincoln. I am proud of your loyalty to Queen Isabelle."

His glance swept over her. "Have you been to the river? You look disheveled, more like a serving girl than a lady in waiting."

"Yes," she improvised quickly. "Isabelle was expecting a boat to bring fresh rushes, holly, and ivy from her hunting park at Banstead. We are garlanding the hall for Yuletide today. I'll go and change and meet you in the Great Hall."

Brianna hurried off, relieved that Lincoln Robert

accepted her lame explanation, yet guilty that she had so easily deceived him.

In an amazingly short time, Brianna arrived at the Great Hall wearing a pale green velvet gown with matching ribbons in her hair. Her betrothed was engrossed in conversation with young Blanche FitzAlan, the Earl of Arundel's daughter, whom they both knew well. Brianna was amused to see Blanche gazing up at Lincoln Robert with adoration, hanging on to his every word. *I won't ruin her day by telling her we are betrothed.*

"Hello, Blanche. It's lovely to see you at Windsor."

"Hello, Brianna. Did you know that Lincoln was one of the nobles who besieged Leeds Castle? He is so gallant and brave!"

"Indeed. I believe I will present him to the queen."

"Ah, Brianna, you are so lucky to be a royal lady in waiting. I wish I were as old as you."

"Are you sure? I'm positively ancient. Excuse us, Blanche." She took Lincoln's arm and drew him across the room to the queen. "Cheeky monkey! She's only a year younger than I."

"Her remark was purely innocent. I think Blanche FitzAlan is a sweet young lady."

"Oh, I agree. Sugar wouldn't melt in her mouth." Brianna smiled her secret smile. She felt so self-assured with Lincoln Robert. She felt safe and in control when they were together. *He will make me a very good husband.*

"Your Grace, it gives me great pleasure to present Lincoln Robert de Warenne. Both he and his father, the Earl of Surrey, are loyal queen's men."

When Lincoln bowed, Isabelle smiled. "I am honored by your devotion. Lynx de Warenne is my friend Jory's brother, if I am not mistaken, though he has seldom graced my court."

"The Earl of Surrey, like the Earl of Warwick,

makes a better warrior than courtier, Your Grace," Brianna explained.

"I am delighted you are here, my lord. Will you spend the Christmas festivities with us?"

"Thank you, Your Grace, but my parents have sent me to bring my betrothed to Hedingham for the Yule, if you could find it in your heart to release her from her duties."

"You are betrothed? Brianna, I had no idea. How romantic." Isabelle sighed wistfully. "I absolutely insist that you go and spend the Yule with your future family."

Well, it seems I have little say in the matter. But it will be lovely to spend Christmas at Hedingham.

Chapter 12

"I intend to stay the night at Flamstead, if you have no objection, Lincoln." Brianna had the ever-vigilant Deveril riding behind her and her betrothed was attended by Taffy, his newly appointed squire who had served Lynx de Warenne for two decades.

"I was going to suggest it. I'd like to have you to myself before my family descends upon you. Once at Hedingham, you'll spend hours in the stillroom with Mother and I wager my brother Jamie will be underfoot most of the time."

"I love and adore your family, Lincoln. 'Tis one of the reasons I agreed to marry you," Brianna teased.

"And Flamstead is one of the reasons I agreed to marry you."

"I thought you told me it was because I am Warwick's daughter."

"That too," he jested.

"So you admit you have more than one ulterior motive?"

"Many more, and speaking of marriage, now that you have turned seventeen, why don't we have a Christmas wedding?"

"Christmas sounds delightful . . . *next* Christmas of course." She quickly changed the subject. "I know exactly the right gift for your mother, but I haven't the faintest notion what to give Jamie, or you, for that matter."

"You know what I want," he said with a leer.

"Indeed I do, Lincoln Robert de Warenne. And it doesn't take a crystal ball."

The afternoon light was fading by the time they arrived in Flamstead's bailey. The castle was much smaller than Warwick. It had no soaring towers and therefore it was less intimidating. There were no fighting men garrisoned at Flamstead, only a few guards. There was a castle household of servants, but the rest of the inhabitants were horsemen, grooms, and stable hands.

"I love Flamstead. It is always so welcoming. I think it's because of all the open pastures where the horses roam freely."

Lincoln dismounted and lifted Brianna from the saddle. They knew Simon and Taffy would tend their mounts and, hand in hand, they crossed the bailey and entered the castle.

"Good afternoon, Hornby, we are on our way to Hedingham and decided to stop for the night. Simon Deveril and Lincoln's squire, Taffy, are with us. Would you be good enough to plenish them a chamber?"

The steward, who'd known the pair all their lives, greeted them warmly. The Great Hall was small enough that it needed only one fireplace and Brianna was drawn to the blaze immediately.

"Surely you cannot be cold, wrapped in your sable fur?"

"No, it's my feet that are cold, Lincoln."

He sat her down in one of the big chairs, went down on one knee, removed her riding boots, and began to massage her feet.

She wiggled her toes. "How very gallant you are."

"Warming you is more pleasurable for me than you, I warrant."

Hornby brought them hot cider and before they had drained their tankards, Simon and Taffy arrived.

Lincoln quickly covered Brianna's feet with her fur cloak.

His action sent her off into peals of laughter. "There is no formality at Flamstead, my love—they've all seen my feet before."

Simon and Taffy concealed their grins and busied themselves taking Brianna's and Lincoln's luggage to the private living quarters, which were up only one flight of stone steps. There were four roomy bedchambers, and all present, with the possible exception of Lincoln Robert, took it for granted that the couple would occupy separate rooms.

Before the evening meal was served, Brianna asked the steward if he would summon various craftsmen who lived and worked at Flamstead. She spoke with the harness maker and asked to see some of his bridles. She chose a red leather one for Jane de Warenne, because she always rode a white palfrey. "Could you attach some silver bells to the bridle? I'm sure the blacksmith has some."

The blacksmith spoke up. "Lady Warwick enjoys the tinkle of bells on her harness. I know just what you have in mind."

Brianna turned to Lincoln. "Do you think Jamie would like some spurs stamped with his initials?"

"That's a brilliant idea. He won't be able to sneak up on us. He'll strut about in them and we'll be able to hear the young devil a mile away."

"Lincoln, be a love and get me some more cider, please?" When he went off to find Hornby, Brianna spoke to the armorer. "I'd like to give Lincoln a sword. I know there's always a supply of new weapons in the guardhouse. I also know you are a talented artist, Toby. Could you inscribe a small lynx on the hilt and a matching one on the scabbard? Will you have enough time?"

"I'll do it tonight, Lady Brianna."

"Thank you so much." She gave each of them a gold coin from the supply her father had given her when she went to Windsor.

Lincoln returned with her cider. "What about a gift for my father? I'm having a devil of a time wondering what to get him."

"What about a hunting dog? When I was here a few months ago, one of Father's prized wolfhound bitches had just had a litter. We'll go to the kennels before we leave and you can help me choose one. It can be a mutual gift from both of us."

"I like your suggestion. We are a most compatible couple."

"That's because we have known each other all our lives. I can often read your thoughts." She doubled up her fist and playfully punched his chest. "Especially the lusty ones."

"I'm a man, Brianna!"

To me you are still a boy, Lincoln. That's why I'm so comfortable around you. You pose absolutely no threat to me. Thoughts of another male tried to intrude, but she firmly pushed them away and forbade them to return.

After the evening meal, they made their way back to the fire. Once the serving men cleared all away, they left the hall and gave the young couple their privacy.

Lincoln threw down cushions before the hearth, and they stretched out together in companionable silence, watching the flames. Gradually, he inched closer, slipped his arm about her, and the kissing began.

Brianna felt so cozy and warm, she became drowsy and drifted off to the edge of slumber. The arms about her gradually became more powerful, the kisses more masterful. She felt her breasts being caressed and her nipples became erect with arousal. She moaned softly. "Wolf, no."

"Wolf?" Lincoln asked, puzzled.

Brianna raised her lashes and stared at him. Wolf Mortimer had transformed into Lincoln de Warenne. Her hand flew to her throat. "My wolf touchstone. I'm not wearing it. Your mother will be unhappy with me."

"You can do no wrong in Mother's eyes. You are the daughter she always wanted," he assured her.

"I think it is time I went to bed . . . I almost fell asleep."

"I dream of you falling asleep in my arms." Reluctantly, he allowed her to arise, and followed her up the flight of stone steps. They stopped at her chamber door and again he took her into his arms and kissed her deeply. His lips moved to her ear. "Let me share your bed, Brianna."

She pulled away and looked up at him. She knew he was fully aroused and had no control at the moment. She was tempted to let him have his way. Then she came to her senses. *I'll have to take control.* "You rode off so gallantly to avenge the queen's honor. Tonight it is my honor you must protect. Good night, Lincoln."

"Brianna! Welcome, darling. I'm so happy you could come." Jane dropped down to her knees before the young wolfhound that accompanied her son and his betrothed. "How do you do, sir? Dare I hope that you have come to stay?"

"He is our gift to Lynx. We knew *you* would love him, but what about the lord and master of Hedingham?" Brianna asked anxiously.

"Lynx will be thrilled. He's always envied your father having Brutus as his constant companion, and I'm glad this one is gray, so we'll be able to tell them apart."

Brianna laughed. "I believe Brutus is the third black wolfhound Father has had by that name—he's very attached to it."

"I'll take him to the stables," Lincoln said.

"You'll do no such thing. Bring him into the castle." The dog gave Jane a look of adoration. "Follow me, sir."

Brianna spoke to Taffy. "Will you find Simon a chamber or will I speak with Hedingham's steward?"

"I'll find him accommodation near mine, my lady."

Taffy carried Brianna's luggage up to her chamber, including the gifts she'd brought from Flamstead. Jane's maid, Rose, was plenishing Brianna's room. She took one look at them and fled.

"Taffy, whatever have you done to Rose?"

"Nothing that I know of, my lady. I think she's just shy."

After he left, Brianna hung up her clothes and put the gifts in the bottom of the wardrobe, and then she went down to join Jane. "May I help you decorate the hall for Christmas?"

"That would be lovely. We'll do it tomorrow. In Scotland, we celebrate Yuletide from Christmas Eve until Twelfth Night when all the trappings are removed. We observe the holy days at Christmas, and the festivities and celebrations are held at New Year."

"Oh dear, I can't stay until New Year, Jane. I must return to Queen Isabelle the day after Christmas."

"Of course you must. I was just reminded of the Twelfth Night festivities we had in Scotland, when Robert Bruce and his brothers came to celebrate with us. Your mother and I had such great fun. It was a magical time."

"I knew that the late Lady Bruce was my mother's godmother, but I didn't realize that the King of Scotland was such a close personal friend." *Mother has never spoken of Robert Bruce to me.*

"It was a long time ago, before Robert became king."

"Lincoln Robert was named for the *Bruce*! I didn't realize." Brianna smiled. "Was he enamored of you, Jane?"

"Heavens, no! The Bruce had eyes only for Jory."

"Robert Bruce was in love with my mother?" *Good God, how many conquests did she have?* "Was she in love with him?"

"She loved him very much, but because the Scots would never accept an English queen, she made a great sacrifice and selflessly left Scotland so he could fulfill his rightful destiny as king."

They were lovers! Brianna was shocked to think that her mother may have given herself to a man other than her husband.

Just then Lincoln strode into the hall. "Father and Jamie are coming. My brother has Stalker with him— perhaps we'll have a dogfight. I think I'll go and warn them."

When Lynx came in, the wolfhound loped toward him, planted his front paws on his master's chest, and wagged his tail madly.

Lynx scratched his ears. "Well, am I your boy, or are you mine? I'll have to think of a good, noble name for you. How about Sir Lancelot?"

Jamie brought in Stalker, who took one look at the wolfhound's size and dropped to the floor in submission. "Well, that settles the pecking order."

Lynx laughed and enfolded Brianna in his arms. "Thank you for the gift." He held her away from him. "You don't look any worse for wear after your ordeal, but it must have been frightening."

She pushed the disturbing thoughts about her mother aside. "I'm over the shock of what happened at Leeds." Brianna lowered her voice. "I do want to talk to you in private, though."

He searched her face. "Very well." He raised his voice so the others could hear. "Come to the library with me, Brianna. I have a book on horse breeding I think you'd like." When Lincoln started to follow them, his father put up his hand. "I'll guard her with my life—word of honor."

Lynx closed the library door. "Your father's book collection at Warwick puts mine to shame." He held a chair for Brianna and then propped himself on the edge of his massive oak desk. "Something is troubling you."

"Troubling me and troubling the queen. I told Father, and I think I should tell you. King Edward assured Isabelle that Leeds Castle was hers. He lied! In reality it still belonged to the Badlesmeres. She believes he sent a royal guard with her to deliberately provoke an attack. It was a clever ploy to stir the people's outrage and have the nobles take their men-at-arms into Kent to avenge the insult to their beloved queen."

Lynx shook his head at his own gullibility. "Lincoln and I wanted to show our loyalty to the queen."

"Father said it was a scheme to divide the barons. He remained neutral and returned to Warwick."

"An infamously wise man." Lynx ran a hand through his tawny hair that was now sprinkled with gray. "Pembroke would never have incarcerated women and children. When Edward saw the size of the forces that had gathered, he took over and without proper process of law, clapped the Badlesmere family into prison." Lynx bit back a curse. "It was the first military victory of his entire life and he didn't even have to draw his sword from his scabbard."

"A few days ago I heard something that put fear in my heart."

Lynx leaned forward with a frown.

"The Earl of Norfolk told me in confidence that Edward has no intention of disbanding the army. He intends to use it to reclaim his royal prerogative. He wants to destroy the Marcher lords and the barons who forced him to banish the Despencers."

"Christus!"

I must not tell anyone that I sent word to the Mortimers. "I said nothing to Isabelle. I did not want to alarm her, after what happened at Leeds. But since you and Father pledged to support the Marchers, I thought you should know."

"Edward has us in a cleft stick—damned if we do, damned if we don't. Did you send word to Warwick?"

"Not yet. Shall I send Simon Deveril?"

"I'll send one of my men," he assured her. "Try not to let this upset you. Most likely the best thing your father and I can do is stay completely out of it. Thank you for confiding in me."

Brianna hesitated as thoughts of her mother came flooding back.

"Will you confide in me? Were Robert Bruce and my mother lovers?"

"Splendor of God, that was such a long time ago, and none of my business. I interfered enough in your mother's love life. If there's anything you want to know about the affair, you'll have to ask her." He put his arm about her shoulders. "Let us go and enjoy our Christmas."

Before Brianna fell asleep that night, she thought about her mother. She had always wanted to be just like her, but the things she had learned today shocked her and made her realize that Jory was far more reckless and spirited than she had ever imagined. Her mother's words came back to her: *I want to protect you from making the foolish mistakes I made.* Brianna smiled into the darkness. *Taking a lover must be wildly exciting!*

Brianna awoke early and when she was dressed she decided to visit Jane's amazing stillroom. She wanted to take Isabelle some scented candles but hadn't yet decided on a fragrance.

When she entered the room, she saw that Rose was already at work with pestle and mortar. "Good morning. You're up early."

Rose almost jumped out of her skin. She dropped the bowl, and its contents spilled on the flagstone floor. "Oh Lord."

"I'm sorry. I didn't mean to startle you." Brianna knelt to pick up the bowl and the pungent smell of pennyroyal took her breath away. She saw that Rose was pale as death and frightened.

Brianna grasped instantly what the little maid was about. She took both her hands and led her to a bench.

"Rose, you are having a baby. You mustn't try to destroy it. You think it's the only way out of your trouble, but you are wrong. You'll never forgive yourself . . . It will haunt you always."

Rose covered her face and began to quietly sob.

"You must tell Jane. She is the sweetest, most understanding lady in the entire world. She will help you, Rose, I promise. I swear to you I won't reveal what I know, whatever you decide. But I truly hope you will search your heart and find the courage to confide in Jane."

Rose fled without a word, and Brianna cleaned up the mess. *She is covered with shame, yet it could happen to any of us.* She thought of the night she and Lincoln had spent alone at Flamstead. *We almost made love.* Yet Brianna knew that if she were in the same trouble, she and Lincoln would be able to wed immediately. *Unfortunately, it's not so simple for poor Rose.*

It was Christmas Eve and snow had begun to fall. After the hall was decorated with fir boughs, holly, ivy, and mistletoe, Lincoln took Brianna on a sleigh ride all around Hedingham's property. They revisited the stream that was now frozen and the picturesque woods where he had asked her to marry him. The cold air was conducive to cuddling and kissing, and on the ride back to the castle, Lincoln Robert taught her how to drive the sleigh.

Just before the evening meal, the men dragged in the Yule log. Lynx and his two sons, his squires and his knights, along with the castle stewards and even Simon Deveril, participated in the annual tradition. The huge pine tree was heavy and more than one male ended up falling on his arse. Raucous laughter accompanied the good-natured taunts that flew about the hall like barbed arrows. The hounds, Stalker and Sir Lancelot, whose name had been shortened to Lance, joined in the fun and howled their approval. The men, fortified by mulled cider and winter ale, finally managed to haul it across the entire floor of the hall and prop it upright beside one of the huge fireplaces. Cheers broke out, followed by toasts and snatches of ribald song. Jane and Brianna wiped tears of mirth from their eyes as they sipped on spicy hippocras.

They were entertained by jugglers at dinner, and a jester with cap and bells named young Jamie the Lord of Misrule. After the meal, Taffy recited an epic poem of valor, and some of the Welsh bowmen played their harps and sang poignant ballads.

When the hour grew late, they all put on their warm

cloaks and went to Hedingham's chapel to observe midnight Mass. Brianna and Lincoln held hands throughout the service and she made a wish that everyone she loved would be as happy as she was tonight.

A short time later, as Brianna made her way to the lovely chamber that used to be her mother's, a movement at the end of the hallway drew her eye. In the dim light she saw two figures; when they moved toward the solar, Brianna recognized Jane and Rose. *Thank God she found courage. I know Jane will be gentle with her.*

Jane lit the candles and closed the solar door. "Rose dear, don't cry. Sit down and tell me why you are so troubled."

Rose did not dare to look at Lady de Warenne. "I've done something terrible, my lady."

"Share your burden with me, Rose."

"I'm . . . I'm going to have . . . a baby," she whispered.

Jane covered her surprise. *These things happen. She is young and pretty and only human.* "Well, my dear, it's not the end of the world. A baby should bring joy, not dread." *I hope she knows who the father is—of course she does—she's not promiscuous.* "Rose, does the father know?"

The young girl nodded.

"Will he not marry you?"

Rose shook her head. "He—cannot, my lady."

Jane felt outrage that a man, already wed, had taken advantage of the little maid. "Tell me his name, Rose."

"I cannot—I promised," she whispered.

"Wed or not, he must take responsibility for the child, Rose. Many men have natural children. There is no shameful stigma if he gives the child his name

and educates him. *At least, not in Scotland there isn't.*
"Tell me his name," she coaxed.

Rose bowed her head. "De Warenne," she murmured.

Jane gasped. *Why am I so shocked? She and Jamie are the same age—it's simply human nature.* "Jamie will acknowledge the child," Jane said firmly.

Rose raised her head; a look of misery marred her pretty features. "Not Jamie . . . Lincoln."

Jane was aghast. *Lincoln is betrothed—how could he have done this thing? He has dishonored Brianna as well as poor Rose!*

Lynx entered his son's chamber, dropped the lit torch into the wall bracket, and swept the bedcovers to the floor.

Lincoln Robert sprang from the bed. "What the *devil* . . . oh, it's you, Father," he said with dull resignation.

Lynx strived valiantly to keep his fury leashed. "It is true? Are you the father of Rose's child?"

He thought about lying, but changed his mind when he saw his father's eyes. "It's . . . possible," he admitted with reluctance.

Lynx wanted to strike him. "What about Brianna?"

"Yes, Rose's problem could very well complicate the betrothal. That's why I tried to keep it quiet over Christmas until Brianna goes back to Windsor."

Lynx's hand ached to grab him by the throat. "Rose's problem? It's *your* bloody problem!"

"It's all right, Father. Brianna needn't know. Jamie has agreed to say the child is his."

Lynx's powerful fist shot out and his son hit the floor with a sickening thud. "You selfish young coward!"

Lincoln Robert swallowed the bile that rose up in his throat and, using the bed, slowly pulled himself upright. "It's not cowardice, it's expedience. If I do the honorable thing and legitimize the child, and it is a male, he will be my legal heir. The Warwicks would dissolve the betrothal immediately if Brianna's child could not inherit the earldom of Surrey."

Lynx groaned and uttered a foul oath.

Chapter 13

On Christmas morning, Brianna arose late. *I won't be the only one. None of us got to bed much before two o'clock this morning.* A serving woman brought her breakfast on a tray and, shortly after, two other servants brought hot water for her bath. When she was done, Brianna took her time selecting just the right gown for the special day.

She donned a frilly lace petticoat and chose her newest gown of cream velvet. The bodice and tight sleeves were embroidered with green oak leaves and the buttons were shaped like acorns. She brushed her red-gold curls until they shone, and decided to wear her hair uncovered. As a final touch she fastened a gold clip decorated with the Warwick staff and bear emblem at each temple.

As soon as she opened her bedchamber door the air became redolent with the tempting smells of roasting meat, game, and spicy mince pies. Beyond the castle kitchens were outdoor cooking pits, where whole oxen and boar had been turning on spits since dawn for the Christmas feast.

When Brianna arrived in the Great Hall she found it filled with the laughing, excited children of the men and women who served Hedingham. Jane was smiling and serene. "Merry Christmas, darling. It does my heart good to see them all so happy."

"Just look at the toys!" Each girl had a doll and a carved cradle and every boy had a painted shield and a wooden sword. "The Welsh archers are such gifted artists. The animals they carve are so detailed and realistic."

Trestle tables were piled with nuts, dried fruit, and sweetmeats, and the children were stuffing themselves without fear of reprimand. Barrels of ale were stacked beside the fireplaces, along with buckets of chestnuts for roasting.

Jamie was capering about with the dogs and when he saw Brianna, he came to wish her Merry Christmas. "You look extremely elegant today, Lady Brianna." He produced a sprig of mistletoe, held it over her head, and stole a kiss.

"Hands off, Lord of Misrule. The lady is mine."

Brianna turned with a teasing smile that fled the moment she saw his face. His cheekbone was badly swollen and bruised. "Lincoln, you're hurt! How on earth did that happen?"

"I warrant it must have happened when I was hauling in the Yule log. Didn't show up until this morning."

"Come to the stillroom and I'll bathe it with angelica."

"Don't fuss, Brianna, you are embarrassing me."

"I'm sorry. Let's go for a walk. I brought my cloak so I could go to the stables and give Venus an apple."

Once they were outside, Brianna scooped up a handful of snow, packed it into a ball, and reached up to hold it against his cheek. She hid a smile. When no one was watching, Lincoln welcomed her fussing.

It was a Christmas tradition to present every household member of Hedingham with new cloaks and footwear. As well, each family was given bolts of gaily dyed wool and finely woven linen for new garments.

After this the Yule feast began and lasted all afternoon and into the evening. Finally, the de Warennes withdrew into their private living quarters to exchange their gifts.

Brianna watched eagerly as Jane unwrapped her present.

"A red bridle with silver bells! I love it. I've always secretly envied your mother's jingling bridle bells."

The moment Jamie unwrapped his spurs, he put them on to show them off, then boldly gave Brianna a kiss of thanks.

She held her breath as Lincoln unwrapped his sword and scabbard. His eyes told her how much he liked the gift.

He hugged her to him and murmured, "I don't deserve you, Brianna." He gave her a small silver casket. "Happy Christmas."

She opened it and was thrilled to find a pair of cabochon emerald earrings. "How perfect! Emeralds were favored by Venus, the Goddess of Love." She whispered, "I love you, Lincoln."

Lynx carried in a large chest made from cedar wood and presented it to Brianna. "Jane suggested it."

Brianna ran her fingers over the exquisitely carved scene of mares with their foals. When she opened the chest, it was filled with woodruff-scented bed linen, embroidered with the de Warenne name and crest. "Oh, Jane, your gift is beautiful and practical, just like you. I thank you both with all my heart. I will keep it here at Hedingham until Lincoln and I are wed, next Christmas."

They finished the night off with fruitcake and wine and when Brianna retired to her chamber, she packed her clothes, ready for the journey back to Windsor. Then she knelt beside the bed and gave thanks. It had been one of the happiest days of her life.

* * *

The next morning she went to the stillroom to collect the jasmine-scented candles she had made for Isabelle. Jane was already there, removing the wax candles from their molds, and Rose was helping her. The moment Brianna appeared, Rose fled.

"Oh, Jane, my heart goes out to her. I urged her to confide her trouble to you."

Jane looked startled. "Rose told you?"

"Oh no . . . I guessed. But I knew you would help her."

Jane pressed her lips together. "Lynx and I have spoken at length about it. We have decided to acknowledge the child as ours. Whether Rose has a boy or girl, the child will be given the de Warenne name and made legitimate." Jane's face flushed to the roots of her hair.

Brianna stared at her in shocked silence. *Lynx is the father of Rose's baby? My God, how could the wicked devil be unfaithful to you?* "Jane . . . I am so sorry for the burden you must bear."

"An innocent babe will never be a burden to me. Don't be shocked, Brianna. Many good men have natural children. When you are older and wiser in the ways of the world, you will realize there are worse sins than infidelity."

On the ride back to Windsor, Brianna was lost in thought most of the way. It had been a revelation that her mother had taken a lover, and that Lynx had dishonored his marriage vows. She glanced at Lincoln. *I wonder if he knows about his father and Rose. I mustn't speak of it—Lincoln would die of shame.* He was not in a talkative mood, and she assumed he looked glum because they would soon be parted.

When they arrived, Lincoln Robert lifted her from the saddle and Simon Deveril took her horse to the stables.

"You will stay and dine with me, won't you?"

He shook his head. "My face would prompt too many questions. Taffy and I will stop at an inn for supper."

She gently touched her fingertips to his damaged cheekbone in a loving gesture. "Poor Lincoln, I hope you're not in pain."

"I am, but it's my heart that aches because we must part." He enfolded her in his arms and kissed her good-bye.

"I promise to write to you, Lincoln. If we exchange letters every month, it will keep us from missing each other so much."

Simon came back from the stables with her luggage. "I'll take these upstairs for you, my lady."

Brianna stood and waved good-bye until Lincoln and Taffy were out of sight; then she slowly made her way to the queen's apartments. All her thoughts were with Jane. *She may not have been born noble, but she is without doubt the gentlest, kindest, most selfless lady in the entire realm. Jane sets an example of noble womanhood that I will try to emulate.*

Brianna changed from her riding dress and boots and emerged from her chamber to find Isabelle's ladies had gathered to greet her. Their anxious faces warned her to expect trouble.

"Praise God you are returned," the Countess of Pembroke declared. "The queen refuses to leave her bedchamber."

"Isabelle is unwell, Marie?"

"She cannot stop crying," Marguerite Wake confided.

Arbella Beaumont murmured, "She keeps asking for you."

"I'll go to her." Brianna slipped quietly into Isabelle's bedroom. The queen was sitting in a chair with a look of panic on her face. Her eyes were swollen from crying. Brianna crouched down before her and took her hands. "Tell me what has happened."

Isabelle raised hopeless eyes. "He's coming back."

Brianna did not need to ask whom she meant. Only the return of Hugh Despencer could have such a devastating effect on Isabelle. "How do you know?"

Isabelle handed her a crumpled paper, which was unsigned. "I received this anonymous letter telling me the king ordered the Archbishop of Canterbury to convene the clergy at Saint Paul's to annul the banishment of the Despencers. They are to return to England under Edward's protection."

"Hell and furies! Their persecution of you and of the barons will start all over again."

"Four months . . . I've been free of Hugh Despencer for only four months! Edward agreed to Mortimer's and Lancaster's demands with every intention of flouting them and bringing back his lover the moment the barons left London. Brianna, do you think there is any chance they will ride to my rescue a second time?"

How can I tell you that the king intends to hunt down his enemies with the large army he gathered under the pretense of avenging you? "There can be no doubt that Mortimer and Lancaster will be outraged at the greedy Despencers' return, for their own sake as well as yours."

"I cannot rid myself of hopeless despair and dread."

"You mustn't allow yourself to become despondent like this, or Hugh Despencer will have defeated you before he even returns. Always remember you are the Queen of England. Don't allow him to turn you into a victim. Every day you must don a beautiful gown and jewels. They will lend you a regal self-assurance."

"Brianna, I'm so glad you're back. You bolster my confidence."

"I wager you haven't eaten. I shall order food immediately. We will dine in your chamber tonight. Then I think you should write to your brother Charles. The newly crowned King of France must condemn Edward's recalling the Despencers. Perhaps your brother can influence Pope John to voice his displeasure also."

"I shall write the letter tonight," Isabelle said with determination. "Marie communicates regularly with family members in France. Her correspondence won't be suspect—I can conceal my letters inside hers."

It suddenly occurred to Brianna that perhaps King Edward had never actually been parted from Hugh Despencer. They had doubtless been meeting secretly. *How easy for Hugh Despencer to anchor his ship off the Isle of Wight when Edward visited Portchester Castle. Together they plotted the trap at Leeds Castle and now Despencer will urge the usually docile king to take revenge on the Marcher barons because they soundly defeated Hugh in the Welsh Borders.* Brianna poured Isabelle wine. *I must tell her, but not tonight. She would sink back into hopelessness.*

Wolf Mortimer and his uncle of Chirk met up with his father and the other Marchers at Doncaster in Yorkshire, where Thomas of Lancaster had called a hasty parliament.

Roger Mortimer embraced his uncle. "How are you faring?"

"I'm well enough," the older man said gruffly.

Wolf's gray eyes met his father's and he shook his head in silent communication. The three men joined Hereford, Audley, and d'Amory in the castle's Great Hall where Lancaster awaited them.

"My spies have reported that Edward has secretly had the banishment of the hated Despencers annulled and they are on the verge of returning." When angry voices rose in protest, Lancaster held up his hand.

"My spies also report that Hugh Despencer sank a Genoese merchant ship in the English Channel, but not before pirating its treasure. This was done with the king's blessing. The pair have been in communication for months."

Roger's eyes again met his son's. Wolf had been right—Edward and Hugh had never parted.

"I have here a Doncaster Petition that I intend to send to London telling the people that their king is recalling his degenerate favorite."

Roger Mortimer spoke up. "I have it on good authority that Edward took revenge on Leeds Castle to set an example. The king intends to keep the military force that gathered to avenge the queen's honor, and use it against any who oppose him."

"My petition spells out Edward's perfidy in supporting Despencer's piracy. I will undermine the support the king has gathered in London and, in the public's interest, I will rid the realm of the Despencers' evil influence."

Loud cheers went up in Doncaster's Great Hall. Thomas of Lancaster signed the petition with a flourish. "I want every baron present to affix his name and I will see that it is sent on its way to London today."

Wolf Mortimer moved closer to his father. "Lancaster fancies himself to be the great Simon de Montfort, uniting the barons and safeguarding the people of England. Don't put your trust in him."

Hereford signed immediately, but as Audley and d'Amory were waiting their turn, Adam Orleton, the warriorlike Bishop of Hereford, entered the hall with a half dozen men-at-arms. Adam had been born at a Mortimer manor and was rumored to be the natural son of the Baron of Chirk.

"Thank God I found you. Because of the long absence of the Marcher lords, the Welsh have chosen this opportune time for a massive uprising."

"Peste!" Roger swore. "We will have to return. Adam, get word immediately to Rickard de Beauchamp in Ireland and tell him to bring his fighting men."

Wolf Mortimer cursed. "I foresaw a threat from the west and should have realized the Welsh would take up arms in our absence."

Roger passed the news of the uprising to the other Marcher lords and they agreed they must leave without delay. Wolf's warning about Lancaster was foremost in Mortimer's mind. He told Thomas they were returning home and challenged him outright. "In the event Edward's army moves against us, can I rely upon you to join forces with us?"

"Sign the Doncaster Petition and I pledge to bring my fighting force to join the Marchers and defeat Edward."

As the Marcher barons left the hall, Wolf decided to reveal a strong premonition he had about Lancaster, prompted by the sound of bagpipes only he could hear. "I believe Thomas is seeking aid from Scotland."

"A pact with Robert Bruce would be treason—a hanging offense," Mortimer declared.

Hereford spoke up. "The Bruce and Edward are formidable enemies. It would be one sure way to depose our degenerate king."

"I agree. Our enemy's enemy is our friend," d'Amory declared.

Roger was outraged. "I've fought the Bruce in Scotland and in Ireland. He is England's enemy. I'll have no part of it!"

"I have decided to take down Lancaster from his high perch. Once I've dealt with Thomas, I will repeal the Ordinances the whoreson forced upon me," Edward confided to Hugh as they lay abed at Gloucester Castle. Despencer had sailed up the Severn to celebrate the New Year with his royal lover.

Hugh reached between the king's legs and rolled his flaccid member between his palms. He had learned it was a surefire method of arousing Edward. Once he had inflamed the king's desire, it was child's play to bend him to his will. "You promised to avenge me, my love."

"And so I shall, Hugh. Lancaster has sent a petition to the people of London, accusing you of piracy and vowing to rid the realm of your influence."

"Your royal cousin is a mere annoyance. He is filled with hot air, but the coward won't venture far from his cushy castle of Pontefract, I warrant. We can deal with him anytime."

Hugh moved down in the bed and pressed kisses along Edward's inner thighs until the king's cock began to pulse with need. Hugh suddenly stopped and raised his head. "I want you to go after Mortimer. The whoreson bastard led the Marchers and took sixty-three of my manors. They robbed me of property worth fifty thousand pounds, and I lust for revenge. You will assuage my lust, won't you, Edward?"

"Yes, yes! Haven't I promised you whatever you desire, Hugh?"

"I desire that tomorrow you order your levies to gather at Cirencester and that you immediately march to capture Mortimer."

"Why, in the name of Christ, did you not remain in Ireland where you were safe, madam?" Roger Mortimer could not hide his fury that his wife, Joan, who had chosen to live apart from him for years, turned up at Ludlow Castle two days after he arrived. It had been a long trek from Doncaster; they had already fought off a Welsh raid on his lands at Wigmore, and his temper was vile.

"What a charming welcome," she drawled. "I'll come to Ludlow when I wish. Don't forget I brought you this castle when we wed."

"You never let me forget. I should have known it was concern for Ludlow, rather than your children, that brought you back." He made no effort to hide the distaste he felt at the sight of her. Once attractive, though she was always self-centered, her body was now stout from overindulgence, her face petulant with dissatisfaction.

Mortimer turned on his heel and left her presence.

Joan's eyes narrowed with something akin to hatred. She had an insatiable desire for the virile, arrogant bastard, though she could no longer lure him to her bed. She lived apart, hoping he would seek her out, but he never did. "A pox on you, Mortimer!"

Roger went to the stables in search of Rickard de Beauchamp and found him and the men he'd brought from Ireland, feeding and watering their horses. "You should have left her in Ireland, but I imagine the dominant bitch overruled you."

"I pointed out the danger, but she insisted I make room on the ship for her." Rickard had made sure his own wife, Catherine, who was Roger's sister, remained in Ireland. He looked at his friend with shrewd eyes. "It's not just the Welsh we must worry about."

Roger shook his head and told Rickard the whole story. "The Welsh on one side and the king's forces on the other will have us in a vise." He gave a confident laugh. "We've been in tight places before. You and I will survive, Rickard."

"Is my father in danger from the king?"

"I don't honestly know. Warwick was the one who told me not to ride to Leeds Castle. He had sense enough to stay out of it."

"I warrant you have scouts on the other side of the River Severn, watching for any sign of the king's forces?"

"I do, and so has Hereford." Roger and Rickard de Beauchamp had been friends for twenty years, since they'd been knighted together. They never hesitated to confide in each other. "Wolf suspects that Lancaster is in secret negotiations with the Scots."

Rickard whistled in surprise, then considered for a minute. "Thomas has always fancied himself king. If he thought the Bruce could depose Edward and put him on the throne, he wouldn't cavil at traitorous dealings with Scotland."

"The Marcher barons have a pact with Lancaster."

"A pact whereby Thomas will expect us to go to his aid. The question is, will he come to ours?" Rickard asked.

"I don't know the answer, but Wolf is certain that he won't."

All at Ludlow worked until midnight, readying armor, weapons, and horses. They were prepared to fend off raids from the Welsh, and protect their landholdings and livestock, but they also needed to be ready to defend themselves if Edward's army threatened.

Roger bade his sons good night and climbed the stairs to his own chamber. He yawned and stretched his arms over his head, to ease the muscles in his shoulders. The moment he closed the door, he knew he was not alone.

Joan lay stretched out on his bed sipping from a goblet. Her robe was undone, exposing heavy thighs. "I'm tired of waiting."

"While I'm simply tired." His voice was curt. "You seem to have lost your way, madam."

She drained the wine. "Poor little lamb has losht her way."

Lamb? More like tough old mutton. He knew she was flown with wine. Roger went to the bed, pulled her robe to cover her, and lifted her into his arms. He could hear her laugh deep in her throat as he carried her to her own chamber. Her head suddenly fell back and when he looked down, he could see she had fallen into a drunken sleep. He laid her on her bed with a gentleness that belied his true feelings and covered her with a warm blanket.

Chapter 14

"Marie has just told me something I think you should know." Brianna had brought Marie to the queen's chamber the moment the nursemaids took the children away to put them to bed.

Marie hesitated, then blurted out, "The king has ordered my husband to take the army to Cirencester in Gloucestershire."

"Did Pembroke tell you why?" Isabelle asked.

"Because the king is at nearby Gloucester Castle and has chosen Cirencester as a mustering point for the royal forces."

"The king's brothers left this morning with their men-at-arms," Brianna added.

Isabelle was surprised and puzzled. "Does Edward intend to march his army against the Scots?"

Brianna shook her head. "No—Edward's target is the Marcher barons—Mortimer, Hereford, and the others who took their Welsh Borderlands back from the Despencers and forced their exile."

Isabelle's hand fluttered to her throat. "But Edward issued royal pardons for the Marcher barons."

"The king's pardons are not worth the paper they're writ on." Brianna clenched her fists. *I warrant Despencer is demanding revenge. The greedy swine must be back . . . if he ever left.*

"Will you excuse me, Isabelle?" Marie implored. "I'd like to spend time with my husband. He leaves at dawn."

When she left, Isabelle turned to Brianna. "I didn't want to say anything to upset Marie, and I pray for Pembroke's safety, but the Mortimers and Lancaster have a pact. They will easily defeat the king's forces, as they always have in a showdown."

" 'Tis rumored the ranks of the royal forces are swollen to near thirty thousand. Edward raised them in your name. Men will flock to Cirencester because they prefer him as a warrior king to the weakling he has always shown himself to be."

Isabelle was suddenly filled with anguish. "The people of England will fight for love of me. They have no idea they are being manipulated. I don't want men dying in my name!"

A picture of Wolf and Roger Mortimer flashed into Brianna's mind. "Amen to that, Your Grace."

Warwick, with a troop of two dozen knights, rode into Ludlow. He dismounted and removed his helm to speak with Roger Mortimer. "I heard a rumor the Welsh heathens are raiding again. I thought you might like some help."

"I have help. I recalled your son from Ireland."

"Rickard is here?" Guy de Beauchamp's face lit up.

Warwick's heir emerged from the armory when he heard the clatter of hooves. "Father! Who told you I was here?"

"No one—perhaps I sensed it." The two embraced warmly.

"Tell your men to rest," Roger advised. "We have a foray planned for tonight. Wigmore has been hit twice this past week. Wolf had a vision they were holding our sheep and cattle at Radnor. He rode into Wales under cover of night and confirmed that his sixth sense was right as usual."

"We'll teach them a lesson they won't soon forget," Warwick pledged. "As soon as we've fed and watered our mounts, we'll join you in the hall for some thirst-quenching Ludlow ale."

Rickard accompanied his father into the stables. His sire had aged a good deal since he'd last seen him. "Roger tells me you had the good sense to stay out of the Leeds debacle and advised him to do the same."

"Your sister Brianna is serving as lady to Isabelle. She was with the queen at Leeds and learned it was a deliberate plot. I saw clearly its purpose was to divide the barons. Expedience told me that the Mortimers and I should not involve ourselves."

Rickard put his hand on his father's shoulder. "We are expecting trouble from the king. I hope that expedience once again tells you not to involve yourself."

"I came to fight," Guy de Beauchamp staunchly declared.

"The Welsh, yes . . . the king, no. It is not your fight."

At dinner that night, Guy de Beauchamp was shocked at Lady Mortimer's appearance. He remembered her when she was a youthful beauty, and he could not believe how her figure had thickened to resemble a barrel. Above a heavy double chin her mouth looked petulant. Warwick was a romantic at heart, and replied with charm when she made cutting remarks, but he sent up a silent prayer of thanks that his wife, the great love of his life, was still exquisitely lovely both in face and form.

Guy's glance moved to the table where the two Mortimer daughters, who were still unwed, were sitting. He paid close attention to young Katherine, who had been suggested as a match for his son, Guy Thomas. He was relieved to find no fault with the pretty child. She was obviously innocent and sweet tempered, unlike her mother.

When it was full dark, Warwick and his men joined those of Mortimer and Mortimer of Chirk. Added to the men Rickard had brought from Ireland, they numbered about two hundred and fifty.

Wolf was in the vanguard, unerringly leading the men to the Radnor encampment, through the pitch-dark night. A surprise attack gave the Borderers the advantage over the Welsh, though they were outnumbered two to one. These odds, however, were undaunting since the Marchers had better armor and weapons.

The Welsh were fierce fighters, but their reckless courage often proved detrimental when pitted against the more disciplined English. The tactics they used were calculated. They would fight like demons, then scatter as if fleeing in fear, only to circle back and surround their enemy. This drew their opponents closer to mountainous terrain, giving them the advantage. Once in the mountains, other Welsh tribes joined them.

Mortimer of Chirk had dropped out of the fighting hours before, and Wolf and Edmund Mortimer led his men along with their own. It was dawn before the Welsh raiders were vanquished. The dead and wounded lay strewn over miles of frozen terrain. The Marchers drew rein to allow the Welsh to retrieve their injured, but all at once a warrior inflamed with bloodlust launched himself at Warwick with a battle-ax and unhorsed him. There was a sickening crack as Warwick's head smashed against a boulder, and his helmet was split in half.

Rickard, his heart in his mouth, witnessed the combatants roll on the ground, entwined in a death grip. He bolted from his saddle to aid his father, but before he could reach him, Warwick withdrew his knife from his attacker and staggered to his feet.

"Christ, Father, are you all right?"

Guy put his hand to his helmetless head. "Almost knocked my bloody brains out—what few I have!"

The pair laughed with relief and Warwick whistled for his horse and remounted. "I'm getting too old for this."

The Borderers' work wasn't finished yet. When they got back to the Radnor encampment they had to round up the Mortimer sheep and cattle and drive them back to Ludlow.

Late the next day, two of the scouts Roger Mortimer had sent to keep watch for the royal army rode hell-for-leather into the castle courtyard. Roger, Wolf, and Rickard greeted them warily.

"The king was staying at Gloucester with a negligible number of guards. Early this morning he left and rode to Cirencester. When we followed, we saw Pembroke already there with hundreds of men-at-arms. Hundreds more poured in by the hour. By the time we left, there were thousands, not hundreds."

"Does Hereford know?" Mortimer asked.

"Aye, his scouts saw what we saw."

Rickard spoke with the Mortimers. "I ask that you don't tell Warwick. He'd send for more men, and I want him well out of it."

"Agreed," Roger said grimly. "Unlike Chirk he's still a formidable warrior, but it's not his fight." Mortimer dispatched two messengers to notify Thomas of Lancaster that a large number of his forces was needed in the Marches immediately.

Hugh Audley arrived with his fighting force of two hundred, but he also had his wife and young son with him. "I couldn't leave them alone. I couldn't leave men behind to guard them. I believe Margaret and James will be safer at Ludlow with your daughters."

Mortimer greeted Margaret. "Welcome. We have plenty room at Ludlow." He grimaced. "I should warn you, my wife, Joan, is here, though I wish she had remained in Ireland."

They all went into the castle, and then Audley, Mortimer, his sons, and his lieutenants went to Ludlow's war room to study the maps and plan their strategy.

Rickard went to the bathhouse where his father was soaking his battered body. It wasn't Warwick's aching muscles that troubled Rickard, it was the goose egg on Guy's skull and the blood in the whites of his eyes. Rickard deliberately played down the threat.

"Pembroke has brought an army of a few hundred to Cirencester. Fortunately, Lancaster is on his way with reinforcements."

Warwick nodded. "Thomas has spies everywhere. What if the levies at Cirencester are larger than you anticipate?"

Rickard shrugged. "Then we will negotiate. We're not fools."

Guy de Beauchamp nodded again. "If we do what's expedient, we won't go wrong."

"*We*? I want *you* to return to Warwick. Today. And I want you to lie low. The name of de Beauchamp must not be involved in this treasonous fight with the Crown."

"Last I heard, *your* name was de Beauchamp."

"None but the Mortimers know I'm here. I'm dark enough to pass as a Mortimer. You on the other hand are recognizable to all."

"True enough. Why are you so adamant to keep me out of it?"

"To preserve Warwick and our other castles. If worse comes to worst in this fight with the king, our landholdings would be confiscated. Leave today, Father. Say hello to Jory and my brother for me. I've no idea when I'll be able to see them."

When Guy de Beauchamp went into the hall he was surprised to see Margaret and her young son. She was the daughter of his late friend Gilbert de Clare and Princess Joanna. Warwick's wife, Jory, had been with Joanna when Margaret was born, and she was her godmother. Warwick embraced Margaret and felt her despair.

"I've told her there is naught to fear." Joan's voice dripped with contempt for Margaret's apprehension. "The king is an inveterate coward. He won't dare come into Marcher country!"

Loath to alarm Joan, Guy chose not to argue with her. He did wish to offer Margaret his protection, however. "I am returning to Warwick today, my dear. Why don't you come with me? Jory would be overjoyed to see you and James."

Joan, jealous of the younger woman's beauty and noble pedigree, urged her to go.

Warwick gallantly extended the same offer to Joan, but she refused with utter disdain.

Rickard de Beauchamp was relieved when his father, accompanied by Margaret Audley and her son, departed before the afternoon light faded. His relief was short-lived, however. When the inhabitants of Ludlow arose the following morning, Rickard found that seventy of the hundred men he had brought from Ireland had melted away in the night and deserted.

"The whoreson cowards!" Roger Mortimer declared. "Once they learned the size of the king's force, their backbones collapsed."

Rickard was both angered and frustrated, and yet he understood the desertions. The men had served in Ireland for four years; now they were home and they'd had a bellyful of fighting. They'd slunk off to their families, and who could blame the poor bastards?

The following day, Hereford's sons, John and Humphrey de Bohun, arrived at Ludlow with two hundred men, which was only half of Hereford's forces.

"Where is your father?" Roger Mortimer asked.

The brothers looked at each other, and their fair skins flushed. "He took a force of men to meet Lancaster. He told us to join our forces with yours. He said you would know enough to remain on our side of the River Severn and keep the enemy from crossing."

"Set up your campaign tents for tonight. We'll leave tomorrow. I'll send word to d'Amory to bring his forces to join with ours." Roger was worried about his Uncle Chirk. He didn't have the stamina to lead men in a campaign.

Wolf spoke up. "Edmund and I will keep our eye on Chirk's men. They'll take orders from us." He waited until the de Bohun brothers left to confer with their men, and then he spoke up. "Hereford hasn't gone to meet Lancaster. In spite of his assurances to bring his great strength to support us, Thomas won't come. Hereford has ridden north to hole up with Lancaster and make a deal with the Scots."

Roger stared grim-faced at Wolf. "Ride swiftly to see if d'Amory has done the same fucking thing."

Wolf Mortimer had ridden less than four miles when he encountered a messenger d'Amory had sent. They returned quickly to Ludlow.

Wolf gave his father the message. "D'Amory has taken his men to Lancaster's castle of Tutbury, hoping to meet him there." Wolf held up his hand to stay his father's curses. "Roger d'Amory didn't desert. He naively believes Lancaster will come to our aid and will soon be at his castle of Tutbury."

"Then he is a misbegotten fool to put his trust in a man with Plantagenet blood!"

Wolf shuddered as if a goose had walked over his grave, or more to the point, d'Amory's grave.

The next day the large Marcher force left Ludlow and rode toward the great River Severn. When it came into view, they turned and rode south. They were about to make camp when a Mortimer scout on a lathered horse caught up with them.

"The king's forces are on the march!"

"They will go to Worcester where they can cross the Severn." Roger countermanded the order to make camp. "We must press on immediately." He turned command over to Edmund, Chirk, Audley, and the de Bohun brothers. "Rickard, Wolf, we must ride full speed and get to the Worcester Bridge before Pembroke!"

The three men covered the twenty miles in two hours. When they got to the bridge that crossed the river and led to Worcester, they dismounted and tethered their horses a safe distance away.

"I warrant we should fire the bridge from both ends." Roger looked directly into Wolf's eyes. "Tell me straight—are you confident you can swim back, or will I do it?"

Without hesitation, Wolf said, "I'll do it—you are indispensable."

Roger and Rickard each lit a torch, while Wolf removed his boots and leather jack. They handed him the pair of blazing torches and Wolf strode across the long bridge in his bare feet.

When he reached the far side, he fired the wooden struts, knowing his father and Rickard would be doing the same at their end. He crouched down on his haunches, waiting to make sure the heavy wood burned through, so the bridge would be totally destroyed.

As Wolf stared into the flames, he had a vision of the royal forces. The horde he saw approaching was so large, he questioned his second sight. He saw the royal banners and those of four earls—Pembroke, Norfolk, Kent, and Arundel—and was convinced his overactive imagination was clouding his true inner vision.

As the acrid stink of burning timber filled his nostrils and the crackle of flames roared in his ears, he suddenly had a vision of a female swathed in a black cloak. She pushed back the hood and her glorious red-gold hair was more brilliant than the flames. Brianna de Beauchamp beckoned to him. Wolf fought the craving to go to her, yet at the same time he had the uncanny feeling that whether he fought his desire or not, he would soon be with her.

A great crack rent the air, the burning bridge crashed down into the river below, and his vision was instantly extinguished. He watched as the raging river, swollen from an early January thaw, carried great sections of the wooden bridge away.

Wolf slid down the steep riverbank, filled his lungs, and plunged. The roiling water closed over his head, his arms thrust upward, and when his face surfaced he had to fight the fierce current that threatened to drag him after the splintered bridge.

He forced his mind to block the icy coldness and focus on his goal. Midway, his powerful strokes lessened and he was carried downstream; then suddenly Brianna was swimming alongside him. The river was no longer the Severn in winter, but the Avon in summer. He knew his towering male pride could not allow her to win the race. With renewed strength, he vigorously kicked and stroked through the water until he neared the riverbank.

Wolf grasped hold of his father's outstretched arm and then he grabbed Rickard's too. They hauled him out and he lay on the ground, his chest heaving, his lungs dragging in cold fresh air.

"Good man," Roger muttered.

The first to arrive were Edmund and Chirk with the Mortimer forces, followed by Audley and his men. Dusk had come early and Wolf stood gazing across the Severn for any sign of the enemy. Once again he envisioned a host of men; an army so large it was almost beyond comprehension.

He moved away from the river and joined the others just as John and Humphrey de Bohun arrived with the Hereford forces.

"As soon as the king's army arrives at Worcester and sees we have destroyed the bridge, they will march double time to the next one. Bridgnorth is a good twenty-five miles from here but we must burn it before they get there. If we wait until morning it could be too late," Wolf insisted.

"The king's army won't match our speed—large numbers of troops are unwieldy. But Wolf is right, we cannot wait until morning. We'll rest until midnight, then move north. Light no fires."

In his father's campaign tent, Wolf stripped off his wet clothes, wrapped his body with a saddle blanket, and fought the apprehension he felt. The fear was for the Mortimer family, not for himself. The king would force a confrontation; it was inevitable. Wolf knew they must hold it off as long as possible.

He conjured a vision of Brianna that was so palpable, he was able to wrap his arms about her and hold her tightly against his body. Her naked flesh warmed him and the smoldering desire she aroused in him turned his blood hot as it surged wildly through his veins. He slid his marble-hard erection to lie along the valley between her thighs and buried his lips in the warm hollow of her throat. Gradually his heartbeat slowed and he drifted in and out of blissful repose as if he had found sanctuary.

Wolf groaned when his father stirred and awoke him. He was wide-awake in seconds and dressed quickly. His clothes were cold and damp, but at least his stockings and boots were dry, as was his leather jack. He sprinted toward the river and his spirits sank as he saw campfires on the far side of it. More were being lit as he watched, telling him the army was only just arriving. In the darkness, perhaps they had no idea the bridge was gone. He sensed the number of men was massive.

Wolf ran back, forcing himself not to panic. "The soldiers are just arriving and setting up camp. Pass the word quietly."

Roger and Rickard were already mounted. "The three of us will ride ahead to Bridgnorth—we'll be there before dawn."

Wolf saddled his horse and rode after his father and Rickard within minutes. He had a short-handled whip that he seldom needed to use. His horse sensed urgency and plunged through the darkness at full gallop. As he rode, he envisioned what had happened to Lady Badlesmere and Edmund's bride, once Leeds Castle had been forced to surrender, and a feeling of dread rose up in him.

When they had ridden seven or eight miles, Wolf realized that they were passing Wigmore, which lay a few miles inland from the Severn. He tried to throw off the dread, but as the trio galloped another four miles, and they were parallel with Ludlow, Wolf felt compelled to draw rein.

"What the hell are you doing?" Roger shouted over his shoulder.

"Keep going! You fire the bridge—I'm for Ludlow!"

Wolf dug in his heels and urged his horse to gallop west. When he got to Ludlow it was still full dark, around three o'clock in the morning. He was out of the saddle and running before his horse came to a stop.

He roused the guards and then the stable hands and ordered them to ready two wagons. He ran inside the castle. "Up! Up! Everyone up!" He ran through the Great Hall and vaulted up the stairs to the adjoining, luxurious chamber block that had been built only two years ago. He threw open the door of the room his young sisters shared. "Katherine, get up and help Joan to dress."

"Wolf, what's amiss?" Katherine cried, jumping from her bed.

"Nothing if you do as I bid you."

The serving women gathered in the corridor, roused by Wolf's alarm. "Quick, pack the girls' clothes. I'm taking them to sanctuary . . . You can come too, though I doubt you're in danger." His voice deepened. "Christ, don't stand there gaping—*move*!"

Wolf ran back to the other end of the Great Hall to where the solar palace had been built. He entered his mother's chamber and ordered her out of bed.

"What the hellfire are you about?" she demanded.

He swept the blankets from her. "Get up and pack your things. Anything of value. I'm taking you to sanctuary."

"Go to the devil, you arrogant young lout! You're just like your father," she hissed.

"I'm taking the girls and you to sanctuary with the nuns at Wigmore Abbey. Get dressed!" he commanded.

"Put me in a *nunnery*? Piss off! Ludlow is mine and none will take it from me!"

Wolf remembered the whip he was clutching. He uncoiled it and lashed it at his mother's ankles. When it cracked, Joan screamed and jumped away. "*Obey*, or suffer the consequences." He raised the whip again with every intention of using it.

Joan knew better than to defy a Mortimer in this deadly mood. She immediately capitulated.

Chapter 15

Brianna suspected she was dreaming when she heard Wolf Mortimer's voice. "I'll race you."

She dove beneath the water, heading toward the middle of the River Avon where the tide ran more swiftly. She cut through the warm current with long, strong strokes, thoroughly enjoying herself by showing off her prowess.

Suddenly, the water turned icy cold, the current of the turbulent river was too much for her to battle, and she was swept away like a bobbing cork. Wolf was beside her. She threw him a desperate look of panic and then she heard his voice in her head.

Together we can make it. If we join the power of our minds and stick close, we will prevail.

Relief washed over her as they reached the far bank and were pulled from the icy water, but Brianna was freezing cold and feared she would perish. She turned over in bed and was immediately enfolded in warm arms. She clung to the powerful male body willingly, eagerly, as their bare flesh became infused with delicious heat. She sighed as she felt his lips nuzzle her throat and was thankful it was only a dream. She could not be accused of faithlessness for imaginary dalliance with the dark devil.

Brianna woke with a start, unable to recall her dream, but she suddenly thought of Wolf Mortimer and had a strong premonition that she would see him soon. *That's not possible!*

Thoughts of Wolf Mortimer made her feel decidedly guilty and she picked up the letter she had received yesterday from Lincoln and reread it. He was not the world's greatest correspondent, which was the reason Brianna found his letter endearing. It was short and sweet and told her how much he loved her and missed her. He had written one bit of news that was a pleasant surprise. Taffy, Lynx's squire, had married Rose. *It fills me with happiness that Rose will be able to keep her own baby. Taffy is a good man.*

Before she went down to breakfast, she sat down and answered Lincoln Robert with a ten-page letter of her own.

"Where are the rest of the forces? Did you send them north?" Wolf asked his father when he caught up with them at Bridgnorth. He saw that Rickard, Chirk, Edmund, Audley, and the de Bohuns were with Mortimer, and wondered who was leading the other men.

Roger Mortimer took his son aside. "We burned the bridge and successfully prevented the king's army from crossing the Severn, but when our troops saw the size of Edward's force, they began deserting in droves. Our only hope is if Lancaster and Hereford come with reinforcements."

"Then all hope is lost. They are not coming, Father."

"The army will cross at Shrewsbury. We cannot prevent them and we do not have a large enough force to defeat them in battle."

Wolf remained silent. He did not suggest their only alternative. It must come from the dauntless Mortimer.

"I will have to make terms with Edward," Roger said decisively.

Wolf nodded. "I put Mother and my sisters in sanctuary at Wigmore Abbey. You needn't worry about their safety, when you negotiate for terms."

"I'm relieved the girls are safe—no thanks to me."

"You had more than enough to occupy you."

"Well, I've dealt with Pembroke before. I can do it again. The fine we'll have to pay will be astronomical—we'll have to sell some of our land to meet it. I may even have to spend time in custody," Mortimer said with resignation.

"You will do what is expedient, Father," Wolf said confidently.

The royal army crossed the River Severn on January 14, and the following day at Shrewsbury Castle, King Edward ordered the arrest of the Mortimers and the Earl of Hereford and issued a safe conduct so they could come to him unharmed.

Roger Mortimer did what he always did when summoned by the king. He ignored the order.

Edward sent another messenger with an arrest order for Roger Mortimer, Mortimer of Chirk, and Hereford and again issued them a safe conduct to Shrewsbury.

This time Roger sent a message to Edward, trying to make terms. He told him that Hereford was not with him and that Mortimer of Chirk was ailing and must be excused. He offered to lay down his arms in return for clemency.

The king was outraged. He handed the courier a message that read:

Mortimer, I promise you nothing. You have committed treason by rising in arms against me, defying my commands, and supporting my enemies. Your safe conduct expires on January 20.

On January 21, when the Mortimers did not show up, the Earl of Pembroke came to mediate. Rashly, he assured them that if they submitted to the king, their lives would not be in peril and they would be pardoned.

Roger thanked Pembroke and told him that he and his Uncle Chirk would present themselves to King Edward the next day at Shrewsbury Castle.

When Pembroke left, Roger called the leaders and lieutenants into his tent. He looked at his friend Rickard. "De Beauchamp, I thank you for your support. I want you to leave *now*. They don't know you are here and I want neither you nor the men you brought from Ireland to be in jeopardy." Roger's eyes moved to Audley. "Since the arrest warrant does not bear your name, I advise you to make yourself scarce."

That night as Wolf stared into the flames of the campfire, he sensed the jaws of the trap closing. He tried to reconjure the visions he'd had when they'd camped beside the Thames and he had foreseen the finger of death touching three Marcher barons. Wolf felt certain that Uncle Chirk was one of them, but the identity of the other two remained unknown. He was in a dilemma—should he tell his father what he felt in his bones and take away his hope? When Roger joined him by the fire, Wolf suddenly realized that his father had decided against fighting, to save his Borderers from a bloodbath. Wolf chose to give him only strengthening words. "Father, you *will* prevail."

The following day, Mortimer and Chirk rode into Shrewsbury and surrendered to the king. The moment the pair dismounted, they were surrounded by royal guards and were put into chains.

Roger was stunned. "Mortimer of Chirk is a sick man! Release him and take your revenge on me, Edward."

"I fully intend to take my revenge. There will be

no pardon for either of you. I hereby confiscate for the Crown all the lands and properties that belong to any with the name Mortimer. I also order the arrest of Lady Mortimer and your sons." Edward waved his hand. "Throw them in Shrewsbury's dungeon. When we have dealt with the rest of the traitorous Marchers, you will be incarcerated in the Tower of London to await trial for treason."

Mortimer's gray eyes stared into Edward's with burning hatred. *Misbegotten degenerate! You are the poorest fucking excuse for a king England has ever known.* "I curse you, Edward Plantagenet! Remember this day, for I will bring you low!"

On the third day of February, Brianna opened her chamber door and read the words on a note the page boy handed her: *I have news. Come to the stables.* It was signed Simon Deveril.

Brianna donned a wool cloak and went to meet him immediately.

Simon was standing at the stable entrance. He put his finger to his lips. "You have a visitor."

Wolf Mortimer! I had a premonition I would see him soon. She started toward the box stall, when she saw a dark male currying her palfrey, Venus. He put a warning finger to his lips. *Rickard! You're supposed to be in Ireland.* For a moment, her heart lifted with joy, and then it plummeted. *Dear God, my brother is here to bring me ill tidings!*

"You have become a rare beauty, as I always knew you would. Brianna, I am sorry to be the bearer of sad news. The king took Roger Mortimer and his Uncle Chirk prisoner at Shrewsbury twelve days ago and confiscated everything they own. Arrest warrants were issued for his wife and sons."

Brianna stared at Rickard, aghast. Her heartbeat hammered in her eardrums. "How do you know?"

"I was there. I returned from Ireland because of a Welsh uprising. We soon put that down. Father even came to help, but when the royal army threatened, we insisted he go back to Warwick and lie low."

"You lost the battle?" she whispered, clutching his hand.

Rickard pressed grim lips together and shook his head. "There was no battle. Pembroke assured Mortimer that if he submitted to the king, he would be pardoned. The Marcher forces were outnumbered thirty-to-one. Mortimer ordered me to leave. Then he surrendered to save his men."

"What of his sons?" Her hand went to her throat.

"They were taken into custody. They could have fought off the royal force that came to take them, but it would have put their father in jeopardy. Wolf would never do that."

He knew he would be taken, that's why he brought Shadow to me.

" 'Tis certain Edward will not leave the Mortimers at Shrewsbury for fear they will be rescued. Almost certainly they will be transferred to the Tower of London, where escape is impossible."

"Edward has confiscated everything at Ludlow and Wigmore?" she asked in disbelief. "He left the Mortimers nothing?"

"Nothing. Wolf took his mother and sisters to a nunnery for sanctuary. Edward's army swept south and took every Marcher castle in his path. He has claimed everything that belongs to Hereford, Audley, Mowbray, and d'Amory. Yesterday, Berkley Castle surrendered and Lord Berkley and his son, Maurice, were cast into prison."

"Berkley's son is wed to Mortimer's daughter Margaret."

"Exactly. Let's hope they had enough foresight to get her to sanctuary." Rickard lowered his voice. "Edward is mad with power. No one is safe. I'm on my way to Warwick to warn Father to keep his mouth shut and do nothing. Will you let me take you home, Brianna?"

"No, no, Rickard. I cannot leave Isabelle. Edward has petitioned to have the Despencers' banishment annulled. If Hugh returns to the king, she will need me. She will be devastated."

"Hugh Despencer is already with the king—they spent Yule together."

Brianna's heart constricted. "I knew it! He has confiscated the Marcher lands to give to the insatiable Despencer."

"I must go. Let no one know that I am in England. I will be in touch with you, whenever I can. Be careful, Brianna."

"Thank you for coming to see me, Rickard. When you see Mother, Father, and Guy Thomas, tell them that I love them dearly."

Brianna returned to the castle slowly. Her heart was heavy at the thought of Roger Mortimer losing everything, including his freedom. She pushed thoughts of Wolf away; they were too painful to even contemplate.

She did not relish the task of imparting the news to Isabelle, but tell her she must. Keeping the queen in ignorance would be both insulting and dangerous. Though Isabelle was only twenty-seven, she had been forced to cope with many demoralizing situations that would have daunted all, and defeated most, women. *Isabelle is stronger than she realizes. I must reinforce that resilient strength every day.*

Brianna found the queen in baby Joan's nursery. Isabelle had decided that her little daughter was old enough to eat solid food.

"She takes the bottle so hungrily. Most likely milk isn't enough to satisfy her voracious appetite." Isabelle glanced at Brianna. She had the soft brown eyes of a doe that reflected her feelings, if she did not veil them with her lashes. "Brianna, you have learned something that saddens you." She handed baby Joan to her nurse. "Come, we can be private in my chamber."

They walked side by side in silence until they reached the queen's bedchamber. They went in and Brianna closed the door.

"Please sit down, Isabelle. My news will distress you."

"Oh no!" She sat and gripped the arms of the chair.

Brianna sat down facing her. "The king's army so outnumbered the Marcher barons' forces that Roger Mortimer surrendered to save his men. The Earl of Pembroke assured Mortimer he'd be pardoned, but Edward chained him and imprisoned him at Shrewsbury Castle."

All the color left Isabelle's face. "Who told you this?"

Brianna shook her head. "I can only tell you that it was someone who was there, someone I trust with my life."

Isabelle wondered if it was her betrothed, Lincoln de Warenne.

"The king confiscated all Mortimer landholdings. Then he did the same with all the castles and lands of the other Marcher lords." She took a deep breath. "Hugh Despencer spent Yule with the king. I warrant it was done at his urging."

Isabelle had loosened her grip on the chair. Her fists were clenched so tightly, her fingernails dug into her palms. Her eyes were two glittering slits and her lips were drawn back in a snarl that bared her teeth. "I hate, loathe, and detest the swine." Her words were halfway between a whisper and a hiss.

"Hugh Despencer is an evil, degenerate influence."

Isabelle shook her head. "No—not Hugh." She let out a shuddering breath. "I've always been cautious speaking of Edward. I've thought it, but not said it because it is treasonous to speak ill of the King of England. But if I don't spew the venom that is building inside me into someone's ears, I will die of the poison!"

Brianna went down on her knees before the queen. "You can say anything to me, Isabelle. I will never betray your confidence."

"I loathe Edward Plantagenet with every fiber of my being. As a bride of thirteen, I fell in love at first glance. He starved me of attention and lavished it upon Gaveston, his lover. Edward allowed, nay, encouraged him to feed my jealousy until it ate into my soul and shattered my heart.

"Edward was so obsessed by his pretty plaything, he allowed Gaveston to make my life a living hell. He and his entourage of Gascons bled the treasury dry. Edward was so weak, he became addicted to venery and sexual perversion, and his lover was able to lead him about by his prick! He abdicated his role as king and allowed the country to fall into chaos, while he and his lover indulged in pleasure and slaked their lust.

"When Thomas of Lancaster executed Gaveston, not for crimes against me, but against the kingdom, Edward turned to me for solace and companionship. He begged me to forgive him for the sins he had committed against me and asked that I be his friend. A tiny flicker of hope rekindled inside me, and even though I knew he was flawed and weak and immoral, I swallowed my hurt, my humiliation, my pride, and finally became his wife. I could not bring myself to love Edward, though I became a dutiful wife and accepted him as my husband. And there is no denying that I love and adore the children he gave me.

"When Hugh Despencer became chamberlain of the royal household and I learned Edward had gone back to his old habits, I was stunned. The thing that devastated me, and for which I will never forgive him, was that he shared my bed and used my body at the same time he was being intimate with Hugh. He fathered my last child before I learned of his debauchery. Edward dishonored me and covered me with shame and humiliation.

"To add injury to insult he permitted Hugh Despencer to become the uncrowned king. Edward allowed him to treat me like a serf, rather than a Princess of France and the Queen of England. Despencer sent away my ladies, packed my servants off to France, and took away my dower castles, so that I was penniless. But it was the whoreson *Edward* who permitted this to happen. He is unstable. He disgusts and repulses me and I *abhor* him!

"Roger Mortimer released me from my purgatory and got Hugh Despencer banished. Now Edward not only has had the banishment annulled, he has delivered Mortimer to his lover so he may take his revenge. Edward Plantagenet, I spit upon you. I *curse* you!" Isabelle broke down and began to sob.

Brianna, totally caught up in Isabelle's vehemence, wrapped her arms about her. "Get it all out. Don't let the poison fester."

When Isabelle's tears became dry heaves, Brianna said, "Once you are all cried out, you must make a vow to yourself that you will never cry again because of Edward. It is good that you got mad and your anger exploded, but now you must get even. You must be avenged for the wrongs done to you, Isabelle. The only way you can do that is by becoming stronger. Each day you must strive to become stronger than the day before. All things come at their appointed time. You must have infinite patience, but when the opportunity comes, you must be ready."

Isabelle raised her tearstained face. "I feel so guilty.

I started all this trouble when I went to Leeds Castle. It is my fault that Roger Mortimer has been taken prisoner!"

"It is *not* your fault. King Edward is to blame. I, too, am heartbroken that Roger Mortimer has lost everything, including his freedom. I cannot bear the thought that his sons have been taken into custody. But neither one of us must let anyone know our true feelings. Not by look or word must we appear to be anything other than indifferent. Never let anyone see a chink in your armor, or they will strike you to the heart. Promise me, nay, *promise yourself*, Isabelle!"

"I do so promise . . . I *swear* it!"

"Both the king and Despencer have sown the seeds of their own destruction by these unlawful acts against the Marcher barons. Their enemies will be legion. England will cry out for justice."

That night in bed, Brianna could not sleep because of the heavy thoughts that pressed down upon her. It was untenable to think of the gallant Roger Mortimer in prison. Even worse, the thought of Wolf's incarceration was unbearably painful. *He has a natural wildness. It will be unendurable for him to be fettered or caged.*

Brianna's chest began to tighten. She tried to breathe deeply, fighting the hands that squeezed inside her chest. The old terror from her childhood stole upon her. The children at her eighth birthday party had been playing hide-and-seek and she had hidden in a heavy oak settle. She had been trapped for hours in the dark, confined space that had no air, and imagined she was going to die. Panic began to slowly choke her. She couldn't move. She couldn't scream. She couldn't think. She couldn't *breathe*!

Brianna's eardrums began to pulse and gradually, she realized it was the sound of rain against her windowpane. It broke her trance and she shot up out of bed and drew in gulps of air. She remembered that it was ten-year-old Lincoln Robert who had freed her from that heavy oak settle, and knew that was the moment she had begun to love him.

Brianna still felt too confined and was compelled to go outside. She put on her dark cloak and went up to the crenellated castle roof. In the lovely fresh air, she lifted her face to the raindrops and breathed deeply. She felt better, but sad thoughts of Wolf Mortimer's confinement lingered. *I cannot free Wolf, but tomorrow I will visit Shadow and make sure she has a day of freedom in the forest.*

"Margaret, I cannot tell you how happy I am to have you and James here at Warwick. I know you must be sick with worry for your husband, but knowing you are safe here with us will lessen Hugh's burden." Jory had always loved Princess Joanna's daughter.

"I wish we had news." Margaret's voice was apprehensive.

Jory too was anxious about the Marchers. She was especially worried about the Mortimers and her husband's son, Rickard de Beauchamp. Guy had been unusually silent and somewhat remote during the fortnight he had been back at Warwick and Jory assumed it was caused by anxiety for his son and heir.

Jory gazed from the tower chamber window, scanning the horizon for a nonexistent messenger. Her eye was drawn to the figure of her husband. He walked alone, save for his ever-present companion Brutus. The tall wolfhound and Guy had been inseparable since his return from the Marches. *They communicate without words. A touch is all that is necessary between them.* Jory smiled. *Rather like Guy and myself.*

That night, when they retired to their bedchamber, Guy became particularly attentive to his wife. He cupped Jory's face with loving hands and gazed down at her as if memorizing every detail, treasuring her delicate beauty, appreciating the feel of her soft skin, cherishing the caress of her silver-gilt hair as it brushed against his fingers, inhaling her intoxicating woman's scent, and savoring the feel of her lips against his. "Have I told you how lovely you are, my beauty?"

Jory smiled up at him. "Incessantly, but I never tire of it."

His fingers brushed the tendrils back from her temples, and then he traced her brows and her cheekbones. "I'm the luckiest man alive." He drew a fingertip down her nose and outlined her lips. "You look exactly the same as the day I first saw you."

She laughed softly. "I'm forty years old."

"Jory, to me you will never grow old." He picked her up, carried her to bed, and made gentle love that lasted for hours.

For the next few nights, it became a ritual, beginning with Guy cupping Jory's face to gaze down at her, and ending with hours of lovemaking. During the day, Jory watched her husband with adoring eyes, and slowly, it came to her that he was keeping a secret.

A few days later, Rickard rode in alone. Guy was in the stables, and his wolfhound began to bark excitedly. "It's someone you know, Brutus."

"Father!" Rickard embraced Guy and scratched the grinning hound's ears. "My news isn't good, I'm afraid."

"Well, it isn't all bad. At least you're safe."

Rickard quickly told him what had happened, and Warwick shook his head with regret at the injustice of it. "We have no choice—we have to tell Jory and Margaret Audley what has happened. Guy Thomas has taken young James hunting. In spite of the news they'll all be happy to see you. Lead the way— come, Brutus."

Jory's face became stricken as she listened to Rickard catalogue the disastrous events that had come to pass.

"Margaret, your husband, Hugh, is safe. He is in hiding with some of his men. Roger Mortimer told us to leave before he surrendered to the king. Sadly, the Crown has confiscated your home and your lands."

Margaret burst into tears and Jory put a comforting arm about her. "Audley's not a captive, Margaret. You and young James must make your home with us, for now."

"I too have a force of men. We will bide our time and wait upon events. None know I have returned from Ireland, and I want to keep it that way. Roger will expect me to recruit an army in the Welsh Marches and be ready to strike, if he gives the signal."

Rickard gave Jory an intense look that told her he wished to speak with her in private. "It's good to have you home at Warwick, if only for a little while. Come, we'll find Mr. Burke and have him plenish your old chambers for you."

As soon as they were alone, Rickard took Jory's hand. "I absolutely implore you to do everything in your power to keep Father out of this. He will want to right this injustice, but he must not draw attention to himself. If the greedy Despencer fancies Warwick or any of our other castles, Edward will confiscate them in an instant. If he challenges the king, he will throw him in prison. You must convince him to lie low and stay at home. You are the only one he might listen to, Jory."

They entered Rickard's old bedchamber and Jory closed the door. "Warwick won't be rushing off to avenge anyone, my dear. I promise you he will lie low and I will keep him at home with me."

He let out a long breath. "Christ, that eases my mind, Jory."

She shook her head. "No, it won't ease your mind, Rickard. I'm afraid Warwick is going blind."

He stared at her in horrified disbelief. "Are you sure? He recognized me instantly and had no trouble making his way from the stables into the castle."

"He recognized your voice. Brutus leads him everywhere. He thinks I don't know. His towering pride wants to keep it secret."

"Jesu, in combat in Wales, his helmet was cleaved in two. He took a terrible blow to the head and the next day his eyes were full of blood."

"I assumed he'd taken a fall. If he tells you, don't let on that I know. Blind, the Infamous Warwick thinks himself less of a man. He will tell me in his own good time."

Rickard enfolded her in his arms. "Of course he will. Father knows how lucky he is to have you."

Chapter 16

"Isabelle, on the ride back from Chertsey, a daring idea came to me." Brianna was in such a hurry to speak with the queen that she hadn't yet changed from her riding dress.

"Accompany me to the wardrobe chamber and help me select material for the new gowns I've ordered. If Despencer is back and orders economies, it will be too late to affect the way I dress."

Brianna gave her a look of approval. "You are learning expedience. My idea is also expedient. We know the Mortimers will be brought to the impregnable Tower of London, where their loyal friends cannot free them. I remember you told me the Queen's royal palace apartments there are in sad disrepair with leaking ceilings. Why don't you have them plastered and painted and refurbished? That way you will have need to visit the Tower as often as you wish without arousing suspicion. You could even take up residence there from time to time."

"Brianna, that's a brilliant idea! I shall set the wheels in motion today."

Brianna pushed away her feelings of guilt. She knew that she was manipulating Isabelle, but it was the only way she knew of perhaps being able to see and speak with Roger Mortimer.

"The Tower has a new constable. I shall order my barge to take us downriver so I can make the acquaintance of Sir Stephen Segrave and inform him of the repairs I am ordering."

The following day, the royal barge arrived at the Tower and Queen Isabelle and her ladies alighted. She was swathed in her ermine cape and Brianna wore her sable cloak, lined with blue velvet.

The constable's sublieutenant, Gerard Alspaye, had alerted him that the royal barge was approaching, and the two men rushed down to the Coldwater Gate at the Tower Wharf to greet the queen.

Brianna and Isabelle had concocted a plan to dazzle, flatter, and seduce Segrave with their considerable feminine wiles so that each would hold him in the palm of her hand.

Queen Isabelle raised the constable from his deep bow. "Sir Stephen, I'm delighted to make your acquaintance. 'Tis obvious you are a gentleman, unlike the coarse fellow you replaced, who was sent packing for dereliction of duty and displeasing his queen."

"Your Grace, I am honored to be of service. Permit me to introduce my sublieutenant, Gerard Alspaye. He has strict orders to accommodate you and your ladies and fulfill your wishes."

The queen then introduced her ladies, further dazzling the two men with their noble names. "Sir Stephen, lend me your arm and escort me to my royal palace apartments." The constable was stunned at the intimacy.

Brianna gave young Gerard Alspaye a radiant smile and tucked her arm beneath his. She could almost hear his heartbeat quicken.

The queen's royal apartments occupied the upper floors of the Hall Tower, so named because it gave access to the Great Hall. The lower floors held the guardrooms. Isabelle removed her arm from Segrave's and pointed to the damp marks and chipped plaster on the ceilings. "My lovely royal chambers are going to wrack and ruin. I have ordered the entire place be redone. When my plasterers arrive, I am sure you will allow them free rein, Sir Stephen."

"I shall put Alspaye in charge. He will accommodate them in every way, Your Grace."

"Splendid. Once the place is refurbished, I shall take up residence for a time, and since you will be my host, so to speak, you must take supper with me on Friday evenings."

Segrave was flattered beyond reason. "You do me great honor, Your Grace."

Brianna spoke up. "Queen Isabelle, you wanted me to remind you to visit Saint Thomas's Tower where the Royal Wardrobe is housed." Saint Thomas's Tower also held the king's royal apartments.

"Thank you, Lady Brianna. The Wardrobe is a repository for furniture as well as royal robes and garments, to say nothing of my jewels. I would like you to do an inventory of the furnishings we may use in my chambers."

Segrave bowed again. "Alspaye has the keys. I'll let the lieutenant do the honors."

"I mustn't keep you one moment longer from your important duties as constable. Good-bye, Sir Stephen, until we meet again."

When the queen and her ladies arrived at the Wardrobe, and Alspaye selected a key from the iron ring that hung at his belt, Brianna murmured, "Gerard, perhaps you could have a duplicate key made for me, so I may come and go without . . . disturbing you." The intimate smile she gave him told him she was quite aware that she already disturbed him.

The Tower Wardrobe proved to be a treasure-trove. Not only was it a repository of wine, foodstuffs, and furniture, but it stored royal garments, furs, footwear, bolts of plush French velvet, cloth of gold, silk, satin, and brocade. Isabelle took what she fancied. "I shall soon be back for more. If I don't claim these luxurious items, others, who shall remain nameless, will do so."

The queen saw two black velvet cloaks. She chose the one with red satin lining and gave the one with fuchsia lining to Brianna. Isabelle also took her own jewels and put the gem casket that held them in Brianna's keeping.

On the barge ride back to Windsor, Brianna urged Isabelle to share the news with her other ladies.

"I am sorry to tell you that Roger Mortimer and his uncle of Chirk are prisoners of the king."

Marguerite Wake gasped and went pale.

"I know your father, Lord John, is Mortimer's cousin. I hope and pray he is not made to suffer for it. The king also has brought the Despencers back from exile."

Arbella Beaumont looked stricken. Hugh Despencer had dismissed her mother from the queen's service and her father was an enemy of Despencer.

The queen continued. "I refuse to be in Hugh Despencer's presence. If Edward brings him to either Windsor or Whitehall I shall withdraw to the Tower. Marie, have you not heard from Pembroke about any of this?"

Marie blushed. "I have not heard from my husband since he left for Cirencester. He but follows the king's orders."

And the whoreson king follows Despencer's orders, Brianna thought angrily.

Isabelle patted Marie's hand. "At least you know Pembroke is safe. Apparently there was no fighting."

Maude FitzAlan flushed. "My brother Arundel also is with the king's royal forces."

"Aye, unfortunately the barons' allegiance is split, but that is no reason for us to be at odds. I know I have your loyalty."

As they disembarked, Isabelle took Brianna aside. "When we visit the Tower, it would be safer to leave Marie and Maude at Windsor, so they can carry no tales, inadvertently or otherwise."

Brianna gave Isabelle a look of admiration. "You grow wiser and stronger every day, Your Grace."

A few days later, Marie displayed a letter she had just received from Pembroke and she read out parts of it to Isabelle. "My husband is sorry, but he won't be coming home. He says the king has ordered a general muster of men at Coventry at the end of February to march against the Scots."

"That's an ambitious undertaking," the queen declared. She gave Brianna a look that said: *It will keep him away from me, thank God!*

Brianna bit her lip. It seemed that her worries were multiplying. Neither her father nor the de Warennes would ever support the king against the Scots. Lynx and Jane were friends of Robert Bruce, and her mother had once loved him. *Coventry is near Warwick. I hope Father doesn't quarrel with the king over this.*

Marie read from her letter again. "The Mortimers are being sent to the Tower until their trial. The sons of Mortimer and Hereford are to be confined here at Windsor."

Brianna was astonished. *Here at Windsor? Hell's teeth, I had a strong premonition that I would see Wolf Mortimer again soon. I must learn to trust my instincts.*

"Hereford's sons, John and Humphrey de Bohun, are the king's nephews. I am relieved they are being sent to Windsor. Their freedom will be confined, but their living quarters will be suitable for young men of royal blood." Isabelle turned to Brianna. "I don't believe I've met Mortimer's heir, but I did meet his second son when we rode to Saint Albans. He had a dark, proud and fierce look about him."

A picture of Wolf came full-blown into Brianna's head, and her pulse quickened.

"Mortimer's heir is wed to Badlesmere's daughter," Marie said.

"Yes, he will fare better at Windsor than his poor wife who is imprisoned at Dover," Isabelle said with relief.

"Poor wife, indeed! I don't know how you can have sympathy for anyone named Badlesmere," Marie declared.

"She is a young bride . . . Nothing that happened at Leeds Castle was her fault, Marie."

I will keep watch for Wolf Mortimer. I must find a way to communicate with him, Brianna vowed. *I will convey this news to Simon Deveril. He will learn where the four are to be housed.*

On her next visit to the Tower, Isabelle again took all of her ladies. The plasterers were busy repairing the ceilings and resurfacing all the walls and Marie could not hide her utter boredom. This was the effect Isabelle was hoping for, so that next time she could leave the Countess of Pembroke at Windsor.

Brianna made sure that she spent time alone with Alspaye so that she could cultivate his friendship. She was just going to bring up the subject of Roger Mortimer when the sublieutenant spoke to her in confidence.

"We are about to receive a pair of most exalted prisoners, Lady Brianna."

"Really, Gerard?" She gave him her undivided attention.

He lowered his voice. "Roger Mortimer, Baron of Wigmore, and his uncle, the Baron of Chirk."

"May I confide in you, Gerard?" She knew he would be flattered to share confidences with the Earl of Warwick's daughter.

"Absolutely, my lady."

"Roger Mortimer was present the day I was born. I have known him all my life. He is the most gallant gentleman you will ever meet. He is an outstanding military leader who faithfully served the king as Justiciar of Ireland, but that counts for naught now that the king's favorite, Despencer, has been recalled."

"I did not know he had been recalled, my lady."

"I hope I may trust in your discretion, Gerard?"

"You have my word on it, Lady Brianna."

"Where will the Mortimers be held?"

"It hasn't yet been decided. Since there are two and their noble status will allow them a servant, it will have to be one of the larger cells. Sir Stephen Segrave will make the final decision, but I warrant he will listen to my recommendation."

She smiled at him. "He trusts your judgment, as do I, Gerard." Brianna said no more. She was laying the groundwork for some contact with Roger Mortimer. *A delicate touch will serve me better than a heavy hand.*

When Brianna arrived back at Windsor, a letter awaited her from Lincoln Robert. She opened it eagerly and read:

My Dearest Brianna:

I am moving to Farnham Castle so that I can take over running the estate and oversee this year's crop planting. Father has given me a score of men-at-arms for the defense of the castle where we will live when we are married. Mother suggested I ask you which herbs you want planted in the kitchen garden.

I want you to come for a visit soon and decide what new furnishings you would like. I know you will be impressed with the castle. It has a trout stream and a mews complete with hunting birds

*and a competent falconer. Surrey is lovely and I
know you will be happy there.*

　　*Send your reply to Farnham Castle. I miss you,
Brianna, and can't wait for you to visit me.*
Fondest love,
Lincoln Robert.

Brianna set the letter down. She thought it was a
wonderful idea that her betrothed was moving to
Farnham Castle. It would be no small undertaking to
run the large estate that had belonged to the late John
de Warenne.

　　She found it strange that Lincoln Robert made
no mention of the dreadful events that had befallen
the Marcher barons and the cold-blooded revenge the
king had taken on those who opposed him. That the
Mortimers were imprisoned in the Tower of London
and had all their castles and lands confiscated was a
monumental injustice that consumed her thoughts.

　　*Perhaps Lincoln is wary of putting things down on
paper. The retaliation of the king and the Despencers
is so vicious that all the barons must be cautious.*

　　Though Brianna acknowledged she would like to
see Farnham Castle, she hoped Lincoln would not
press her to visit any time soon. *My life has become
so involved in Isabelle's affairs, I am strangely reluctant
to leave. Farnham Castle seems a world apart from the
queen's court here at Windsor.* Brianna immediately
felt guilty. *How selfish I am! It would be too unkind
to refuse the man who loves me.*

　　The next morning, Brianna spotted Simon Deveril
by the stables, and knew he was waiting to speak with
her. She made sure no one was watching before she
joined him. They fell into step and walked a short
distance from the stables before he spoke.

　　"The gentlemen have arrived."

Brianna's eyes widened. "All four of them?"

Simon nodded. "They are housed in the Lower Ward. Their chambers are over the guardrooms."

"Damnation! There will be guards everywhere."

"It could be worse. They will take their meals in the barracks and use the communal bathhouse and privy, but each will have his own well-furnished private chamber."

"Thank you, Simon. I must think of a way to visit them."

It didn't take Brianna long to concoct a plan. As she donned her favorite riding dress, she pushed away the feelings of guilt that always assailed her when she intended to manipulate someone. *Perhaps I shouldn't . . . but I shall!* She made her way to the tiltyard where Prince Edward took lessons in swordsmanship and weaponry most afternoons. The prince waved to her and when his lesson was over, he joined her.

"Spring is in the air, Lady Brianna. I haven't seen you all winter. I've missed our rides."

"I've neglected you shamefully, Your Grace."

"You used to call me Teddy."

"And you used to call me Brianna," she teased.

"Ride with me around the park," he suggested eagerly.

They went to the stables for their horses, and Prince Edward, who was now taller than Brianna, helped her into the saddle. He waved to the groom who intended to accompany them. "Don't trouble yourself—we are only riding in the park."

They talked of horses, the prince's favorite subject. Then Brianna said, "Did you know that your royal cousins John and Humphrey de Bohun are at Windsor?"

"I had no idea. They haven't been to visit me yet."

"Well, they aren't exactly in a position to visit you."

"What do you mean?"

"Hereford's sons, and Mortimer's sons, are being confined here at Windsor."

"Do you mean they are *prisoners*?" he asked doubtfully.

"Yes. Your father is in conflict with the Marcher barons and considers them enemies. Roger Mortimer surrendered to save his men. Apparently the Earl of Hereford escaped, but his sons and Mortimer's sons were taken into custody and sent here to Windsor."

"Let's go and visit them. Do you know where they are?"

"Yes, I do know. Will you get into trouble, Teddy?"

"I don't really care. My tutors tell me nothing. I must make sure my cousins are housed as befits their royal status, and I'm eager to meet Mortimer's sons. Roger Mortimer is a renowned military leader whom I greatly admire. I cannot think of him as an enemy when he has kept both Wales and Ireland secure for us."

Brianna led the way from the park into the Lower Ward; they rode past the stables and dismounted at the guardhouse barracks. When they entered, the large room fell silent. The guards could not remember Prince Edward visiting their barracks before.

The royal prince strode past the guards with Brianna in tow. His face broke into a smile when he saw his cousins. "John, Humphrey, it is so good to see you, though the circumstances are less than ideal." He moved forward and shook their hands warmly. "I had no idea you were here until Lady Brianna informed me."

"Edward, you have grown apace since last we met," John declared. The heir to the throne was physically and mentally mature beyond his years.

Humphrey said with resignation, "Since we are to be confined, Windsor is the best possible place."

Both de Bohun brothers gazed at Brianna with appreciation; the guards too ogled her.

Brianna did not notice. She stood rooted to the spot, staring across the room, her gaze held by a pair of intense gray eyes. Though there were a score of people present, they were invisible to Brianna. She was aware of only one man. The look they shared awakened every one of her senses. She could feel her heartbeat in her throat and her mouth went dry.

Edward and his cousins crossed the room and John introduced the prince to Edmund Mortimer.

Brianna heard Wolf's voice in her head. *Come to me.* Slowly, she followed the others until she was standing beside him. She murmured low, "They are coming to the Tower. I'll try to get word to your father that you are safe."

"No!" A forbidding look came into his eyes. "Do not put yourself in danger."

She stepped back, furious that he thought he could dictate to her, even when he was in confinement. *We cannot be in the same room without my temper flaring!*

Edward spoke to Wolf Mortimer, telling him how much he admired his father. Before they left, the prince said, "I shall visit you often. If there is anything you need to make your detention more bearable, don't hesitate to ask." He crossed the room and spoke with the guards. "Who is in charge of the prisoners?"

Captain Lionel Colby stepped forward. "I am, Your Grace."

"Have they given you their parole, Colby?"

"They have indeed."

"Good. They are men of honor. You may take them at their word. They will give you no trouble."

"The Mortimers won't, because the well-being of their father depends upon it. That is the point of their confinement, sir."

Edward fixed Colby with an icy blue stare. "And the de Bohuns won't, because they are royal."

Hell's teeth, don't antagonize their guard, Teddy! Brianna looked at Colby, gave him a conspiratorial wink, and was relieved to see his lips twitch with amusement.

"I want the bottom half of the walls wainscoted and the top half whitewashed and painted with roses," Isabelle told the workmen who were decorating her royal apartment at the Tower.

Brianna could see by the expression on Alspaye's face that he was bursting to tell her some news and she guessed that the elder Mortimers had arrived. She went into the Great Hall, which led to the royal kitchen, knowing he would follow.

"Where are they?" she asked quickly.

"The Lanthorn Tower. It's next to this one." He gazed about the large room for a minute. "The kitchen actually runs between this tower and the Lanthorn Tower."

Brianna closed her eyes for a moment, overcome by the thought of the handsome, gallant Roger Mortimer in captivity. Her pulses raced that he was so close, yet so far.

"Their cell is far from elegant. It is long and narrow with lofty ceilings. Only threepence a day has been allotted for their maintenance. 'Tis a blessing they brought their own servant to do their laundry."

"Surely nobly born prisoners should be comfortably housed, fed, and allowed privileges," she said passionately.

"You were right about him being a gentleman. He has shown no animosity toward me, in spite of the fact that I am his gaoler."

"He has immense pride and courage. I am sure it would greatly ease his mind if you could tell him that his sons are safe at Windsor." Brianna bit her lip. "I'm so sorry, Gerard. Please forget that I asked you to do such a reckless thing as pass along a message from

me. I have no right to compromise your integrity."
She lowered her lashes so he could not see how
pleased she was with her clever speech.

During their next few visits, Isabelle worked her
enchantment on Sir Stephen Segrave, asking his advice
on refurbishing her Tower apartments and flattering
him with attention and compliments. Meanwhile, Brianna took pains to ensure her friendship with Gerard
Alspaye blossomed. The pair of conspirators worked
toward one goal—to be able to communicate with
Roger Mortimer. Some way, some day, each hoped to
converse with him face-to-face.

Brianna sat up in bed. Her neck prickled and her
eyes searched the darkness for something that had disturbed her. She knew it was long past midnight, yet
dawn had not begun to lighten the sky.

"It's me."

When she heard Wolf's voice coming through the
darkness, she thought she was dreaming. When he
stepped from the shadows and drew closer to the bed,
she knew he could not be there, and believed she was
still fast in the arms of Morpheus.

He lit one candle and the flickering light illuminated
his wild, dark features. "You're not dreaming."

Brianna believed him. "More like a nightmare! How
did you elude the guards?"

"It's best that you not know, Brianna."

His words piqued her defiance. "I passed a message
to your father that you were safe, despite your
warning."

"I would prefer that you not endanger yourself on
my behalf," he said firmly.

She tossed her head in a defiant gesture. "I do it
on Roger Mortimer's behalf, not yours!"

"You are determined to involve yourself." It was a
statement, rather than a question.

"Wolf, if I can help your father, or you, I shall do so."

"I would never ask it of you."

"If I did not wish to do this with all my heart, your asking could not make me."

"Brianna," he said softly, "I could seduce you into doing anything I wished."

No, you could not! Well, mayhap you could, you devil. She shuddered and pulled the covers up to her chin.

"If you wish to help us communicate, I will be most grateful. But I promise I will never lure you to it, no matter how much you tempt me. My integrity wouldn't allow it."

"You mean your pride!"

He ignored the taunt. "My father, on the other hand, would not cavil at seduction. Be warned, Brianna."

She refused to believe the accusation.

"I saw Shadow not long ago. We spent the day in the forest."

"Thank you, Brianna."

She noticed he was dressed all in black. She watched him slip a black silk hood over his head, and when he snuffed out the candle with his fingers, he completely disappeared.

"Wolf?" she whispered. There was only silence. He had vanished as quickly as he had appeared.

Chapter 17

"Lord Mortimer," Brianna said softly as her heart beat a wild tattoo inside her breast. She had arranged with Gerard Alspaye to be at the door that led to the Tower garden when he brought Roger Mortimer for his daily outing.

"Dearest Brianna." His gray eyes kindled with affection. "You are very brave."

Alspaye opened the door and drew his prisoner outside.

Brianna was grateful to have seen Roger and thrilled beyond belief that he had spoken an endearment to her. She remained where she was, guarding the door, acting as lookout because Isabelle was in the garden. It was mid-April; it had taken weeks to arrange this brief meeting between the queen and Mortimer.

Brianna was not surprised that Roger had soon made Alspaye his friend and confidant. His young gaoler was dazzled by the dark Borderer's charisma and magnetism. Brianna also had worked her charm on Gerard until he finally agreed to make it possible for the queen to meet his prisoner.

Roger Mortimer stepped beneath a shade tree that would shield him from observation from the Tower windows. The queen was there before him, waiting impatiently to meet the courageous Marcher lord who had risked and lost everything.

Isabelle held out beseeching hands. "Lord Mortimer, my guilt overwhelms me. It is my fault you are a prisoner."

Roger took her hands. The moment he touched her, something akin to lightning sparked between them. As he gazed down at the small, exquisite female, a desire to make her happy engulfed him. No woman had ever had this effect on him before, though he had known many intimately.

He took her fingers to his lips. "*Ma belle*, you are more a prisoner than I will ever be. My heart aches for you."

Her lovely blue eyes sparkled with tears as she gazed at him with a poignant look of sorrow mingled with admiration.

In that moment she was the most feminine creature he had ever seen; a supplicant begging him for forgiveness. Her beautiful, heart-shaped face, framed by delicate blond tendrils of hair, cried out to his overt, dominant masculinity.

"There is nothing to forgive, my queen. You must not shed one tear for me, Isabelle. I forbid it."

"I never knew a man with such strength and courage. What can I do to ease your captivity?" she implored.

He shook his head. "I will survive. My Uncle Chirk ails—he'd benefit from a doctor's visit."

"I'll send my own physician," she promised.

"Go, now," he ordered. "You must not be discovered with me."

Isabelle obeyed, though she was reluctant to leave him.

It pleased Mortimer that though she was the Queen of England, she willingly did as he bade her.

Isabelle slipped through the door where Brianna stood waiting. Wordlessly, the pair of conspirators hurried back to the queen's elegantly decorated apartments.

It was Friday, and Isabelle had invited Sir Stephen Segrave to sup with her that evening. She had installed a cook and small kitchen staff so they could provide meals whenever she visited. They had been given rooms in another part of the Tower, away from the royal apartments, so that when they finished their work in the kitchen, they would retire to their own chambers to give the queen privacy.

"I have a dozen potent bottles of wine I brought from the Wardrobe storage," Brianna confirmed to Isabelle. "When I serve you tonight, I will keep Segrave's glass filled constantly. We want him to fall in the habit of overindulging on Friday nights so that he sleeps like the dead."

"I can tell by his florid complexion that he is a man who is addicted to drink. I know the signs of a drunkard well, since I am wed to one." Isabelle shuddered with distaste.

That evening the constable arrived promptly at six o'clock and for the next three hours he set about devouring enough food and wine to fell an ox.

Isabelle entertained him, flattered him, and encouraged him to talk about himself. All the while, Brianna plied him with dazzling smiles and potent wine.

When Isabelle believed that his tongue was sufficiently loosened, she said, "Sir Stephen, your position as Constable of the Tower carries so much responsibility, especially now that you have two notorious noble prisoners."

"One of them doesn't look long for this world, Your Grace."

"I shouldn't want you to get the blame if anything happened to the wretch. For your own safeguard, Sir

Stephen, why don't you have my physician take a look at the fellow?''

"Mayhap you are right . . . try to keep him alive at least until he stands trial.''

It was after nine o'clock when Segrave rose to leave. When he bent over the queen's hand to bid her good night, the constable swayed on his feet and Brianna knew she had done her job well.

An hour later, Brianna opened the door to Alspaye and Mortimer's servant. She gave them the meat and bread left over from the queen's supper and added a bottle of wine. Her heart was a little less heavy, knowing that Roger would eat tonight.

Isabelle lay in bed in her newly furbished bedchamber unable to sleep. Though her day had begun early and ended late, and had been filled with activities, the only minutes that meant anything to her were those she had spent in the garden with Roger Mortimer. She relived their encounter over and over again in her mind.

It was the first time a real man had looked at her with appreciation for her femininity. His bold gray eyes told her frankly that he found her sexually attractive. It was a new and thrilling experience and she responded like a flower lifting its face to the sun. She hungered for a man's attention, his admiration and approval, his strength and his tenderness. Today, when he touched her, he had imbued her with his vitality and his power. She marveled that though he was in captivity, they would never be able to cage his spirit.

Before Roger Mortimer lay down on the narrow bed in his cell, he fed Chirk a full cup of wine and waited until he slept. Then, with his eyes fixed on the stars visible through the small, high window, rather than the water droplets trickling down the damp stonewall, he thought about the rendezvous in the garden.

On a physical level, Isabelle's delicate, blond beauty appealed to all his masculine senses. He tried to pinpoint the thing that aroused his intense attraction. It suddenly dawned on him that it was her *innocence*. Even though she was twenty-seven years old and a mother, she was not yet a woman. Her female sexuality had not yet been awakened. She had mated and procreated, but she had never been taught that sex could be for pleasure. That still lay before her and he anticipated that he would be the one who would introduce her to sensuality. What made her extremely tempting and enticing was the fact that she was ripe and ready, perhaps without even being aware of it. She was alluring and tantalizing, with the added fillip of innocence, which made her both desirable and utterly irresistible.

On an intellectual level, Isabelle is even more appealing. She is the reigning Queen of England, beloved and revered by the people, yet seemingly unaware of the infinite power she possesses. With a woman like Isabelle at my side, there is nothing I could not accomplish. If I make her love me and she yields to me in all things, I could rule England!

The following day, Isabelle's physician reported back to her after he had attended Mortimer of Chirk.

"I believe the elderly Chirk suffers from a malignancy of the stomach. It is doubtful he will recover at his advanced age. Though their living conditions are less than ideal, Roger Mortimer does an admirable job of nursing him. I left him a decoction of poppy to ease the pain and will order more."

When Brianna returned to Windsor, Simon Deveril sent her a message to meet him at the stables. On the pretext of riding in Windsor's vast park, Deveril led her through the trees to where her brother, Rickard, was waiting for her.

Brianna's mother, Jory, had given him strict instructions to keep the knowledge of Warwick's blindness from her daughter, but there was other shocking news that he wanted his sister to pass along to the young nobles who were in confinement at Windsor, and to Roger Mortimer, if such a thing were possible.

Brianna dismounted, ran to where her brother sat waiting with his back against a stout oak trunk. "Rickard, you have news?"

"Most of it bad. The king issued a general muster for the Scots, but instead he moved against Lancaster. They took his castle of Tutbury where Marcher baron d'Amory was in hiding. D'Amory died in battle. Lancaster's army met the king's at Boroughbridge and was defeated. His fighting men deserted in droves and Lancaster surrendered to the king. The Earl of Hereford was with him, but he too was killed in battle."

Brianna's hand went to her throat. "Ah, no! How can I tell the de Bohun brothers that their father is dead?"

"I would do it myself, if there was any way I could communicate with them, Brianna."

"That's impossible. I don't want you discovered and taken into custody. It's difficult for me to communicate, but I'll manage. Rickard, please tell me that you kept Father from going to Lancaster's aid?"

"Father remained at Warwick. At the end of March, Thomas of Lancaster was tried as a rebel in his own castle of Pontefract by the king and the elder Despencer, and found guilty of treason. He was taken outside and beheaded on his own land."

Brianna's eyes widened. "The king executed Thomas of Lancaster? But he has royal blood—he is Edward's kinsman. Queen Isabelle will be horrified!"

A feeling of dread washed over her. "If he would kill Lancaster, he could do the same to Mortimer!"

"Exactly. A way must be found for Roger to escape."

"No one has ever escaped from the Tower," Deveril pointed out.

"I have an army. Adam Orleton, Bishop of Hereford, has an army, and we are gathering more every day. Try to get word to Roger."

"That will be the easy part. I have a way to communicate."

"Brianna, I don't need to tell you how dangerous this is. Have a care for yourself. Promise you won't do anything reckless."

"You have no need to worry, Rickard," she assured him. *Recklessness is second nature to me. It's in my blood!*

On the way back to the stables, Brianna asked Simon, "Do you have any contact with Wolf?"

"Most nights the guards gamble and dice in the barracks. I often join them as do the Mortimers and de Bohuns, but there is no way I can speak openly to them and pass along this information."

"It is only necessary to pass one word to Wolf."

"One word?"

"Just say *Brianna.* Wolf Mortimer will do the rest."

Isabelle noticed Brianna's windblown hair. "Were you out riding? Now the weather is fine, I too must get some exercise."

"I met with Simon Deveril. He told me some terrible news." Brianna would tell no one that Rickard de Beauchamp was in England, not even Isabelle. "The king's army fought a battle with Lancaster's forces."

"Though Thomas is his cousin, Edward has always hated him."

"The Earl of Hereford was killed in battle."

"*Mon Dieu*! De Bohun was Edward's brother-in-law. John and Humphrey will greatly mourn their father's death. Why must there always be fighting?"

"Lancaster surrendered and was tried for treason at Pontefract Castle and was found guilty."

Isabelle's hand flew to her throat. "I must write immediately and intervene on Thomas's behalf. He has always defended me against injustice. I will beg that Edward reprieve him."

"Isabelle, it's too late. Lancaster is dead—he was beheaded."

The queen burst into tears. "Perhaps it isn't true. Mayhap Deveril is just repeating wicked rumors he has heard."

At dinner, however, Marie showed the queen a letter she had received from Pembroke that confirmed the horrific news.

"He writes that they discovered evidence that Thomas had a pact with the Scots!" Isabelle cried with disbelief.

The queen was too upset to eat. She retired to her chamber with Brianna and railed against her husband. "Edward killed Thomas out of pure revenge. Lancaster beheaded Piers Gaveston, the love of Edward's life, and the king has harbored hatred for him ever since. I warrant his vengeance was cruel and merciless."

Brianna did her best to comfort Isabelle, and did not leave her until she had cried herself to sleep.

When Brianna sought her own chamber, she did not undress. She laid her black velvet cloak on the far side of her bed, she blew out all the candles, then lay down on the bed, pulled the covers up to her chin, and waited for her visitor.

It was long after midnight when he arrived exactly as he had the last time. Brianna didn't even hear her chamber door open and close. She did not see Wolf until he lit the candle and it illuminated his face.

Her pulse fluttered at the sight of him and when he stepped close, she could hear her heartbeat thudding in her eardrums.

"Let me start with the good news," she said. "There is little of it, I'm afraid. I saw your father and he is well. I was able to pass some food and wine to him from the queen's kitchen."

"Thank you."

"Rickard was here. He asked me to get word to your father that he has an army . . . Adam Orleton has an army and they are gathering more recruits every day."

"That is heartening."

"The rest of the news is terrible." Brianna licked her lips.

"Just tell me."

"King Edward mustered the army for Scotland, but instead he moved against Thomas of Lancaster. They took Tutbury Castle and d'Amory was killed. There was a battle at Boroughbridge and the Earl of Hereford was killed." Brianna hesitated. "You don't look surprised."

"I've sensed for some time that three Marcher lords would die."

Brianna gazed into his eyes. "Wolf, do you have second sight?"

"Occasionally I see the past, sometimes the future," he acknowledged.

"You knew you would be confined, that's why you brought Shadow to me. You knew your father would be captured!"

"Neither of us was *captured*. We surrendered."

"I am so sorry you must tell John and Humphrey de Bohun that their father is dead."

"John is now the Earl of Hereford."

"That is so—I didn't realize." She took a deep breath. "At the Battle of Boroughbridge, Lancaster's forces deserted him and he surrendered."

"If Lancaster had kept his word and ridden to support us, we would have defeated the king's forces. He got what he deserved."

"They tried him for treason in his own castle of Pontefract."

"If Lancaster made a pact with Robert Bruce and the Scots, he was guilty of treason."

Pembroke's letter said they found evidence he had made a pact with Robert Bruce. Wolf, how on earth do you know these things? "They beheaded Thomas of Lancaster a week ago."

"Christ! No English noble has been executed for treason since the Norman Conquest."

"You foresaw three deaths . . . Lancaster was not one of them?"

"I foresaw three *Marcher* deaths. My Uncle Chirk is the third."

"Then you know he is ailing." A lump came into her throat.

Wolf felt Brianna's sadness and the urge to comfort her rose up in him. He had vowed he would do nothing to seduce her. It was almost impossible for him to resist enfolding her in his arms. He cursed silently. "If Edward would execute his own royal cousin, there isn't a nobleman in England who is safe."

"That's why Rickard said your father must escape. But that is impossible. No one has ever escaped from the Tower of London."

"To a Mortimer, nothing is impossible."

Brianna watched him don the black silk hood; he snuffed the candle and literally vanished. Her heart pounded as she pushed back the covers and swept up her black velvet cloak. She intended to follow Wolf Mortimer to learn how he was able to disappear from his chamber, evade his guards, and return without being detected. She threw on her cloak, pulled the hood close to conceal her face, and opened the door.

He was gone, of course, as she knew he would be. She ran down the stairs and went outside into the Upper Ward. Instinct told her to keep close against the buildings, as he must do, to get back to Windsor's Lower Ward.

It was the dark of night and she saw and heard nothing—not the least hint of a movement anywhere. *He moves like a shadow. Perhaps he learned it from his wolf. Nay, stealth is innate to his nature. Wolf Mortimer has inherited the ancient Celtic traits and mystic power from his ancestors.*

Brianna stood in the shadow of a tower at the top of the Lower Ward and allowed her glance to travel slowly along the guardhouses and barracks. Then she raised her eyes to the second-story chambers where the Mortimers were confined. She detected no movement and was convinced Windsor's Lower Ward was empty.

Her gaze moved to the buildings on the opposite side and stopped at the doorway of the Chapel of Edward the Confessor, which had been built by the king's grandfather in the last century. Brianna wasn't absolutely sure, but it seemed as if the door, deep in the shadows, had just closed.

She pulled her hood close and crossed to the chapel. Inside, the vaulted church was cold, dark, and silent as a tomb. Sunday services in the chapel drew some of the guards, but otherwise it was seldom used and was completely unoccupied in the middle of the night. The altar at the far end held a pair of flickering tapers, which gave off a meager glow that barely penetrated the surrounding darkness.

Brianna moved silently up the chapel nave, listening carefully for any rustle or creak that would tell her she was not alone. She concluded no one was there and was about to retrace her steps when she decided to go behind the altar. She stood still, wishing her eyes would adjust to the darkness. When they didn't, she moved to the back wall and ran her hand along the stone. She drew in a swift breath when her fingers detected a wooden door.

Suddenly, a hand clamped across her mouth and Brianna almost jumped out of her skin. Her heart hammered in her breast and her knees gave out. A powerful arm wrapped about her waist from behind was the only thing that kept her from sliding to the floor.

"What the hellfire are you doing?" Wolf hissed. When he sensed she would not scream, he removed his hand from her mouth.

"I'm following you."

He pulled her round to face him and removed his silk hood. "You are putting yourself in danger!"

She could just make out his features in the dim light, and his expression was fierce. "There must be a passage between the chapel and the buildings that house the guards!"

His hands gripped her shoulders and he shook her like a rag doll. "If you reveal the secret you put me in jeopardy," he growled.

"I swear to you I'll guard the secret with my life."

"Go back to bed, you little hellcat. You cannot come to me—I'll come to you."

Wolf was implacable. His voice held such a forbidding tone, Brianna did not dare argue. "I understand," she whispered.

"Go! Now!"

She nodded and hurried from behind the altar. Her feet carried her down the nave until she came to the third pew. Then she stepped inside, slid to her knees, and put her head down.

Brianna waited, hardly daring to breathe, until she gauged that half an hour had passed. The smell of must mingled with the faint pungent aroma of incense made her nostrils quiver as she left the pew and crept back up the aisle. She took one of the thin tapers from its candlestick and gasped when a drop of hot wax fell on her hand. She stopped breathing and listened.

If Wolf were still here he would have heard my gasp. With slow steps she went behind the altar. She held the taper high and its light revealed the wooden door. She gripped the iron ring, turned it, and pushed. She almost fell down the steep steps of the gaping dark cavern that opened beneath her feet.

Brianna recoiled in horror. Dread from her childhood washed over her and panic threatened to engulf her. Nothing could ever induce her to go down into that airless, dank, black hole that led underground. She closed the door and backed away, her heart still hammering with fear. *Wolf is right . . . I can never go to him. He will have to come to me.*

Chapter 18

"Which gowns shall I pack for your visit to the Tower?"

"Ah, Brianna, I dread going this week. I know we must find a way to inform Roger Mortimer of what has taken place, yet when he learns of these horrific events he will be devastated. Perhaps we can stay at Windsor and keep him in blissful ignorance."

"Mortimer is not a man to flinch from the truth, Isabelle. If Thomas can be executed for treason, Roger could be sentenced to the same fate, if he is found guilty at his trial. Forewarned is forearmed—he must prepare his defense."

Isabelle was shocked out of her listlessness. "Holy Father, say it isn't so!"

"I will write everything down and ask Alspaye to deliver the letter. Tomorrow is Friday and I urge you to entertain the constable at dinner. It is better if we keep to the routine."

"You are right, Brianna. It is important that Lord Mortimer get meat and wine from my kitchen. He is on starvation rations the rest of the week."

On Thursday, Brianna, accompanied by Alspaye, went to the Tower Wardrobe department where the wine was stored.

"I had a key made for you, Lady Brianna. There will be times when the queen will need things from the Royal Wardrobe and it will be inconvenient for you to come searching for me."

"Thank you, Gerard. You are so very considerate. The queen will never forget your service to her."

Brianna had written out all the horrendous news that Rickard had brought her so it could be passed to Roger Mortimer. She knew it was a risky thing to do, since the lieutenant could easily give the paper to Constable Segrave, but she breathed easier now that Gerard had given her the key, allying himself against the authority of the Tower.

When Alspaye readily agreed to pass the note, she slipped him two gold coins for his trouble. The money was Brianna's, but she implied it was the queen who insisted he be rewarded.

Later in the day, when Gerard confirmed he had passed the letter, he expressed his great shock that Thomas of Lancaster had been executed for treason. "He is the king's royal cousin!"

Roger shared the news with him. He would not take Alspaye into his confidence if he were not completely sure of his allegiance.

"The queen was distraught at the news. With Mortimer in prison and Lancaster dead, no one in England is safe."

"Hugh Despencer rules the king. The people hate the Despencers, my lady. When news spreads about what has happened, Londoners will curse the day the evil, greedy swines were brought back from exile."

"When Sir Stephen dines with the queen tomorrow, we will not breathe a word about any of this. The constable and the rest of London will learn of it soon enough. If you come tomorrow night around eleven o'clock, I will have the food and wine ready."

*   *   *

Brianna fastened the row of buttons down the back of Isabelle's pale blue gown. "This delicate color makes you look ethereal."

"Do you think I should wear my fleur-de-lis diamond brooch?"

"Yes! It will remind Segrave that you are a princess of France, as well as his queen. It's beautiful. I shall pin it here at the décolletage to draw attention to your breasts."

Brianna picked up Isabelle's brush. "I'll pile your curls high like a coronet and fasten them with this dark blue velvet ribbon."

When she was done, Isabelle stared at her reflection in the mirror. "What would I do without you?"

The Constable of the Tower arrived promptly, as always. The moment he knocked, Brianna poured two goblets of wine. Isabelle pasted a smile on her face and greeted him warmly. "Sir Stephen, I so look forward to our Friday evenings."

During the next few hours, whenever the conversation lulled, the queen encouraged Segrave to talk about himself, and the words flowed apace with the wine. The constable did not take his reluctant leave until almost ten o'clock, but when he departed his eyelids were heavy, his speech slurred, and his gait unsteady.

Isabelle rolled her eyes. "I feared the fat swine would fall asleep where he sat." She paced about restlessly. "The evening was interminable."

"I had better go to the kitchen and make sure the staff leaves. I told Alspaye to come for the food at eleven."

Brianna made her way through the Great Hall and when she arrived in the kitchen was relieved to see that the staff had already departed. She took a linen cloth and wrapped up the two game birds that were left over from dinner. She added a loaf of fine white bread and put a bottle of wine into the food basket.

Not long after, she heard a low knock. Carrying the basket, she retraced her steps into the Great Hall and opened the door. She stepped back, startled that the man with Gerard Alspaye was Roger Mortimer. "My lord," she gasped as they stepped inside.

"Dearest Brianna, I've come to see the queen."

"I will take you to her," she said breathlessly.

He shook his head. "I would rather you guard the door."

"Yes, of course." Alspaye remained at her side and they watched Mortimer stride down the hall and enter the queen's private chambers.

"I'll go outside and keep watch. Lock the door after me. If anyone approaches, I will knock to signal you. Don't unlock it to anyone."

Brianna moved a chair close to the door and sat down to wait.

Isabelle stopped pacing and stared at the tall figure that filled the doorway. "Lord Mortimer, you take a great risk!"

"The risk is worth it, *ma belle*." He closed the distance between them and took her small hands into his. He raised her fingers to his lips and kissed them with reverence.

"Roger, you have sacrificed everything. I am so fearful for you. I have only just learned that they executed Thomas of Lancaster. I would have begged Edward to reprieve him, but it is too late, the deed is done."

His powerful grip tightened. "I never want you to beg Edward for anything. Begging ill becomes a Princess of France and a Queen of England, Isabelle."

She gazed up at him in wonder. "In spite of all the terrible news, and your own imprisonment, your spirit is undaunted. I truly believe you are descended from King Brutus."

"Isabelle, you are unearthly fair, just as Guinevere must have been. You dazzle my eyes." His gaze licked over her like a flame as if he were memorizing every delicate feature of her face. "I want to take away your sadness and fill your heart with joy."

He loosened her hands and she lifted her fingers to touch his cheek, marveling that he had shaved before coming to her. His closeness took away her breath, and the worshipful gaze of his gray eyes made her feel as if she were the most beautiful and desirable female in the world.

He unfastened the velvet ribbon holding up her hair, and the shining golden mass tumbled down about her shoulders. He gathered it in his hands and shuddered at the sensual feel of it. He lifted a tendril to his lips to taste it and it was Isabelle's turn to shudder.

Roger cupped her heart-shaped face between his palms, holding her captive for his mouth's ravishing. There was nothing tentative about his kiss. It was possessive, passionate, and demanding; designed to steal her senses.

His lips traveled a path to her throat, his bold arms encircled her waist, and his knowing fingers unfastened the buttons that ran down the back of her gown. Before she realized it, he had her naked to the waist and was cupping her breasts with powerful hands. She whispered his name. "Roger, Roger." He was the daring, dominant male she had always craved. He made her feel delicate and fragile. Above all, he made her feel precious.

Mortimer swept her up in his arms and carried her to her bedchamber. He laid her down and removed her gown and undergarments with gentle hands. He threw off his doublet and shirt, then sat down on the bed to remove the rest of his clothes.

When Isabelle saw his muscled body and his powerful chest covered with its dark pelt, she wanted to scream with excitement. Her arousal had begun the moment she saw him fill the doorway, and with every look and touch it had spiraled higher.

Roger began at her toes and kissed and caressed every inch of her smooth skin. He licked across the soft flesh of her belly and the sensitive underside of her breasts. His teeth toyed with her nipples until they became diamond-hard jewels.

Isabelle had been starved for praise, starved for affection, and starved for a man's love for so long, she responded like a woman awakened from a trance. She clung, and writhed, and panted with desire, inflaming Roger with a white-hot passion that was reeling and urgent. When she was frenzied with need, he mounted her. With one driving thrust, his marble-hard cock was seated to the hilt and he felt the hot pull of her tight sheath around his throbbing sex. She opened willingly, wantonly, yielding everything to him. "You're so eager for me, you make me feel like a man more than any woman I've ever known."

She gasped as his plunging heat made relentless demands on her, and the pulsing fullness inside her made her cry out her pleasure. Roger covered her mouth with his own and took her cries into himself. Isabelle became aware of her whole body from her tingling scalp to the soles of her feet, from her fingertips to the tips of her breasts.

She arched her body up to his and with three deep thrusts he brought her to climax. It was cataclysmic for Isabelle; it was a revelation that she could respond to a male in this way. When her last quiver subsided, Roger took his own release. She felt his heat and his power seep into her and it filled her with a soaring confidence she had never known.

He gathered her to him and held her in a possessive embrace until her body softened with surfeit. He whispered thrilling words of love that melted her heart and made her feel cherished. Roger knelt above her and brushed her disheveled hair back from her temples. He gazed down into her eyes with an intensity that made his face hard with passion. "From this moment on, you are mine alone, Isabelle!"

Roger was virile enough to make love more than once, but shrewd enough to control his lust, knowing that if he held back, her desire for him would become ravenous.

Mortimer felt omnipotent. He had just made love to the Queen of England and brought her to sexual fulfillment for the first time in her life. As he gazed down at her, he knew that Isabelle was the key that would unlock his prison; she was the device that would lead to his freedom; she was the instrument that would enable him to avenge his enemies and perhaps rule the kingdom!

Roger donned his clothes quickly and pulled on his boots. Then he knelt and touched his lips to hers in a long, lingering kiss. "Come, let me help you." He lifted her to a sitting position and began to dress her. He pulled her to her feet and fastened the buttons that ran down the back of her gown. "It's long past midnight— it's May Day. You are the loveliest May Queen in England." He lifted the mass of curls from her neck and set his lips to her sensual nape. "Be happy, Isabelle."

She watched him leave, though every fiber of her being cried out for him to stay. *I'm mad in love with you, Roger Mortimer!*

Brianna opened her eyes when she felt someone touch her hand. She jumped to her feet. "Lord Mortimer."

"Thank you, Brianna."

Surely I didn't fall asleep? She unlocked the door and handed him the basket of food. She had no idea what time it was or how long Roger had been with the queen.

She walked down the length of the Great Hall and entered the queen's private rooms. She bent down and picked up the velvet ribbon that lay on the carpet.

Isabelle came out of her bedchamber. Her face was radiant. "Lord Mortimer is an incredible man. He has more courage than any man breathing. Though he is a prisoner, his spirit is undaunted."

"He is indeed brave . . . and proud . . . His pride will not allow him to show fear. It is a Mortimer trait."

"He is a man in a million!" Isabelle declared passionately.

Brianna sighed. *She has fallen under his spell because he took a great risk to come and talk with her. Roger is the antithesis of the man she married—she is bound to compare them.* "I will rest easier knowing his hunger has been assuaged tonight."

Isabelle drew in a quick breath. "What are you saying?"

"I gave him game birds and wine," Brianna explained.

Isabelle let out her breath and smiled. "Thank you. We will both rest easier tonight." *Roger certainly assuaged my hunger.*

"Here is your ribbon. I'm sorry your hair fell down."

Isabelle took it and her smile deepened. "May has arrived . . . It is a time for renewed hope. Go to bed, Brianna. I have everything I need tonight."

During the month of May, however, King Edward with Hugh Despenser at his side exacted a bloody vengeance on those who had supported Lancaster. His widow, Alice de Lacy, and her elderly mother were imprisoned and he threatened to burn Alice alive if she did not turn over all her lands and pay a massive fine.

More than a hundred barons and knights were slaughtered. Badlesmere, who was found hiding at the

Bishop of Lincoln's house, was hanged, drawn and quartered, and the bishop was removed from his Episcopal office. All the leading barons were issued crippling fines. The nobles of England were bullied by threats and penalties and the harsh tyranny of the king increased to such an alarming degree that none dared to cross his will.

When the Earl of Pembroke protested Edward's savagery and injustice, the king turned on him because he had urged the Despencers' exile. Edward demanded that he pledge his body, his land, and all his goods to obey the king and not ally with his enemies.

At Warwick, Jory de Beauchamp had taken over the account books because of her husband's increasing blindness. When she received notice of a huge fine, she kept the upsetting news from Warwick and paid the twenty thousand pounds quietly.

Edward made the elder Despencer an Earl of the Realm, and bestowed upon Hugh all the confiscated lands of Marcher barons d'Amory and Audley. He gave him the lordship of Gower and made him the unopposed ruler of South Wales.

At the end of May, Edward and Hugh focused their attention on the Mortimers. The king ordered that the Mortimers be tried at Westminster Hall for Notorious Treason. He ordered that all the lands of their followers be seized and commanded a review of Mortimer rule in Ireland, determined to uncover treachery and financial misdeeds.

Isabelle had gone to the Tower every Friday in May. She had entertained Constable Segrave at interminable dinners and looked forward to Roger Mortimer's visits with the anticipation and longing of a young girl in love for the first time in her life. Every week she had been doomed to disappointment, however. Finally, with the connivance of Alspaye and Brianna, the queen met Mortimer in the Tower garden.

She ran to him and pressed her small hands to his broad chest. "Roger, why have you not come to me? I have been desolate!"

"Isabelle, my dearest love, the risk to you was too great. Extra guards have been assigned until our trial next week."

Her hands clutched his shirt. "I'll come to Westminster Hall."

"No! I absolutely forbid it! That is why I risked this meeting today. You must not attend the trial and you must not come to the Tower. I want you safe at Windsor. Do you understand, Isabelle? You must show no interest whatsoever in the affairs of the Mortimers. Promise you will obey me in this?"

"I faithfully promise to do your bidding, Roger," she vowed.

He took her in his arms and kissed her. Isabelle clung to him desperately, with her heart in her eyes. "I love you, Roger."

"Je vous adore, ma belle."

Wolf Mortimer indulged in games of chance almost every night with Windsor's guardsmen. At first when he had gambled with Captain Lionel Colby, he considered putting the man in his debt. Then he realized that if the guard ended up owing him a huge amount, Colby could easily arrange an accident to dispose of him. Shrewdly he decided to let the captain win. If Wolf owed Colby money, he would keep him alive in hope of receiving it someday.

Wolf held up his hands. "No more tonight, my friend, I'm in danger of losing my soul to you." He threw down the cards, stood up, and stretched his muscles. Before he retired, he glanced at Simon Deveril and cocked an eyebrow.

When he entered his chamber, he crossed to the window and stared into the darkness with unseeing eyes. Tomorrow, his father and Chirk were being tried for Notorious Treason, and Wolf knew he must learn the verdict ahead of time.

He pictured Westminster Hall in his mind, but it was empty and he knew he was recalling it from memory. He knew he must give up his control to a higher power, if he was to envision the future. Wolf allowed his mind to float free, his breathing began to slow, and suddenly he was there in the Great Hall. It was packed with spectators and a long row of men in robes, along with the king and the two Despencers who were sitting in judgment.

Two men stood silent in the center of the room. They had been forbidden to speak in their own defense. One was Wolf's father, his proud head held high, his gray eyes blazing their defiance. The older man was Mortimer of Chirk. He seemed shrunken, diminished; his body slumped with pain and the weary acceptance of his fate.

When the verdict was announced, a loud murmur went around the court. Wolf was not surprised that the Mortimers were found guilty of Notorious Treason. It was a foregone conclusion. Hugh Despencer wanted a guilty verdict, and the king and his jury were avid to please him.

It was the *sentence* that Wolf wanted to learn. What penalty would the degenerate bastards demand that the Mortimers pay?

He didn't have long to wait. In an indecently short time, the sentence was pronounced: *Forfeiture and Death.*

A gasp of disbelief rose up from the spectators, and with a jolt, Wolf found himself back in his chamber, standing at the window, his unseeing eyes staring into the black, starless night.

Simon Deveril lay sleepless. He was a Warwick man and the de Beauchamps were staunch allies of the

Mortimers. He would attend their trial tomorrow at Westminster Hall and was troubled how he would bring himself to inform Lady Brianna if the Mortimers were found guilty of Notorious Treason.

Gradually, Simon became aware that he was not alone. Someone was in the room with him. As he sat up and lit a candle, Wolf Mortimer removed his black silk hood.

"How in the name of Christ—"

Mortimer put a warning finger to his lips. "Tomorrow night I will need a horse," he said low.

"You would escape?"

Wolf shook his head. "I'll be back long before dawn."

Simon thought it over. He had only one horse, but Flamstead would supply him with another if it were not returned. "I'll tether my mount in the woods by the river."

"Good man." Wolf snuffed the candle and disappeared.

On the day of the trial, Brianna asked Isabelle if she intended to go to Westminster.

"Absolutely not!" she said emphatically.

Brianna was in turmoil. She did not dare to think about the outcome of the trial, but her heart was filled with apprehension. "You prefer to wait at the Tower?"

" 'Tis not what I want, 'tis what Roger wants! He made me promise I would remain at Windsor, though how I will fill the hours, God only knows."

Brianna nodded. "It is the wisest and safest course, Isabelle, though certainly not the easiest. We must keep busy."

"If I do not, I will run mad!"

Brianna realized the queen too was in turmoil and quickly devised a plan that would occupy them for most of the day.

Isabelle and her ladies spent the morning with the royal children. They played raucous games on the lawn, allowed Princess Eleanor to splash in the fountain, and then watched young Prince John parade around on his pony.

After lunch, which neither Brianna nor Isabelle could eat, the queen and her ladies went to watch Prince Edward practice his swordsmanship. After that he gave them a demonstration of his prowess with the longbow. When Brianna saw Isabelle begin to pace up and down in agitation, she suggested they take their horses for a long gallop and follow the River Thames to Runnymede and back.

When they returned to the castle in the late afternoon, the queen's other ladies went off to change from their riding dresses. Brianna accompanied Isabelle to her chamber to help her dress for dinner. Neither of them had any appetite, but changing clothes and going to the hall for the evening meal would fill a few hours.

When they arrived at Windsor's Great Hall it was abuzz with the momentous tidings of what had happened at Westminster. Like all hasty news it had traveled by word of mouth with lightning speed. The same question was on the lips of everyone in the dining hall: "Have you heard that the *Mortimers* were sentenced to *death*?"

Brianna went icy cold. She felt stunned, like a bird flown into a wall. *No! No! Roger! No, it cannot be!*

Brianna felt disoriented. She stared about her as if she did not know where she was. The room tilted and then it righted itself, leaving her dizzy and nauseated. She turned to Isabelle, but she wasn't there. She looked at the others. "Where is the queen?"

"She was here a moment ago," Marie confirmed.

"I saw Her Grace leave," Maude FitzAlan told Brianna.

"Excuse me." Brianna turned and made her way back to the queen's private chambers.

As soon as she opened the door, she heard sobbing. She found Isabelle facedown on her bed, absolutely distraught. "The news is terrible. I, too, am devastated."

The queen sat up. "You don't understand . . . I cannot bear it! I cannot bear it!" Isabelle beat her fists against her breast.

"I *do* understand . . . I feel exactly the same way."

"No, Brianna, you *don't* understand. I love him, I love him!" The queen flung herself from the bed, tears streaming down her face. "He cannot die! He must not die! He is the only man I have ever loved—the only man who has ever loved me! If he dies, I don't want to live!" She collapsed onto her bed again, sobbing.

"You allowed Roger Mortimer to make love to you?" Brianna's voice was a shocked whisper. A woman who committed adultery was considered worse than a whore in a brothel. Her husband had the legal right to kill her.

"We couldn't help ourselves . . . *We are in love!*"

Brianna sat down in stunned silence while the queen lay crying out her heart. Brianna's girlish infatuation for Roger Mortimer began to dissolve. Wolf's voice came winging back to her: *My father would not cavil at seduction. Be warned, Brianna.*

As she thought about it, Brianna realized she *did* understand. Mortimer was desperate and Isabelle was an exquisitely attractive woman, who was also the Queen of England. A vulnerable Isabelle, starved for a man's affection, would be drawn irresistibly to Mortimer's powerful charm. The dark, dominant male was the antithesis of her weak husband, whom she had come to hate and despise. What other man breathing would have the bold audacity to seduce a queen? *Isabelle and Roger were meant for each other.*

Brianna's thoughts swept away her illusions. She bade them good-bye with little regret, along with her naiveté. She was a woman, not a child. The world was ofttimes cruel, peopled by evil men, and it would take a strong will and determination to survive. *Jane was right—there are worse sins than infidelity.*

"Isabelle, you had better stop crying and dry your eyes. Roger is going to need your strength to help him escape."

The queen sat up and stared at her. "Escape from the Tower? That is not possible."

"To a Mortimer, nothing is impossible."

Chapter 19

Wolf Mortimer, garbed from head to foot in black, made his silent way through the dark labyrinth of ancient corridors known as Westminster Palace. It was three hours past midnight and even the guards posted outside the royal apartment were asleep. He entered the king's bedchamber and stood motionless. All five of his senses were heightened, while he allowed his sixth sense to roam about seeking knowledge of everything in the room from the furniture to its occupants. Through the darkness he saw the massive bed. He heard the slow, heavy breathing that a drunken stupor produced, and his nostrils flared at the pungent odor of wine and semen. He touched the knife at his belt and unwound the heavy black cord he had tied beneath his doublet. Then he moved to the opposite side of the bed, away from the heavy breathing.

Before Hugh Despencer opened his eyes, he was aware of the prick of the sharp knife at his throat. Cautiously he opened his eyes and saw only darkness. He tried to touch Edward surreptitiously to awaken him, but realized his arms and his legs were bound tight. "Who are you?" His voice was ragged with fear.

"I am *Death*."

"The Angel of Death? There is no such thing."

"Angel—Devil—take your pick." Wolf pressed the point of the knife until he drew blood. "The king sleeps like the dead—he won't awaken for hours."

"What do you want?" Hugh whispered hoarsely.

"I want you." His voice was cold, implacable.

"No! Please! I'll give you money."

"Money is no good to me. I deal only in life or death."

"Name your price!"

"Persuade the king to rescind Mortimer's death sentence. *Tomorrow!*" Wolf twisted the tip of the knife. "The choice is yours. Mortimer lives, or you die. I shall be back to collect you tomorrow night, Hugh Despencer." He let the silence stretch out for a full minute. "No, I can read your thoughts. I will elude any guard you set for me, as I did tonight. I am invisible. Only those who are about to die can see me. *Bon nuit*, I quite enjoy these nocturnal visits."

The next day, King Edward commuted the Mortimers' death sentence to perpetual imprisonment in the Tower. All were astonished and offered their own reasons for this change of heart. Many said it must have been Pembroke's doing, but others who had been present when the Mortimers surrendered said King Edward was afraid of the curse Roger Mortimer had put on him that day.

The news swept from Westminster to Windsor and beyond like wildfire, and it was on everyone's tongue.

The queen felt elation and despair at the same time. "Brianna, I am so relieved that the horrific death sentence has been lifted, but my heart is filled with anguish to think he must remain trapped in the Tower."

"My emotions mirror yours exactly, Isabelle. We must hold on to our hope and never let go. Traps can be sprung."

"I must take Roger the news."

"No, Isabelle. Alspaye will have heard the news and brought word to him. The Tower will be abuzz with it. It will be best to stay away until things settle down."

Brianna wanted to get the news of Mortimer's commuted sentence to Wolf and Edmund as soon as possible. She knew it would be cruel to keep them in ignorance for even one day. But as the afternoon shadows lengthened and twilight fell, she knew she could not face entering the dark, musty underground passage behind the altar in the chapel. She sent up a prayer that Mortimer's sons would hear it from their guards, and cursed herself for a coward.

The following week Marie received word that Pembroke was ailing. She left court immediately and returned to her husband's wealthy estate in Surrey. A few days later Brianna and Isabelle visited the Tower of London.

Brianna went directly to the Royal Wardrobe and let herself in with her key. She knew Gerard Alspaye would meet her there. It was a safe haven where they could talk.

"Mortimer of Chirk is dying. Roger made a special request to Constable Segrave for the Bishop of Hereford to administer the last rites. We are expecting him any hour."

Brianna clenched impotent fists. Mortimer of Chirk had been most gallant to her when they met at Warwick. "The trial was too much for him. How cruelly ironic to have his death sentence removed, then die a short time later." She crossed herself. "If it is at all possible, Gerard, could you bring the Bishop of Hereford to the queen's apartment?"

"I'll see what I can do, Lady Brianna."

When she told Isabelle that Roger's elderly uncle was near death, the queen became visibly upset. "Living in a cramped cell with not enough food to sustain him has hastened his death. Oh, dear Lord God, I don't want Roger to die in this accursed place!"

"Roger Mortimer is a survivor, Isabelle. He is a man at the peak of his strength. We must arrange for his escape."

"I love him so much, I would do *anything* to save him."

When Adam Orleton, the Bishop of Hereford, arrived he had two priests with him. Constable Segrave welcomed them and accompanied them to the Lanthorn Tower where he unlocked the Mortimers' cell door and ushered them inside.

Roger shook Segrave's hand. "I thank you, Sir Stephen, for your kindness in this matter. I am forever in your debt."

Chirk was still alive, and the constable stepped back and watched the bishop and priests give the old man the last rites.

Adam Orleton approached Segrave and lowered his voice. "We will keep the death watch. It won't be a protracted period of time before he meets his Maker. When it is all over, we will take Mortimer of Chirk's body back to his lands in the Welsh Borders for burial."

Segrave, realizing he would be relieved of a troublesome burden, summoned his sublieutenant and ordered him to plenish suitable accommodation for the Bishop of Hereford and his priests.

Mortimer of Chirk died that evening. Two hours later, Brianna opened the door of the queen's apartment and admitted Adam Orleton. "Your Grace, the vigil is over. Chirk has passed. Tomorrow we will take him to his final resting place at Wigmore Abbey."

"Thank you for your loyalty, Bishop Orleton . . . Adam. My thoughts and my fears are now centered on Lord Mortimer."

"Do not fear unduly, Your Grace. I am his close friend and ally. He has told me you are interested in his welfare."

Brianna feared they must not tarry, and spoke quickly. "Bishop Orleton, Rickard de Beauchamp is my brother."

"Lady Brianna, it is my pleasure to meet you. Your brother and I are in close contact. Plans are afoot to aid the Border Lord on the outside, once he is free of these walls. Now what is needed is aid on the inside."

"I will do everything in my power, Adam. I swear it," Isabelle vowed passionately.

"Be guided by Roger in all things. I charge you both, do not take unnecessary risks."

Brianna cautiously opened the door and beckoned Gerard Alspaye to take the bishop back to his chamber.

Isabelle paced the room restlessly. "I don't think I can stay here tonight. The sadness is so oppressive, it is making me feel ill and my head aches vilely."

"The oarsmen sleep aboard your barge. If we hurry, we can catch the tide and be back at Windsor by midnight."

At Windsor, Brianna left the queen's apartment and sought her own chamber. She stared at her bed and knew she would not be able to sleep. Her emotions swirled in a maelstrom, filling her with a restless energy that cried out for release. Sorrow mingled with anger over injustice for the Mortimers, and frustration that she could do nothing to right the wrong filled her with misery. At the same time a small glimmer of hope that Roger might be able to escape from the Tower refused to die. Above all, a feeling of longing made her heart ache and she knew the cure was Wolf Mortimer. Yet fear kept her from seeking him out.

Fortune favors the bold! How often she had heard

her father say those words. Disgust at her own cowardice compelled her to try to conquer her fear. Quickly, before she could change her mind, Brianna took the black cloak from her wardrobe and pulled up the hood to cover her hair.

Outside, she kept close to the buildings until she reached the Lower Ward. Then she crossed over and entered the ancient chapel. When she opened the door, her nostrils were assailed by the unique smell that permeated all places of religion. The odor, a combination of wax, incense, and must, made her shudder.

She walked down the dimly lit knave, counting her steps to occupy her mind and keep her fear at bay. When she reached the altar, she took one of the lit tapers from its holder and with determined resolution made her way behind the altar. As she approached the door in the wall her hand was shaking, but she was oblivious of the hot wax that dripped onto her skin.

As she stood before the door, her courage faltered and her knees felt like wet linen. She took a deep breath and gritted her teeth. *Do it now!* She opened the door and felt her throat tighten as the dark void loomed before her. She shielded the taper's flame with her hand, terrified that it would go out, as she forced her feet to descend the stone steps.

The passage was narrow and as a cobweb brushed against her cheek, Brianna felt trapped. Suddenly she couldn't breathe. She fought the panic with determination and told herself there was plenty of air—it was her fear that was making her throat close.

She noticed that the floor beneath her feet sloped upward, and hope kindled that she would soon reach the end of the dank passage. She lifted the taper high, and stared in dismay at the wall before her. There was no door! She pushed against the wall with one hand, but nothing happened. She set the taper on the floor and was engulfed in blackness as the flame snuffed out.

Her heartbeat hammered inside her ears and she stifled a scream that threatened to erupt from her throat. Slowly, determinedly, Brianna gathered her scattered thoughts. *There is a way out, and I will find it!*

She sank to her knees and put both her hands on the wall in front of her. As she pressed, it moved sideways and a section of wall slid into itself, leaving a narrow opening. Relief flooded over her as she squeezed through, but immediately she came up against another barrier that blocked her way.

She was assaulted by the pungent odor of ale, and as she reached out in the darkness, her hands came in contact with the familiar shape of barrels, stacked one upon another. Her fear began to dissolve and she fought the impulse to laugh as she realized she was in a storage room.

Brianna stood still until she caught her breath, and as she breathed deeply a small measure of calm returned. With caution, she maneuvered around the obstacles in the room and located the door. She found herself in a dimly lit hall with many doors and a staircase at each end.

She ascended the stairs that were closest to her and found another hall. She was thankful that this one was carpeted and would muffle her footsteps, but she now faced another dilemma. *Which chamber belongs to Wolf Mortimer?*

Brianna had no choice but to let instinct guide her. She noticed that only one door showed light beneath it and decided to take a chance. As she reached out, it swung silently open and she found herself staring into fierce gray eyes.

A powerful hand pulled her into the room and the door swung closed. She saw a muscle tick in his jaw, then saw his eyes cloud momentarily with sorrow as he realized what had brought her. "When?" he asked.

"Tonight. Wolf, I'm so sorry." She slipped her arms

about him to comfort him. She felt his strength seep
into her and it was Brianna who received comfort.
Her cheek was pressed against his chest and when she
felt his steady heartbeat, her agitation began to dissolve and was replaced by Wolf's quiet calm.

When she stopped shaking, he took her hands and
held them tightly. "His suffering is over."

"The Bishop of Hereford gave him the last rites
and will take him to Wigmore Abbey for burial."

"Adam Orleton is Chirk's son."

Her eyes widened. "How hard tonight must have
been for him."

"To a Mortimer, life without freedom is not worth
living. Adam will take comfort that his father is now
free."

"The queen and I had a chance to speak privately
with him. Orleton and my brother Rickard are making
plans to aid your father's escape, once he is free of
the Tower."

"He will need help on the inside, as well as the
outside."

"He has made an ally of his gaoler, Gerard Alspaye,
and the queen vows she will do all in her power to
help your father."

"He has become her lover."

Brianna withdrew her hands from his. "How can
you know that?"

"I know my father. Isabelle is his greatest asset."
He searched her face. "You are shocked that men and
women use each other. You are a true innocent,
Brianna."

She raised her chin. "I am becoming less so with
every day that dawns."

Suddenly, the door was thrown open and Captain
Lionel Colby entered. "Lady Brianna, what the devil
are you doing here?"

She captured Wolf's hand to give her strength.

"Captain Colby, we are betrothed. Have you any idea what it is like to be so close, yet forever kept apart?"

Colby stared at Mortimer.

"It is a secret betrothal. I hope we can rely on your discretion, Captain," Wolf said calmly.

"I'll turn a blind eye to an occasional visit."

"I am indebted to you, Captain."

"Indeed you are. Say your good nights—I'll wait outside."

Brianna was stunned. "He's willing to keep quiet and let me visit you again?"

Wolf touched her cheek. "Little innocent. Females come to the barracks every night to visit the guards, and our confinement doesn't preclude the service of a wench or two. Now that John de Bohun is an earl, he has to fight them off."

Brianna blushed furiously. "Colby will allow me to visit because he thinks I'm servicing you!"

"You're the one who said we are betrothed," he said solemnly.

She thumped him on the chest. "You bugger!"

"It will give us a perfect cover, and I think you would rather appear brazen than go through that dreaded tunnel again. Brianna, I do know what it cost you to come tonight."

You know too much about me . . . You can read my every thought. "Good night. I see no reason to sully my reputation by coming again."

Isabelle was consumed by thoughts of Roger, and the following Friday she and Brianna returned to the Tower. It was extremely difficult for the queen to hide her impatience while she entertained Sir Stephen at dinner, but she called upon the skills of artifice she had developed dealing with Edward and the despised Hugh Despencer. A sweet smile masked thoughts and emotions that would shock the devil himself.

Brianna too played her part well, filling and refilling the constable's wine goblet so that by the time Segrave left, he was legless. Two hours later she opened the door and admitted Roger Mortimer into the Great Hall. Then she turned the key in the lock and sat down in a comfortable chair, fully prepared to guard the lovers' privacy into the small hours of the morning.

Isabelle stood awaiting him in her bedchamber. The moment she saw him, she ran into his arms. "Roger, I'm so sorry about your Uncle Chirk."

"He was like a father to me. Escape was out of the question while he was alive—I had to stay and care for him. Now that he is gone, we can make plans for our future."

"Our future?" Isabelle asked breathlessly.

"Plans for us to be together, my lovely. A future without you would be unendurable." Roger spoke with complete sincerity. She was the most exquisite female he had ever made love to and she worshipped him. That she was also the queen made their union perfect.

His first kiss told him that she was ravenous, and he was wise enough to make love to her and satisfy her most urgent cravings before he discussed plans that would enable him to escape.

As she lay replete in his arms, he kissed and caressed her, showering her with whispered love words that made her feel cherished. His persuasive mouth and knowing hands molded her body and her will to his.

"The Bishop of Hereford deplores the misgovernment of Edward and the Despencers. Because of his years at the papal Curia he is a friend of the pope and of the King of France. He has written to your brother, asking him to give me safe haven."

"France? Of course! I too will write to my brother," she said eagerly. "Charles will receive you with great honor and offer you a place at his court."

"If I go to Paris, will you promise to join me there?"

"Yes, Roger, I swear I will find a way. But how will you escape this stronghold? It has never been done."

"Alspaye has access to a plan of the Tower. He has drawn me a copy. The Lanthorn Tower is next to this one. My cell butts up against the royal kitchen. A few removed stones would be all the space I'd need to squeeze through. The chimney of the kitchen's great fireplace leads to the roof. With a rope ladder I can scale down the outer bailey wall to the wharf."

Isabelle's heart began to pound with excitement that there was a possibility it could actually happen. She knew Mortimer had supreme confidence in his own ability and was reckless enough to risk all to attain his freedom. These were the very qualities that made her love him so much.

"I know *how*. The only question that remains is *when*."

"But what about all the guards and the night watch who make the rounds?" She trembled, realizing if he were caught trying to escape, he would be executed.

His arms tightened possessively to ease her fear. "The first day of August is my birthday. I thought of having a small celebration and drugging the wine, but my bereavement makes that seem inappropriate."

"August first is the feast day of Saint Peter ad Vincula, the patron saint of the Tower garrison. There is always a celebration that night. It won't seem at all inappropriate."

"Then August first is a definite possibility. I shall think long and hard on it." His lips brushed against her ear. "Speaking of long and hard, do you see the profound effect you have on me, my beauty? Let's not waste any more precious time talking. This night was made for love."

Brianna was awake and watchful when Roger Mortimer left the queen's apartment and traversed the

Great Hall. She stood to unlock the door and Roger stopped to speak with her.

"Thank you for your loyalty to Isabelle and to me, Brianna. I have a request, but will understand if you cannot help me."

"What do you need, Lord Mortimer?"

"My son Wolf has an uncanny intuition. I would like his thoughts about a certain date. August first is a fateful day for me when either good or bad things can happen. I need to know if that date will be propitious this year."

Your gray eyes are identical to your son's. They compel me to do your bidding. "I will ask him and bring you his answer."

"You have a generous heart, Brianna de Beauchamp."

Chapter 20

"**Y**our father seeks your advice." Brianna blurted out the words so that Wolf Mortimer would know it was his father's needs that prompted her visit, not her own. She was filled with chagrin that she'd had to return so quickly after telling him she would not be back. Her cheeks still held the blush put there by Captain Colby's knowing wink when he allowed her into the building and boldly watched as she climbed the stairs to the second floor.

"Won't you sit down? You look ready to flee."

She took the seat he offered. Isabelle had shared Mortimer's daring escape plan with her, but she did not relay it to Wolf. "He wants to know if August first will be a propitious day."

"That is Father's birthday . . . a fateful day indeed." *He's planning to escape that day and wants to know if he'll succeed.* Wolf paced to the window and stared out into the night. When it came, his vision was amazingly detailed. He saw his father and another man on the roof tiles of the Tower. He saw them scale down an outer wall to the wharf where men in a rowboat were waiting. The scene faded and he saw Rickard de Beauchamp with a small party of men and horses waiting on the Surrey shore of the Thames. When he saw the sails of a merchant ship, he realized his father would escape to France.

Wolf turned from the window and saw Brianna's face was pale with apprehension. *She truly cares about the fate of the Mortimers.* "August first will indeed be a propitious day." He closed the distance between them. "Your brother Rickard will provide the outside help. He will need swift horses."

"Rickard can get horses from Flamstead."

"Can you get a message to him?"

"I can give the message to Simon Deveril—Rickard keeps in touch with him."

"They will need a ship. The Mortimers have always done business with Ralph de Botton, a London merchant with cargo ships. Tell them the port of Southampton will be far safer than London."

"August is only a month away." Anxiety made her breathless.

"When you are entrapped, a month seems like a lifetime." He saw her lovely dark eyes cloud with compassion and knew some of it was for him. He didn't want her consumed with worry and decided a taunt was the quickest way to dispel her dread.

"Have you called off your betrothal to de Warenne yet?"

She sprang up from the chair, her dark eyes now blazing with fury. "Why would I do such an outrageous thing?"

Without hesitation, he swept her into his arms and took possession of her lips. The kiss was so powerful, she clung to him and opened her mouth for his ravishing. When he released her, she staggered on unsteady legs.

"*That* is why."

Brianna turned and fled.

When she was back in the safety of her own chamber, she cursed Wolf Mortimer for taking advantage of her vulnerability, but Brianna, deep down, blamed herself for allowing the intimacy. Honest to a fault, she admitted that she had enjoyed the kiss. As she thought about it, she realized that a kiss meant little to Wolf Mortimer. He had likely done it to distract her from her fear. If so, it had certainly worked.

The next morning she sought out Simon in the stables. "I need to get a message to Rickard. Is it possible?"

Deveril lowered his voice. "Your brother is at Flamstead. I was about to saddle up and ride there."

"I'm coming," Brianna decided impulsively. "Saddle Venus for me and I'll join you shortly."

She hurried to the queen's apartment and found Isabelle with her children and their nursemaids. "I am on my way to Flamstead with Simon Deveril. There is an urgent matter of business concerning the horses." She threw Isabelle a speaking look that told her it was in connection with the secret that consumed them. "I will try to be back tonight, Your Grace."

"Don't scold me for coming, Rickard. I have an important message for you."

He lifted her from the saddle. "I won't scold you, Brianna. You are a grown woman and quite capable of making your own decisions. You must be thirsty after your long ride. Come inside and make yourselves comfortable."

Brianna sipped her wine, while Rickard poured Simon some ale. "It's such a relief to be able to speak openly. I know you are in charge of the escape plan."

Rickard nodded. "I have six men, all close loyal friends of Roger."

"You will need swift horses, which Flamstead can easily supply. Take whatever you need." Brianna blushed. "I'm sorry, Rickard. You are Warwick's heir, you don't need my permission."

"Flamstead will be yours someday."

"Wolf Mortimer says you will need a ship. There is a London merchant called Ralph de Botton who will supply you with one, and Wolf warns that Southampton will be a safer port than London. Do you have enough money? The Mortimers have nothing."

"Warwick gold is financing this venture. Father is generous. Do you have any notion how Roger will manage to escape the Tower?"

"Yes, let me draw a rough sketch for you." Brianna took a sheet of paper from the desk and, with a piece of charcoal, drew two towers. "The queen's private apartment is in this tower. This is the Great Hall and this is the connecting Royal Kitchen. Roger is in the Lanthorn Tower and his cell butts up against the kitchen. He has tools to remove enough stones to crawl through. The huge kitchen chimney leads up to the roof. He will scale down the outer wall of Saint Thomas's Tower to the wharf."

Rickard's finger traced the escape route. "We'll be waiting here with horses, on the Surrey shore. When is it to happen?"

Brianna hesitated. Roger clearly had a specific date in mind and Wolf had confirmed that date would be perfect. "On the night of August first," she said confidently.

Rickard grinned. "That's his birthday—he is sure to succeed. With only a month to finalize the plan, we've no time to waste. When I have secured the merchant ship, I will get word to Simon."

After lunch, Brianna spent a delightful hour in Flamstead's verdant pastures among the horses she loved. She talked to the mares, and praised the new colts they had dropped, never doubting for a moment that they understood every word she said. It brought her a measure of calm serenity.

That night, after she had returned to Windsor, she reread Lincoln Robert's latest letter. He was asking her to set a firm date when she would visit Farnham in Surrey.

Though Brianna longed to see the castle that would be their home once she and Lincoln were married, she knew she could not possibly leave Windsor during the crucial month of July. The plans for Mortimer's escape must be finalized and all loose ends tied up. Nothing could be left to chance, if it were to succeed.

The queen also was depending on her to accompany her to the Tower for her last secret trysts. Isabelle had given her heart to Roger Mortimer, and their parting would be poignantly bittersweet.

Brianna dipped her quill and wrote to her betrothed.

My Dearest Lincoln Robert:
Your letters are a constant source of pleasure to me. I am so looking forward to spending time with you, and of course visiting Farnham Castle. I have decided to come in mid-August when it will be at its loveliest, and all will be in bloom.

Brianna lifted her quill and felt guilty for putting him off. She firmly pushed away the remorse and wrote two more pages, asking questions about the crops he'd planted and the herd of cattle he'd bought. Then she avowed her love and signed the missive.

The following day, Isabelle and Brianna visited the Tower and the queen followed the same routine of entertaining Constable Segrave at dinner. She brought up the subject of the Tower garrison's celebration of its patron saint. "It is an annual tradition and a reward to the guards for the vigilant job they do. I hope you will not frown on allowing them wine on such a special occasion, Sir Stephen."

When Roger Mortimer arrived just before midnight,

Brianna locked the door and this time accompanied the Border Lord to the queen's apartment. Brianna saw the look of adoration on Isabelle's face and knew Roger was the sun and the moon to her. *Their time together is so short and so precious.*

"Lord Mortimer, I was able to visit Wolf and ask him about the date you gave me. While I was there, I believe he had a vision that August first would be most propitious. He told me you would need a ship that could be supplied by a merchant named Botton, and warned that Southampton would be a safer port than London."

"Wolf is one step ahead of me, as always. That's the advantage of having second sight, though sometimes he thinks it a curse."

"I passed the information on to my brother Rickard. He will arrange for the ship and will have swift horses waiting on the Surrey shore. I felt confident enough to tell him the plan was set for the night of August first."

He gallantly kissed her fingers. "I will be forever indebted to the de Beauchamps."

"My lord, do you intend to swim across the Thames?" Isabelle gasped, terrified at the thought.

"I would not hesitate, if that were the only way. Alspaye has arranged for a rowboat to meet us at the wharf. The lieutenant is coming with me. 'Tis the only way to save him from hanging."

"We couldn't have met without the lieutenant's help. I am most grateful to him. I spoke with Segrave about the celebration of the garrison's patron saint to ensure he would allow the guards to imbibe wine that night."

"I have a good supply of the decoction of poppy your physician left me for Chirk. The sleeping draught works like a charm—the guards won't know what hit them."

Brianna stood and bade the lovers good night, and then she went to the Great Hall to sit vigil.

*   *   *

One week before the celebration of Saint Peter ad Vincula, Brianna met Gerard in the Royal Wardrobe and gave him thirty bottles of wine. Alspaye dosed each one with syrup of poppy and carefully fit the corks back into the bottles.

That night, Roger held Isabelle in his arms for hours, quieting her fears and erasing all doubts that everything would go according to plan. "*Ma belle*, you must not come again. I want you nowhere near the Tower for a week before my escape. When they rouse from their drugged sleep and find the bird has flown, all hell will break loose. You must remain at Windsor and be above suspicion. Swear it to me on your life, Isabelle."

She cried that this must be their last time together and Roger kissed away her tears. "I will find a way to join you in Paris," she vowed fervently. "I love you with all my heart!"

"Marie, I am so happy you have returned to Windsor. This must mean that Pembroke has recovered from his illness." Isabelle gave her cousin a warm kiss of greeting, happy for any diversion that would make the last week of July go by more quickly.

"My husband is far from well, yet the king insisted Pembroke accompany him and Despencer to Pontefract. Since Lancaster's death, soldiers have been deserting the army in droves. Apparently there is a rumor of miracles taking place at Thomas of Lancaster's tomb and people are flocking there, calling him *Saint Thomas the Martyr*. King Edward is livid. He has issued a proclamation forbidding pilgrimages and has ordered Pembroke set a guard at the tomb."

Brianna and Isabelle exchanged a look of pure relief that King Edward and Hugh Despencer would be far away up north when the first day of August arrived.

"Your Grace, I have brought you a letter from your

brother Charles. When I received it this morning, I decided to come to Windsor immediately."

"Marie, that was so thoughtful of you. I will let you in on a secret. The King of France is planning to marry again. My brother's bride-to-be is Jeanne of Evreux."

Isabelle retired early, anxious to read her brother's letter. As Brianna hung the queen's gown in her wardrobe, she listened avidly to the things Charles had written.

"He will receive Lord Mortimer with all honor." Isabelle looked up from her letter. "The King of France detests Hugh Despencer's tyranny and his influence on Edward. Charles says he has written to Edward summoning him to do homage for Gascony and Ponthieu, and if he delays one more time, my brother will send in his army and occupy Gascony!"

"The Despencers will never allow Edward to go to France and leave them in England. Without the king's protection, their enemies would destroy them," Brianna declared.

"Edward fears war with France. I will offer to go and make peace! It will take months, but perhaps by Christmas I will be able to join Roger in Paris. If the plan works out and I am allowed to go to France, will you come with me, Brianna?"

"I'm afraid I cannot, Isabelle. My year as lady in waiting will be over. I am to be married at Christmas."

"Of course you are. How lucky you are to be able to wed the man you love." Isabelle sighed.

The last week of July finally crawled to a close and the fateful day that Isabelle and Brianna both anticipated and dreaded arrived. "My nerves are taut as fiddle strings. I can't stop biting my fingernails—I don't know how I'll get through the day."

"We must keep busy. Why don't we gather roses and verbena from the garden and make perfume? At

least that will occupy our hands. After that we can
take the children and their dogs for a romp in Windsor's park," Brianna suggested.

"That's a lovely idea. John can ride his pony and
Eleanor can feed the carp in the fishpond. Children
need watching every moment and will divert my
thoughts from endless worry."

"This afternoon we can watch Prince Edward practice with the longbow, and perhaps we could have a
lesson in archery."

Because the queen and her ladies filled their day
with activities, it passed without too much anguish.
The night, however, was another matter. Dinner in
the Great Hall took up a couple of hours, though all
Isabelle and Brianna did was push the food about on
their plates and make a pretense of eating.

When they returned to the queen's apartment, Isabelle paced about her favorite chamber restlessly. It
had marble pillars and stained-glass windows with
casement seats. One wall was painted with a mural of
the *Wise and Foolish Virgins* and Brianna watched the
queen stare at it with dismay.

Finally, Isabelle took pity on her ladies and dismissed them for the night. "Thank heavens they are
gone. I could not mask my emotions any longer, pre-
tending to be calm and collected when in reality I
am frantic!"

"Both of us are agitated . . . Perhaps we should go
to the chapel."

"Oh yes . . . I do need to pray."

The queen's chapel was next to her apartments. Isabelle's pew was in the upper gallery where she could
pray in private. On Sundays her household worshipped below.

Brianna followed Isabelle into her pew and they
both knelt and bent their heads. A picture of Roger
Mortimer came full blown into Brianna's mind, and

though she knew he was courageous and daring, the thing he was attempting tonight was against all odds. He had lost everything and his cause seemed hopeless.

> *Oh Holy Saint Jude, Apostle and Martyr,*
> *Great in virtue and rich in miracles,*
> *Near kinsman of Jesus Christ,*
> *The faithful intercessor of all who invoke your*
>   *special patronage in times of need.*
> *To you I have recourse from the depths of my*
>   *heart,*
> *And humbly beseech you, to whom God has*
>   *given such great power,*
> *To come to the aid of Roger Mortimer on this*
>   *fateful night.*

When Brianna said Roger's name, a small measure of serenity came over her. *I must never give up hope. Hope is all we have in the face of cruel adversity and impossible odds. If anyone can pull off a miraculous escape from the Tower of London, it is Roger Mortimer.* Brianna raised her eyes heavenward. *With a little divine intervention.*

Brianna felt Isabelle take her hand and they prayed together. When they left the chapel, they went to the queen's bedchamber and talked until midnight.

Brianna plied Isabelle with full-bodied red wine, hoping it would make her sleep. The queen was emotionally exhausted, her nerves were in tatters, and eventually she agreed to undress and get into bed. When her eyes began to close, Brianna tiptoed from the room and sought her own chamber.

Though she kicked off her shoes and lay down on the bed, she knew she would not be able to sleep. Her body might be at rest, but her mind was overactive, as her chaotic thoughts chased each other in neverending circles.

Brianna heard a distant church bell chime four and knew she could lie there no longer. If she didn't arise and go outside, she would suffocate. *Lots of people start their day at four o'clock in the morning. Only the privileged lie abed.*

As she put on her shoes and donned her cloak, she realized her worries had changed from last night. How on earth would she get through the day, not knowing if Mortimer had succeeded or failed?

How in the name of God will Isabelle get through another day? They could not go to the Tower. They could not make any inquiries whatsoever. They would have to wait until the news was brought to them. Brianna racked her brains for a solution to the dilemma.

Finally, an idea came to her. Since the news would have to be brought from London, she hurried down to the vast kitchens where the workday had already begun, and made her way out to the yard where the produce wagons were being unloaded.

Fish carts arrived from the London docks, but the drivers seemed to have no exciting rumors to pass along. She walked among the wagons bringing sacks of flour for the thousand loaves baked every day at Windsor, but no gossip was being exchanged.

Brianna lingered among the carters bringing everything from meat to fresh-cut rushes for the floor of the Great Hall, but to her great disappointment she learned nothing.

Dawn had begun to lighten the sky, so Brianna walked down to the river and waited at the water stairs. Two wherries, transporting people from London, pulled in at the same time, and as the two groups disembarked, they began lively conversations with each other.

"Blimey, did ye hear the news? Mortimer disappeared from under their bloody noses! Heads will roll over this, mark my words."

"Drunk as bleeding lords, every last one of 'em!"

"Mortimer's pulled off the greatest escape in history. No wonder they call him *Notorious*!"

Brianna's heart lifted with joy. She wanted to ask a dozen questions, but kept her mouth tightly closed. She had learned the one thing that mattered and she could not wait to share the glad tidings with Isabelle. She cautioned herself not to break into a run, and instead walked sedately back to the castle.

After a brief knock, she entered the queen's bedchamber and carefully closed the door. Isabelle was sitting on the edge of her bed. Her face was deathly pale and she had mauve shadows beneath her eyes.

Brianna broke into a wide grin that ended in a ripple of lighthearted laughter. "Isabelle, he did it!"

"How do you know?" she whispered, not daring to believe it.

"I went down to the water stairs, knowing the first wherries from London would be arriving. The people disembarking could talk of nothing else but Mortimer's miraculous escape!"

"Thank God and all the saints in heaven!" Isabelle sprang up and the pair, giddy with relief, threw their arms about each other and danced around in circles.

They sobered for a moment and Isabelle wiped tears of joy from her cheeks. "I can't believe it. I just cannot believe it!"

"I never doubted for one minute!"

The two friends erupted into laughter again at Brianna's barefaced lie.

"I need a bath . . . and food." Isabelle, delirious with happiness, was suddenly ravenous.

"I shall order you both. Remember to curb your elation in front of your other ladies and the servants. You must pretend complete indifference when you hear the news."

As Brianna left the queen's apartment, all she could

think about was finding a way to let Wolf Mortimer know his father was free. *He will be jubilant!*

She walked down to the Lower Ward and knocked on Simon Deveril's door. He opened it and she stepped inside.

"Simon, everything must have gone according to plan. The staff who arrived from London this morning brought the news that Mortimer has escaped from the Tower!"

"God be praised," he said solemnly.

"We must get word to Wolf . . . and his brother of course. If you see them in the mess hall, send a signal—a thumbs-up sign would be enough to convey the message."

"I won't be seeing Wolf, Lady Brianna. All four of them disappeared in the night." Deveril's face broke into a grin. "With the aid of some well-placed horses Rickard provided."

Brianna was stunned. "They're gone?"

"Wolf decided it was the expedient thing to do. Once the king learned of Roger's escape, he could use threats against his sons, to lure him back into the trap."

"Of course. Edward and Despencer wouldn't hesitate to throw them in the Tower and use them as bait." Her hand went to her throat. "The moment Captain Colby finds them gone, he'll sound the alarm and scour the countryside for them."

"He'll be looking for four men, but they won't stick together. They planned to ride their separate ways. They got a good head start—they left at two this morning."

"Do you think they will flee to France?"

"France, Wales, Ireland . . . anywhere but England, I warrant."

"Thank you, Simon. Thank you for helping them."

As Brianna walked back to her own chamber, she

felt dazed. All her joy was seeping away, and in its place she felt an overwhelming sense of loss.

Back in her room she caught a glimpse of herself in the mirror and realized she was still wearing the clothes she'd had on yesterday. She removed them, washed herself, put on fresh garments, and began to listlessly brush her hair.

What the devil is the matter with me? I should be elated that Mortimer's sons and the de Bohun brothers are no longer captives. An hour ago, I was ecstatic to learn that Roger had escaped from the Tower, yet now my heart is heavy with despair.

"Wolf." She whispered his name.

"I may never see you again."

The thought was unendurable. She felt lost and empty inside.

"I cannot bear to lose you!"

Suddenly, her heart began to thud and her pulse became wildly erratic. "*Shadow.* You wouldn't leave without *Shadow*!"

Chapter 21

"I must get to Chertsey before it's too late!"

Brianna hurried to the stables and saddled Venus. She told no one where she was going, nor did she ask the queen for permission to leave. She had only one thought, one goal, and it blocked out everything else. *I must get to Chertsey before it's too late.*

Brianna rode the seven miles at full gallop. All manner of doubts assailed her. What if he hadn't gone to Chertsey? Or, if by some miracle he had, would he be long gone before she arrived? She tried to banish her doubts, for with each successive mile her need to see Wolf Mortimer grew stronger.

When she arrived at the castle, the hour was still early. She slid from the saddle and led her horse into the stables.

"Wolf!" She cried out his name, overjoyed to see him, praying that he was real and not an apparition. "You're here!"

"I was waiting for you . . . I hoped you'd come." His dark face, usually so fierce, broke into a grin.

The sight of him made her giddy. She deliberately slid her betrothal ring from her finger and slipped it into her saddlebag. "He did it! He escaped from the Tower!" She ran into his arms and he picked her up and swung her about. They were both laughing and so filled with joy they were euphoric. Suddenly the world seemed an enchanted place and Chertsey Castle the most glorious spot on earth because they were there together.

Shadow, who had been at Wolf's side when Brianna came into the stables, stretched her head back and let out a rejoicing howl. The elemental cry sent them off into another paroxysm of laughter and Brianna clung to Wolf so she wouldn't fall down.

Brianna sobered for a moment and wiped away tears of mirth. "Shadow is exultant that you are free, and so am I."

"Let's spend the day together. We can have a wild ride through the forest and let her hunt."

"Yes, just the three of us. There's nothing I would rather do, nowhere I would rather be than here with you."

"You haven't eaten."

"Not for days. Have you?"

He shook his head. "I was waiting for you." He took her hand. "Come on."

Suddenly, the thought of having breakfast together, sharing food, filled her with delight. "Have you met Mrs. Croft, the steward's wife?"

"I met them both around three this morning. I didn't have to waken them—apparently Shadow did that, padding about and howling like a lunatic. Her wild instincts told her I was coming."

Just as your wild instincts told you I was coming.
"Didn't the castle guard stop you?"

He grinned down at her. "Eluding guards is my favorite game."

Her eyes sparkled with admiration. "The Mortimers do it so well."

"We do everything well," he assured her.

"Cocksure Welsh devil!"

"And then some." His gray eyes lit with amusement.

"It's good to see you laugh. You are usually so stark and fierce, you frighten me."

"Little liar." He drew her fingers to his lips. "You are afraid of neither man nor beast." He growled deep in his throat and pretended to bite her.

She laughed up at him, delighted that he could be playful.

When they entered the kitchen, Mrs. Croft beamed. "Lady Brianna, Shadow's master told me to expect you. Sit down and eat, everything's ready."

She served them oatmeal porridge with rich cream and golden syrup. She also set a platter of gammon ham, poached eggs, and lamb sweetbreads on the table, along with hot baked scones and freshly churned butter. Then she brought them a jug of ale and had the grace to disappear, so they could relish the food and savor each other's company in private.

Brianna poured cream on her oatmeal. "Shadow's master? Mrs. Croft hasn't the faintest notion who you are."

He dipped the spoon in the syrup and ladled it on her porridge. "She thinks we are lovers, and this a secret rendezvous."

Their gazes met. "Don't take that away," she said breathlessly. "I like to lick the spoon."

He held it to her lips and smiled into her eyes. "Lick away."

The very air was charged with anticipation. Her thoughts became sensual, her senses heightened. The sound of his deep, lyrical voice was like haunting music. The taste of the syrup was ambrosia on her tongue, and the smell of the hot baked scones aroused her hunger for food and for something more. She suddenly had a tactile urge to touch things and experience what they felt like. Her glance roamed over the dark shadow on Wolf's cheeks and she wanted to run her fingertips across the prickle of his jaw. Her gaze lowered to the open neck of his black shirt and her fingers itched to feel the rough linen and slide inside to stroke his darkly tanned skin.

Wolf had a healthy man's appetite and she enjoyed watching him eat. She was aware that he seldom took his eyes from her, and whenever she stopped eating, he fed her with his fingers. His offerings tasted so delicious, she licked her lips, then licked his fingers too. He poured ale into a goblet and they shared it like a loving cup. Brianna smiled a secret smile. She heard the echo of her mother's wise words and at last she was beginning to understand: *The heart wants what it wants.*

Finally, he pushed away from the table and held out his hand. "The day promises to be glorious. Are you ready to ride out?"

"It would be my great pleasure." She put her hand in his and they returned to the stables where Shadow awaited them. When he lifted her into the saddle, the feel of his powerful hands sent a frisson of longing through her body, making her shiver.

She watched him saddle a black horse and realized it was a Warwick animal from Flamstead. "His name is Drago—Celtic for dragon." A warm blush tinted her cheek as she remembered the dragon on his thigh.

He smiled, knowing exactly what had prompted the blush. "Drago is a superb horse. I will take good care of him and promise to return him someday."

"Keep him, if you think him worthy."

"You give with a generous heart."

She watched as he swung a long, powerful leg across the rump of the stallion and mounted with one lithe movement that kept his back ramrod straight and his head erect. His black hair fell to his shoulders and his face looked more regal than any king's. When he stood in the stirrups, she knew he was going to give her a run for her money.

The summer day was heavenly. The color of the grass and the trees was so brilliantly green it hurt the eyes. Shadow loped before them as they thundered across a meadow of deep clover, sending clouds of butterflies dancing on the breeze.

As they approached the forest, Wolf watched Brianna, and his heart lifted as she rode full out, never hesitating over imagined dangers that might lie ahead. He knew that was part of why he was irresistibly attracted to her. He had a deep love of wild creatures like hawks, and bobcats, and wolves because they could never be fully tamed. If you could earn their trust, it was a prize to cherish.

They rode from the trees into a forest clearing so fast they startled a roebuck with a full set of antlers. It poised majestically before leaping away. For the thrill of the chase they thundered after it, their hair streaming behind them like banners on the wind.

They lost the stag and, laughing, slowed their pace. Suddenly, the smile was wiped from Wolf's face. He vaulted from the saddle and snatched up an iron trap that had been set beneath a tree. He smashed it against the oak's trunk until it was completely destroyed.

His face and his demeanor turned so fierce, she was momentarily afraid. Then she realized he must hate them with a vengeance because both he and his father had been entrapped. His good humor returned when he caught a glimpse of Shadow streaking through the trees, intent on some quarry she had marked as hers.

He took hold of Venus's bridle and led the two horses toward a stream so they could drink. He held up his arms for Brianna and without hesitation she came down into them with an eagerness that made her wildly beautiful. He held her against his heart and brushed his lips across the fiery tendrils that curled at her temples. Then he set her feet to the ground and handclasped they walked along the stream to where it widened into a forest pool.

Wolf stretched himself in the long grass beside the water and pulled her down beside him. They lay prone, their bodies touching, and gazed down into the pool. They were mesmerized by their reflections and smiled into each other's eyes. They were so at one with nature, their spirits touched and merged.

Wolf rolled onto his back and pulled her over him in the dominant position. Her red-gold hair cascaded down onto his chest and he took off his shirt so he could feel it whispering against his skin. They needed no words to communicate. Both wanted to rid themselves of the impediment of their clothes and enjoy being nude together as nature had made them. Laughing, they stripped off their garments and when they were naked, they gazed at each other enraptured.

He worshipped her with his eyes, missing no finest detail of her vibrant beauty. Her disheveled red-gold hair cloaked her shoulders and wispy tendrils curled possessively about her lush, high-thrusting breasts.

Slowly, his gaze moved lower, over her delicate rib cage to her waist and her satin-smooth belly. His glance followed the curve of her hip to her long, slim legs and fine-boned ankles, then moved back up to her soft thighs and the fiery curls that sat atop her high mons.

Brianna gazed at his impossibly wide shoulders and the rippling muscles of his powerful chest. Inexorably, her eyes were drawn down across his flat belly to the dragon that adorned his thigh. As he flexed a muscle, it grew larger and flicked its fiery tongue. Her avid glance sought his manhood that thrust up proudly from its nest of black curls. Her natural curiosity tempted her to reach out and touch him and his cock bucked beneath her fingers. Her glance flew to his and she laughed into his fierce gray eyes.

"I once dreamed that I was Shadow and you were a black wolf who lured me from my den," she said.

"We ran together faster and faster, in a wild frenzy of joy, relishing our freedom, ecstatic that we had found each other."

"But it was my dream, not yours."

"It was *our* dream, Brianna . . . I sent it to you to gratify our secret desires. We came upon a clearing in the heart of the forest."

Brianna gazed about her in wonder. "This was the clearing." She felt the primal heat of arousal in her belly. "We mated here."

"We did. But that was only a wishful dream, Brianna. The reality is far more complicated." He knelt before her and pulled her down to face him. "At this moment, more than anything in the world, we want to make love to each other. I want you for a lifetime, but I cannot have you. I am a fugitive with not a stick or a stone to my name. I cannot offer you marriage. You are the daughter of an earl and I am nothing."

"To me, you are everything. My father is wealthy— he would give us a castle and land, but I know your towering pride and I'd not insult you by offering it. I don't care that you cannot give me marriage. I love you! We cannot control love. It controls us. The heart wants what it wants." Every female instinct told her that if she did not seize this moment, she would regret it for the rest of her life.

"This short time together is all we have. I'm willing to grab it if you are, Wolf, and consider myself the most fortunate female alive to be loved by you."

"Your love is precious to me."

"I give it with a generous heart."

He enfolded her in his arms and they lay back in the tall grass. His lips touched her face and began

their slow seduction. He kissed her temple, and
brushed his lips along her eyebrow. When she lowered
her lashes, he very gently kissed her eyelid. His tongue
traced along her cheekbone, and then finally his lips
captured hers. He kissed her for an hour—gentle
kisses, soft kisses, short quick kisses, and slow, lingering kisses that melted her very bones.

She became aware of the scent of the man who held
her—leather, horse, male flesh. She felt his breath
upon her skin and knew she wanted Wolf Mortimer
more than anything she had ever wanted in her life.
She opened her mouth to his seeking tongue and surrendered herself to her need for him.

He cupped her bare breast with the palm of his
hand and stroked over her nipple with his rough
thumb.

She gasped as a frisson of purest pleasure shot from
her nipple, spiraling down through her belly to her
woman's core. As Wolf's hand continued to fondle
and caress her, the rippling sensations of desire increased. His hands stroked down her body and the
fiery touch of his fingers on her naked flesh almost
scalded her. She clung to him, loving the taste, the
smell, and the feel of him as she pressed her soft
curves against the hard length of his body. The crisp
hair on his chest abraded the sensitive tips of her
breasts, and she dug her nails into his shoulders, reeling from the delicious roughness.

Wolf moved over her, straddling her hips, and
looked into her lovely, soft brown eyes. "My sweetheart, this will hurt."

"I know," she said breathlessly, "I welcome it."

He stroked his palm down across her belly and
cupped her mons. He watched her eyes turn smoky
with feral need as she arched her hot center into his
hand. His fingers felt her wetness start and he knew
he could wait no longer. He positioned the head of

his phallus against her cleft, and with one powerful stroke, thrust through her hymen. Then he held absolutely still.

He watched her closely. If the pain became too much, he would withdraw. But to his amazement and delight, after her initial cry of pain she arched her body up to meet his, fiercely, sweetly, trusting him to bring her exquisite, heart-stopping pleasure. Clearly, Brianna loved his fullness inside her and yielded her body generously as he slowly slid in and out of her satin sheath.

They both moaned at the unbelievable pleasure they gave each other. She was tight and scalding hot and her passion matched his own. As he felt the brush of her thighs against his own, fire snaked through his loins. They moved in an undulating rhythm that made him think of hot, rippling silk.

Brianna experienced a budding, a blooming, as if some rare exotic flower inside her opened its petals wide to receive him. Unfurling, uncurling, she arched against him until suddenly the blossom deep inside exploded and splintered into a million fragments. She cried out his name. "Wolf! Wolf!"

He withdrew before he allowed himself to spend. Her fulfillment was reward enough for him. He would not take the chance of getting her with child. He enfolded her in his arms and held her against his heart. They lay entwined, their heartbeats thudding against each other, conjoined as if they were one being. "I love you, Brianna." Love was all he had to give and he prayed that love would be enough.

With his lips buried in the warm hollow of her throat, they drifted to the edge of sleep in a blissful cocoon where only they dwelled and the rest of the world didn't exist. After an hour, Wolf kissed her awake. Invigorated, and laughing like children, they slipped into the forest pool and swam together. Now the joyous experience of their lovemaking was added to the euphoria of the Mortimers' escape, and their spirits overflowed with happiness.

As the afternoon shadows grew long, they dressed, and Wolf whistled for Shadow. When she arrived, he mounted Drago and lifted Brianna before him. Venus followed willingly as they returned to the castle. None seeing the pair together could doubt that they were bound lovers, impatient for nightfall so they could claim each other again.

They dined together, but paid such scant attention to the food, they could not recall what they had eaten. The anticipation of sharing a bed and sleeping together for the first time blotted out all other thoughts.

Brianna chose the spacious master bedchamber where Guy de Beauchamp and Jory always slept. It was far more inviting for making love than her own small chamber.

"I was in such a fever to get here, I brought no clothes." She threw open her mother's wardrobe and found some of Jory's elegant gowns and pretty undergarments.

Wolf came up behind Brianna and slipped his arms around her. "Oh, bugger. Can we pretend you didn't find these things? I'd much prefer to keep you unclothed."

"I shall so pretend . . . at least for tonight, you Welsh devil."

He began undressing her immediately. When he had her down to her shift, he plucked it from her triumphantly and flung it across the room. Not to be outdone, Brianna unfastened his shirt and removed it, then playfully unsheathed the dagger he wore at his belt and pointed it at him. "Strip and show me the dragon, or I'll slit yer throat!"

"If ye ask me nicely, wench, I'll let ye ride the dragon."

"Oh, yes, please." She licked her lips in anticipation.

They caught a glimpse of themselves in the polished mirror, and the contrast between their bodies acted like an aphrodisiac. Their reflection showed them to be complete opposites. His hard, muscled body emphasized her soft femininity. His jet-black hair made her red-gold curls look like brilliant tongues of flame. Her smooth, creamy flesh played counterpoint to his swarthy skin that was tanned to a deep copper. Yet under the skin they were perfectly matched, not only sexually, but also temperamentally.

When Brianna saw the dragon on his thigh, she dropped to her knees and kissed it. Then she traced its outline with the tip of her tongue. Her feathered fingertip caresses and the effect of her sleek tongue sliding over the hidden, intimate parts of his body made him quiver with desire. "You enthrall me. I never believed anything could be as exciting as my visions of you, but I was wrong."

Wolf swept her up and carried her to the bed. He lifted one foot and kissed her instep, and then he proceeded to anoint every inch of her creamy flesh, worshipping her with his mouth. Tonight, he wanted more than her body, he wanted to enter her blood, her heart, and her soul. His love words were so intense they held her in thrall. His lovemaking was passionate and she knew she could never escape the power of this man. She did not want to escape it, now or ever.

He lay back and lifted her onto his body in the dominant position. "Ride me, ride the dragon, Brianna."

There was nothing passive about her tonight. She made love to Wolf with a wanton passion she did not know she possessed. She had a ravenous desire to make him groan with a hunger of his own and her lovemaking became splendidly uninhibited.

Though he usually had an iron control, at this moment it did him no good. He too began to move. She rode him faster and harder and he held her lush breasts cupped in his strong palms. Finally, she arched backward and released a cry of shattering bliss into the night.

He withdrew so he would not impregnate her and gathered her close against his heart. Later, they lay curled together in the big bed and talked. Neither wanted to waste the precious hours they had left in sleep.

"You looked afraid today, when I smashed the iron trap."

"The trap brought out a violence in you that you keep hidden."

"Shadow was only a few days old when I found her. She was huddled against her mother, who had lain in agony in a trap for at least three days. The hungry, suckling mother had been lured by the bait. She tried to eat off her leg to free herself. I arrived too late to save her. I had to put her out of her misery."

"Shadow's love is your reward."

"I have an affinity for wild creatures. That's why I cannot resist you," he teased.

"This has been the happiest day of my life," Brianna murmured. "Your father is undoubtedly safe in France by now."

"His work has only just begun. He will start gathering an army to invade England so he can rid her of a useless king. It may take years, but he can be relentlessly patient when necessary." He kissed her tenderly. "I have a massive job ahead of me. I have to secretly unite all the barons who are against Edward and Despencer. When my father comes, we must be ready."

"Wolf, I will wait for you, no matter how long—"

He silenced her by placing his fingers against her lips. "No undying vows, Brianna. I have taken enough from you. I have taken today and tonight—I must not take all your tomorrows."

They stole another day together. And as lovers always had done before them, they rode, walked, and swam, moving their bodies together in the same rhythm, imitating what they really wanted.

They went fishing, and laughed and splashed in the stream so much, it was a miracle they caught anything. Wolf cleaned the trout and then cooked them over a wood fire he built.

Shadow went hunting and brought Wolf back a token of her love in the form of a hare. Since it was already dead, he skinned it and cooked it over the fire.

That night, Wolf's lovemaking brought a lump to Brianna's throat. His kisses were so sweet, so gentle, and so breathtakingly tender that she felt cherished. His sole intent was on giving her pleasure. His caresses were unhurried, and his whispered words made her feel beautiful and deeply loved.

Later, as they lay entwined together, Brianna knew that he had changed her life forever. She felt completely safe and secure locked in his arms, warmed by his powerful body. The heavy, strong, sure beat of his heart lulled her to sleep.

When Brianna opened her eyes at the first flush of dawn, she felt the loss immediately. She sat up in a panic, knowing that he had already left her. On her pillow lay the wolf touchstone that she had given to him so impulsively on the day he had brought Shadow to her for safekeeping. As her fingers closed over it, her eyes flooded with tears. "God keep them both safe."

Chapter 22

"I must face Lincoln Robert and ask him to release me from our betrothal." As Brianna brushed her hair before the mirror, she spoke to her reflection.

She felt no guilt over loving Wolf Mortimer and had not the slightest regret that they had spent the last two glorious days and nights together consummating that love. There had been sparks between them from the first moment they met, and the attraction had flared stronger and deeper with every encounter, until it had ignited into a fire that would burn forever. Though she had denied it, her heart knew all along that she had fallen in love with him, and when she finally acknowledged it, her spirit had been set free.

Brianna did, however, feel great remorse over Lincoln Robert. She had pledged to marry him and now she would have to hurt him by asking him to release her. She now realized that what she felt for Lincoln was a natural affection for a brother or a cousin. It had nothing in common with the tumultuous, all-consuming passion she felt for Wolf.

Since she was already in Surrey, Brianna decided to ride the few miles to Farnham Castle and tell Lincoln Robert, face-to-face, that she could not marry him.

When she arrived at Farnham, she saw that the

property was even lovelier than Lincoln had described in his letters. She gazed about the estate where she and her betrothed were supposed to begin their married life. *Lynx and Jane were so generous to give us this castle that belonged to the late Earl of Surrey. They will think me an ungrateful wretch when I ask to be released from the betrothal contract.*

In the courtyard, Farnham's steward greeted her.

"Good morning. Can you tell me where I may find Lincoln Robert?"

"He returned to Hedingham yesterday, Lady Brianna. He will be sorry to have missed you. He spoke of your visit often. Do come inside and enjoy Farnham's hospitality."

"Thank you for your lovely invitation, but I had best return to my duties at Windsor." Brianna could not help feeling relief that the confrontation with her betrothed had been postponed. As she left, a voice inside her head accused: *Coward!*

"Where on earth did you disappear to?" Isabelle asked Brianna when she got back to Windsor.

"I rode to Farnham Castle to see Lincoln de Warenne. I kept postponing my visit until after August first." *It's not really a lie—I did actually ride to Farnham.*

· She saw the concerned look on the queen's face. "Never fear, Isabelle, I did not confide any secrets to my betrothed."

"Thank you, Brianna. We must trust no one. I have news for you. While you were gone, it was discovered that Mortimer's sons and the de Bohun brothers were no longer at Windsor. By some miracle they escaped their confinement."

"That is a great relief, though we must pretend complete indifference."

"It was my son, Prince Edward, who told me about

it. He was quite happy they were no longer prisoners. I wouldn't be at all surprised if he had a hand in helping his royal cousins escape."

Brianna decided not to disabuse her of her suspicions.

Two days later, King Edward and Hugh Despencer arrived in London, incensed that Roger Mortimer had escaped from the Tower. Though the constable blamed his sublieutenant Alspaye for aiding and abetting the notorious prisoner, the king had Segrave slapped in irons and the entire garrison of guards punished.

King Edward was in a state of near panic. His royal army was shrinking by the day. Mortimer at liberty could be the focus for a concerted opposition to his rule. He issued orders that Roger Mortimer must be recaptured, dead or alive, and raised the hue and cry all over England. Both Edward and Despencer took it for granted that the notorious traitor would have gone to either Wales or Ireland, and ordered Pembroke to send men-at-arms to scour those infernal places.

"This could not have happened at a worse time. I am beset on all sides," the king raved to Pembroke. "You were up north with me. Not a day went by that the accursed Scots did not mount raids into England! Your army is useless, Pembroke. We have never been victorious fighting the Bruce!"

The Earl of Pembroke, aging and not in the best of health, dared to tell Edward the truth. "Sire, war with Scotland is one that can never be won. Your father emptied England's coffers conquering the Scots, but they refused to stay conquered."

"Each time we sign a truce, the accursed Scots break it. God rot their heathen souls! You must go and negotiate a long and lasting truce with Robert Bruce that he will not break after a few months."

"Sire, may I suggest that you send the earls of Surrey and Arundel with me to Scotland? They have been friends of Robert Bruce since boyhood. I warrant if any man can persuade the Bruce to a lasting peace with England, it will be Lynx de Warenne."

Edward turned to Despencer, who was busy stamping deeds with the Royal Seal of England. "What do you think, Hugh? Your advice in these matters is indispensable."

Hugh Despencer dominated the king, who had given him all the confiscated lands of Mortimer, d'Amory, and Audley, making him the unopposed ruler of South Wales. The insatiable Despencer was not satisfied, however. He spent his days amassing estates, land, and wealth, which in turn increased his power. Since he hated women, he took particular delight in preying on widows and other vulnerable females who owned property. He had his own network of enforcers that did his bidding because he paid them well. Since these men did not hesitate to commit violence, the women surrendered their manors and their lands. The people of England both feared and hated him, and secretly lusted for his downfall.

Hugh Despencer had been closely following the conversation. "Since de Warenne has come into the earldom of Surrey, he has done little to prove his loyalty to the Crown."

"He brought his forces to help siege Leeds Castle," Pembroke pointed out.

"That proved his loyalty to the queen, not the king," Hugh declared. "Summon de Warenne and set the task before him. If he is reluctant, gentle persuasion can be brought to bear."

Rickard de Beauchamp visited the London merchant Botton and picked up secret correspondence from France. Mortimer asked that Rickard pass messages to his son Wolf and to Adam Orleton, Bishop of Hereford. He also asked him to get word to the queen that he had arrived safely in Paris.

Accompanied by Simon Deveril, Brianna met her brother Rickard in the woods by the river. She saw that he now sported a beard to help disguise his features.

"Roger sent a message for the queen. He arrived safely at the King's Court in Paris and was warmly welcomed by Isabelle's brother Charles."

"Thank you, Rickard. She will be greatly relieved. Did he send a message for Wolf?"

"He did," Rickard confirmed.

"Then you know where he is!" Brianna said quickly.

"I know how to get in touch with him," he said evasively. "He moves from place to place. His mission is the same as mine—to unite those who oppose the tyranny of Edward and Despencer. Adam Orleton is secretly uniting the bishops. We all have our work cut out for us. Roger Mortimer will raise an invading army. When he lands, we must be ready."

"Thank you, Rickard, for risking your neck to bring us a message. Is there any safe way I can contact you?"

"If it's absolutely necessary, send Simon to Flamstead."

On the way back to the stables, Brianna said, "Thank you for not asking where I disappeared to last week."

"I didn't need to ask," Simon said quietly.

"Oh." Brianna blushed. "I must go to Hedingham, as soon as the queen can spare me for a few days."

"I will escort you, my lady."

"Thank you, Simon. I am most grateful." *You know my secrets, yet you are still loyal to me.*

By late August, Brianna knew that in all conscience she could no longer delay her visit to Hedingham.

When she asked for permission from Isabelle, she did not tell the queen that the purpose for her visit was to end her betrothal. *Lincoln Robert must be the first to know.*

When Brianna and Simon Deveril rode into Hedingham, Jane, who was in the courtyard, broke into a radiant smile. "Oh, how wonderful you are here. I was just about to write you a letter to invite you. I have such exciting news, Brianna!"

"Hello, Jane." *Oh dear, you look so happy, and I am about to ruin it.* Simon helped Brianna from the saddle and took Venus to the stables.

"I see you are wearing the touchstone I painted for you. Do you believe in the wolf's mystic power to bring you secret knowledge, and to guide you on the path of life?"

"Yes, I do. The wolf is absolutely the right symbol for me," Brianna said truthfully.

"Come inside and I'll tell you the news."

Jane led the way into her solar and poured them dandelion and burdock wine she had made herself.

"Lynx was summoned to Westminster by the king. I knew he was reluctant to go, though he didn't tell me why. But when he returned yesterday, his worries seemed to have been put to rest and he was full of plans."

"What did Edward want?" Brianna was immediately wary.

"The king wants Lynx and the Earl of Arundel to accompany Pembroke to Scotland to negotiate a lasting truce with Robert Bruce. I will be able to visit my family at Dumfries Castle and show off my sons. I haven't been to Scotland for almost eighteen years. I am very excited!"

"Jane, I am so happy for you. It will be wonderful to return to Scotland and see your family after all these years."

"We want you to come too, Brianna. The first thing Lincoln Robert said was how overjoyed you would be."

"That is most generous of you, Jane. I . . . I don't know what to say." *Dear God, I must tell Lincoln I want to be released from the betrothal. I cannot just fling it in Jane's teeth.*

"You will be able to visit Wigton Castle, which will be yours when you wed. And you will meet Robert Bruce, the King of Scotland. You will love him—everyone does."

"Yes . . . indeed," she said faintly. "Where is Lincoln Robert?"

"He's gone to check on the harvesters. We hope to get the early hay crop in before we leave. He should be back any minute."

"I think I'll go and meet him."

"Off you go, darling. Let him tell you about Scotland. Don't let on that I spoiled the surprise."

Brianna felt wretched. *I'm the one who will spoil the surprise.*

She began to walk to the hay fields, which lay beyond the orchard. She got as far as the first row of apple trees when she spotted him returning. Brianna stood still and waited.

He let out a whoop when he saw her and slid from the saddle. "You didn't keep your promise about coming to Farnham," he teased.

"I . . . I did go to Farnham, but you had already left."

"Did Mother tell you we are going to Scotland?" He picked her up and swung her about.

"Lincoln, please put me down. I have something serious I must discuss with you."

"Me too." He set her feet to the ground. "Why don't we get married at Wigton Castle?"

"No, Lincoln . . . that is impossible."

"Then Scotland. We could have the wedding in Scotland."

Brianna took a deep breath. "Lincoln, I ask that you release me from our betrothal."

His face turned grim. "No!" he shouted. "I absolutely refuse to release you!"

"Lincoln, you must." She searched for words that would not hurt him, but failed. "I have come to realize that my love for you is that of a cousin. We were childhood friends, and I thought that was enough, but—"

"Friends don't do this to each other!"

"I am so sorry. I am filled with remorse, Lincoln. But I cannot marry you, because I don't love you that way."

"I don't give a damn, Brianna! The contract is legal and binding and I won't allow you to break it."

"You must release me, Lincoln. I will not marry you."

"Love has nothing to do with it. You are the daughter of an Earl of the Realm. You signed it and you will honor it!"

"Are you telling me that noble titles are more important to you than love?" Brianna began to feel angry.

"Signed betrothal contracts take precedence over love. Our fathers, both Earls of the Realm, also signed the contract. It is a fitting match between equals. Love will come after we marry."

"We will never be married, Lincoln. I will speak to Lynx and Jane about this."

Lincoln immediately changed his tactics. He stopped demanding and started cajoling. "Brianna, you would never be so cruel as to speak of this to my mother? It would be heartless to spoil her visit to Scotland after she has waited all these years."

"I don't want to hurt Jane," Brianna protested. "She is the sweetest and most gentle lady I know."

"Then do not hurt her, I beg you. For my mother's sake, say nothing about breaking the betrothal until she has enjoyed her visit and we return home. Our wedding was planned for Christmas. That gives you lots of time to think about it and perhaps change your mind. When December comes, if you still feel the same, I will release you."

Brianna hesitated. "Lincoln, I would feel much better if we made a quick, clean break."

"*You* would feel better? Forgive me, your feelings are paramount in this matter." His voice dripped sarcasm. "Forget you are the daughter my mother has always wanted. Forget that this will break her heart."

"I am covered with guilt that I must hurt her, but I feel that Jane will understand."

"Yes, my mother is indeed selfless. She is a most understanding lady, who always puts others before herself."

Brianna drew in a deep breath. "I suppose I could wait until you return from Scotland. But, Lincoln, I want you to understand that I will not change my mind."

"I quite understand how stubborn you are."

No, Lincoln, you haven't the faintest idea!

"Brianna, how's my imp of Satan?" Lynx de Warenne teased.

She flushed. His words made her feel like a handmaiden of the devil. Lynx had ridden over to Colchester to discuss the upcoming journey with Richard FitzAlan, Earl of Arundel, but had returned in time for dinner.

"When I told FitzAlan I was taking my family with me to Scotland, he decided to take his daughter, Blanche. He offers his ship, which he keeps at Colchester, for the journey to Edinburgh. That would be far less fatiguing for the ladies than riding all the way to Scotland."

"That is most generous of Lord Arundel," Jane declared happily.

"Brianna and I think Blanche FitzAlan a very sweet young lady," Lincoln Robert declared.

Young Jamie rolled his eyes and Brianna choked on her wine.

After dinner, Brianna followed Lynx into his library and closed the door. "I find it strange that you are eager to do the king's bidding. Edward and Despencer are nothing but tyrants."

"Indeed they are, but there is method in my madness. If I negotiate a truce with my friend Robert Bruce, my castles and lands will not be forfeit."

"They have threatened you?"

"Not in so many words, but it is implied that if I am successful, my estates will be safe. I know I can trust your discretion, Brianna. Don't let on to Jane. Lincoln returned from Farnham to warn me that our neighbor's property that runs parallel with ours has been sequestered by Despencer."

"He's a vicious, greedy swine! If you were approached by those who would unite against this tyranny, would you join them?"

Lynx stiffened. His face set in stern lines. "I will not discuss treason with you, Brianna. Do not involve yourself in men's affairs. Splendor of God, you are just like your mother. You may trust me to do what is best for my family."

"Yes, of course. I'm sorry."

His face softened. "Jane will enjoy showing you Dumfries, and perhaps you and Lincoln can visit Wigton Castle, which is just across the Solway Firth from Jane's old home."

Brianna opened her mouth to protest, and then closed it. She had agreed to keep quiet about ending the betrothal until Jane returned from Scotland.

"When do you plan on leaving?"

"We'll try to sail in a week. I'd rather not wait any later than the first week of September. Autumn comes early to Scotland, and winter weather soon follows. Don't forget to pack your furs."

The evening passed in a blur for Brianna. When Lynx and Jane retired early, she suspected it was so that she and Lincoln Robert could be alone. "I'm tired. I think I'll go upstairs too."

Alone in the lovely chamber that had belonged to her mother, she found that she could think more clearly. She readied herself for bed and then her fingers sought the wolf touchstone. She clasped it tightly. *Please guide me on the right path.*

Lynx and Jane took it for granted that she was going to Scotland with them, but in truth she had no desire to go. Since she had agreed not to break off the betrothal until after the trip, it would mean that she would have to live a lie every day of the journey, and she shrank from it. *Don't be such a hypocrite, Brianna. You are quite capable of lying and practicing deceit. You've been doing it for months to help Isabelle and Mortimer.*

As she pondered her dilemma, she realized that she could make an excuse to Lynx and Jane why she could not go to Scotland, without disclosing her intention to break her betrothal with Lincoln Robert.

She pulled on a bedrobe over her nightgown and went down the long hallway that led to Lynx and Jane's bedchamber. Their door was slightly ajar and when she heard her name spoken, something made her stop and listen.

"Brianna has Robert's eyes. Their large, soft brown Celtic eyes are identical. I've often suspected the Bruce is her father."

"You mustn't say such things. Many people have brown eyes," Jane admonished her husband.

Brianna was stunned. *I cannot possibly be the daughter of the King of Scotland!* She stood in the dim hallway, her heart pounding, her head spinning, and her feet rooted to the floor. When the dizziness passed, she silently backed away from their chamber and returned to her own room.

She went to the mirror, raised her thick dark lashes, and saw the large brown Celtic eyes staring back at her. Brianna's fingers closed over her wolf touchstone. *You brought me secret knowledge.* The reflection of the room behind her evoked her mother. Jory's spirit seemed tangible in the very air.

You left Scotland and immediately married Guy de Beauchamp. The Earl of Warwick is not my father! Anger and pain rose up in her. *How could you? How could you both deceive me?*

Chapter 23

"Simon, may I trouble you to take this letter to Hedingham for me? The de Warennes invited me to sail with them to Scotland and coward that I am, I find it easier to make my excuses in a letter than in person."

"It's no trouble, Lady Brianna. The weather is lovely and I fancy a ride."

"Good. I have every intention of riding to Warwick soon." Brianna's anger and pain had not lessened one whit after she returned to Windsor, and she knew she would find no peace until she journeyed to Warwick and confronted her parents.

When Brianna asked Isabelle for permission to go home for a visit, the queen gave her consent. "I shall try to manage without you. After all, if you had gone to Scotland with your betrothed, your absence from Windsor would have been far longer."

Brianna began to pack. It was a seventy-mile ride to Warwick and would take three days. When Simon Deveril returned, it would take him only a day to ready himself and the horses.

Simon brought her two letters from Hedingham. She opened the one from Lincoln Robert first.

My Dearest Brianna:
I regret that you are not coming to Scotland,

*but hope the time apart will allow you to reflect
upon your foolish decision to break our betrothal.
Our families have set their hearts on this marriage
and it would be both cruel and selfish to disappoint them. I feel confident that by the time I
return, you will have changed your mind.
Fondest regards,
Lincoln Robert de Warenne.*

She sighed, well aware that she was cruel and selfish
without being told by Lincoln. She opened the letter
from Jane.

*Darling Brianna:
I am so sorry that your duty to Queen Isabelle
prevents you from sailing to Scotland with us. I
will miss you sorely, as will Lincoln Robert. As
soon as I learned about Lynx being asked to negotiate a truce with Robert Bruce, enabling me to
visit my family at Dumfries, I dispatched a letter
to your mother telling her that you were coming
with us to Scotland. Perhaps you could let her
know you were unable to join us.
I am so excited and happy about this visit. For
me, it is like a dream come true. I intend to enjoy
every moment.
All my love,
Jane de Warenne.*

Though Jane was the Countess of Surrey, Brianna
noted that she did not use her title to sign her letter.
*Jane is so unpretentious. I'm glad I kept the news from
her about breaking my betrothal. It would have ruined
her visit.*

As prearranged, Wolf Mortimer met up with his
brother, Edmund, the de Bohun brothers, and Adam
Orleton in Hereford. Because Orleton was the Bishop

of Hereford, it was a safe haven where they could rendezvous.

Since Wolf was usually aware of impending danger, he had deliberately chosen to recruit in the Welsh Marches. He rode at night, often following the royal troops who had been sent to search for and capture his father. Though Edward had given Despencer title to the lands of Mortimer, d'Amory, and Audley, Wolf Mortimer recruited the people who inhabited those lands to secretly pledge their support for Roger Mortimer.

"I also have pledges from Chepstow, Usk, Raglan, Clifford, and Hay," Wolf said with a grin. "I'm working my way north. I'll be visiting our own castles of Wigmore and Ludlow tomorrow."

Edmund shook his head in wonder at his brother's reckless daring. "I believe I have persuaded Aylesbury and Woodstock."

John de Bohun had pledges from Tewksbury and Gloucester, and his brother, Humphrey, had recruited Dorchester and Oxford. Next they intended to recruit in Cambridge, a strategic city, and then secretly contact nobles along the east coast.

"A remarkable achievement for only one month," Orleton praised. "I have been in communication with the bishops of Bath, Lincoln, Norwich, and Winchester. All condemn the tyranny of Edward and Despencer, and fortunately bishops have the powerful protection of the Church and the ear of the pope."

"Rickard de Beauchamp is adept at getting messages to and from my father in France. If necessary, he is prepared to cross the Channel to meet secretly with Roger Mortimer," Wolf told them. "We need the backing of the most powerful earls such as Chester. I will ride there, but first I will seek out Thomas of Lancaster's brother Henry Plantagenet. The king not only executed his brother, but also deprived him of

Lancaster's earldom and possessions. He is bound to
be bitterly opposed to Edward and Despencer, and
lust for their downfall."

"Somehow, sometime, someway, someday!" Wolf
Mortimer swore the vow and awoke with a start. Once
again he had been dreaming of Brianna. Since the
two days they had stolen at Chertsey, when they had
consummated their love, her image was ever before
him. Last night, as he lay in bed he had tried to conjure her, so he could transcend the physical and join
her in spirit, as he had often done before. Since he
had returned her touchstone, he possessed no object
that held traces of her essence, and no matter how he
willed it, a vision of Brianna did not materialize.

His dreams, however, were amazing. Sometimes
their lovemaking was highly erotic, like riding wild
horses on a magic carpet. At other times it was sweet
and gentle, and breathtakingly tender. As he lay with
his lips buried in the warm hollow of her throat, it
was as if he had found sanctuary.

Last night Wolf dreamed Brianna was at Warwick.
Unlike his mystic visions when he experienced true
second sight, he knew dreams were unreal and ephemeral, prompted by wishful thinking. *Perhaps my dream
was trying to tell me something.* His longing for her
was so great, he decided to stop at Warwick on his
way to visit Henry Plantagenet at nearby Kenilworth
Castle.

"Wolf Mortimer, it is an honor to welcome you to
Warwick." Jory de Beauchamp gave her unexpected visitor a kiss of greeting, and said fervently, "I thank God
for your father's escape from the Tower last month."

"I assure you God had nothing to do with it,
Lady Warwick."

"Of course you are right," she acknowledged. "It

must have taken a great deal of planning by courageous men."

"And women," Wolf added lightly.

"Rickard came for one night and told us Roger had escaped and that you and the de Bohuns had managed to free yourselves from confinement. Guy Thomas had a hundred questions, but Rickard was amazingly closemouthed."

"That is because we are hunted fugitives. If caught, we would all lose our lives, including Rickard."

Jory took Wolf into the hall and poured him ale. "Brace yourself for his questions. Guy Thomas will be overjoyed to see you. He has taken on a lot of Warwick's responsibilities since his father's accident."

"Accident?" Wolf's brows drew together.

"Early in the year, my husband suffered a blow to the head and ever since he has been losing his sight. It is not completely gone, he still can see shadows, but his days of combat are over."

"That is most regrettable, my lady. Please accept my sympathy—I would not dare offer it to Warwick."

Jory smiled. "How very astute you are."

He longed to ask about Brianna, but controlled the impulse. If she were at Warwick, he would soon know. *If she is here, I cannot ask her to marry me. I am still a fugitive.* His senses became drenched with her. *Perhaps I will ask her to wait for me.* Wolf's heart contracted painfully. He clenched his fists. *That would be totally self-serving. Before we parted I told her I wanted no undying vows. She must be free to make her own choices.*

"Here comes Margaret," Jory said. "News of your arrival is spreading like wildfire."

Wolf turned and saw the pale, poignant face of Margaret Audley. Her eyes were wide with apprehension.

He smiled. "I have some encouraging news, my lady. I saw Sir Hugh a fortnight ago and he was hale and hearty."

Her hand went to her breast. "Thank heaven! Can you tell me where he is, Wolf?"

"Your husband has regrouped all his fighting men. He has made secret contact with the people of Audley and has their allegiance, but he is no longer in perilous South Wales. He has gone to d'Amory's Hampshire castle of Odiham, a safe refuge."

At that moment, Guy Thomas came striding into the hall. Margaret's son James was trying to keep up with him. "Wolf Mortimer! I cannot believe you are here in the flesh!"

Wolf grinned. "Are you growing taller, or am I shrinking?"

"*I'm* growing taller," young James asserted.

"You are indeed. Your father will be most impressed when he sees you." Wolf restrained himself from tussling the boy's hair and treating him like a child.

Guy Thomas said, "He follows me about just as I did with you. I'll try not to ply you with a million questions."

When Warwick arrived with the ever-present Brutus at his side, Wolf bade Shadow, "Stay." She went down on her haunches and made no move toward the black wolfhound.

Guy de Beauchamp shook hands with Mortimer and invited him to the library where they could talk in private. He sat down at the desk and Brutus stretched at his feet. "It's the height of irony that I have one of the best book collections in England that I can no longer read."

"I warrant you've read every book and will retain the knowledge." Wolf took a seat. "My father arrived safely in Paris and received a warm reception from King Charles."

"Undoubtedly it was Queen Isabelle who arranged a safe haven for Roger at her brother's court."

"Aye. Perhaps Lady Brianna told you that he charmed the queen into helping him escape?"

"You mean he *seduced* her. I hear the censure in

your voice. Don't fault him, Wolf, for manipulating her. She is using him too. Isabelle must clearly recognize that Roger Mortimer is the only man capable of ending the tyranny of Edward and Despencer."

When Warwick made no mention of Brianna, Wolf went on to tell him what he and the de Bohuns had been doing since they left Windsor. "Adam Orleton is uniting the bishops and tomorrow I will ride to Kenilworth and ask Henry Plantagenet to pledge to our cause. In theory, he is the highest magnate in England."

"I believe Henry will commit to you. He has petitioned Parliament for his brother's earldoms of Leicester and Lancaster, though he knows it's futile so long as Despencer rules the king. I pledge you my Warwick men-at-arms. Rickard will lead them."

"I thank you, sir. I don't know how we will ever repay you."

"The Mortimers and the de Beauchamps have a bond of blood. Our fortunes are inextricably tied together."

Wolf flushed. *The Mortimers have no fortune. We are reduced to beggars.*

"I hear the bell summoning us to dinner. Come, Brutus, it would be rude to keep the ladies waiting."

Jory sat at her husband's right hand and placed Wolf beside her. Guy Thomas quickly took the seat beside him.

Wolf held his breath as his glance swept about the hall, hoping that Brianna would show up for the evening meal. When she did not arrive, his hopes plummeted.

In spite of his promise, Guy Thomas plied him with questions and Wolf strived to answer him with honesty and humor.

Halfway through the meal, Jory decided her son had monopolized their guest long enough. "I received a letter from my brother's wife, Jane, yesterday. It seems King Edward has sent Lynx de Warenne to Scotland to negotiate a lasting truce with the Bruce. Jane was born in Dumfries and is excited to visit her family."

"I wonder if Brianna will get seasick," Guy Thomas pondered with little sympathy.

"Brianna?" Wolf's heart thudded as he murmured her name.

"Brianna and her betrothed, Lincoln Robert, have sailed with them," Jory explained. "It will give them the opportunity to visit Wigton Castle, which my brother placed in Brianna's dower."

Wolf's heart stopped and turned over in his breast. His gut knotted with distress. *She did not end the betrothal.* The expression on his face remained calm, masking his inner turmoil.

"I have no idea how long they will remain in Scotland. When they return, it will be time to make plans for their wedding."

Wolf's food turned to ashes. He set down his fork and tried to swallow the lump in his throat. He didn't succeed. *Choking might be a merciful death.*

He heard no more of the Countess of Warwick's conversation. The loud thunder hammer of his heart deafened him. He stared at her beautiful face, so like the one he loved, except for the eyes.

Jory motioned for his wine goblet to be filled.

Wolf picked it up and drained it. *Her family is looking forward to her marrying de Warenne. Brianna could not bring herself to be cruel and disappoint them.* An inner voice mocked him. *She is quite capable of being cruel. I warrant she is far too beautiful to be kind.*

The hour after the evening meal was a complete blank to Wolf. He retired early to the chamber that had been plenished for him. He lifted the jug of wine, then set it down again. Drowning his sorrow was not the answer. Truth must be faced.

Brianna's words came echoing back to him: *This short time together is all we have. I'm willing to grab it if you are, Wolf.* They had seized the moment passionately, without reserve, and he knew that neither of them would ever regret it. He loved her deeply, but warned himself that his love must not be selfish. Did he love her enough to want what was best for her? He did not know the answer. The thought of her wed to another was torturous.

He picked up his saddlebags on the verge of riding to Scotland, forcing her to end her betrothal, and bringing her back. *If you do this thing, you can neither propose marriage nor in all conscience ask Brianna to wait.*

He strode to the window and Shadow padded after him. He stared out into the darkness with unseeing eyes, longing for one glimpse of her, aching to hear her voice, craving to hold her, willing her to come to him. Slowly, one by one, he mastered his emotions and accepted the inevitable.

Brianna has made the wise choice. She has not allowed her heart to overrule her head. I made that same choice when I decided we could not marry.

He knelt down and buried his face in Shadow's fur. In that moment Wolf realized he had not mastered all his emotions.

He prowled the room to avoid sleep. The last thing he wanted was dreams. In the small hours of the night, Brianna's bedchamber beckoned to him, luring him to her private sanctuary. Initially he resisted the temptation but finally he gave in and succumbed to the enticement. Silently, he made his way to Brianna's chamber. He laid his hand on her pillow until all his senses overflowed with her essence.

Wolf lit a small candle in hope of finding some object that belonged to Brianna, but her dressing table was bare. He opened her wardrobe and touched her garments. He rubbed his cheek against a velvet cloak and inhaled her delicate fragrance. The intoxicating scent of verbena stole to him, and he realized it was coming from the lit candle.

He snuffed it and removed it from its holder. If Brianna had made the verbena-scented beeswax candle, he knew it would be imbued with her essence.

Wolf returned to his chamber, slipped the small candle into his saddlebag, and with Shadow at his side, made his silent way to the stables. *I must not dwell on the past—I will focus on the future. By first light I should be at Kenilworth.*

"Brianna!" Jory's face lit with delight at the sight of her daughter. She quickly descended the front steps of Warwick Castle. "This is such an unexpected surprise. Darling, I am so relieved you didn't go to Scotland."

Brianna allowed Simon Deveril to lift her from the saddle and waited until he led Venus across the courtyard toward the stables. "I can well understand your relief, but it will be short-lived." Her fists clenched and her dark eyes glittered with anger.

Jory was immediately wary. "Is something wrong?"

"Something is *very* wrong." Brianna raised her chin. "You have deliberately deceived me, allowing me to believe all these years that Guy de Beauchamp is my father, when in truth I am the bastard of Robert Bruce!"

Jory's hand flew to her heart. The secret she had guarded from Brianna all her life had been revealed. Her daughter's accusation, though true, sounded so ugly. "Where did you hear this?"

"At Hedingham. I overheard Lynx tell Jane my brown Celtic eyes are identical to Robert's and that he had often suspected the Bruce is my father."

The blood drained from Jory's face, leaving it waxy pale.

"Is it true?" Brianna cried. *Please tell me it isn't true.*

Jory bit her lip. "Yes, it's true," she whispered. "Guy de Beauchamp never—"

"Never wanted me? Ah, but he always wanted the beauteous Jory de Warenne and the only way he could get you was to take me too."

"Brianna, stop! It wasn't like that."

"It was exactly like that."

At the sound of horses entering the far end of the courtyard, Brianna turned. "Here comes the Infamous Earl of Warwick now."

Guy de Beauchamp, accompanied by his steward, dismounted and almost walked into a stack of barrels outside the brewery. Brutus barked and Guy's hand shot out to feel the barrier; then he stepped around it and patted his wolfhound's head.

Brianna drew in a swift breath. "What's the matter with Father?"

"It's his sight, I'm afraid. It's almost gone."

"Oh my God! Oh my God! Why didn't someone tell me?" Brianna lifted her skirts and ran across the courtyard. Her priorities in life underwent an instant transformation, and were rearranged in order of importance. "Father," she cried, breathlessly. She fiercely dashed the tears from her cheeks, so he would not discern that the sight of him had made her weep.

He held out his arms and she went into them eagerly. She saw the look of joy on his face as he embraced her and lifted her from the ground. "Brianna! You didn't go to Scotland."

"What the devil would induce me to go to that god-forsaken place, when I had a chance to come home to Warwick and visit you?"

He set her down and reached out to touch her hair

in wonder. "I can see the color of your fiery curls. That's amazing—I usually see only gray shadows." He cupped her face and gently traced her cheeks with his thumbs.

Brianna was weak with relief that she had wiped away her tears. *This is the man who lifted me onto my first pony. He taught me how to read and allowed me to tear pages from his precious books. He tutored me in the skills of horse breeding and ingrained in me a love of all animals. He gave me the confidence to be my own woman. He is the only father I will ever want, the only father I will ever need, the only father I will ever love.*

"I'm happy you came home for a visit."

She slipped her hand into his. "Father, I missed you so much."

The de Beauchamp family talked and laughed their way through the evening meal, thoroughly enjoying their precious time together. When the candles were lit, Warwick insisted he could see their faint glow, and it brought hope to their hearts.

Brianna promised to ride out with her father in the morning and asked Guy Thomas to take her fishing in their old skiff on the River Avon.

It was late when she retired to her bedchamber. Five minutes later, Jory knocked and opened her door. "May I come in?"

"Mother, I'm sorry for the things I said."

Jory closed the door and shook her head. "As soon as you were old enough to understand, I should have told you."

"Lord, I must be a sore trial to you sometimes," Brianna lamented.

"You've never given me a moment's distress since the day you were born. I'm sorry you had to learn about it from Lynx. I honestly believed Guy and I were the only two who knew. I never told Robert."

"I'm glad you didn't. And Lynx was only guessing. Jane told him he shouldn't say such things—lots of people have brown eyes."

"I forgot how shrewd Lynx is. There's little that escapes him."

"True. He always tells me I am exactly like you."

Jory laughed. "Like two peas from the same disgusting pod."

"Mother, I hope I am exactly like you. I have strived for that goal my entire life."

They embraced and stood holding each other for long minutes.

What a self-righteous wretch I am to condemn my mother for taking a lover, when I did the very same thing.

"I love you, Mother. You are so forgiving and understanding." *I long to confide in you that I intend to break my betrothal to Lincoln Robert, but I don't want to upset you, and especially not Father. Perhaps I'll find the right words before I return to Windsor.*

As Brianna readied herself for bed, thoughts of Wolf were so vivid, his presence felt tangible. When she looked in her mirror, her imagination conjured him standing behind her. She sighed wistfully. *I hope with all my heart that we can be together someday.*

Not long after she laid her head on her pillow, her wishes became reality, at least in her dream. She and Wolf rode together, swam together, lived, laughed, and loved together. In her sleep, a secret smile curved Brianna's lips.

Chapter 24

"Whoreson! Idiot-brained French frog!" King Edward flung down a letter he had received from King Charles of France. "Because I didn't rush to Paris at his command to pay homage for my French possessions, the avaricious swine has declared Gascony forfeit!" He thrust the offending letter at Hugh. "The only reason I wed his sister was to keep Gascony and Aquitaine!"

"You have the means for revenge at hand, Edward. Isabelle is his sister. Punish her and you punish the King of France."

"You are brilliant! Advise me. What shall I do?"

"Declare all the queen's estates forfeit and take them back in your own name. Sequester her dower lands in Cornwall with their valuable tin mines. The Crown allows her eleven thousand marks per annum for personal expenses—cut it to one thousand."

"Prepare the papers and I'll sign them," Edward directed.

"By Order of Parliament we must banish all subjects of the King of France from your household and that of the queen, and order them back to their own country."

Edward waved his hand. "Do it! You have the Royal Seal."

"We should immediately warn our English subjects in Gascony to arm themselves in the event Charles sends in an army to try to take possession."

Edward appointed his half brother, Edmund, Earl of Kent, as the Lieutenant of Gascony. In early September, he led the English who lived in Gascony in an attack on some masons who had begun to build a fortified town at Agenais and killed a French sergeant. The French people in general, and King Charles in particular, were outraged.

Roger Mortimer instantly offered his sword to the French king, offering to fight against King Edward's subjects in Gascony.

Charles sent a dispatch to Edward, demanding that he hand over the English subjects who had committed murder, and ordering him to come immediately to pay homage for his possessions in France.

When Edward learned that Charles was harboring the notorious traitor Mortimer, his Plantagenet rage was so great he frothed at the mouth. And bolstered by Despencer, he accused King Charles of assisting Mortimer in his escape. Edward refused to turn over the murderous culprits or travel to France to do homage.

King Charles immediately sent an army into Gascony and took possession of it.

Edward flung down the dispatch from the King of France, delivered by an English knight whom Charles had sent.

"Whoreson, scab-arsed baboon! This is an act of war!" Edward's outlet for anger was physical. He picked up a wooden chair and smashed it, then kicked the pieces across the room.

Hugh Despencer's response was cerebral and far more vicious. "Retaliation against the French is now justified. You must issue an order that any Frenchmen left in England be arrested, imprisoned, and their property confiscated."

*   *   *

"Your Grace, I beg you relieve me from your service." Arbella Beaumont clutched a letter from her mother, as tears streamed down her face. "My father has been arrested and thrown into prison."

Isabelle's face went white. "On what charges?"

"Mother says he refused to swear an oath of loyalty to Despencer, but she says the real reason is that Henry Beaumont is a friend of the queen. Forgive me, Your Grace."

"There is nothing to forgive. You must go home to your mother without delay. I'm sure your father's brother, the Bishop of Durham, will be outraged, as am I!"

Later that day, Queen Isabelle was officially informed that everything she owned in England had been sequestered and put into the king's name. She was also notified that her allowance from the Crown had been cut from eleven thousand marks to one thousand per annum. Isabelle demanded to see the king.

The following day Edward arrived at Windsor with Hugh Despencer. As Brianna had taught her, Isabelle arrayed herself in garments that befitted a queen and put on her jeweled coronet.

Being loved by Roger Mortimer had given the queen newfound confidence. Though her knees trembled, Isabelle held out the official paper and demanded in her most regal voice, "Sire, what is the meaning of this?"

"Your brother has sent his army into Gascony and taken possession of it. Gascony is mine! This is an act of war!"

"What does that have to do with rendering me a pauper?" she demanded with daring.

Despencer stepped forward. "Madam, you are a Frenchwoman. You are the enemy."

Isabelle gathered her courage. "I am indeed *your* enemy. I am the Queen of England. You will address me as *Your Grace.*"

Edward's eyes blazed. "Madam, you will not speak to my dearest friend with such wanton disrespect."

Isabelle lost control. "He is a prick licker!"

All the royal attendants in the chamber gasped.

Despencer hissed, "You, *madam*, will swear an oath of loyalty to me personally, here and now, or you will be treated as an enemy of the state."

Fury was the only thing that kept her knees from buckling. Isabelle raised her chin and drew herself up to her full height. "That I will never do. I will die first!"

Livid, Despencer turned on his heel and strode from the chamber. Edward followed him like a lackey and his royal attendants followed silently.

Isabelle sank down on a brocaded couch and Marguerite Wake brought her a cup of wine. "You were so brave to stand up to them, Your Grace," she said, wide-eyed.

Isabelle gave a shaky laugh. "I don't feel brave . . . I feel exceedingly vulnerable. With Arbella Beaumont gone, we need someone to bolster our ranks. I shall write to Brianna at Warwick and ask her to return to Windsor immediately."

Back at Westminster, Hugh Despencer paced the royal chamber silently raging with spleen, plotting his revenge. The retribution he inflicted on Isabelle must stab her to the heart. Edward trotted after him trying to placate his beloved.

Finally, Hugh stopped in his tracks; a thin smile hovered about his cruel mouth. "As a Frenchwoman, Isabelle could easily encourage her children to commit treason against you, their father. They will have to be removed from her custody immediately for the safety of the realm."

"Are you sure, Hugh? I love my children. I want no harm to come to them."

"It is precisely because you love them that they must be removed from the Frenchwoman's vile influence. They will be given into the care of my dear sister, Lady Monthermer, at Marlborough."

"I must return to Windsor without delay." Brianna handed her mother the letter that Queen Isabelle's messenger, John Sadington, had brought to Warwick.

"Hell's teeth, the hated Despencers did all this before when I was dismissed from court." Jory was filled with impotent rage that Isabelle was again being persecuted. "The Beaumont family has been friends of the queen since she was first wed to Edward. 'Tis pure vitriol that Henry has been imprisoned. Who will be next? Promise me you will be extremely careful, Brianna."

"The queen's lands have been taken from her and her allowance has been cut to a pittance. I know it is Hugh Despencer who is behind all this, but Isabelle blames Edward's weakness, and she is right. King Edward is the root of all her troubles."

"While you pack, I will get you money from your father. Feel free to use it on Isabelle's behalf if she becomes desperate."

"You are both so generous, and I know Isabelle appreciates it as much as I." Brianna hesitated. "There were so many things I wanted to talk about, but our time has been cut short."

"Write me a long letter, darling. By the time you return to Windsor, everything may have changed for the better."

"Taken your children?" Brianna was aghast to learn when she arrived back at Windsor Castle that things had changed for the worse. "I don't understand."

"Because my brother Charles marched into Gascony, Edward says it was an act of war. As a French-woman I am being treated as an enemy of the state. His malice toward me is unendurable."

"What about Prince Edward?"

"Thank heaven, he remains at Windsor. Because he has his own household, they do not fear my influence over him."

"Then they are bloody fools. Who could possibly have more influence than a loving mother?" Brianna asked. "Inform your son what has happened and ask him to make a formal protest to his father. He will be outraged when he learns his brother and sisters have been removed from your custody."

"I'm so glad you are back, Brianna. Your advice is invaluable and your presence bolsters my confidence."

"Have you written to King Charles about all this?"

"I was about to write him regarding my sequestered lands depriving me of my income, when this happened. It was such a vicious blow, I am still reeling from it."

"Write down everything, starting with the children. Tell him of your anguish. Inform him that you are being treated as an enemy of the state. Everything is being taken from you—your children, your income, your friends, and your husband's protection. You have lost your status as Queen of England. It has been reduced to that of maidservant. Be sure to tell him all Frenchmen are being arrested, imprisoned, and their property confiscated."

"I will do it now. We will ask Marie to smuggle it in one of her letters to France."

"No, no!" Brianna protested. "Marie is a French-woman. Her correspondence could easily be seized and examined. I will take your letter and pass it on to someone who can get it to France quickly and safely."

"Brianna, the risk is so great. How do you know we can trust this man?"

"Because the man is my brother, Rickard de Beauchamp. I trust him with my life. He is Roger Mortimer's friend and ally. I have never mentioned his name before, because it is best that none know he is in England."

That he was a friend of Roger Mortimer was enough for Isabelle. She sat down at her desk immediately and wrote her letter to her brother.

Brianna waited until nightfall, and then escorted by Simon Deveril she rode to Flamstead. She was disappointed that Rickard was not there, but a trusty Warwick man rode to the Abbey of Saint Albans where the Benedictine monks provided a safe meeting place for Rickard de Beauchamp and Adam Orleton, Bishop of Hereford.

The following day, Brianna was overjoyed when her brother rode into Flamstead. "Rickard, Queen Isabelle is in desperate need of your help. Because she is French, she is being treated as an enemy by the king. Her children have been taken away from her and placed in the custody of Hugh Despencer's sister at Marlborough. She has written a letter to her brother Charles, cataloguing her vicious treatment, and asks that it be delivered to the King of France."

Rickard took Brianna's hands and led her to a chair. "The queen is indeed fortunate to have such a loyal champion. Give me the letter and I will see that it is put directly into King Charles's hands. However, I want you to know that the King of France is being kept fully informed of all that has happened to his sister, as well as the other French people living in England. Orleton and the rest of the bishops know and they are in communication with the pope."

"Rickard, I am so relieved. Isabelle has done naught to deserve this cruel punishment."

"I know that a reprimand is on its way from the pope to Despencer condemning him for causing hatred between the King of England and the King of France. The papacy instigated the marriage of Edward and Isabelle to ensure peace between England and France. Now the two countries are on the verge of war and the pope will not countenance it."

"I had no idea of the extent of the communication. All those allied with Roger Mortimer are taking great risks."

"It is not solely for Roger that we risk all. It is for England and her people who are being persecuted. It is also for Prince Edward who is the heir to the throne. Mortimer is simply the catalyst—the only man strong enough to end the tyranny of Edward and Despencer. The King of France and the pope both recognize this."

"May I tell Isabelle the things you have told me?"

"Aye. You may also tell her that Roger Mortimer is working tirelessly to gather a great force." Rickard hesitated about telling his sister more, but then he relented. "There is something I'd rather you didn't divulge in case the plan doesn't come to fruition and Queen Isabelle is sorely disappointed. Roger and King Charles are working through diplomatic sources to get the queen to France."

"Thank you for confiding in me, Rickard. I swear Queen Isabelle will not hear it from me. You have reassured me that things are not as black as they seem. You have lifted a great deal of the heaviness from my heart."

Rickard embraced her. "I cannot stay. Look after yourself."

"Before you go, there's something I must tell you. I just returned from Warwick. Father could see the color of my hair, rather than just gray shadows, and the night before I left, he swore he could see the glow from the candles in the Great Hall."

"That's wonderful news. Wouldn't it be amazing if he regained part of his sight? You have lifted some of the heaviness from my heart. Godspeed, Brianna."

*   *   *

"Were you able to put my letter in safe hands?"
Isabelle had counted the hours until Brianna's return.

"Yes, I warrant it has already reached King Charles.
But I have amazing news. It seems that your brother
is being kept fully informed of all that happens to you
and to all the Frenchmen who live in England. Adam
Orleton has united most of the bishops and is corres-
ponding with the pope. His Holiness has sent a letter
of reprimand to Hugh Despencer for the way you are
being treated, because it causes strife between Edward
and Charles that could lead to war."

"That is encouraging, but it will take more than
a reprimand to make Despencer return my children
to me."

"Isabelle, if you can somehow endure what is unendurable for a little while, there are secret forces uniting to end the tyranny."

The sadness in the queen's sigh was palpable. "Yes,
I must keep hope alive in my heart. It is most gratify-
ing that the good people of England love me enough
to risk much on my behalf."

"I also have it on the best authority that Roger
Mortimer is working tirelessly to gather a great invasion force."

Isabelle's hand went to her heart. "He does it for
love of me. Love is the greatest force on earth. It can
move mountains."

Brianna thought of Wolf. *If only it were true.*

"Jesu Christus! Mortimer is in Hainault successfully
raising troops. The notorious traitor intends to invade
England!" Edward's hand shook as he set down the
letter that he'd received from his English envoy at the
French Court.

Hugh Despencer was busy reading an official letter
from the pontiff. "I am being accused of instigating
war between England and France. The whoreson pope

should be strung up by the balls! It is King Charles who is threatening war with England."

Edward almost shit himself as he suddenly realized the prospect of war with France was very real, and now he also faced the threat of invasion led by Mortimer. "I must write to William of Hainault and protest his harboring of the notorious traitor."

"That will do little good. Our relations with Hainault are nonexistent because of trade disputes."

Edward was in a panic. "I think we should burn these letters. I don't want the council to learn there is a threat of war."

King Charles and Pope John, however, made it their business to inform King Edward's Royal Council about the impending war.

The Royal Council held a meeting and an emergency Parliament was called to deal with the critical situation. Parliament decided that any expedient was preferable to the disaster of war. They urged Edward to go to France without delay and pay homage to King Charles for Gascony and Aquitaine to defuse the crisis.

It was now Hugh Despencer's turn to panic. "Edward, my dearest love, our enemies want you to desert me. The moment you cross the Channel, they will descend upon me and hack me to pieces! Promise you will not go and leave me unprotected?"

"Hugh, you are my entire world. I will never leave you. I will suggest that my brother Edmund pay homage in my stead."

The suggestion that the young Earl of Kent represent King Edward was immediately rejected. Moreover, they considered it an insult. Edmund had led the English in Gascony to take up arms against the French, thus alienating Charles and the country.

"Where the devil is Pembroke when I need him? What the hellfire can be taking so long in Scotland?

They've been gone over a month. There had better not be trouble brewing there too."

"You are the only man who ever beat me in wrestling." The laugh lines on the face of Robert Bruce deepened as he grinned openly at his old friend, Lynx de Warenne.

"You are being generous. I believe I only bested you twice." Lynx placed his hand at the small of his wife's back and urged her forward. "Here is Jane. She insists she always knew you would be King of Scotland."

Robert did not embrace Jane, but his face was wreathed with smiles as he gazed at her. "In spite of the fact that he made you the Countess of Surrey, you were always too good for him."

Lynx grinned. "Truer words were never uttered."

They were in a private chamber of the king's at Edinburgh Castle. The Earls of Pembroke, de Warenne, and Arundel had been received formally a few days before, but this was the first chance the two boyhood friends and Jane had been alone together.

Today, the Earl of Pembroke had taken to his bed, Arundel had returned to Leith to check on his ship, and it was clear that the peace negotiations would be worked out between Lynx and Robert.

"Congratulations on the birth of your son, Robert. I trust Elizabeth is well?" Jane had always been fond of his wife.

"Yes. She prefers to live at Holyrood Abbey, rather than this barren pile of stone. You must come to dinner tonight. Elizabeth is looking forward to showing off David."

"You chose a braw name for your son. I have a brother by the same name. I shall be going to Dumfries to visit my family."

"How I would love to travel with you and visit

Lochmaben. Alas, my duty keeps me in Edinburgh," Robert said ruefully. "Jane, why don't you go and visit Elizabeth now? I'll have you escorted down the hill to the abbey. As soon as your husband and I have thrashed out this truce, we will join you."

Once they were alone, Robert asked, "How many years' truce were you seeking?"

"What would you say to a dozen years?" Lynx asked cautiously.

"Done! In fact, let's make it a baker's dozen."

"Why would you agree to thirteen years?"

The Bruce began to laugh. "Why not? The bloody truce won't be worth the parchment it's written on. I can dishonor it any time I fancy. But if you return with a truce signed for thirteen years it will put that degenerate weakling you call king in your debt."

Lynx laughed. "You always were a wily swine, Robert. I warrant that's what it takes to rule the Scots."

"We'll have the truce drawn up and I'll sign it before you and Jane leave for Dumfries. Will my namesake, Lincoln Robert, be joining us tonight?"

"Aye. Since my elder son was born in Scotland, I brought him to see his native land. Arundel brought his daughter, Blanche."

"Are they betrothed?"

"No. Lincoln Robert is betrothed to Brianna de Beauchamp. They are to be wed when we return."

"Jory's daughter." A faraway look came into Robert's dark brown Celtic eyes. "I warrant she is a rare beauty."

Chapter 25

"I have messages for you." Brianna entered Isabelle's private chamber and found the queen sitting at her desk writing letters to her children at Marlborough Castle. Brianna had ridden out early on the October morning and Simon Deveril had passed the verbal messages he'd been given by Rickard de Beauchamp.

"Are they messages of hope?" Isabelle could not dispel the aura of sadness that clung about her.

"Yes, indeed. The pope has written to Edward with the suggestion that he send you to France to mediate for peace with your brother Charles. It seems the only solution to avert war and settle the dispute over Gascony."

"Oh, Brianna, do I dare to hope? Without money or status or my children, Windsor has become a prison to me. You have no idea how I long to escape to France. The thought of being with Roger again has lately seemed like an impossible dream."

"The king and Despencer will likely refuse outright, but there are political and religious powers that will put pressure on Edward to agree to this solution."

"It cannot come soon enough for me," she declared passionately.

"If and when Edward and Despencer approach you on the matter, I advise you not to seem eager. If you appear too keen they may become suspicious of your motives. First show a little reluctance and then indifference. Let them think they must persuade you. Then appear to be resigned and accept it as a duty."

"That's shrewd advice, Brianna."

"I hope it is. Despencer will be providing Edward with shrewd advice, so we must outwit them."

Fortunately for Isabelle, Pope John also sent his suggestions to the English Parliament and they debated the matter at once and concluded it was a sensible solution.

Despencer knew he had made a bitter enemy of the queen and feared she would plot against him if she was sent to France. Parliament pressured Edward and his favorite, and then the Bishop of Norwich and the Bishop of Winchester intervened.

They said that the King of France had promised that if the King of England would create his son Duke of Aquitaine and send him to France with the queen, then Charles would restore all the lands he had taken. Hugh Despencer's father persuaded his son that this was an offer that must not be refused.

When Isabelle was approached she told them she could not leave her children in England while she went to France. When told that Prince Edward would also be sent to France, she agreed to consider the idea. She tried to bargain, saying she would go if her lands and castles were returned to her. Edward and Despencer came back with a counteroffer saying her status as Queen of England would be restored and as ambassador, she would go to France with full royal accoutrements.

"Brianna, I cannot believe it! They are going to let not only *me* go, but my son also. I hid my fury and my hatred for Edward so well that he truly believes I will be a loyal wife and uphold his interests. His stupidity borders on insanity!"

"That Edward is eager for you to go proves that he and the vicious Despencer were lying when they accused you of being an enemy of the state."

"I have so many people to thank for making this possible."

"My brother, Mortimer's sons, and Adam Orleton have been working tirelessly, uniting a secret opposition party of barons and bishops to support you and your son, Prince Edward. They won't stop when you leave—they will only become more diligent."

"They are all allies of Mortimer. I have Roger to thank for this. I am so excited, I can hardly breathe. I wish you were going with me. It would make everything quite perfect."

"Well, at least I will be here to help you ready a spectacular wardrobe and help with all the other preparations for your visit."

"My very lo-oo-ng visit. I'm sorry I will miss your wedding, Brianna."

There will be no wedding. I dare not tell you or I would find myself on a ship to France. "Don't think about me. Think about seeing your brother again and showing off your handsome son to the French. Think of how you will be feted and fawned upon in Paris. Think about your reunion with Roger. You must make up for seventeen years of being without love."

Isabelle's eyes became dreamy. "Roger Mortimer could do that for me in one night."

These Mortimer men are the very devil.

"At last it is official. I am to travel in state with a retinue of thirty people. Edward has issued letters of protection for everyone in my train, and my brother Charles has sent me a safe conduct."

Brianna rolled her eyes. "The king wants to show your brother that you travel as befits a queen, but most of these people are loyal to Edward and have likely been included so they can spy on you. I suggest you object to some names on the list and substitute a few who are loyal to you."

"I want Lady Marguerite to come and I'd also like her father, Lord John Wake, who has always been a loyal member of my household. I surely don't want Reynolds, the Archbishop of Canterbury, who was responsible for bringing back Despencer."

"Substitute the Bishop of Norwich and the Bishop of Winchester. You are in a position of power, Isabelle."

"I'll do it! 'Tis obvious Edward doesn't want to displease me. He is sending my former treasurer, William de Boudon, and has given him a thousand pounds from the Exchequer for my expenses." Isabelle turned to Marie, who had just arrived. "I am certain you would enjoy a visit to Paris. Shall I add your name to the list?"

"I would truly love it, but I've just received a message from Pembroke. His health is deteriorating and when he returns from Scotland, I must try to nurse him back to health."

Brianna caught her breath. *Perhaps Marie has news of when the de Warennes will be returning.* "When do you expect him back?"

"Apparently, Robert Bruce signed the truce, and then the Earl of Surrey took his wife to visit her home in the Scottish Borders and Arundel's daughter went with them. They rejoined Arundel's ship at Newcastle and my husband says he should arrive in London in a couple of days. After he sees the king, he hopes to be able to go home to Surrey by the first day of November."

"You won't have long to wait. November will be

here in a week," Brianna said, knowing she must travel to Hedingham as soon as possible after Lincoln Robert returned home.

"I hope to be in Dover by then," Isabelle said. "Give Pembroke my love, Marie, and tell him to rest and get his health back."

The next week melted away and before they knew it, it was time for Isabelle to make her departure. The night before she left, the queen spoke privately to Brianna in her bedchamber. "Since Edward and Despencer insist on accompanying me to Dover, we won't have a chance to say anything confidential in the morning."

"Then I shall say my good-byes now. A new chapter is beginning for you, Isabelle. I warrant it will be the most important time of your life. I am so happy you have grown strong and confident."

"Yes. My time has finally come and I am ready. Edward and Despencer have sown the seeds of their own destruction."

All things come at their appointed time. Isabelle's vengeance will be justified. "I will write to you in Paris and let you know what is happening in England."

"Yes, I can trust you to tell me the truth. I will write to you also, Brianna. Shall I send the letters to Hedingham or to your castle at Farnham?"

"It will be far safer to send your letters to Flamstead. That way they will not fall into the wrong hands. I love you, Isabelle." Brianna embraced the queen. "Go with God."

The day after Isabelle left Windsor, Brianna spoke with Simon Deveril. "I have begun to pack. Tomorrow we will go to Flamstead. The de Warennes have returned home from Scotland, so we must go to Hedingham without delay."

"Very good, Lady Brianna, I will be ready."

"Simon, I haven't told anyone except Lincoln Robert, but I intend to break my betrothal when we go to Hedingham. I wanted to do it months ago, but he persuaded me to wait until Jane had enjoyed her visit to Dumfries."

"Do your own parents know?"

Brianna shook her head with regret. "I had every intention of telling them before I left Warwick, but then I got the urgent letter from the queen to come back to Windsor, and somehow I couldn't find the right words."

"They will understand that your heart lies elsewhere."

"Hell and Furies, am I so transparent?"

"Like calls to like. You and Wolf Mortimer have the same indomitable spirit."

The following morning before Brianna left Windsor, she received a letter from her mother telling her that they were leaving Warwick for Flamstead to make preparations for the wedding. Brianna felt more than a twinge of guilt that they would have the journey for nothing. *Father loves Flamstead. He will be eager to be with his beloved horses.* Her brows drew together in consternation. *Don't excuse yourself. He won't be eager to hear the news of your broken betrothal.*

That same afternoon Brianna, riding Venus, and Simon Deveril, leading a packhorse with her baggage, left Windsor for Flamstead. The autumn weather was still glorious. The trees had turned vivid yellow, orange, and red, and the leaves had begun to float to the ground and create a rustling carpet for their horses' hooves.

Brianna unpacked and retired early, and she spent the following day reuniting with all the equines at Flamstead, most of which had been bred there. She created names for the dozen colts that had been born in the spring. She talked endlessly with the horse handlers about winter fodder, broodmares, and cures for various ailments. Realization dawned that she much preferred life at Flamstead to being at the Queen's Court of Windsor. *A year was long enough to be a lady-in-waiting and get it out of my system.*

That night as she readied for bed, she decided that tomorrow she must go to Hedingham and face the music. If she waited any longer her mother and father would be arriving, and in all conscience she owed it to Jane and Lynx to tell them first. When she blew out the candles and got into bed, her thoughts drifted to Isabelle and her reunion with Roger Mortimer. She smiled into the darkness. *It will be one of the happiest times of her life and she deserves to enjoy every moment of it.*

"When I saw you this morning, my heart stopped. When you did not greet me, Roger, I thought I would die of unhappiness."

"Isabelle, beloved, my heart pounded like a sledgehammer." He took her hand and drew it to his chest. "Feel—it's still at it." He captured her lips and a dozen fevered kisses followed before he withdrew his mouth and explained things to her.

"We must be discreet at all costs. Your reputation must be unsullied, Isabelle. If fate had not conspired, I could not even be here in Paris. I've been in Hainault with the count, who is helping me raise troops for the invasion of England. Your cousin, the Countess of Hainault's father, has just died and I escorted her to Paris for his funeral."

"Roger, I don't want to be discreet, I want to shout to the entire world that I love you!"

Roger threw back his head and laughed. "Little wanton. I know what you need . . . what we both need. The time is not for talking, but for loving. Let me undress you."

"Yes, please. Hurry, I am starving for you."

Roger Mortimer was an accomplished lover and he knew there was no need to waste time on foreplay with Isabelle tonight. It would have been cruel to prolong the anticipation. Her eager hands helped with her disrobing, and then he swiftly stripped off his own clothes. He swept her up in his arms and carried her to the bed, where he unleashed the fierce desire that had been riding him for months.

Isabelle was so aroused she began to bite him and left a row of teeth marks along his shoulder. When he brought her to her first climax, she screamed over her release. Her sexual relief was so great she began to sob and covered his heart with her tears.

He held her possessively. "You are *my* woman, Isabelle. I will never allow you to go back to Edward."

Isabelle thrilled to his dominance, his assertiveness, and his strength. Roger Mortimer was the only man she would ever love.

They mated a second time before he began to talk and tell her the things she must do and the things she needed to know. He was shrewd enough to keep part of himself from her while demanding that she yield all. That way, the beauteous Queen of England would always do his bidding.

"Your reputation must not be despoiled by the vile sin of adultery, Isabelle. We must never flaunt our relationship. The people love you and we must do nothing to tarnish that love."

"I feel we commit no sin in the eyes of God, Roger."

"Perhaps not, but in the eyes of the Church and State our sin would be considered abominable."

Isabelle sighed. "I will try to be discreet."

"In public, we must be formal with each other at all times. I want you to accept the offer of an alliance with Hainault. It is a prosperous country that will give England trading advantages."

"I am sure that Charles will also help us."

"He has assured me that he will, but he cannot do it openly. Invading England with a French army would lose you the support of the English. Charles will form a secret alliance with Hainault to mount a joint invasion of England. In diplomatic negotiations you must pretend that your goal is to remove only the Despencers. Vengeance against your husband would risk society's condemnation."

"I feel only revulsion for him," she said passionately.

"My love, we have both been victims of his evil malice."

"He took everything from you and forced you into exile."

"He did the same to you, but never fear, Isabelle, I shall restore us both to greatness."

"You have all my trust as well as all my love, Roger."

"There are many English exiles here in France. They are all enemies of Edward and Despencer, who have scores to settle. You will attract them like a lodestone. They will surround and support you. The moment Henry Beaumont was released from prison he came to France."

"Henry has always been loyal to me, and I have the allegiance of the Earl of Richmond, who came to France with me."

"I have already won over Edward's half brother, the Earl of Kent. He wants to wed your lady-in-waiting, Marguerite Wake, who happens to be a cousin of mine."

"I didn't realize Lord Wake was related to you."

"The Mortimers are connected, one way or another, to most noble families in England."

"I doubt that is coincidental."

Roger laughed, pleased that she recognized his shrewdness. " 'Tis the result of careful planning." He brushed the pale strands of disheveled hair from her forehead and kissed her deeply. "I have no idea when we will have the opportunity to be together again, Isabelle, but remember that the bond we have forged can never be broken."

She clung to him fervently, secure in his strength, his powerful determination, and his love.

"Simon, I truly appreciate your vigilance in looking out for me this past year. I'm sure you would have preferred Warwick." Brianna and her escort were almost at Hedingham.

"Being at a royal castle broadened my knowledge of human nature, as I'm sure it did for you, Lady Brianna."

"Indeed. Oh dear, we are almost there. I wish I didn't have to hurt the people I love. Jane has always been so good to me, and Lincoln Robert is loath to break our betrothal."

Deveril kept a wise silence as they rode into Hedingham Castle's courtyard. He helped Brianna from the saddle and took the horses to the stables.

Brianna was surprised to see Lincoln Robert appear from nowhere, almost as if he had been watching for her. She girded herself for her betrothed's protestations.

"I'm glad you're here. There's something important I want to ask you. Let's walk to the orchard where we can talk in private."

If you ask me to marry you one more time, I will scream. Brianna pulled her cloak about her to keep warm, yet knew it was a defensive gesture. "I hope you enjoyed Scotland."

"I had a marvelous time." Lincoln took a deep breath. "Brianna, I want you to speak up immediately and tell my parents that you have decided to end the betrothal."

"I am glad you have come to terms with it. It's best to get it over and done as soon as possible, I warrant." She held out the betrothal ring.

He took the ring. "Yes, that is best. I have proposed to Blanche FitzAlan and she has agreed to marry me."

Brianna's mouth fell open.

"It would embarrass you if I cried off. I'd rather play the gentleman and tell my parents *you* wish to break it off."

"A gentleman indeed. Do you know, Lincoln Robert, I believe you and the Earl of Arundel's daughter were made for each other." *A bloody match made in heaven and here's me feeling guilty as sin.* Brianna didn't know whether to laugh or to cry and suspected before the day was over, she would probably do both.

Brianna gave Lincoln credit for escorting her into the castle. She thought he might bolt at any moment and leave her to it.

Jane greeted her with her usual warm enthusiasm. "Brianna, how I wish you had been with us when I visited my family at Dumfries."

Brianna listened attentively as Jane described her great adventure in detail. When Jane was done, Brianna said with sincerity, "I'm glad you had a marvelous time. You truly deserved it after waiting all those years."

When Lynx joined them in the solar, Brianna was relieved that she could deliver the news to both at the same time, yet was slightly intimidated by his grave air of authority.

"I congratulate you on negotiating the peace treaty between England and Scotland. I won't plague you for details, since you likely consider it *men's affairs*."

Lynx's mouth quirked with amusement, which vanished the moment Brianna made her announcement.

"Jane . . . Lynx . . . I have something to tell you. I am asking you to release me from my betrothal to Lincoln Robert."

"Oh, Brianna, is it because of Rose?" Jane asked with concern.

"Rose?" she asked blankly. *Oh my God, Lincoln Robert is the father of Rose's child!* "No, no, I assure you it has nothing to do with that. I have come to realize that what I feel for Lincoln is the love of a cousin, not of a wife."

Brianna could see that both Jane and Lynx were trying to understand what she was attempting to convey. They stared at their son, but he remained silent. "I made the decision before you went to Scotland, but Lincoln begged me not to speak of it until you returned. And in all conscience, Jane, I realized it would be cruel to spoil your visit."

"Are you sure about this, Brianna?" Jane asked quietly.

Brianna nodded. "I think the idea of becoming your daughter and being part of your family appealed to me more than becoming Lincoln's wife. It would be completely unfair of me to marry him when I feel this way."

Lynx stared at his son. "Don't you have anything to say?"

"I am in complete agreement with Brianna."

"Thank you, Lincoln." She could not keep the irony from her voice.

"What about Jory and Guy? Do they know about this?"

"No, Jane. They are on their way to Flamstead to make preparations for the wedding. I thought I should tell you first."

"There will be a wedding," Lincoln Robert blurted. "I've asked the Earl of Arundel's daughter to marry me."

"Blanche FitzAlan?" Jane sounded mystified.

"I see," Lynx said dryly.

"Please don't hate me," Brianna said softly.

"We love you . . . We could never hate you, darling," Jane said.

"Broken off your betrothal to Lincoln Robert? Jane and Lynx will hate you, Brianna. What maggot has gotten into your brain?" Jory stared at her daughter as if she had lost her senses.

"Lincoln and I were childhood friends. I love him like a cousin and that isn't nearly enough for me."

"It's a simple case of wedding nerves. I'll speak with Jane and Lynx and smooth everything over."

"Jory, you are not *listening* to her," Warwick declared.

Jory took a deep breath and smiled at her daughter. "I'm sorry, Brianna. Tell me everything."

"The young devil has thrown her over and she is trying to put a brave face on it," Guy de Beauchamp said to his wife when they retired to bed that night.

"Throw over Brianna for Blanche FitzAlan? You must be mad."

"The Mad Hound of Arden—I've been called that before."

"I think our daughter is enamored of someone else," Jory said.

"Enamored? To be determined enough to break off her betrothal, she must have experienced the *grand passion*."

"How exciting! I wonder who it could be."

"Don't pry. She'll tell you when she is ready."

"Me, pry? Wherever do you get such notions?"

Warwick bit his tongue and pulled her into his arms.

Chapter 26

"I will never forgive Edward for executing my brother," Henry Plantagenet declared to Wolf Mortimer. "Our father was a royal prince and Edward our cousin. I will not be avenged until he is dethroned."

"Thomas's murder will be avenged with Despencer's blood. My father is raising men to invade England, and once they arrive, we'll need your support to remove Edward from the throne." Wolf Mortimer gazed about the Great Hall, thinking of the momentous events that had happened since he was last at Kenilworth.

"Once they land I hereby pledge my unconditional support."

Wolf, determined to make Henry keep his pledge, held out the infallible bait. "If young Prince Edward is crowned King of England, you, as highest noble in the land, will be his official guardian."

Used to being deprived of any royal prerogatives, Henry had not aspired to such heady heights. "I am your ally—I swear it!"

"Before the month is over, I intend to visit Lincoln Castle, which legally should be yours."

"It was appropriated by Despencer. You take a great risk."

"I wager the castle keepers of Lincoln will not be loyal to the hated Hugh Despencer."

Wolf stayed at Kenilworth for a few days, enjoying Henry's hospitality; then he departed and rode to the City of Chester. Chester Castle had been used for over a century by the Marcher lords and by England's barons to mount raids into Wales, and Wolf knew that the Earl of Chester had always been a staunch ally of the Mortimers, and would need little persuasion to back them now.

Wolf, in Chester Castle's map room, pointed out the earls and barons who had pledged to a secret alliance with the Mortimers.

"You have wrought a miracle, uniting so many," Chester declared with approval.

"All are angered by this hateful regime and have endured Edward and Despencer's evil overlong. They are desperate for a strong leader willing to take up arms."

"November arrived with a vengeance in these parts. Allow me to offer you the hospitality of Chester Castle."

"I appreciate your generosity, my lord earl, but I am on my way to Lincoln and warrant I had better set out before the winter weather worsens."

"I understand that Despencer now owns Lincoln Castle. I advise you to break your journey at Bolsover Castle. At least you will receive a warm reception there."

Wolf's secret visit to Lincoln Castle proved worthwhile. When he departed and rode south, the late November weather was much improved and when he arrived at Cambridge, it had turned mild.

He met up with the de Bohun brothers, who told him that the Earl of Surrey had returned from Scotland and had successfully negotiated a truce with Robert Bruce for King Edward.

"Lynx de Warenne is not a known king's man," Wolf stated, "but he and the Bruce were childhood friends. No doubt Edward took advantage of that when he pressed him into service. Since Hedingham is only a few miles from here, I shall ride over and recruit de Warenne to our cause."

"De Warenne's heir was wed yesterday. Most likely the celebrations will last for days. You can join the revelry."

Humphrey de Bohun's words pierced the iron carapace Wolf Mortimer wore to shield his emotions. He abruptly excused himself from their company, mounted his horse, and rode into the countryside. His senses were drenched with Brianna and he knew physical exertion was the only antidote.

Just before the afternoon light faded, he spotted a small boat. He dismounted, tethered Drago to a tree, and with Shadow sitting before him, Wolf rowed out into the Cambridge Fens.

"She married him!" Shock was followed by anger. When he finally worked off his fury, Wolf felt bereft.

Shadow watched him closely; her ears lay flat against her head.

Wolf rested the oars, and stared off into the darkness. He wondered when night had fallen.

"Fuck it all. I've done everything I can for the cause. Tomorrow we'll go home to the Welsh Borders. I've had enough of these *civilized* English ladies and gentlemen."

Shadow howled her approval.

"That was quick. I shall refrain from using the word unseemly." Jory handed Brianna the letter from Jane telling them that Lincoln Robert had wed Blanche FitzAlan. She watched her daughter's face closely to gauge her reaction. When she discerned neither sorrow nor joy, she prompted, "What do you think?"

"I think that Lincoln Robert will be far happier with Blanche than with me. She is younger than I and, I wager, a good deal more amenable than I would ever be. At the same time, she fulfills Lincoln's first priority for a wife—she is the daughter of a noble Earl of the Realm."

"That's rather cynical, darling."

"Yes, I am sometimes cynical . . . shocking in a female who is about to celebrate her eighteenth birthday." Brianna's mouth curved slightly. "I recall once telling someone about my betrothal to Lincoln Robert and they said, *Poor lad. You will ride roughshod over him.* An astute observation, don't you think?"

"And who was this *someone*?"

Brianna smiled her secret smile. "I forget."

"You certainly have a convenient memory," her mother teased. Then she surprised a haunting, wistful look on her daughter's face that told her Brianna had memories and hidden depths that were fathomless.

"You know me well because we are so alike."

"Well, we may not be having a wedding, but we shall certainly celebrate your birthday, and then we'll stay and celebrate Christmas at Flamstead. We shall be festive and rejoice and carry on inordinately. What do you think?"

"I think it's time you stopped worrying about me."

"What are we giving Brianna for her birthday?"

Guy de Beauchamp knew immediately what would please his daughter most. "A new palfrey. There is a sleek black yearling, part Arabian, that runs like the wind. It would suit her to perfection."

"An excellent choice. And I think I'll give her one of my emeralds, since she gave back her betrothal ring."

"That's both generous and selfless, Jory, but then you need no jewels to enhance your beauty."

"Flattery will get you nowhere, you infamous devil."

"On the contrary, it always gets me exactly what I want." His possessive hand unerringly found her bottom.

"I believe it might snow soon. Why don't you use up some of that sexual energy and refurbish the sleigh that we keep in the stables? Nothing is more romantic than a ride in the snow."

Wolf Mortimer arose at dawn and packed his saddlebags. The air was no longer mild and had a decidedly sharp nip to it today. He needed an early start for his journey to the Welsh Borders, where winter arrived early. He fed his horse, and suddenly felt remorseful. The qualities he prided himself on, courage and loyalty, would be compromised if he deserted the Mortimer cause. He thought of the sacrifices his father had made, and the even greater sacrifice of Mortimer of Chirk. Before he had finished saddling Drago, Wolf knew he would ride to Hedingham and try to recruit the de Warennes.

Wolf was in no hurry as he rode the twenty-odd miles from Cambridge. He had little desire to see the bride. By the time he rode into Hedingham Castle's courtyard, his fists were unclenched, his face was impassive, and he was focused on his mission.

At the stables Lynx de Warenne greeted him warmly, and he turned Drago and Shadow over to Taffy, Lynx's squire, for safekeeping.

"Congratulations on negotiating a truce with Scotland, Lord Surrey."

"Thank you, Mortimer. News travels swiftly. I salute your father for escaping the Tower. He is the first man in history to accomplish the feat."

"My father is a resolute man when he puts his mind to it. On that head I'd like to speak with you in private, my lord."

"You don't mind if I include my son, Lincoln Robert? He is newly wed and will soon command a de Warenne force of his own."

Wolf felt his back stiffen and forced himself to relax.

"Here comes the groom now," Lynx declared.

"Congratulations," Wolf said woodenly.

Lincoln grinned. "My head is still splitting from the celebration."

"Let's go into the castle, the wind is bitter today."

Bitter was exactly the way he felt today, Wolf realized.

In the hall Lynx stopped long enough to serve his guest mulled ale, and then the three men went into the small library.

With an iron will that forbade his mind to wander, Wolf told the de Warennes how many earls and barons had secretly pledged to support an invading army led by Roger Mortimer to remove Edward and Despencer. "Warwick is an ally. His son will lead his men."

"Guy Thomas is little more than a boy," Lincoln Robert protested.

Wolf did not say he had meant Warwick's heir, Rickard de Beauchamp. "Guy Thomas acquitted himself well when we took back the Despencer holdings in Wales." He felt smug satisfaction when the bridegroom flushed.

Lynx de Warenne said matter-of-factly, "We will stand with you when the time comes. Keep in mind, however, that an invasion could render the truce with Scotland null and void."

Wolf saw immediately that he was right. The most expedient strategy to invade a country was when another enemy was invading it. "Thank you. I *will* keep that in mind."

"Let me extend Hedingham's hospitality. We've just celebrated a wedding, so we are still feasting."

"That is most generous, but I must decline," Wolf said firmly.

As they left the library and headed back to the Great Hall, a fair-haired young lady appeared.

"Permit me to introduce my bride," Lincoln said proudly. "Blanche FitzAlan is the Earl of Arundel's daughter."

Wolf stared hard at the female, hoping his eyes were not deceiving him. She stepped timidly behind her new husband, as if she needed protection from the dark, fierce Welshman.

Wolf did not kiss her hand, fearing she would faint if he actually touched her, but his gallantry came to the fore. He bowed gravely. "I wish you every happiness, my lady."

Inside, Wolf did not feel grave, he felt elated. *Brianna broke off the betrothal!*

In the stables, he thanked Taffy for taking care of his horse and his wolf. He rode off in silence, keeping his jubilation inside until he was off de Warenne property; then he let out a whoop of joy. "Shadow, she didn't marry him!"

Shadow looked up and grinned.

Wolf no longer noticed the bitter wind. He was so absorbed in his thoughts that he rode rather aimlessly, with no destination in mind. When he stopped for food at Great Dunmow, he realized he was heading west and if he kept going he would reach Saint Albans before nightfall.

He arrived at the Benedictine monastery at twilight. He stabled his horse and asked if either Adam Orleton or Rickard de Beauchamp were now at the abbey and learned they were not. The abbot assigned him a spartan room with a small window and whitewashed walls. He put his saddlebags on the bed and poured water for Shadow.

Though Wolf Mortimer was not a particularly reli-

gious man, he was deeply spiritual and he suddenly
had the urge to give thanks for his good fortune. He
bade Shadow stay and made his way to the abbey. He
walked down the long nave, slid into a pew, went
down on his knees, and bowed his head.

Prayers, he had been taught, were supposed to be
sober and said with reverence. Wolf, however, found
it impossible to be somber or even staid. Truth be
told, he felt exultant. *Hallelujah!*

"She is absolutely beautiful! You couldn't have chosen a better birthday gift." Brianna realized it was her
father's idea, and the sleek, black palfrey was his
choice. *She has the same bloodline as Wolf's horse.
Drago would make a perfect mate for her.* A lump
came into her throat and she dutifully pushed away
wistful thoughts that would make her melancholy. Her
loving parents did not deserve to see their daughter
moping about in a pensive mood on her birthday. "I
shall give her the name of a goddess, as I did with
Venus. What do you think of Athena?"

"The Greek goddess of wisdom—I like it," Warwick declared.

"Ah," Jory teased, "and here's me thinking Venus
was named for a heavenly body."

"All goddesses have heavenly bodies," Warwick
jested.

"I think I'll take her for a gallop. Will you join me?"

"Yes, but since it snowed this morning, I'd prefer a
sleigh ride. Guy, have the horses harnessed and we'll
follow Brianna's lead," Jory suggested.

"Will you trust me to drive?" Guy asked his wife.

"I have more good sense than to trust you in any
way, but risk adds to the enjoyment."

"Actually, the brightness of the snow aids my vision,
but I'll do something risqué to give you enjoyment,"
he promised with a wink.

"Men!" Jory rolled her eyes. "They always have their minds on one thing."

"I'll saddle Athena." *They are still in love after all these years. Mother fell in love with Guy when she was my age, but had to wait five years before they could be married.* Brianna sighed. *Dear God, I don't want to wait that long.*

Brianna enjoyed her gallop on Athena, but observing her parents' intimacy on the sleigh ride emphasized her longing for Wolf. Seeing her mother cuddle up close to the man she loved made Brianna crave the warmth of Wolf's powerful arms. The laughter they shared ignited a fiery hunger in her belly.

That night, after the evening meal, Jory presented her daughter with one of her coveted heavy gold chains from which hung a huge cabochon emerald. It could be worn around the neck or the waist. The dangling jewel was designed to be provocative, either lying in the cleft between the breasts, or worn lower to decorate the mons.

"Mother, I never expected anything like this. I know how precious your emeralds are to you." Since she wore the wolf touchstone about her neck, she fastened the chain about her waist.

"Unexpected gifts bring the most pleasure."

Warwick stood, lifted his goblet, and addressed all the people of Flamstead. "Join me in a toast to my beautiful daughter who turned eighteen today. Someday she will be the chatelaine of this castle. Brianna has brought me joy every day of my life."

"Hear! Hear!" The shouts went up around the hall and Brianna blushed prettily at the near adulation in their voices.

She got to her feet and replied to the toast. "Thank you. Flamstead and all its people hold a special place in my heart. You surround me with love. There is nowhere I would rather be on my birthday than here with you."

The horsemen banged their knife handles on the trestle tables to show their approval.

It was late when the de Beauchamps retired. Brianna kissed her parents good night and when she closed her bedchamber door, the solitary atmosphere was in high contrast to the one that had pervaded in the Great Hall tonight.

Perhaps because it was her birthday, perhaps because her wedding had been canceled, perhaps because her parents had such a loving relationship, tonight her heart ached unbearably for Wolf.

She lit the candles, lifted off her touchstone, and gazed at it with a tremulous longing. "Come to me, Wolf. Please come to me."

Wolf Mortimer sat on the narrow bed in the cell-like room at Saint Albans Abbey, staring at the blank, whitewashed wall. He was happy tonight and felt receptive to what the future held.

Gradually, a vision formed before him like a play unfolding upon a stage: *He saw a huge fleet of ships make anchor on the Suffolk coast. Queen Isabelle and Roger Mortimer were met and made welcome by the king's half brother, Thomas, Earl of Norfolk. Wolf recognized a score of earls and barons who had pledged their support, and relief swept over him that they had kept their word.*

The scene changed to the City of Cambridge, where Adam Orleton, Bishop of Hereford, acted as spokesman for all the other bishops who had gathered to assure Queen Isabelle and Mortimer of the rightness of their cause. Wolf saw that his father commanded a force of only seven hundred and was amazed at his courage, invading England with so few men. Mortimer's instinct had been correct. The people flocked to support their queen, Isabelle the Fair, whom they had always loved, and Mortimer's army now swelled to two thousand.

Again the vision changed. *Wolf watched a horrific scene where Hugh Despencer was castrated, his heart cut out and thrown into a fire. Then his body was hacked to pieces by a vengeful crowd.*

As if by magic the scene changed once again. *Henry Plantagenet, Earl of Leicester, knighted young Prince Edward, and then the prince was crowned King of England and the Great Seal delivered into his hands. At the coronation, Roger Mortimer's vast landholdings and castles were returned to him, and he was made the Justicier of Wales for life.*

Mortimer rewarded his son Wolf by giving him all of Mortimer of Chirk's estates and possessions.

Wolf surged to his feet, astonished at his good fortune. His vision faded and disappeared, and once again he found himself staring at the blank white-washed wall of his cell-like room.

He was absolutely convinced that he had seen the future. He had been given no indication when these events would come about, nor any hint of the time between when the ships anchored and when he would be endowed with his uncle of Chirk's landholdings. He was certain, however, that these things would come to pass.

Wolf was immensely proud that his father was the catalyst that would bring about these beneficial changes for England and her nobles. *Roger Mortimer is fulfilling his destiny.*

His heart swelled with joy that he now had the chance to fulfill his own destiny. He closed his eyes and a picture of Brianna came to him full-blown. "Brianna Mortimer!"

Wolf opened his eyes and realized that he was faced with a dilemma. He spoke to Shadow. "Where is she? She certainly isn't at Hedingham. Her mother told me she had gone to Scotland. Did she remain in Scotland or did she ever go there?"

Shadow didn't seem to know the answer.

"Brianna would not remain at Windsor after the queen left. Did she decide to join Isabelle in France? Perhaps she went home to Warwick. That seems a logical choice."

Shadow cocked her head to one side as if to say, "You're the one with the second sight."

"You're right." Wolf opened his saddlebags and began to search. At the bottom, he found what he was looking for. He lifted out the candle he had taken from Brianna's bedchamber when he had visited Warwick Castle.

He replaced the tallow candle, in the pewter candlestick that was on the bedside table, with the perfumed one that belonged to his beloved. When he lit it, the lemon scent of verbena spiraled into the air about him, evoking haunting memories.

Wolf sat down on the bed and stared into the flame. Almost at once he saw her. She too was sitting on a bed, gazing at something she held in her hands. He realized it was her mystic touchstone painted with the image of a wolf that looked identical to Shadow. He breathed deeply and his senses became drenched with her. He realized that it was her birthday and heard the sound of her voice faintly as if from a long distance. *Come to me, Wolf.*

He still had no idea where Brianna was. He knew his spirit could walk two paths—one in the physical world and one in the supernatural. He could transcend beyond what was perceptible to the five senses and, with his sixth sense, could conjure real imagery. His inner eye drew back from Brianna's chamber to give him an overview of her surroundings. He saw pastures and an abundance of horses. "She's at Flamstead!" he cried.

Shadow grinned happily. *We're going on a night ride!*

Chapter 27

"Come to me, Wolf. Please come to me." Brianna whispered the words. Her longing for him came from her soul.

There was an ancient custom that said you could make a wish on your birthday, and if you didn't reveal the wish to anyone, it would be granted. Brianna closed her eyes. *I wish for Wolf!*

She reclined against her pillows and fell into a daydream about the dark, fierce Welsh Borderer. He was riding Drago, and Shadow loped ahead of him through the night. Brianna schooled herself to patience, imagining that he was coming to her with all speed.

Something roused her from her reverie and she sat up and listened intently. She heard the noise again. It sounded like a faint scratching on the castle door, but of course she realized that Flamstead's stout oak portal was too far from her chamber for her to hear any sound from such a distance.

The insistent scratching came again and Brianna took up her candle, silently descended the steps that led down to the Great Hall, then made her way to the castle's main entrance. She listened intently and heard a faint whimper. In her mind she could actually see Shadow standing on the other side. She threw back the bolts on the heavy oak door and opened it. "You came!" Brianna stood mesmerized. "Wishes really can come true."

Wolf's arms enfolded her and held her tightly against his heart. "My own love, I came because you summoned me."

"How did you get past the guards?"

"Silly question." He hugged her closer. "It's what I do. Shadow taught me how."

Brianna's heart was racing wildly. She put her finger to her lips, took his hand, and led Wolf and wolf upstairs to her chamber.

"Let me have a good look at you." He held her at arm's length. "You called off the betrothal after all," he said, bemused. "I confess that I lost all hope—I visited Warwick and your mother told me you had gone to Scotland with the de Warennes."

"Everyone just assumed I would go. When I told Lincoln I couldn't marry him, he begged me to wait until they returned from Scotland. I agreed because I didn't want to ruin Jane's visit."

He cupped her face in his hands. "That was kind."

She wrinkled her nose. "I'm kind more often than cruel. I worried about breaking Lincoln's heart, and the callous swine married Blanche FitzAlan the moment they returned from Scotland."

"I met the bride. To me they seemed a perfect match. She was terrified of me."

"Mmm, so am I." Brianna lifted her arms about his neck.

Wolf kissed her deeply and continued his kisses until they lost count. When they sank down on the bed, Wolf bethought himself. "Brianna, I have neither stick nor stone. All I have is a towering audacity, and a deep and abiding love for you. Will you marry me?" Wolf knew he should have told her that someday he would be both rich and powerful, but something perverse inside him wanted to know if she loved him enough to marry him when he had nothing and was still a fugitive.

"Yes, I will marry you! And not at some indefinite time in the future. I want to marry you *now*."

"It will have to be secret. If the king found out you had married a Mortimer, he would punish both you and your family."

"I swear I will tell no one," Brianna vowed.

"With the caveat of your parents, of course."

"Are you sure?"

"Yes, we must have their permission, which might not be easy to get. The Earl and Countess of Warwick may consider it anathema for their daughter to wed a notorious Mortimer."

She gazed up at him with a mischievous light in her eyes. "The *Notorious* Mortimers! If I wed you, will I too be notorious?"

"You are bloody incorrigible."

"Yes, I know." Brianna was inordinately pleased at the accusation. She unfastened his leather jack. "Make yourself comfortable." She poured water into her washbowl from the jug and set it on the floor for Shadow. Then she began to undress.

"What are you doing?"

"Going to bed. It's quite big enough for both of us."

"Sweetheart, I can't sleep with you under your father's roof. He'd have my balls!"

"You may only have hours to live. When he discovers you, he may run you through to save my honor. Wouldn't you like to spend your last hours making love to me?"

Wolf pulled her down into his lap. "I *will* spend my last hours making love to you—but that won't be for another fifty years."

"It's almost morning." She threaded her fingers into his long, black hair. "You rode through the night to come to me. How did you know where to find me?"

"When I visited Warwick I stole one of the scented candles from your bedchamber. Earlier tonight, in my room at Saint Albans Abbey, I lit the candle. Because you made it, your essence was on the candle and it illuminated your whereabouts for me."

"Did you know that the abbey was built with stone from the ruins of the ancient Roman city of Verulam?" she asked innocently.

"I don't need a history lesson from you, Brianna de Beauchamp."

"You are right. A lesson in manners would benefit you far more." She laughed up at him, thoroughly delighted that both of them remembered every word they had ever said to each other.

They stretched out on the bed together, his powerful arm anchoring her to his side. "Try to rest, sweetheart. We may have a taxing day ahead of us."

She rubbed her cheek against his heart. "To a Mortimer, nothing is impossible!"

Their banter helped him to control his passionate desire for the exquisite female who lay in his arms. The only thing that kept his raging lust at bay was the heady thought that she had agreed to marry him and would be his for the rest of his life.

Just as dawn was lighting the sky, Shadow went to the door and growled. Wolf and Brianna, who were lying on her bed, sat up.

Warwick threw open the door, and Brutus and Shadow stood nose to nose, with raised hackles. "Good boy, Brutus."

"Father! Wolf and Shadow arrived in the middle of the night. I didn't want to disturb you," Brianna explained quickly.

"Well, you do disturb me." His face was grim. "I'm not as blind as you imagine."

"I'm to blame for this, Lord Warwick." Wolf stood and faced the earl. "I would like to speak with you and Lady Warwick in private, if I may."

"Am I excluded?" Brianna demanded in a challenging voice.

"Yes, you are," Wolf said firmly.

"I think that would be advisable," Warwick declared. "We will see you in the library." He pointedly held the door open waiting for Mortimer to vacate his daughter's bedchamber.

Wolf signaled Shadow to stay, and then left quickly.

He found his way to Warwick's library and saw that it lived up to its reputation. His wait for the earl and countess was rather lengthy and he passed the time by reading all the titles of the books. It was no wonder Brianna was intelligent if she'd read even half of them.

Finally, Guy and Jory entered the library.

"Good morning, Lady Warwick." Mortimer bowed gallantly.

"Wolf, it's lovely to see you again."

Warwick cleared his throat, warning Jory not to be effusive.

Jory smiled at Wolf, blithely ignoring the warning. "Let's sit down, shall we?"

Warwick took the seat of authority behind his massive desk.

Without hesitation Wolf Mortimer spoke up. "I am in love with your daughter, and have been for some time. Because she was betrothed to another, I could not declare myself."

Jory gave Guy a look that said: *I told you so!*

"When my father was in the Tower and I was confined at Windsor, Brianna and I found a way to secretly communicate. Your daughter was instrumental in our escape and I learned that she returned my feelings. Because the Mortimers were reduced to landless paupers, I could not ask an earl's daughter to become my wife, nor even ask her to put her life on hold and wait for me."

"Since my daughter took such dangerous risks for

you, I warrant she must return your feelings." Warwick did not look amused.

"How exciting!" Jory declared.

"She is too much like you for her own good," Warwick remarked.

"I shall take that as a compliment," Jory said blithely, "since I know you wouldn't change one thing about me."

"Sir, you are aware that I have second sight. Though I do not know when, I am quite certain that Queen Isabelle and Roger Mortimer will land with an invasion force and, with little bloodshed, King Edward will be deposed in favor of his heir, Prince Edward.

"My father's lands and castles will be restored to him and he will reward me for my service with Mortimer of Chirk's estates. Since Brianna is no longer betrothed, and in light of my future prospects, I came to ask your daughter to marry me."

"How romantic." Jory was filled with joy for her daughter.

"How bloody audacious!" Warwick declared.

"Guilty as charged, sir. I am willing to wait until the Mortimers' fortunes are restored. Brianna, however, is not willing to wait."

"Oh, please tell me you are not willing to wait, Wolf. Tell me that you are just as impetuous as Brianna?" Jory begged.

"I will wait if you say I must, my lady, but I confess I won't do it willing."

"If you do marry, it must be kept secret, for her safety," Warwick stated flatly.

Wolf did not let the triumph he felt show on his face. The Infamous Warwick was conceding. "I am a fugitive and we both realize her safety and yours would be in jeopardy if it was known that she was my wife."

"Congratulations!" Jory looked radiant.

"Damn it, woman, I won't give my consent until I have spoken with Brianna," Warwick said emphatically.

Jory forwent rolling her eyes. "Of course not, my lord." She smiled at Wolf. "You may escort me to breakfast."

Guy de Beauchamp bade Brutus to stay, and opened Brianna's door. Shadow lay down, put her nose on her paws, and flattened her ears, sensing the dominance of the alpha male.

"Do you love Wolf Mortimer?"

"Yes, Father, with all my heart."

"Agreeing to marry him has nothing to do with Lincoln Robert marrying Blanche FitzAlan, has it?"

Brianna smiled tenderly. "Lincoln and I were childhood friends. Once Wolf and I became close, I realized that what I felt for Lincoln was affection, not love."

"I warrant it would be better if you waited for the Mortimers' fortunes to be restored."

"Better perhaps, but not *best*, Father. You had to wait five long years for your heart's desire. I don't want to wait. The Mortimers' fortunes may never be restored, and I don't even care if they ever are."

Guy realized Wolf had not told Brianna about his vision. This convinced him that his daughter truly did love Mortimer with all her heart. "Who am I to stand in the way of your happiness?" He held out his arms and Brianna moved into them.

A lump came into her throat. "I love you so much, Father."

Guy and Brianna joined Jory and Wolf for breakfast. Their demeanor told the pair who had been awaiting them that all was well. "Father will swear the priest to secrecy and we can be married today."

"Since dusk falls early, I'll ask him to arrange a candlelight ceremony," Guy declared.

Jory turned to Wolf with a radiant smile. "I warrant you had no notion the Infamous Warwick was a romantic at heart."

"How else could he have won the heart of a lady like you?" Wolf asked the beauteous countess.

"Ah, such flattery tells me you have the gallant charm of your father," Jory teased. "Beware, Brianna, beneath the velvet glove is a fist of steel."

"Then he has much in common with my own father, yet I have no fear." Brianna winked at her mother. "You were the one who taught me there isn't a man breathing who cannot be manipulated."

Guy looked at Wolf. "It's a bloody conspiracy!"

"Waiting for dusk will make the day seem endless. Why don't you go for a romantic sleigh ride? The snow may not last."

Wrapped in her sable cloak with a fur lap rug tucked about her, Brianna snuggled close to Wolf as he drove the magnificent pair of matched grays that pulled the sleigh. The air was as crisp as fine wine, and the silver bells on the animals' harness jangled in a merry rhythm that matched their galloping hooves.

Shadow loped ahead of them, occasionally flushing a covey of grouse, or coursing after a hare that got away. Clearly the wolf was enjoying the wild dash through the snow today, far more than the hunt.

"I'm so deliriously happy, I want to shout it to the world." Brianna cupped her hands about her mouth. "I have a secret!" she cried at the top of her lungs.

Wolf grinned down at her, took his hands from the reins, cupped his mouth, and shouted, "I'm in *love*!"

An owl on a birch branch asked, "Whoo? Whoo?"

Wolf shouted, "Brianna de Beauchamp, that's who!"

Brianna lowered her voice and spoke more intimately. "You are a reckless driver, who enjoys taking risks."

He picked up the reins. "You too obviously enjoy taking dangerous risks, or you wouldn't be marrying me, sweetheart."

"I taught Isabelle to take risks, but I never dreamed she would take your father for her lover."

"He seduced her with his notorious Mortimer charm and she threw all caution to the wind."

"Isabelle's risk was far, far greater than mine. She is the Queen of England and her lover can never marry her. They are both committing adultery, yet if God is just, He will forgive her sin."

"True, but I'm not certain He will forgive Roger Mortimer."

She gazed up at him. "Why?"

"Father chose Isabelle, not only because she was a beauteous queen, but because she was the perfect instrument of Mortimer's revenge upon Edward Plantagenet. The day my father surrendered to the king, and Edward put him in chains, Mortimer put a curse on him and vowed he would bring him low."

"But your father hasn't yet invaded and taken his revenge."

Wolf shook his head. "Roger Mortimer took his revenge the night he cuckolded King Edward."

Brianna remembered words Wolf had once said to her: *I could seduce you into doing anything I wished, but I promise I will never lure you to it, no matter how much you tempt me. My integrity wouldn't allow it.*

She smiled up into his dark eyes. "I love you, Wolf Mortimer."

He dragged the horses to a halt and pulled her into his arms. "You had better, my beauty." His insistent fingers found their way beneath the fur rug and inside her sable cloak.

She could feel the warmth of his possessive hands through the material of her gown as he caressed her back, and when she lifted her mouth for his de-

manding kisses she knew that this was her man and
there was nowhere in the entire world she would
rather be on this exciting winter day than on a sleigh
ride at Flamstead, enfolded in her lover's arms.

The horses stamped their feet and blew clouds of
vapor into the cold air. With his fingertips, Wolf
brushed the snowflakes from Brianna's eyelashes. He
slapped the reins and the horses surged into a gallop.
"I'm burning—I forgot it was cold. If I let myself get
any hotter, I shall make love to you in the sleigh."

"That would be heavenly." She slid her hand along
his thigh.

"I'm trying to control myself until we are married.
Behave yourself, English."

She squeezed his thigh muscle. "Fiery Welsh
dragon!"

When they returned to the castle, Jory told Wolf
that she would order a bath be prepared for him.
"Come, Brianna, we must choose something lovely for
you to wear at your wedding. The chapel will be cold
and we shall both have to wear our fur cloaks, but
underneath we must look spectacular."

Wolf said with regret, "I have only leathers to
wear."

"Take a look in Rickard's wardrobe. I'm sure you'll
find something. Go up those stairs and turn left. Rickard's chamber is at the very end. In fact that's where
you can bathe."

A short time later, as Wolf was sponging himself in
the wooden tub, the door swung open and Rickard de
Beauchamp stepped inside. "You are actually going
to wed Brianna?"

"I am. We will be brothers-in-law." Wolf grinned.

"Brianna *is* my sister, but since I am wed to your
father's sister, I'll still be your *uncle*," Rickard taunted.

Wolf refused to be baited. "Uncle makes you sound

old, but take your choice—you can be my uncle or my brother."

"You shrewd sod—you know I'd rather we were brothers." He reached into his doublet and pulled out letters. "I had no idea you were here. I was on my way to Saint Albans to look for you. I have a letter from your father." Rickard set down two envelopes and handed Wolf a towel. "The other is for Brianna from Isabelle."

"It's fortuitous you arrived—you can be my witness. The queen's letter may distract her. I won't give it to her until after we are wed."

"My sister is a female who likes to make her own decisions."

"I am well aware of it, Rickard." Wolf opened the wardrobe. "Truthfully, I wouldn't want it any other way." He pulled out a dark green velvet doublet with a golden dragon embroidered on one sleeve. "May I borrow this? It's Mortimer colors."

"Be my guest. I'll wear the wine velvet."

Wolf grinned. "I leave you little choice, since everything else is leathers."

"Resplendent garments are rather useless on a horse-breeding estate. Did you know Flamstead would be Brianna's one day?"

"Why do you suppose I asked her to marry me?" Wolf jested.

"That's a bloody lie. I know how much pride you have."

It was evident that everyone gathered before the altar in the small, chilly chapel was inordinately proud, as Brianna and Wolf exchanged their wedding vows.

"Who giveth this woman to be married to this man?"

"I do." The Earl of Warwick proudly placed his daughter's right hand in Wolf Mortimer's and stepped back.

"I, Roger, take thee Brianna to my wedded wife, to have and to hold from this day forward, for better for worse, for richer for poorer, in sickness and in health, to love and to cherish, till death us do part, according to God's holy ordinance, and thereto I plight thee my troth."

Brianna had forgotten that Wolf's real first name was Roger, and she smiled her secret smile. "I, Brianna, take thee Roger to my wedded husband." She continued, proudly repeating the solemn words Wolf had vowed.

He gazed down at his bride with loving eyes, and slipped the plain gold ring that Jory had provided onto her finger. "With this ring I thee wed, with my body I thee honor, and with all my worldly goods I thee endow." *With all my FUTURE worldly goods.*

The priest put his hand on top of the couple's clasped right hands. "Those whom God hath joined together let no man put asunder. I pronounce that Roger and Brianna be man and wife together, in the name of the Father, and of the Son, and of the Holy Ghost. Amen."

The newlyweds placed their signatures in the chapel's register, and then Rickard and Brianna's nurse, Mary, signed as witnesses.

Warwick was the first to hug his daughter, and Brianna noticed that his cheeks were damp. "I love you," she whispered.

Jory gave her new son-in-law a motherly embrace, and Wolf wished his own mother were this warm and loving.

Guy and Rickard thumped the groom on the back with hearty blows that would have felled a man with a less powerful build.

When the wedding party entered the castle from the cold night air, the tempting tang of roasted game and meat, layered with the delicious aroma of baked bread, cakes, and tarts, was a mouthwatering assault on the senses.

When Wolf removed his black wool cloak, and Brianna saw the golden dragon on his doublet, she was thrilled.

He helped her from her sable cape and gazed transfixed at the exquisite picture she made. Wolf realized just how lucky he was. *Brianna is a magnificent marriage prize.*

She had chosen a pale green silk gown, because it was a Mortimer color and because her red-gold curls were a vivid contrast. She also wore her birthday chain about her waist, with the large cabochon emerald suggestively decorating her mons.

The hall was filled with the people who lived and worked at Flamstead. Not by word or even look did they let on that they knew this was a wedding celebration. Since they were well aware that the marriage must be kept secret, they conducted themselves with a veneer of normalcy, albeit underneath was a barely suppressed frivolity.

As the food and drink were consumed, the atmosphere became progressively more festive and noisy. Toasts were drunk silently without the usual testimonials. There was no dancing with the beauteous bride, but there was no lack of merry songs sung, both suggestive and otherwise. Finally, Wolf got to his feet and raised his goblet to everyone present. "I thank you with all my heart for making me feel at home."

A cheer broke out and reverberated about the Great Hall.

Chapter 28

"I shouldn't . . . but I shall!"

Using Brianna's favorite phrase, Wolf picked up his bride, carried her from the hall and swept her up the stairs.

"My bedchamber is to the right," Brianna indicated.

"Your mother had Rickard's chamber prepared for us."

"Why?" she asked breathlessly.

"Because your chamber is next to your parents' and Rickard's is to the left, at the far end."

"Ah, obviously they don't want to be disturbed by our cries of passion," Brianna teased.

"I warrant it was in deference to your shyness."

"I am now a Mortimer, for God's sake. Shyness is not in my vocabulary."

"You are incorrigible."

"And then some," she said, using his favorite phrase.

As he reached to open the door he saw that Shadow had been following them. "You can stay out here and guard us tonight."

"With all she ate at the wedding supper, she will be asleep long before we are."

Inside the chamber, scented candles had been lit

and the bed made with fresh linen sheets. A handful of dried rosebuds had been scattered across the pillows. A jug of wine and two goblets sat on the desk, along with the letters Rickard had brought.

Wolf sat Brianna down on the bed and knelt before her. He raised her foot, removed her slipper, and kissed her instep. Then he repeated the pretty gesture with her other foot.

"You make me feel cherished."

"I vowed that I would. I've only just begun."

Brianna drew in a shuddering breath as his hands slid up her legs and caressed her bare thighs; then he pulled off her hose and garters. His fingers stroked her flesh. "Your skin is soft and smooth as silk."

"Thighs are wondrous things," she whispered. "Yours have the power to drive me wild. Perhaps I should get a dragon tattoo."

"Over my dead body, English."

"Will you always hold your Welsh superiority over me?"

"Among other things," he promised.

Brianna removed the gold chain from around her waist.

Wolf took it and set it on the bedside table for safekeeping. "I wish I could give you jewels, sweetheart."

"Wishes can come true," she assured him mischievously.

"I have no doubt of it." He slipped his arms behind her and unfastened the buttons at the back of her gown. "I am about to get one of my wishes."

"More than one, I warrant."

When Wolf removed her gown and her petticoat, his teasing stopped. "You are wondrous fair, my beauty."

Brianna reached out and threaded her fingers into his long, black locks and murmured, "Strip for me . . . It's been so long."

Wolf complied immediately and watched her eyes darken with desire as he revealed the dragon. He flexed his thigh muscle and Brianna gasped with delight as it flicked its fiery tongue.

Gently he pushed her back on the bed, and starting at her toes, began to worship her with his lips. When he got to her knees, he paused and looked at her. When he saw anticipation writ clearly on her face, he continued and trailed kisses up the insides of her thighs. Once more he paused and gazed into her eyes.

"The emerald decorating your mons shamelessly taunted and tantalized me to madness tonight. Will you accept your just deserts?"

"I shouldn't . . . but I shall."

Brianna stared in rapt fascination as Wolf caressed her mons with his lips, then thrust his tongue into her sugared sheath. Never in a thousand years could she ever have imagined a man could make love this way, but the sensations he aroused were so unbelievably sensual that she arched her mons into his demanding mouth and writhed with uninhibited abandon.

"Wolf!" she cried in disbelief as she dissolved in liquid tremors. "I thought I knew everything about making love."

He came up over her. "You've only just begun to learn."

She gazed up into his magnetic gray eyes. "Do you know everything?"

"No, thank God. We'll explore and learn together, sweetheart."

His fingers reached to untangle a rosebud caught in her hair, and then he changed his mind because it looked so pretty nestled in her curls. He spread her red-gold tresses across the pillow and gazed down at her. He watched the tips of her lush, upthrust breasts turn into tiny, hard jewels. To Wolf, Brianna was the most exquisite creature in the world and he exulted that she was his woman.

Brianna wound her arms about her husband's neck and pulled him down to her. She trailed her lips along his jaw, then kissed his ear. "I love how you taste and how you smell," she whispered.

"And how is that?" he asked, bemused.

"Like man, and wolf, and dragon!"

"That's a figment of your vivid imagination."

She arched her mons against his hard, erect cock. "I warrant *that* isn't my imagination."

Wolf's face became fierce and intense as he lowered his hips and with one hot, driving thrust, unleashed the wild desire that had been riding him since before dawn.

Brianna closed sleekly around him and shivered each time his breath swept her neck. She wrapped her legs high about his back and took him all the way inside her, yielding to his dark male dominance with breathless cries of passion.

He watched her face closely and when she peaked in climax he withdrew. Wolf would father no child until he could support it with Mortimer riches.

Wolf spent on Brianna's belly, gently wiped it with the linen sheet, and then he enfolded her in his arms and held her against his heart. They lay still, savoring the closeness and the intimacy of pledged lovers who had just mated. It was as if magic spiraled around them, weaving an invisible yet tangible cocoon that kept them private and separate from the entire world.

After the quiet time, Wolf stirred and kissed her brow. Brianna stretched, enjoying the feeling of languor that seeped through her limbs. He rolled with her so that she was in the dominant position; then he opened his legs so that Brianna lay between them. "Are you comfortable, sweetheart?"

She gave a heartfelt sigh. "I may never move again."

"When I was at Saint Albans, I had one of my visions."

Brianna gazed at him, enthralled. "Was it about the future?"

"It was." He brushed the red-gold tendrils back from her forehead. "I saw a fleet of a hundred ships make anchor off the Suffolk coast. My father, accompanied by Queen Isabelle, landed with an invasion force. England's earls, barons, and bishops met them with open arms, and almost without bloodshed they forced King Edward to abdicate in favor of his son."

"You have true second sight. Your visions will come true!"

"They always have," he said quietly. "I witnessed the Coronation of Prince Edward. After the ceremony, Queen Isabelle restored everything that had been taken from Roger Mortimer, and young King Edward made him Justiciar of Wales for life."

"I warrant Teddy will make a great king in the Plantagenet tradition of his magnificent grandfather."

"In my vision, my father rewarded me with my uncle of Chirk's vast estates. That is what prompted me to seek you out and ask you to marry me, sweetheart."

Brianna instantly scrambled away from him and knelt before him on the bed. She dug her fists into her hips, tossed back her disheveled hair, raised her chin, and challenged him like a ferocious wildcat. "You Welsh devil! Your towering pride would not allow you to marry me until you knew you would be a wealthy and important nobleman."

Wolf laughed at her. "You are angry because I will be able to provide for you on a grand scale! You are the most maddening and perverse female I have ever known."

She lunged at him and grabbed two fistfuls of his long hair. "Just how many *have* you known?"

Wolf saw the teasing light in her eyes. "Let me see . . . counting you . . . that would be . . ."

"One!" she cried.

"One," he conceded and pulled her down beside him. "I have no idea when all this will happen, Brianna. It could be one year, or even two. Until then, you will have to keep me."

"I'll keep you. I'll keep you in a continuous state of arousal," she promised wickedly.

"Two can play that game," he threatened, caressing her breasts.

"Just one moment." She struggled to sit up. "Why didn't you tell me about your vision before you proposed?" She answered her own question. "You were testing me to see if I truly loved you!"

He grinned. "A damn good thing you passed the test. Pour me some wine, English. This is thirsty work."

Brianna got up and poured them each a goblet of wine, and then she padded happily to the door and let Shadow into the chamber.

"May I read my letter now?" she asked sweetly.

"You knew you had a letter?"

"Of course I knew. Both our letters are lying in plain sight on the desk, but since this is our wedding night, it was important that we put our own needs first." She came back to the bed, handed Wolf the letter from his father, and then sat down cross-legged and tore open her letter from Queen Isabelle.

Isabelle told her how happy she had been at her brother's court in Paris. King Charles of France lived in opulent luxury. She told Brianna that her reunion with Roger had been more wonderful than she had ever dreamed. She said the only thing that spoiled her visit was Edward's constant demands that she return home to him immediately.

I tell him that I will never return until Hugh Despencer is banished, but that is just a stalling tactic. I know that my beloved Roger would kill me before he would allow me to return to Edward Plantagenet under any circumstances.

I have been assured that my children are being well looked after in my absence. My heart aches for them, but I live for the day that I return to England and have them once again in my loving care. I beg you send me any news you have of them, Brianna.

I have accepted an alliance with Hainault, and my son, Prince Edward, is quite taken with one of Sir John of Hainault's lovely young daughters. Any reply to this letter must be sent to me in Hainault where I will be residing from now on.

Brianna, I am most grateful for your friendship. Without it, I would never have escaped the prison I was in. Someday I shall repay you for your unwavering loyalty to me.
Your friend,
Isabelle

Brianna handed her letter to Wolf so he could read it.

Wolf was far more reluctant to let his wife read the letter from his father, but after a moment's hesitation he handed it to her. She might as well learn firsthand of Roger Mortimer's manipulative nature since he was now her father-in-law.

King Charles has secretly agreed to fund my invasion vessels, provided my liaison with Isabelle does not embarrass him with the pope. We are moving to Hainault, where I have a secret pact with the count to make one of his daughters the future Queen of England, once Prince Edward takes his father's crown.

I have the young Earl of Kent in the palm of my hand and ask that you get his brother, the

Earl of Norfolk, to fully commit to us. They are shrewd young devils who will give their loyalty where it will do them most good, and both hate and detest King Edward's bum boy.

I have recruited German mercenaries and promised to finance them with money from your mother's French relatives, the Joinvilles. They may never see a penny of it, but the Germans are not to know that.

You, Rickard, and Orleton have done a credible job recruiting the nobles we will need on our side when we land. The only unknown in this plan is Robert Bruce. He could be the fly in the ointment, if he takes the expedient action of invading at the same time we do.

The letter was signed with only the initial M.

Brianna could not help comparing the information in both letters. Where Isabelle was happy that Prince Edward found one of the daughters of the Count of Hainault appealing, Mortimer had already agreed to make a pawn of Isabelle's son by marrying him to one of Hainault's daughters and make her the Queen of England, in return for money and provisions for his invasion.

"Roger Mortimer makes promises he may not be able to keep."

"To my father, the end justifies the means."

Brianna gave him back his letter. "It obviously takes someone this hardened and determined, and yes, *devious*, to invade a country, depose its king, and set up another in his stead."

"Unfortunately, it does."

She looked at him and smiled. Wolf was very like his father, with one glaring exception. *Integrity!* Brianna thanked God for it. She climbed back into bed beside her husband. "Your father expects you to get the Earl of Norfolk to eat out of your hand."

"I wonder what it will take to make the king's half brother change his loyalties," Wolf mused.

"I believe I can help you. Thomas Brotherton took quite a fancy to me when we were at Windsor together. Norfolk sought me out for every dance," she said coyly.

He slanted a black brow. "It is too bad you won't be traveling with me."

"What the devil do you mean?"

"Our marriage is a secret. Your reputation would be blackened beyond redemption if we rode about in each other's company and sheltered at the same lodging."

"Wolf Mortimer, you don't honestly believe I am going to sit pining for you at Flamstead while you go off on your adventures?"

"You'll be safer here."

"I don't want to be safe. Oh, I know! I'll disguise myself."

"As what?"

"As a boy!"

"How will you disguise these?" He cupped her breasts and kissed her, which effectively put an end to any looming conflict for the rest of the night.

At dawn, Wolf arose and let Shadow out for her morning hunt; then he returned to the warm bed.

When Brianna awoke, she opened her eyes to find her new husband propping his head on his hand, gazing at her.

"This is the way I want to awaken every morning for the rest of my life." Wolf caressed her cheek.

"Then it's settled. When you go to see Norfolk, I'm coming."

"Dressed as a boy, I suppose. If you think that won't raise eyebrows, you are mistaken, my beauty."

"I don't give a fiddler's fart for raised eyebrows!"

"Charming language for an innocent bride."

"Perfectly acceptable for the bride of a notorious Mortimer."

"Will you never let me have the last word, English?"

"Perhaps, occasionally."

"Then it's a good thing actions speak louder than words." He took possession of her mouth, effectively limiting her utterances to breathless whispers.

"I love you, Wolf."

When the newlyweds arrived downstairs, Jory greeted them affectionately. "I would have brought up your breakfast, but I didn't want to disturb you."

"We appreciate your thoughtfulness, my lady," Wolf declared.

"Oh, please, none of this *my lady* business. You must call me Jory, as Rickard does. Brianna, your father and I have discussed it and we think we should return to Warwick and let you two have your privacy."

"Please don't change your plans on our account. I'm sure Brianna enjoys being with her family."

"Perhaps, but not at the expense of her privacy with her new husband. We usually spend Christmas at Warwick Castle with our people, and though Guy Thomas is perfectly capable of looking after things in his father's absence, I'm sure he would appreciate it if we returned to Warwick for the Yule."

Brianna's eyes sparkled as she smiled at her mother. "Thank you. I will love playing chatelaine at Flamstead."

Rickard, accompanied by his father, came into the hall and joined the newlyweds for a second breakfast. "What news from Roger?"

"Both my father and the queen are now in Hainault. He has secret alliances with King Charles of France and the Count of Hainault for his invasion. He also has money to hire German mercenaries."

"He certainly hasn't allowed the moss to gather beneath his feet," Warwick observed with approval.

"When Roger organizes a military campaign, he does a thorough job, as I learned when we fought in Ireland," Rickard declared.

Brianna smiled at her brother. "Thank you for bringing Isabelle's letter. I shall answer her today. Will you take the letter for me, Rickard?"

"All the way to Hainault, if you wish it," he offered.

"Did Isabelle sound happy in her letter?" Jory asked Brianna.

"Immensely happy. I'll let you read it for yourself."

"Before I came to Flamstead, I spoke with your brother, Lynx de Warenne," Wolf told Jory. "He warned me that Robert Bruce might take advantage of an invasion by invading England himself. Though there is a signed truce between England and Scotland, the Bruce has broken it before."

"You can always count on Robert Bruce to do the expedient thing," Rickard declared cynically.

Jory and Brianna exchanged a quick glance. "Darling, why don't I come up and read your letter now? Perhaps I will write to Isabelle and send it with your reply."

Upstairs, in the privacy of the bedchamber, Brianna handed her mother Isabelle's letter.

"I've never asked you, but were you and Isabelle instrumental in Roger Mortimer's escape from the Tower?"

"Yes, we both wanted him free, especially after Mortimer of Chirk died. The intrigue and the risk were immensely exciting. Roger seduced Isabelle . . . They are lovers. At first I was shocked, but she fell head over arse in love for the first time in her life and the virile Mortimer was exactly what she needed."

"And apparently the Queen of England was exactly what Mortimer needed. Speaking of expedience, your brother is right. Robert Bruce will always do what is expedient for Scotland. If Queen Isabelle could offer him something that he lusts for, he would not invade England."

"For what does he lust?" Brianna asked bluntly.

"For England to acknowledge him as king of an independent Scotland. I know, and I warrant Isabelle knows in her heart that a war with Scotland can never be won."

"That is something a female would admit, far more readily than a male. King Edward would never agree to recognize Robert Bruce as King of Scots. I wonder how Roger Mortimer would feel about it. He fought the Bruces both in Scotland and in Ireland."

"I don't know. Perhaps Isabelle could convince him. I convinced Warwick not to fight the Bruce."

"Father agreed for love of you," Brianna pointed out.

Jory smiled her secret smile. "Yes, he did."

"I will suggest it to Isabelle in my letter," Brianna declared.

"Since you intend to put treasonable words down on paper, you had better ask Rickard to take it to Hainault and put it directly into the queen's hand."

"Yes, I had better." Brianna changed the subject. "Did you know Wolf had a vision that the invasion would be successful? He said that Queen Isabelle would restore all the Mortimer holdings and his father would reward him with his Uncle Chirk's estates."

"Yes, Wolf assured us their fortunes would be restored."

"So that's why Father gave his consent!"

"No, Brianna. He withheld his consent until he asked you if you truly loved Wolf Mortimer. Only then did he agree."

"I am so lucky to have Guy de Beauchamp for my father."

"As I am lucky to have the Infamous Warwick for my husband."

After discussing the matter in detail, Brianna and Wolf both replied to the letters they had received, and the following day, Rickard de Beauchamp set out on a secret mission that would take him across the Channel to Hainault.

During the next two days, Wolf accompanied Guy about Flamstead, gleaning all the knowledge he could about breeding horses. It gave him a deeper appreciation of both the animals and the men who worked with them.

Brianna helped her mother pack for her return to Warwick.

"Would you like to keep Mary? I'm sure she would love to stay and mother you, darling."

"No, I think Mary should enjoy the Yule festivities at Warwick. I don't need a maid . . . I have Wolf to undress me."

Jory could see how happy Brianna was and sensed that the pair of lovers had been intimate before they were married. "Take care of each other. The dangers are very real, darling."

When the earl and countess departed, Brianna and Wolf moved into the master bedchamber because it was more spacious and had a large stone fireplace.

That night, Wolf threw pillows down in front of the roaring fire and pulled Brianna down beside him. "This is the first night we've been alone since we were wed. I intend to make it memorable. Would you like to play Tame the Dragon?"

Brianna threw him a saucy look and ran the tip of her tongue over her lips. "I shouldn't . . . but I shall!"

Chapter 29

The snow lasted until Christmas and Brianna, Wolf, and Shadow enjoyed long sojourns into Flamstead's woods almost every day. Most often the newlyweds rode Drago and Athena, but sometimes they enjoyed the warmth of the sleigh.

"Happy Christmas, sweetheart." Wolf caught Brianna beneath the mistletoe they had brought from the woods and hung up only yesterday. With his arms wrapped tightly about his bride, Wolf's kiss was both romantic and sensual. When they heard applause from the horsemen in the hall, they broke apart and laughed.

After breakfast, Brianna distributed the traditional Yule gifts to the household and then she handed Wolf his present. She had put much thought into what to give him. It could not be costly since he had no way to return an ostentatious gift, and the last thing she wanted to do was offend his pride.

When Wolf opened the package, he found a sheepskin saddlecloth, which would prevent his saddle from galling Drago. Brianna had dyed it Mortimer green and embroidered his initials in gold thread across one corner. "Thank you, love. It's such a surprise, though it shouldn't be. Everything you do is thoughtful."

Brianna was thrilled that he liked her gift, and it was her turn to be surprised when she opened her Christmas present from Wolf. It was a small knife for cutting herbs with a carved jade handle. Its soft leather sheath had a slit so that it could be worn on a belt. "Oh, it is exquisite. You are a magic man!"

That night at the Yule feast, the Flamstead household enjoyed roast boar, goose, and venison, followed by flaming Christmas puddings and washed down by dozens of barrels of homemade cider.

After the meal, Wolf entertained them with a poignant Welsh ballad he had learned as a boy. When he was done, the horsemen banged their wooden goblets on the trestle tables and began to sing Yuletide carols.

At midnight when it was time to retire, Brianna got to her feet and staggered a little.

"You are flown with cider, English. I'm afraid I'll have to carry you."

She swayed toward him. "A clever ploy on my part, I warrant."

The following day when they arose, they found the snow had melted in the night. They immediately made plans to visit the Earl of Norfolk at his castle of Walton on the River Naze.

Brianna unearthed a trunk that held some garments that had belonged to Guy Thomas when he was a boy, and she quickly appropriated them. When she donned the leather breeks and jacket, Wolf rolled his eyes.

"Judas, you'd tempt a saint."

"No, I won't. I'll rub dirt on my face."

Wolf cupped her bum cheeks, pulled her close, and pressed her breasts against his chest. "I wasn't referring to your face."

They rode the thirty-mile journey in one day to Walton Castle, which directly overlooked the sea. Though the water of the North Sea roiled pewter gray on this winter day, it did not look nearly as ominous as it usually did in this season.

The guard in the barbican tower let the two male riders through the castle gate and when Mortimer was approached by Norfolk's castellan he asked that he and his companion be provided with separate bed-chambers.

Brianna had brought a gown and a hairbrush in her saddlebags and she changed into her female clothes the moment she closed her chamber door. She blithely ignored the shocked look on the steward's face as he led her and Wolf Mortimer down to the hall to meet Thomas Brotherton, Earl of Norfolk.

The king's half brother recognized her immediately and got to his feet. "Lady Brianna, welcome to Walton! You've arrived just in time to dine with us."

Norfolk stared at Wolf. "You look familiar, sir, though I'm not sure we've met."

Wolf lowered his voice so others would not hear. "I am the son of Roger Mortimer."

"Ah, that explains it. The resemblance is marked. Forgive me for staring at you both—you seem strange traveling companions."

"That is easily explained, my lord earl," Brianna murmured. "My friend, Wolf Mortimer, is here representing his father, and I am here on behalf of my dearest friend, Queen Isabelle."

Norfolk waved aside the servers to guarantee privacy.

"Rumor has it that you left the Royal Court because of differences with your brother, King Edward," Wolf began.

"Rumor is correct! His minion stole some of my land, and my *half* brother condoned the theft."

"Is there a noble breathing who is not sick and tired of Despencer's tyranny?" Wolf asked. "The people of England are suffering oppression under the king's misdeeds. Hugh Despencer's advice has weakened the regime. Your brother Kent has pledged his loyalty and support to Queen Isabelle. My father is gathering an invasion force to dethrone Edward and put his son in his place."

"So I have heard from my brother."

"Would you be open to allowing the ships to land on your territory of East Anglia, my lord?" Wolf asked bluntly.

Brianna spoke up quickly. "You could play a vital role, Thomas. Queen Isabelle would reward you generously."

"You may count on my aid. It must be kept secret, however. If rumors start, I shall deny everything," Norfolk declared firmly.

"I guarantee it will be kept in strictest confidence, my lord. All the leading barons and bishops are united in this cause. The plan will not be set in motion until every detail is in place and success is a certainty," Wolf pledged.

Thomas Brotherton nodded. His glance moved between the man and woman before him with speculation. Brianna de Beauchamp was such a desirable female he concluded she must be Mortimer's mistress.

Brianna retired first, but when Wolf climbed the castle stairs he went directly to his own chamber. When he had not joined her after half an hour, it dawned on her that he had no intention of compromising her reputation. She chuckled at his sense of honor, but when she climbed into the lonely bed, she found she could not sleep. After trying for the best part of an hour, she threw back the covers and padded to the window. She stood in awe, watching the waves of the North Sea crash onto the shore.

The force of the sea is so overwhelmingly powerful. It seems to put the problems that beset England into perspective. A weak, tyrannical king and his incubus

rule a resentful, yet powerless populace. I hope and
pray that Roger Mortimer will sweep in with a force as
commanding as the sea and cleanse the realm of the
putrefaction that plagues it!

Brianna and Wolf returned to Flamstead and spent
the month of January enjoying their solitude, getting
to know the horses better, learning which mares were
pregnant, and trying to discern when they would drop
their colts.

Their nights were spent before the fire, talking endlessly, sharing their secrets, and their hopes and
dreams. After they made love, they slept spoon-
fashion, with Wolf's long body curved about Brianna's, safe in their warm cocoon of love.

At the end of the month, Rickard returned with
letters. Queen Isabelle and Mortimer wrote that they
were willing to offer Robert Bruce recognition as king
of an independent Scotland, in return for a pledge of
peace between the two countries.

Wolf replied to his father's letter, telling him that
he had secured Thomas of Brotherton's permission to
land his ships on the East Anglian coast in the Earl
of Norfolk's territory. He also promised his father that
he would make a secret journey to Scotland and negotiate with the Bruce.

Brianna wrote to Isabelle:

Norfolk is a sworn enemy of Hugh Despencer
because of land he stole from Thomas. Like his
brother Kent, it will please you to know, he has
pledged to switch his allegiance from King Ed-
ward to Queen Isabelle.

Wolf wanted to ride to Scotland in February, yet he
protested it would be too arduous for Brianna. "It is
best if I go alone."

"It is *not* best," she vigorously protested. "I *must*

come with you. We are husband and wife—we are part of each other—we share everything—our thoughts, our actions, our risks, our lives!"

Reluctantly, Wolf agreed to take her. "But we will go by ship. Edinburgh is almost six hundred miles from here—too far to ride in winter. Perhaps Rickard can arrange us a secret passage on a cargo ship. He has connections with a London merchant."

"Thank you. You won't regret taking me. I will be invaluable in your negotiations with Robert Bruce."

"Perhaps you're right. It makes me feel whole and complete knowing we share everything in our lives. I love you, Brianna."

In the Port of Leith, Scotland, Wolf unloaded Drago and Athena from the hold of the merchant vessel. He and Brianna then rode the four miles to Edinburgh Castle. Though the ride was short, Brianna was glad she was wearing her sable cloak.

By the time they were escorted into the ancient fortilace, Brianna's cheeks were flushed rose pink, both from the brisk air and the thought that she was about to come face-to-face with Robert Bruce, her real father, for the first time in her life. Jory had kept the Bruce in ignorance of her existence and Brianna hugged the secret close.

The chamberlain inquired who they were and what their purpose was. Wolf told him they were envoys from England on a diplomatic mission and they hoped King Robert would give them an audience. The dour Scot sniffed when Wolf offered no names, but he grudgingly accommodated them with a chamber.

Servants came in to plenish the room and light a fire in the grate. Brianna stripped off her riding gloves and held her hands to the blaze. "This castle is a monstrous, barren pile of rock."

Wolf grinned at her. "Very like some of the castles in Wales."

"I just hope there are plenty of blankets on the bed."

He waggled his eyebrows. "I'll keep you warm, sweetheart."

Brianna washed her hands and face in the cold water provided and changed into her pale green velvet gown. She fastened the heavy gold chain about her neck and allowed the cabochon emerald to lie in the valley between her upthrust breasts.

Wolf removed his leather jac, put on a snowy, linen shirt, and covered it with a black velvet doublet. His gaze swept over his wife. "Your jewel draws the eye irresistibly to your breasts."

" 'Tis the only jewel I brought. Would you rather I wore it about my waist?" she asked ingenuously.

"Don't play the innocent, sweetheart. You know damn well I don't want the emerald decorating your mons."

"I didn't think so." Brianna smiled sweetly and picked up her brush. Her red-gold hair crackled in the cold, dry air, as she tossed it back over her shoulders.

While they waited for the chamberlain to return, they stood at their chamber window with their arms about each other. The high vantage point of Castle Rock afforded them a stunning view of the surrounding countryside. At this season, all was black and white, but once it turned green in the spring and was dotted with sheep and lambs, the vista would be breathtaking.

After a wait of almost two hours, the chamberlain came to collect them and he escorted them down to the throne room. Brianna bit her lip and caught up her skirts with trembling hands. As the chamberlain opened the heavy doors, she closed her eyes and prayed for courage.

As they were led toward the man seated on the throne, her steps lagged, allowing Wolf to walk a few paces before her.

"Welcome to Scotland." Robert Bruce's voice was deep and rich.

"Sire, what we have to say is for your ears alone," Wolf said.

The king turned to the men who flanked him and dismissed them. When they were alone, he assessed the man who stood before him, and then his eyes were irresistibly drawn to the woman at his side.

When Brianna raised her lashes, her knees turned to water.

"Sire, my name is Wolf Mortimer. I am here as an envoy for Queen Isabelle and my father, Roger Mortimer."

The Bruce stared at the young beauty before him. She was dressed exactly as Jory de Warenne had been dressed when he fell in love with her more than twenty years ago.

She dipped her knee. "Sire, my name is Brianna de Beauchamp."

Wolf's brows rose slightly. His wife's name was *Brianna Mortimer*.

Large brown Celtic eyes looked into a pair that was identical to his own and, in that fateful moment, Robert Bruce recognized her. "You are Jory's child."

Wolf looked from his wife to the king and back again. His sixth sense suddenly took over and he knew that Brianna was the daughter of Robert Bruce. He realized it was a shock to the king. *Damn you, Brianna, you knew all along!*

Wolf stiffened. The sudden knowledge was a mortal blow to his pride. *How could you have kept this secret from me, Brianna?* Wolf bowed stiffly, politely. "I shall leave negotiations in your capable hands, my lady. Kindly excuse me. I warrant you will do better without my intrusive presence."

Mortimer turned on his heel and strode from the throne room.

Robert rose to his feet and stepped closer to his daughter. His eyes never left her face. "Your mother never told me."

Brianna raised her chin. "She never told me either. I overheard a private conversation between my uncle, Lynx de Warenne, and his wife, Jane. He said he had always suspected that you were my father. I went to Warwick and confronted my mother. Only then did she admit the shameful truth to me."

"I'm sorry, Brianna."

"There is no need to be sorry," she said proudly. "I have never thought of you as my father, and I never shall. I have not the least ambition to be a king's daughter. My mother provided me with the best father in the world. I would have no other father than Guy de Beauchamp, just as she would have no other husband!"

The Bruce knew she was rejecting him, but he realized it was a protection against being hurt. "I am honored to have met you."

"I am here on behalf of my dearest friend, Queen Isabelle. Someday in the future when the time is right, she and Roger Mortimer plan to invade England and depose the weak, degenerate king. Queen Isabelle is willing to recognize you as king of an independent Scotland if you solemnly pledge that you will never invade England."

The Bruce smiled. "A pragmatic solution to everyone's advantage. Certain women are far shrewder than men. Your mother is astute, as are you. Dare I hope Isabelle is such a woman?"

"Who do you think taught her? Will you pledge peace?"

"I am more than willing . . . I welcome it."

Brianna drew in a swift breath and reached for his hand.

"Don't touch me!" Robert drew away quickly, but immediately saw the hurt in his daughter's eyes.

"Brianna, I have *leprosy*. The time left to me is short. My son, David, will be a child king. I want peace between Scotland and England for his sake."

The lump in Brianna's throat almost choked her. Her eyes glistened with tears as she realized the unkind words she had thrown at the rightful King of Scotland. "There is a way for your son, David, to have a permanent peace. Isabelle's youngest child, Princess Joan, is almost the same age as your son. I warrant Isabelle could not resist an offer to make her daughter the future Queen of Scotland."

" 'Tis clear you have inherited Celtic shrewdness from me. To marry the children would be to fuse the two countries and be the first step to healing the wounds we've inflicted upon each other."

"I promise I will plant the seed with Isabelle, Sire."

"Lynx told me you were betrothed to his son, Lincoln Robert, and when they returned to England you would be wed."

"Your namesake married the Earl of Arundel's daughter who accompanied the de Warennes to Scotland. I fell in love with Roger Mortimer's son, Wolf. My mother once told me that the heart wants what the heart wants, and I discovered she was right."

"You are wed to the man who just stalked out of our presence?"

"I am." She sighed. "We are about to have our first quarrel. I neglected to tell him that the King of Scotland was my father."

"The Mortimers fought against me in Scotland and in Ireland. I warrant I am their worst enemy, after Edward Plantagenet and Hugh Despencer, of course."

"What is past is past. The Mortimers now need an alliance with you. I assure you that Wolf no longer thinks of you as an adversary . . . At the moment, I fill that role."

"My dearest child, I regret that I have come between you."

"Regrets are useless . . . One cannot alter the past."

She smiled at Robert Bruce. "I bearded one lion in his den today. Now I will go and attempt to beard the other one. I bid you adieu, Sire."

When Brianna opened their chamber door, Wolf, who had been gazing from the window, spun about to face her. His back was rigid, his face grim. "I do not enjoy being made a laughingstock. How in God's name did you keep a straight face when I declared it made me feel whole and complete knowing we shared everything in our lives?" he demanded. *"I will be invaluable in your negotiations with Robert Bruce,"* he mimicked. "Why did you keep this secret from me? You should have disclosed it before we wed."

"As you disclosed that you would inherit Mortimer of Chirk's landholdings and manors?" she asked defiantly, refusing to take the defensive.

Wolf blatantly ignored her question. "Common courtesy demanded you should have at least informed me before I met Scotland's king face-to-face. I was completely blindsided!"

"I didn't know he would recognize me. My mother never told him." Brianna put her hands together in supplication. "Wolf, in my heart, Guy de Beauchamp is my father. I never want him to learn that I know the truth of my parentage. Don't you see I couldn't take the risk of Warwick finding out that I knew Robert was my father?"

Unbending pride raised his head and glittered from his gray eyes. "You couldn't take the *risk*?" he demanded incredulously. Again he flung her own words at her: *"We are husband and wife—we are part of each other—we share everything—our thoughts, our actions, our risks, our lives.* Obviously there is something we don't share. We keep our deep dark secrets to ourselves."

"It wasn't my secret to share," she shouted with defiance.

Wolf swept up his heavy leather jac and strode from the room.

"Devil take you, Wolf Mortimer!"

The black oak door slammed with a resounding crash.

Brianna, stubborn and self-righteous, clung for two full hours to the opinion that she was the one who had been wronged. *I grossly underestimated my husband's towering pride!* At the end of two more hours, however, her thoughts began to change. *Perhaps it was Wolf's capacity to be hurt that I underestimated. I think him strong and invincible. I had no notion he had a vulnerable spot.*

When he did not return that night, she cried herself to sleep.

Chapter 30

Wolf Mortimer saddled Drago and rode from the castle stables. The cobblestone path down Castle Rock was treacherous, so he exercised caution. The only road he knew led to Leith, and he picked up speed as he headed north toward the coast.

His emotions had taken control and he recognized the slippery slope as clearly as he had seen the dangers on the steep hill. Wolf knew he needed to cool his temper so that he could think rationally. As he neared the port, he became aware of his surroundings and saw that there was more than one squalid alehouse-cum-brothel that catered to sailors and dockworkers.

He hadn't many coins on him, but when he dismounted, he chose a braw lad of about twelve to watch his horse. He gave him a penny and told him there would be another when he left the tavern.

Smells of food assailed his nose as he entered, but since he didn't have enough money for both food and drink, he ordered ale from the blowsy-looking female who greeted him.

Wolf sat down with his back to the wall. His eyes slowly swept the room and its occupants. He saw that his muscular build and dark coloring blended in well with the other customers. The only visible difference was that his clothes were of better quality.

The male voices were loud and boisterous, but unfortunately their Scots brogue was thick as porridge and he could discern few of their words. He saw some of the men eye him, assess his fierce swarthy features, and decide to give him a wide berth. The background noise was gradually drowned out, as his thoughts seemed to increase in volume and take precedence.

She didn't trust me! She couldn't take the bloody risk, begod! He downed half the ale, thinking to soothe his pride. Wolf Mortimer had long been averse to putting himself in another's shoes, since inevitably that kind of thinking played advocate to your adversary. This time, however, he reluctantly tried to examine Brianna's point of view.

She desperately wanted to protect Warwick, no matter the cost to Robert Bruce or to me. Grudgingly, he acknowledged that proved Brianna's deep love for the man who had played the role of father with honor and devotion. *That showed loyalty.*

Since Wolf was stubbornly opposed to being appeased, he stepped into the mind of Robert Bruce. *The king was shocked. Though he was Jory de Warenne's lover, he had no idea he had fathered her child. Females make expert cheats. Breathes there a bloody woman who can be trusted? Did the beauteous countess deceive the Infamous Warwick? Like mother, like daughter, I warrant!*

Wolf downed the rest of his ale and slammed his empty mug on the rough-hewn table.

"D'ye fancy havin' yer knob polished, laddie?" The blowsy lass had a thick brogue, but Wolf understood her meaning perfectly.

"The only thing I fancy is another ale."

"Och, man, don't blame me fer yer impotence!"

The corner of his mouth quirked at the lass's temerity. *I must look a dour son of a bitch. Then I open my mouth and add uncouth to my sins.* When she brought his ale, he winked by way of apology.

I wonder how long Brianna has known the Bruce is her father? What did she feel when she found out? Anger? Betrayal? Pride that she is the daughter of a king? Or humiliation that she is a bastard? He felt a pang of heartache for her dilemma, and quickly crushed the emotion.

Wolf gulped down the ale and called for another. His money was gone, so he nursed the brew as carefully as he nursed his mauled pride, lingering over it as if it were the elixir of life. Suddenly, he saw the picture he made. *I am bloody pathetic!* Wolf laughed, but there was little mirth involved.

Tenacious as a terrier, the barmaid returned and gave him a speculative look.

"I am a pauper, love. Otherwise I would have had yer back on this table and polished yer knobs hours ago."

"Are ye English, laddie?"

"Welsh."

"Ah, that explains it, Taffy!"

"Cheeky sod." This time he laughed with genuine amusement.

A picture came to him full-blown of Brianna beseeching him to understand. In their entire relationship she had asked him for little, while he had asked her for much. *She has been unfailingly generous. Yet when she came to me as a supplicant, I scorned her.* Suddenly, he saw himself as clearly as he saw his visions, and he was covered with shame. In a heartbeat, Wolf made his decision, tossed down his ale, and rose to his feet.

He emerged with empty pockets, wondering what excuse he could give the lad who was watching his horse. Drago whickered, but the braw laddie had slung his hook. Wolf threw back his head and roared with laughter. Things usually had a way of working themselves out. *Pray God that fate will help me with Brianna.*

The road leading from Leith to Edinburgh was deserted at this hour long past midnight. Drago's hooves echoed eerily in the cold, dark night, but the sound buoyed his spirits as it measured off the evershortening distance between him and the one he loved with all his heart.

Brianna awoke with a start but she could see nothing in the darkened chamber.

"It's me," Wolf murmured gently.

She reached out to touch him and her hand brushed across his heart. "You came back." The relief in her voice was palpable.

They spoke in unison, "I'm sorry, sweetheart." They did it again. "No, no, it was *my* fault!" Then they laughed together.

Wolf sat down on the bed and gathered her in his arms.

"I was afraid you wouldn't come back."

"I was afraid you wouldn't have me back." He kissed her brow and then he lit a candle so that he could see her lovely face.

"I didn't mean to hurt you, Wolf. I wasn't even aware you could be hurt. I thought you invincible."

"You are my Achilles' heel, Brianna." He kissed her nose. "I'll have to kill you, now that you know my secret."

She brushed the back of her fingers across his unshaven jaw, and love swelled her heart to almost bursting. "I didn't find out about the Bruce until after Isabelle left for France. When I went to Hedingham to break my betrothal, I overheard my mother's brother Lynx tell Jane about his suspicions that his friend Robert was my father."

"You must have been shocked."

"Shocked and angry. I'd never been so furious in my life that they had kept it from me. I rushed home to Warwick to confront my mother. When she confessed the truth to me, it did nothing to assuage my fury. Then I saw Guy de Beauchamp and realized he was blind. I knew instantly how much I loved him, and what a devoted, loving father he had always been to me. My love for him is all-encompassing. I want and need no other father."

"Does Warwick know about Robert Bruce?" he asked gently.

"Yes, my mother told him before she would agree to wed him."

"Not many men would be that generous."

"He has a big heart, filled with love."

"I will try to emulate him," Wolf promised.

"I have another secret," she whispered solemnly. "I can only share it with you if you promise to tell no one."

"I promise on my sacred honor."

"The Bruce told me he has leprosy. His years will be short. He welcomes the truce with Isabelle because his son, David, will be a child when he becomes King of Scotland. Robert risked telling me, knowing his enemies will use the information against him if it becomes known."

"He obviously trusts you."

"He told me I had inherited his Celtic shrewdness."

"When did he say that?" Wolf asked, bemused.

"When I suggested he wed his son, Prince David, to Isabelle's youngest daughter, Princess Joan."

"You *are* a shrewd little wench, one who enjoys dabbling her fingers in royal affairs, I warrant."

"I told the Bruce that I'd plant the seed with Isabelle."

"Brianna Mortimer, queen maker!"

"When you left, I told him I was married to you."

"What was his reaction?"

"He said he was the Mortimers' worst enemy, after Edward and Despencer. He said he was sorry to cause trouble between us."

"I caused the trouble. Will you forgive me?"

"I shouldn't . . . but I shall."

Wolf growled low in his throat and took possession of her mouth. "Give me a minute to shave and I'll be right back."

"No, don't shave. I like you all bristly for a change." She helped him remove his leather jac and watched avidly as he removed the rest of his garments. She licked her lips. "You taste of ale. I do believe you've been drinking, my lord."

He waggled his eyebrows. "That's not all. I was propositioned by a buxom Scottish whore in a squalid alehouse."

"And what did you say?"

"I told her I couldn't afford her. I'd spent my last penny on ale, and she was a tuppenny whore."

"You Welsh devil!" Brianna threaded her fingers into his hair and gave it a good yank.

"Hellfire, two can play that game," he teased. He grabbed two handfuls of her lovely red-gold tresses and buried his face in them. "You smell provocatively inviting."

"Better than the whore?"

"Mmm, more like an expensive courtesan."

"And how many expensive courtesans have you bedded, my lord?"

"I don't have enough fingers to count."

Brianna gave a little scream. "Your wicked fingers are doing more than counting."

"That's another secret I've learned . . . You're ticklish!"

"Aren't you?"

"Not usually, though I admit you tickle my fancy."

Brianna reached down and stroked her fingers along the entire length of his erection. "And fancy it is. I think I'll call it *Dragoncock*! Does it have a fiery tongue?"

Wolf winked. "I'll supply the cock—you'll have to supply the fiery tongue."

Brianna gasped at his erotic suggestion. "Just as I think I know everything, you always manage to surprise me."

"That's because you are my sweet innocent virgin bride."

"I won't cavil at innocent, but I'm not sure about sweet. Perhaps tart would be a more apt description."

She pushed him back on the bed and hung over him for a long, tantalizing moment. Then her vivid hair tumbled down across his limbs, concealing the actions of her playful fiery tongue. She felt her woman's power as Wolf writhed and groaned with pleasure. He arched up from the bed and cried out as he spent.

He enfolded her in his arms and rolled with her until he was in the dominant position. In this heightened moment of intimacy, Wolf felt intensely protective of her. He kissed her gently. "Brianna, don't ever feel compelled to tell me your secrets unless you want to. You are your own woman, and I love you exactly the way you are."

"With all my faults?"

"Your virtues far outweigh any imagined faults you think you possess," he assured her.

"My *virtues*?" Brianna couldn't think of any.

"You possess every virtue that I admire. First and foremost, you are courageous, and you inspire those around you to find their own courage. Then, when you agreed to wed me and share all your worldly goods, I learned that you have generosity in abundance. The other virtue I admire is loyalty. If you give me one-hundredth part of the loyalty you have bestowed upon

Warwick, I will consider myself the luckiest husband alive. I love you, sweetheart."

She kissed his ear and whispered invitingly, "May I have a demonstration of that, Dragoncock?"

Epilogue

June 1, 1327
City of Hereford, England

"I was born to play the role of Queen Guinevere!" Isabelle, sitting in the lists with Brianna, Jory, and an array of other noble ladies, made a radiant picture of sublime happiness.

"Who else was courageous enough to challenge King Arthur in the joust?" Brianna asked. Earlier, Roger Mortimer, in the guise of King Arthur, had thoroughly trounced the Earl of Kent, the Earl of Richmond, and the Earl of Norfolk, who had generously allowed him to come ashore on his lands.

"One of the de Bohun brothers. They look so much alike, I always get them mixed up," Isabelle confessed.

"John is the Earl of Hereford. Humphrey is a year younger," Jory explained. "Being in Hereford makes me feel I have come full circle. When I was eighteen, I was wed to their uncle, Humphrey de Bohun, and he brought me to Goodrich Castle, just ten miles away. The place is the same, but I am a very different woman."

"Aren't we all?" Isabelle's laughter was infectious. "I never dreamed I could be this happy! For the first time in my life I have a strong man on whom I can lean. Jory, now I enjoy the happiness you have always had, married to Warwick."

Brianna bit her lip nervously. "This next joust is between Wolf and my brother Guy Thomas. I am utterly torn!"

"You cheer for Wolf and I'll champion my son," Jory declared.

Brianna watched Wolf Mortimer, mounted on Drago, thunder down the lists, his lance couched, his powerful arm an extension of his weapon. In seconds his opponent lay flat on his back in the dust.

Both Brianna and her mother rose to their feet, apprehension turning their faces pale. "Wolf should have let him win."

"Of course he shouldn't," Jory said, regaining her composure. "Guy Thomas would have been covered with humiliation if Wolf had let him win unfairly. As it is my son has a ready excuse. He will insist his wedding night sapped all his strength."

The day before, everyone had gathered to celebrate the double wedding of two of Roger Mortimer's daughters. Katherine had married Guy Thomas de Beauchamp, the son of the Earl and Countess of Warwick, and young Joan Mortimer had been joined in matrimony to James, the son of Margaret and Sir Hugh Audley.

"Speaking of weddings," Isabelle said happily, "plans are going forward to betroth Princess Joan to David Bruce. My son Edward approves wholeheartedly of the match. As the newly crowned King of England he would like to see a lasting peace between his country and Scotland."

Brianna and Jory exchanged a look of satisfaction. It felt quite heady to have a hand in events that might change history.

"Roger is next." Isabelle's hand went to her throat.

"I don't think I can watch. De Bohun is half his age and has twice the reach—Lord God, I know not what I'll do if aught happens to him."

"You have little to worry about, Isabelle. Roger has the benefit of experience, to say nothing of fierce determination."

Brianna stood and took Isabelle's hand. "King Arthur jousts for Queen Guinevere. Besides, the Mortimers have too much pride to eat the dust of the lists. You saw what Wolf did to my poor brother."

The three ladies watched the contest avidly, with only one of them having any doubt about its outcome. At the last moment, Roger Mortimer swung his shield to deflect the young Earl of Hereford's lance, and unseated his challenger to a roar of approval. Gallant as ever, he dismounted and helped John de Bohun to his feet. The spectators stood up and applauded wildly.

Isabelle was visibly relieved. "I'm glad it's over. I need a cool drink before I present the prizes."

"Good idea, my bum went to sleep an hour ago." Brianna rubbed her bottom and followed Isabelle from the stands.

Refreshments were laid out in abundance on the vast lawns of the magnificent Episcopal Palace that now belonged to Adam Orleton, Bishop of Hereford.

Rickard de Beauchamp was there with his wife, Catherine Mortimer, and their little girl. Rickard had finally deemed it safe enough to bring his family from Ireland. This gathering was the first time Catherine had seen Brianna in many years.

"The jousting was truly exciting, Cathy. Didn't my brother want to take part?" Brianna asked her sister-in-law.

"Rickard was acting as Roger's squire today."

Brianna made sure Isabelle couldn't hear her. "Behind every great man is an even greater man who doesn't crave applause." She picked up Cathy's daughter, Marjory, and admired the circlet of rosebuds decorating her hair. "You are the prettiest girl in Herefordshire!"

Marjory giggled. "Would you like to wear my roses?"

"No, darling. The red buds are perfect for your dark hair."

Cathy smiled at Brianna. "Your own tresses are such a lovely shade of red gold. I cannot believe you are twenty years old. Where did the years go?"

Brianna turned as an elegantly dressed lady approached. "Marie, how lovely to see you. I don't believe you know my brother Rickard's wife, Catherine. This is the Countess of Pembroke. I don't need to tell you she is a Parisian—her clothes give away her secret." Marie had been widowed for more than two years. Her husband, the long-suffering Earl of Pembroke, had been buried at Westminster Abbey.

"I am delighted to meet you, Lady Pembroke."

"I have to give out the tourny prizes. Won't you come with me?" Dowager Queen Isabelle asked her companions.

By the time the ladies arrived at the dais where the prizes were displayed on a velvet-covered trestle table, the combatants had been divested of their armor, bathed, and changed their clothes. Young King Edward and his bride, thirteen-year-old Philippa of Hainault, arrived to stand beside Queen Guinevere. The winners were each given a silver cup to much raucous applause. Brianna glowed with pride when Wolf stepped forward to receive his prize. Then Isabelle held up her hands for silence.

"I am delighted to announce the Grand Champion of the Round Table Tournament is none other than King Arthur himself. He unseated more opponents than any other jouster here today. Long may he reign, undefeated."

As Isabelle presented the gold cup to Mortimer, the tumultuous cheering was deafening.

Brianna smiled at her mother. "Everyone adores them. Isabelle is the overwhelmingly popular mother of their beloved young king, and Roger is the destroyer of the hated Despencers."

A short time later, everyone gathered on the palace lawns for refreshments at the sumptuous outdoors buffet that the Bishop of Hereford had arranged.

Wolf Mortimer came to join Brianna, and Guy Thomas took the hand of his bride, Kate. Then Guy de Beauchamp, who had regained partial sight, and had squired Guy Thomas in the tournament, joined the party. "This is the first time our entire family has ever been together."

Rickard slipped his arm around his wife and hugged her close. Cathy looked at her nephew Wolf with speculative eyes. "We are surrounded by newlyweds. When are you going to make a commitment to this beautiful lady?"

Brianna's laughter spiraled into the warm afternoon air. "Wolf and I have been secretly married for over two years!"

Wolf grinned. "We had better be wed. My wife will be presenting me with an heir in about six months."

Brianna gasped. "You know?"

"Of course I know. Give me credit for some intelligence, sweetheart." He hugged her close. "The question is, why did you wish to keep it secret from me?"

"I was afraid."

Her parents and her brothers laughed at the blatant lie.

"Why were you afraid?" Wolf asked with skepticism.

"Your accursed pride, of course! You kept spouting all that nonsense about not having a child until you could support it with Mortimer wealth. Since you were just granted your Uncle Chirk's landholdings, I swear I was going to tell you tonight."

Jory hugged her daughter. "Congratulations, darling. I'm so happy—the role of grandmother is far more rewarding than mother."

Wolf dipped his head and put his lips close to Brianna's ear. "Why don't we slip away and have our own joust?"

Brianna laughed up at him. "I shouldn't . . . but I shall."

Wolf bowed to the family. "I am sure you will excuse us. We have a pressing matter we must attend to." He took possession of his wife's hand and drew her in the direction of the stables.

With a straight face Brianna murmured, "A pressing matter?"

"A secret I haven't told you about."

"Tell me immediately, you Welsh devil."

"I prefer to show you." He took her into the stables and saddled their mounts.

As they rode side by side through the lush countryside, Wolf teased, "Anticipation is half the pleasure. Not all Chirk's holdings are in Wales or on the Border. He also had a Herefordshire estate that now belongs to us."

"So that's why you left me at Flamstead on the pretext that you needed to spend a few days with Adam Orleton."

"Guilty as charged," Wolf admitted with a grin. "Adam was born on the estate. I told you that Mortimer of Chirk was his father."

They rode through a tiny village called Bromyard and were almost immediately on Mortimer pastures filled with sheep and lambs. "Are these your flocks? I love their black faces, but they are on the small side."

"They are *our* flocks. They look small because they

were shorn in May. They are tough Welsh mountain sheep."

"Perhaps we could crossbreed them like we do with the horses at Flamstead. We could perhaps breed larger ewes."

Wolf laughed and teased, "I warrant you are preoccupied with breeding at the moment."

"Look! Here comes Shadow, racing like a mad thing to greet us. I can't believe you trust her to run free with all these sheep."

"She's never killed sheep. She prefers to hunt small game in the forest . . . creatures that venture forth in the night."

They drew rein in front of a lovely old manor house, covered with rose vines. "It's beautiful! I love it already," Brianna said.

Wolf lifted Brianna from the saddle and a stableman took their horses. She bent down to embrace Shadow and got her face licked. She looked up at Wolf with wide eyes. "I think she's with pup. There's a bulge in her belly."

"Your imagination is overactive." He crouched down and stroked his hands across the she-wolf's belly. "Well, I'll be damned. It must have happened in the woods of Flamstead. I had no idea there were wild wolves so close to your castle."

"*Our* castle—at least it will be someday. Our family is starting to grow and it fills me with joy. Does your mother know we are married?"

"Yes, I told her yesterday at the double wedding of my sisters. She seemed inordinately proud to have another bond with the de Beauchamps."

"I was most surprised to see how friendly she was with Isabelle. Surely she grasps the situation between her husband and the queen?"

"Grasps it and encourages it. Through Isabelle, her wealth and landholdings were restored. I warrant she believes her husband's infidelity is a small price to pay."

"Faithfulness to me is beyond price."

"That's why I love you, Brianna."

In the front hall, the housekeeper curtsied. "Would you like me to gather the servants, my lord?"

"Perhaps later, Mrs. Hadley. My lady cannot wait to see the bedchambers. Ask the cook to make us something good for dinner."

Though Mrs. Hadley covered her mouth, it was impossible to hide her mirthful grin.

As Brianna and Wolf climbed the stairs, she whispered, "She knows what we are up to."

"By the look of her smile, she approves." Wolf picked her up and carried her over the threshold of the master bedchamber. "I want you to choose a name for the manor." He set her down on the wide bed and knelt to remove her shoes.

"We also need to choose names for the baby. What do you think of Gwyneth? I believe it's a Welsh name."

"Gwyneth is completely unsuitable."

"Why?" she demanded, ever ready to challenge his authority.

"Because we are going to have a son."

"You don't know that!" she accused.

"Of course I know. Have you forgotten my second sight?"

"How could I forget? All your visions proved true. Your father and Isabelle returned to England and conquered the country without any bloodshed. Edward was forced to abdicate in favor of his son and the evil Despencers received their just deserts. Roger Mortimer was made Justiciar of Wales for life and you were given Mortimer of Chirk's landholdings, just as you foresaw."

"Second sight can be a curse as well as a gift. I hope our son doesn't inherit it."

"Truly?" She placed her hand on her belly in wonder. "I'm truly having a boy?"

"Yes, I warrant from now on you will lavish all your attention on the little devil. I brought you upstairs in the hope that you will spare a little for me."

As he began to undress her, Brianna gave him a seductive glance. When she was naked she climbed onto the bed and challenged him to come after her. "There's something about you that refuses to be ignored . . . Its wicked name is *Dragoncock*!"

Author's Note

Deposed King Edward II was imprisoned at Berkeley Castle. Many rumors surrounded his death, but most historians agree that on September 21, 1327, he was murdered by the ingenious method of a red-hot spit inserted into his bowels through his rectum, so that no marks would be found upon his corpse. The order for this foul deed was said to come from Roger Mortimer, and in 1330 he paid the ultimate price.

Dowager Queen Isabelle survived her husband by thirty years. History has not been kind to Isabelle. Because of her marital infidelity, she has been called the She-wolf of France.

King Edward III, who was born in the image of his magnificent Plantagenet grandfather, enjoyed a long, successful reign. His happy marriage to Philippa of Hainault resulted in thirteen children.

New York Times Bestselling Author
Virginia Henley

Ravished

All her life Alexandra Sheffield has longed for
passion and adventure—anything but marriage
to Lord Christopher Hatton.
Instead her body and her heart are weak for
another man—Lord Hatton's devastatingly
dangerous twin brother.

"No one sets fire to the page
like Virginia Henley."
—Christina Skye

"A brilliant author...the best in
romantic fiction." —*Rendezvous*

0-451-20737-8

Virginia Henley

Unmasked

Thirteen years ago, Alex Greysteel
Montgomery, an Earl and double agent, was
betrothed to Velvet Cavendish.
Now that they are reunited, Velvet is
determined to break her bond with Greysteel,
for she has her eye on none other than King
Charles II. But Greysteel is equally determined
to wed the fiery beauty. Now he'll do anything
to conquer—and rule—her heart.

"Virginia Henley writes the kind of book
you simply can't stop reading."
—Bertrice Small

0-451-21627-X

Penguin Group (USA) Online

What will you be reading tomorrow?

Tom Clancy, Patricia Cornwell, W.E.B. Griffin,
Nora Roberts, William Gibson, Robin Cook,
Brian Jacques, Catherine Coulter, Stephen King,
Dean Koontz, Ken Follett, Clive Cussler,
Eric Jerome Dickey, John Sandford,
Terry McMillan, Sue Monk Kidd, Amy Tan,
John Berendt…

You'll find them all at
penguin.com

*Read excerpts and newsletters,
find tour schedules and reading group guides,
and enter contests.*

Subscribe to Penguin Group (USA) newsletters
and get an exclusive inside look
at exciting new titles and the authors you love
long before everyone else does.

PENGUIN GROUP (USA)
us.penguingroup.com